THE COMPLETE

AGENT 13

TRILOGY

THE INVISIBLE EMPIRE
THE SERPENTINE ASSASSIN
ACOLYTES OF DARKNESS

BY

FLINT DILLE and DAVID MARCONI

PULP 2.0
LOS ANGELES, CA

THE COMPLETE AGENT 13®

THE INVISIBLE EMPIRE
THE SERPENTINE ASSASSIN
ACOLYTES OF DARKNESS

First printing: April 1986
Printed in the United States of America

FOR MORE INFORMATION ON THIS AND OTHER PULP 2.0 BOOKS:

WWW.PULP2OHPRESS.COM
WWW.FACEBOOK.COM/PULP2OHPRESS

INTRODUCTION

I was one of the editors, along with Jean Blashfield Black, working at TSR, Inc., when we published the *Agent 13* novels starting in 1986. Much like the novels themselves, the publishing process was fast-paced and action-packed!

The original concept began as an idea for a movie. This was natural, given that authors Flint Dille and David Marconi were screenwriters working on various projects at the time. The idea grew and Flint and David brought it to *Dungeons and Dragons*® creator, Gary Gygax, who thought it would be a great idea for the TSR, Inc. line, *Top Secret*®.

Top Secret was a role-playing game much like D&D, except that the game was set in the 1930s with player characters taking on the roles of crime fighters battling shadowy international crime syndicates instead of wizards fighting dragons. Jean and I were brought in as editors for the three novels, working with the game department as they devised the RPG.

Not surprising when dealing with pulp fiction novels, we were in a race against time! Management wanted the books and the game published together, so we were editing the books as Flint and David were in the process of writing them and the game developers were working on the RPG. This was before the days of email, so chapters and edits were flying back and forth via overnight delivery.

Jean remembers nights spent working on the book in the office after everyone else had left and saying, "No! What!" over the "sheer outrageousness" of the pulp fiction plot lines. Flint remembers that it was a "raucous writing experience". . . "I just started cranking out something that would fall between a very thick outline or a very thin novel. Some was completely written, some of it was a sentence for a whole chapter."

David took over from Flint. David recalls: "I took that pass and went back to Chicago and did my pass, taking all the ideas and grounding them in research and pseudo reality." David drove up to TSR on occasion to work directly with us and the game designers.

There was even mystery and intrigue! As one of the books was on its way to pre-production, I discovered that a crucial chapter was missing. No one knew where it was or what had become of it or if it had even been written. With no time to spare, I contacted David, who dashed off the chapter and sent it to us in the nick of time.

The world of Agent 13 was saved!

We had a great time working with Flint and David on these books. As Jean Black says, "It's great fun to see Agent 13's return and thank Pulp 2.0 for bringing him back to life."

--- Margaret Weis

AGENT 13

CHAPTER I

INVISIBLE EMPIRE

"We can strike anywhere at any time. You and your armies are powerless to stop us..."

INTRIGUE IN ISTANBUL

As the sun sank in the west, long, daggerlike shadows cast by the spiked minarets of Istanbul slid across the Bosporus, foreshadowing the sinister events that darkness would bring.

The noise of honking horns gave way to an impassioned wail to Allah. The people of the day left the streets to the people of the night.

Gypsies danced, as their cooking fires scented the air with exotic spices. Black marketeers lowered their prices and packed their goods, moving quickly to avoid the thieves who drifted from their lairs at night like jackals looking for corpses. Only the self-mutilated beggars remained at their stations, making their final, tearful pleas to the passing strangers for alms to get through the night.

None of this was noticed by the German officer seated comfortably in the back of his Mercedes. The precise, rhythmic purr of the finely tuned engine mellowed the human cacophony into unimportance. The officer stared coldly out the window beyond his chauffeur's shoulder at the colorful crowd that parted like a routed army before his car.

Colonel Schmidt's finger traced the saber slash on his cheek as his steely eyes scanned the streets through the bullet-proof glass. His gaze flicked over the great monuments that stood in ancient, solemn dignity—a marked contrast to the noisy, raucous throng surging around them.

So much for the heart of the proud Byzantine Empire, Schmidt thought. Now the undisciplined masses scurry around this grandeur like rats on a wedding cake. They don't deserve—

"Careful," he murmured as his driver narrowly missed running down a turbanned Sikh who was attempting to cross the street. "We can't be delayed, not tonight."

He eased back into the leather seat, relighting his cigarette. In afterthought, Schmidt mumbled, "I can assure you that these degenerates will be dealt with properly, in due time."

The ambassadorial flags of the Nazi government fluttered defiantly above the gleaming black fenders as the staff-car continued its journey past the Adrianople Gate, the shadow of the Blue Mosque sliding across the hood.

Colonel Schmidt glanced at the passing structure with cynical amusement.

Neither the great religion that built the Mosque, nor the chaotic nation he was visiting, nor even the powerful nation whose black uniform he wore meant anything for him. His duty was to a more ancient cause.

The blood-red sunset silhouetted Hagia Sophia, the church of Constantine, as the Mercedes came to a smooth halt before it. Colonel Schmidt waited as his driver stepped out of the car and scanned the streets for any sign of potential trouble. Seeing none, he opened Schmidt's door.

The German officer emerged, clad in SS black and carrying a heavy briefcase. The driver clicked his heels sharply and saluted. "Heil Hitler."

Schmidt glanced at the young officer, smiled sardonically, and walked past without returning the salute.

Private Hadler, the earnest, young Nazi driver, was shocked by the colonel's action. He was proud of his Fuhrer, as was all of Germany. It was, after all, Adolf Hitler who had delivered them from the shackles of the Treaty of Versailles, the hated symbol of Germany's humiliation.

Regardless of his vicious tactics, Hitler had restored the German people's national honor—a feat that the regimes of the Weimar Republic had failed to do.

The world again respected Germany. It was Hitler who gave the Germans the strength for equality. It was Hitler who delivered the Rhine-land in a bloodless coup, assuring a lasting peace that would sustain the "Thousand Year Reich."

Hitler deserved the salute, Hadler thought, especially from an SS colonel. He glared as the colonel entered Hagia Sophia.

What Private Hadler did not know—would never know—was that this colonel was directly responsible for his Fuhrefs rise to power.

"Schmidt" thought about this as he opened the cathedral door and was wrapped in Hagia Sophia's quiet, ancient shadows. In fact, it was the hidden story of that rise to power that was the subject of the report he was about to present to "interested parties." He rehearsed it in his mind as he walked.

"I arrived in Germany during the later part of 1918, one of several agents the Brotherhood had assigned to keep close watch on the various factions vying for control in that defeated, shattered country.

"My orders were to keep a watchful eye on developments in the military. The Brotherhood arranged to have me placed in the Press and News Bureau of the Army's Political Department. We could see that the Army was becoming deeply involved in politics, especially in Bavaria, which was known as an area of staunch conservatism. I suggested that this might be a prime breeding ground for the country's future leaders.

"My investigation uncovered several interesting possibilities. One of these was a young man whose fanatical anti-Semitism seemed likely to appeal to a defeated country looking for a scapegoat. Unfortunately, he had the horrendous name of Schicklgruber. I suggested he change it, and he is now calling himself Hitler—Adolf Hitler.

"With my help and guidance, this Hitler rose to power quickly. We supplied him with a large Swiss bank account, a chauffeured automobile, a villa at Obersalzburg, and a luxurious apartment in Munich. Most impressive to the masses.

"At last I believed it was time to move. Germany was ripe for plucking. I informed the Brotherhood and received permission to topple the Weimar Republic and begin the 'Thousand Year Reich.'

"It was a simple matter to terrify Chancellor von Hindenburg into resigning, thus paving the way for Hitler's grab at the office. Only one stumbling block remained—Austrian Chancellor Dollfuss—and that was easily dealt with.

"We had, of course, made discreet approaches to Dollfuss, but he continued to oppose Hitler publicly. Under my direction, one hundred and fifty-four members of the SS Standart 89 broke into the Federal Chancellery disguised as Austrian Army troops. Dollfuss was arrested and shot.

"There have since been other minor regrettable 'incidents,' but Hitler is now the unquestioned leader of Germany. Germany is now a world power. Hitler is firmly caught in our web. He does not dare make a move without the Brotherhood.

"And now I have been asked to meet with you here, to make my report on Germany's 'readiness.' I can assure you, we are prepared. It is time to take the next step."

Pausing in a corridor, Schmidt checked his surroundings and smiled in satisfaction, then headed for the doorway at the end of the hall.

Light from the dying sun streamed through a window, turning the cold granite walls to a radiant gold. Stepping through the sun-broken shadows, Schmidt made his way to a small chapel now used only for the collection of archaeological artifacts. He stood in the doorway, his hawklike eyes studying the remains of cracked pillars, broken columns, armless statues, and carelessly stored fragmented frescoes.

The German officer's eyes found the object of his search. Walking quickly, he entered a niche nearly obscured by a half-cracked statue of Neptune rising from the sea.

Scanning the room one last time to make certain no tourist was wandering nearby, Schmidt was arrested by a startling sight. Not ten feet from him was a face twisted in pain! Schmidt reached for his P-38, then suddenly stopped.

"It's nothing but a statue," he sneered to himself, trying to halt the surge of adrenaline through his body. He was drawn to look at the statue once again.

It was a life-sized figure of Christ on the cross. And it was terrifyingly lifelike. The anguish in its pain-filled eyes reminded him of his mother. Resolutely, Schmidt turned away from the Savior's tormented face. Reaching past Neptune into the niche, he pressed on the secret stone. A false wall moved aside, revealing a hidden staircase. He was just about to step inside when he felt himself irresistibly compelled to look back at the statue. Something was odd...

Those eyes... life like ... burning ...

Suddenly, the Savior's hand moved. Pulling one of the "nails" from the cross, the "statue" flung it through the air.

Schmidt gasped, but before he could react, the throwing knife buried itself in his neck. The German pitched to the floor, twisting in death's final spasms. His last impression before the pain exploded his brain was of the figure of Christ descending from the cross....

Still covered in alabaster-colored paint, the killer knelt by the German's side and lifted the man's hand. There was no pulse.

For all the expression that crossed his face, the killer might well have been a statue. He struck a large ring he wore against the stone floor. The room suddenly filled with a sizzling, magnesium-white light. The killer pressed the glowing ring to the dead German's forehead. There was a hissing sound and the smell of burning flesh.

When the killer raised the ring from the German's flesh, a message was left behind—the number 13.

Agent 13 wiped the marblelike make-up from his face. It was a handsome face, or might have been but for the cold, remorseless eyes—the eyes of a trained assassin. He felt no pangs of conscience. He had been trailing this man for four months—four months while the numbers of those murdered by the German stretched into the hundreds. Now Schmidt himself was dead. The world was, by a small measure, a better place.

Turning from the body, Agent 13 slit open the German's briefcase. As expected, it was booby-trapped to go off if the wrong man opened it. With a skilled motion, he disarmed the ticking weapon.

In almost the same motion, he pulled out of the case what appeared to be the purple, velvet robes of a monk. Beneath the robes were several manila file folders. A quick glance showed Agent 13 the nature and importance of their contents.

One dealt with German troop strengths and locations. One contained a detailed synopsis of Hitler's game plan for the war. There were many folders like these. But tucked in among them, almost as if in afterthought, was another folder that had—seemingly—nothing to do with the war. It was a dossier on an American scientist by the name of Dr. David Fischer.

Secreting the files in a hidden location in the chapel where he could pick them up later, Agent 13 robed himself in the purple vestments. He then slid through the hidden door behind Neptune, a door that few knew even existed. Closing it softly behind him, 13 silently descended a narrow flight of winding stairs into a dark and mysterious part of Hagia Sophia.

In the fourth century A.D., palace intrigue threatened the Byzantine Empire. Needing a safe place to forge secret treaties, the bishops and proconsuls developed plans to construct a chamber beneath the church, only to discover, upon investigation, that one already existed.

It had been built nearly a thousand years earlier by the Thracian king, Bizas, whose pagan symbols still adorned the walls. Gratefully taken over by the Byzantines, the chamber was—after conquest of Byzantium by the Moors and then the Turks—forgotten.

Forgotten, that is, by all save the Brotherhood.

This night, after hundreds of years of dusty solitude, the chamber of King Bizas was once more inhabited. Several figures dressed in purple, hooded robes stood together in the light shed by flickering torches. Their identities were concealed from each other by the hooded garb. Of all different nationalities, many had traveled a long way to come and receive their next instructions.

Though each spoke a different native tongue, all joined their voices in the recitation of ancient rites in a language lost to scholars over three thousand years ago.

When the rites were concluded, the torches were snuffed. A chill, damp darkness settled over the chamber. Into the silence came the sound of rock moving on rock. A cold draft whistled through the room, a new light flared. The waiting robed figures slowly turned toward the open secret panel.

Another cowled and robed figure—masked like all the others—stood outlined in a faint greenish glow. A sigh of anticipation whispered through the robed figures as they bowed in homage. "A Rook!" they murmured, impressed.

And now they knew why this meeting had been called. If the masked figure had been a Knight, tonight's gathering would have concerned the infiltration of military or industrial targets. A Bishop might mean Rome was ripe and ready to fall. But a Rook! Rooks resided at the Shrine itself, taking their orders directly from Itsu—the Hand Sinister. With armies mobilized on every border in Europe, this Rook need only cry havoc to let slip the dogs of war.

The Rook's hand went to a large, round amulet hanging from a chain around his neck. With fingers as thin and deadly as the legs of a poisonous spider, the man raised the pendant to one eye.

With no word spoken, the robed figures raised their right hands, palms outward. The Rook looked at each palm through the stone in the pendant. A tattooed number appeared on each palm, framed by the ancient symbol of Omega. Invisible to all save the user of the Seer Stone, the numbers served to identify the figures before him as members of the Brotherhood.

"39," he whispered, "19, 82, 13—" 13!

There was a sudden flare of torchlight, a strange spraying sound, and a noxious green cloud began to fill the room.

Clutching their throats, the robed figures dropped to the floor. Within seconds, nothing moved. The green cloud hung in the damp air, glimmering in the torchlight.

Then the green cloud swirled as another robed figure made its way toward the Rook. The figure bent down and pried the man's fingers loose from the Seer Stone, which he clutched tightly, even in death. The robed figure dropped the Seer Stone into a pocket. Then there was the sound of metal striking rock, a brilliant white light, and the smell of burning flesh.

Half an hour later, a turbanned old man in muslin robes emerged from an alleyway near the dock. The low wail of a ship's horn filled the air, signaling final boarding. The man walked swiftly, heading for a beat-up old freighter that lay at anchor between the brooding darkness of the Black Sea and the soft sea of Marmara.

As the man passed, he tossed an object into the water. The gas mask sank quickly.

Satisfied, he continued on his way, scurrying up the gangplank of the departing ship. Soon the man would be safely through the Dardanelles and into the Aegean Sea.

Only the grimly marked corpses were left behind, evidence that Agent 13 had struck again!

THE INVISIBLE EMPIRE

In 452 A.D., the Scourge of God, Attila the Hun, led his barbaric army toward the gates of Rome. As the Mongol horsemen eagerly advanced to sack the city, they were stopped by a strange and beautiful scene. Looking almost dreamlike in the misty light, Pope Leo I and two of his cardinals rode toward the thundering horde.

Dark-haired Huns raised their small horse-bows, but, at a gesture from their khan, they lowered their weapons. Leaning close to Attila's ear, the white-robed pontiff whispered a few words and—the Holy City was spared.

History has lost the words spoken by the Pope.

History has also lost any knowledge of the two men who really saved the Roman Empire . . . except in one place, where their memories are revered.

One of Rome's saviors was an obscure cardinal, attending (supposedly) His Holiness. The other was one of the maji, serving (ostensibly) Attila.

In the darkness of an early morning two months before Attila's arrival near Rome, both the magus and cardinal received whispered messages, delivered secretly by spectral figures. The two were instructed to stop the invasion.

On receiving this command, from a leader more powerful than any these two ostensibly served, the two set to work.

Before Attila's forces reached Rome's gate, their khan called a meeting of all his spiritual advisors, seeking holy guidance for his final assault on the city.

The oil lamps burned late in the tent of the Great One, as the Ten Magi gathered. One by one, they moved forward and offered their words and visions. Soon, only one remained to speak. He was tall, emaciated, and old. His ancient, withered hands clutched a crusted leather sack. All eyes in the room turned to him expectantly.

"Speak," commanded Attila in a voice that would send most men to their knees, cowering for their lives.

The Old One moved slowly to the center of the tent. Opening the sack, he spread the contents on a small floor tapestry. Attila leaned forward, looking. They were goat entrails.

Studying the entrails for "a sign," the magus gave Attila his reading.

It was a warning. Should Attila ever meet a man in white accompanied by two in red, he must do whatever deed the man in white asked of him. Failure to obey the conditions of the prophecy would result in the Great One's painful death on the tip of a Roman spear and a pestilence upon his kingdoms—the horror of which the world had never known.

The Pope, meanwhile, was told by the cardinal of a "vision" indicating that His Holiness would have the power to turn the pagan horde if he but rode out to face them, accompanied by only two cardinals. All His Holiness need do was speak with the Hun's leader, telling him to leave the city, and the Lord would undertake to see that His Servant was obeyed.

Thus, when the Pope told Attila to turn his horsemen away from Rome, he did so—quickly!

The old magus and the cardinal,

though loyal to their respective camps, both secretly served a more eternal and ancient power—the Brotherhood.

From its inception in the ruins of the once-great civilization of Lemuria, the Brotherhood had acted in the cause of good. Its deeds were not measured in flamboyant actions or bold strokes, but rather in silence—wars that were never fought, wicked kings who never ruled, plagues that never spread, famines that never blighted the land.

Using secrecy as a protective shield from the masses who might seek to corrupt their noble mission, the organization acted quietly, an unseen, benevolent hand guiding world events.

When it was decided, for example, that mankind had learned the lessons taught by the darkness of the Middle Ages, an order was issued to take humankind to the next level.

The Brotherhood's scholars began their task. Working from sacred texts (believed by most to have been destroyed in the burning of the library at Alexandria) and the Crystals of Uru—whose powerful, mystic forces as well as the knowledge contained within the Crystals themselves predated even their own organization—the Brotherhood injected the sweet nectar of renaissance into the fevered body of a dark age.

Soon the great wind of enlightenment swept across civilization. Even the church's high dogma fell prey to the new light.

Thus it was that the Invisible Hand

guided human destiny for so long. And thus it would have continued were it not for universal and immutable laws that balance light with darkness, pleasure with pain, love with hate, and good with evil.

Whether power corrupts or corruption seeks power is a debate for philosophers. Suffice it to say that the august body of the Brotherhood, after centuries of vitality, began to rot from within.

The Invisible Hand grew sharp talons, and the All Seeing Eye took on a sinister gleam.

Slowly, the precepts of goodness were bent to become the precepts of evil, and the line between purity and abomination disappeared.

Slowly, the Invisible Hand reached for the throat of mankind.

As a cancer of an entire body starts with one cell, the shadow of one being fell upon all.

For it was the Hand Sinister, known long ago as Itsu, who seized the Crystals' knowledge for himself—for eternity.

Months after the carnage in Istanbul, the grim murder scene was restaged in the Hand Sinister's secret chamber. After each of the Brotherhood's agents dropped to the floor in mock death, and the actor playing Agent 13 slipped away, the Hand Sinister sat alone upon the throne. Alone, the physical embodiment of Cheated Death and Tainted Life took a deep breath that sounded like the mountain winds of Tibet. He closed his eyes and began to meditate. Deeply entranced, he created a plan to accomplish three objectives:

One, he must regain the Seer Stone.

Two, he must cause a torrent of death to fall from the clouds of war that loomed over the Earth.

Three, he must bring cold silence to Agent 13.

In the calm of darkness, a plot slowly began to form. A beautiful woman ... a ruthless man . .. the Four Primal Fears: Falling, the Dark, Fire ... He would leave the fourth Fear for later. Yes ...

In his isolation, the Hand Sinister smiled.

LIGHTNING STRIKES

It was unseasonably warm for October. A fair wind blew off the Atlantic, and many of the spectators had either opened or removed the heavy wool coats they had carried with them to the Maryland shore.

Before them was a scene that might have been the work of surrealistic artists. A surplus tank from the Great War stood on a decorated platform constructed near the crashing surf. Fifty yards away, three soldiers stood guard around four portable generators, which were all connected with electrical umbilical cords to a gigantic, six-foot-high gun.

But this gun was no ordinary hulking cannon of iron. No, this gun was built of glass tubes, conductors, amplifiers, and dials. Colored gases filled some of the tubes, while a vivid blue glow pulsed in the large, coiled, central tube. The device hummed audibly, as though pregnant with power.

A small observation area had been set up on a low hill overlooking the beach. Its weary white folding chairs were filled by military men and politicians, two of whom were reputed to be very "close" to the President—General Braddock, aging head of the Joint Chiefs of Staff, and a newcomer to the political field—Kent Walters, head of the powerful National Security Council.

In addition to the "elite" in the white chairs, reporters crowded around the demonstration area, continuously clicking cameras at the strange-looking contraption, as if it might have moved.

One reporter wearing a white driving cap took a quick swig of brandy from his hip flask, then offered it to the much taller reporter next to him, who waved it off.

"Well, whaddaya think, Eddie?" Corbett, the short one, asked, pocketing his flask.

"I'm sorry the baseball season's over," Eddie said with a laugh.

"You can say that again. Think the Giants'll do it next year?"

"Naw, go with the Dodgers," Eddie Faulk said in a bored tone. Then he turned toward the shore as the aging General Braddock stepped behind a lectern set between the viewing area and the strange gun.

"Good afternoon, gentlemen." His voice crackled. He fiddled with the microphone and then began again. "As most of you know, I am General Hunter Braddock. Today, we are gathered to witness the demonstration of a weapon that may revolutionize warfare. Its inventor, Dr. David Fischer, calls it—somewhat dramatically—the 'Lightning Gun.' I'm sure that the military would call it something dashing like the 'L-976.'" Braddock paused as the audience dutifully laughed and then went on. "The weapon's inventor is with us today to explain how it works. Dr. Fischer."

A slender, gray man stepped in front of the assembled soldiers, politicians, and reporters.

What a sad case of a man, Faulk thought.

Nature had tricked the scientist into accepting a physique so frail that even the activity of walking demanded full attention. In addition, he had a face so joyless that it was impossible to imagine it breaking out into a full smile.

"What you are about to see is a demonstration of my latest prototype of the Directed Electricity Weapon, known also, as General Braddock has already pointed out, as the 'Lightning Gun.'

"Although I cannot, of course, give you the details of design, I would just like to point out that this test weapon today is powered by only the relatively small generators that you see before you. Therefore it will have a relatively low yield.

"It is my intention, should I receive the funding I have requested, to build a much larger Lightning Gun, whose magnitude and yield would be up to fifty times that which you will see today. Various sized versions could be mounted on everything from flat-bed trucks to battleships. I think I am not being immodest when I say that this weapon could revolutionize the concept of battle."

There was a slight murmur from the crowd.

"Now, if you would all please put on the protective goggles you have been given, we will get on with the demonstration." Fischer stepped away from the lectern. His shoulders slumped as if in relief at being out of the limelight.

General Braddock made a gesture to the three soldiers, who moved into action.

As preparations were being made, Eddie Faulk, the tall reporter, scanned the crowd. His eyes were not those of a journalist but of a secret avenger locked in a deadly battle with the forces of darkness. For Eddie Faulk was none other than Agent 13.

13 knew he was not alone in posing as something he wasn't. Almost certainly, one of the other observers was a member of the Brotherhood. This much he had learned from the papers taken from the dead German's briefcase. Colonel Schmidt had been planning to attend this demonstration. He wouldn't now, of course, but some other member must be here. But who?

The Agent eyed the crowd, but it was a futile gesture and he knew it. It could be one of the soldiers operating the gun. It might be the private who had escorted him to the press area. It might be General Braddock himself.

A moment later, Agent 13's thoughts were jarred by a harsh command.

"READY!"

The Agent, putting on his goggles, saw the soldiers point the strange weapon at the tank.

"AIM!"

They made their final adjustments, then turned their heads, shielding their goggle-covered eyes.

"FIRE!"

A soldier manning the generators threw a switch. A sizzling buzz pierced the air and a blinding flash issued from the gun.

Then, bolts of light, like many whips all cracked by the same master, slammed into the tank.

BLAAAM!

The tank blew. An orange ball of flame rose in the sky. Large chunks of metal flew in all directions. There was a loud cheer and a round of applause from the crowd.

The reporters removed their goggles and ran toward the smoldering heap, cameras clicking.

Agent 13 ran with them, his note pad under his arm, and his camera held ready.

"Yah ask me, I think it's a fraud," Corbett offered from beside Eddie Faulk, who was diligently clicking off frames. "I think there was dynamite inside that thing all along. Military snake oil. Just another way to pry long green out of John Q. Public."

13 didn't reply, but he did surreptitiously examine the rubble for signs that the other reporter's suspicion might be right. There was no trace or smell of the cordite associated with powder blasts. Only the lingering smell of ozone from an electrical arc. The weapon had clearly caused the incredible destruction.

"Well, whaddaya think, Faulk?" Corbett persisted, tugging on his driving cap.

"Damnedest thing I've ever seen," Faulk muttered finally. He didn't have to pretend the amazed tone in his voice—13 was truly astounded by the damage the gun had done.

"Well, I'm not supportin' it. The last thing we need is some expensive new toy for the Army."

Faulk didn't answer. The Lightning Gun hadn't worked like any weapon

13 had ever seen before. It hadn't blown up its target—the gas in the tank had done that. What it appeared to have done was infuse so much energy into the tank that it had blown out every individual rivet, cooked every wire, and set fire to every object within. It was clearly a weapon of mass destruction.

Agent 13 turned and eyed Dr. Fischer, who stood surrounded by reporters. He had shed his natural timidity in this moment of scientific glory.

Two things were certain—the Brotherhood was interested in this weapon, and they must not be allowed to get their hands on it. But a weapon this powerful could be used as a means of maintaining peace as well as fighting a war. If the United States military was truly interested in developing the Lightning Gun for its own use, America's position would be strengthened dramatically.

Dr. Fischer would have to be watched—closely. If the Brotherhood made a move for him, he would have to be rescued and removed from danger. Or, if that proved impossible, the scientist would have to be destroyed—along with his prototype gun, his notes, everything.

Suddenly, 13's thoughts were jerked back to his surroundings by Corbett, the short reporter, tugging on his sleeve.

"Hey, Faulk! Get a load of that!"

A black limousine with a police cherry on top was screaming toward the shore where the observers were still milling around the tank remnants. Immediately, the senior government official present—Kent Walters, the National Security Advisor—ran toward it.

The Agent was among the reporters who dashed along behind Walters toward the limo. Something was up. Something that concerned the National Security Advisor. Everyone was speculating. Could it be war?

By the time 13 reached the limousine, guards had closed in behind the National Security Advisor. Faulk was, after all, just another reporter.

The reporters clamored around the limo, demanding answers to shouted questions while the guards shoved them back. Agent 13's hearing had been trained many years ago to receive and decipher specific noises from the midst of chaos. He focused his attention on Kent Walters, who was speaking to his aide. The fragments of conversation that 13 overheard alarmed him. Elbowing his way past a shouting cameraman, he managed to hear one final bit before the car door slammed shut.

"Set up a meeting of the National Security Council. We'll screen it there! America will not be blackmai—"

"Whaddaya think, Faulk?" asked Corbett. But the tall reporter was busy watching the black limo disappear down the road, speeding toward Washington.

THE CRYPTIC TRYST

The brightly lit Capitol dome glowed against the dark, satiny night. To some, that dome was a beacon of freedom in the murk of growing global tyranny. To others, it was the glowing heart of a benevolent empire. But to Agent 13, observing the gleaming dome through a filthy window in a deserted warehouse, it was an egg about to be knocked from its safe and secure wall. In the autumn of 1937, America's isolationist shell was thin, easily cracked.

When Japanese bombers sank the American gunboat *Panay* in the Yangtze River, few Americans felt that the growling Eastern Empire had anything to do with them.

In a vain effort to avoid entanglement in the impending global war, the U.S. House and Senate ratified three successive Neutrality Acts in 1935, '36, and '37. Even so, the harder the young democracy tried to isolate herself from world affairs, the farther she was drawn into them.

But she faced a worse danger still, though only one man knew of it—the Brotherhood. After viewing the havoc wrought by war-breeding incidents in Europe and Asia, Agent 13 knew that the Brotherhood's next efforts would be directed here—against the Great Democracy. Agent 13 knew he had to stop them... but his position was weak.

His adventure in Istanbul had been a trade-off. Killing the Rook and the German in Istanbul had dealt a devastating blow to the Brotherhood—they would have to find and train a new mentor for their Hitler, and they would be forced to make some time-consuming leadership changes. But it had also severed 13's most important link to the organization.

Still, he had deemed it necessary and now he did not regret his actions—he had the Seer Stone, and with it he could identify any member of the Brotherhood. As long as he had it, the Brotherhood was vulnerable. The Istanbul incident had also revealed the Brotherhood's interest in this Dr. Fischer and his Lightning Gun, an interest that boded well for no one.

No, it had been worth the risk. With the Seer Stone he had the means to destroy the Brotherhood by having the capability to uncover any member. 13 knew that the Brotherhood would stop at nothing to get the pendant back. Therefore, he would use it as bait to bring the most powerful secret society in history down upon him. And thus, he hoped to be able find and destroy their leaders.

It was a risk, but there was no choice, not with the Brotherhood's interest in the Lightning Gun, although Agent 13 was, at the moment, at a loss to see how it might be useful to them. But then, there had never been a choice. Life or death— those were his stakes. Those had been his stakes ever since severing his own bonds with the ancient organization half a lifetime ago.

Closing his eyes, Agent 13 "saw" the Hand Sinister, the Brotherhood's ruler, as he had heard him described: *A gaunt face... burning eyes. "They will drive you mad if you stare into them "A hawk nose... chiseled teeth .. . yellowed skin creased by a thousand wrinkles . . . "He's been kept alive for millennia on infant's blood and jackal's bane" The haunting face... laughing... ancient, rotted breath blowing upon the victim ...*

Then he saw himself at a chessboard, sitting across from the Hand Sinister. Agent 13 made a clever move and a "rook" died among the minarets of Istanbul. Reality within abstraction. Now the shadow of a skeletal hand again hovers above the board, reaching down....

Then, twisting his mind around like a metaphysical Moebius strip, he looked at the board through the eyes of his enemy. Hearing laughter echoing in the ancient skull, peering through ancient eye sockets, he saw the Dead German and the Living Agent 13....

A horrifying possibility broke over him! The Hand Sinister had *sacrificed* the Nazi! It was all part of a scheme as involved as the pattern in a Turkish rug, but he could see only the very edge, the fringes of a scheme within a plot within a battle within a war within an imperial ambition whose complexity was so great that none save the Hand Sinister could grasp it.

13 pounded his fist on a table as—
The phone rang.

He lifted the receiver but did not speak. Customary procedure. His colleagues knew that familiar silence better than their mothers' voices.

"The eyes of—uh—the—uh—Owl see in—uh— many directions."

"Proceed," said 13, smiling slightly.

"The—uh—Falconers con-congregate in . . . damn it! Lemme tell ya straight, boss."

"Go ahead, Benny." He knew what the call was about. The code wasn't necessary for this. Though a trusted informer, Benny had his intellectual limits.

"That meetin' ya wanted to know about. It's tonight at eight."

"Where?"

"All I could get was that it's in some place called 'Eagle's Nest.' That a tavern?"

"Thank you. Now, I want you to tail a man named Fischer, David Fischer. He can be found in the Physics Laboratories at Wilber University. I want to know who he sees and where he goes."

"Gotcha. Anythin' else?"

"No." The line went dead.

Benny the Eye—a member of 13's organization. In the course of his relentless battle with the Brotherhood, the Agent had pulled many lives from the dark shadow cast by that ancient evil. Some of those he saved volunteered their lives to his service, so, in time, he had built up a strong network of agents from all walks of life: police, criminals, sports figures, actors, politicians.

Benny was an odd case. A completely nondescript little man, he had the priceless ability to fade into the woodwork. Thus, Benny the Eye could go anywhere, see all, and hear all—without being noticed. He was also the best "tail" in the business.

Acting on the words Agent 13 had heard National Security Advisor Kent Walters say at the Lightning Gun test, he had put his best operative on the trail, and now it had paid off.

The National Security Council, made up of America's top lawmen, was meeting in emergency session tonight in their secret headquarters. Had the Hand Sinister made his move?

DEATH'S CALLING CARDS

Thousands of Washingtonians drove past the National Security building daily without having any idea of what went on inside. It could have passed for an embassy or even the home of one of the remaining "old" families of Washington. But, in fact, it was the arm of the U.S. Government that attempted to fill the gap between national law enforcement, the State Department, and the War Department.

The midnight oil burned late in a room on the top floor camouflaged as a luxurious penthouse apartment. Inside, behind thick, flowered curtains, a movie projector's beam of light cut through thick cigar smoke that hung motionless in the darkened room. Five men were seated at a massive oak table strewn with file folders. Their attention was focused on the film's images unrolling on the screen at the far end of the room.

Each of the men whose faces flickered in the light of the projector represented a different facet of American law. Together, they made up the National Security Countil.

Assistant Attorney General John Myerson was the horse trader. The slightly overweight politician, who had risen to his position through shrewd and cunning deals made with little fish in order to hook big fish, sat in a leather armchair, puffing on his cigar as he watched the film with a bored expression.

Next to him sat Jack Halloran of Treasury. Strong-jawed, bald as a cue ball, Halloran was a pure-strain gumshoe more at ease on the streets than in a plush penthouse. He invariably rolled a silver dollar over his finger knuckles, no matter where he was or what he was doing.

Kent Walters, the National Security Advisor, was the stoic frontier marshal. A born leader, he had no patience for details and, as an administrator, he didn't need any. All he needed to do was raise posses and chase after the bad guys. Given his quick rise out of the East Coast political machine, he apparently did that quite well. A shrewd judge of character, he was also gifted with a knack for making the right call, especially when it came to events of world-wide importance. Having already seen the film, he watched his deputies more closely than the screen.

Next to him sat Constantin Gyrakos, head of the East Coast division of the Secret Service. Gyrakos was the plodding investigator. "The old man of the department," Constantin had seen and experienced it all, often relating his stories with a dry, biting humor.

The last person in the room was Robert Buck-hurst, Deputy Director of the FBI. Dr. Buckhurst sat in his tweed suit, puffing on a severe pipe that dangled from his lower lip. The "modern scientist" of the group, hand-picked by Hoover to be here, Buckhurst viewed himself as the future of law enforcement. Never one to make a rash or hasty decision before all the evidence and possible angles had been explored, he sat in a cold, unmoving silence.

No one sat too near Buckhurst. He was neither liked nor trusted. Everybody knew that whatever was said in his presence went straight back to his boss. But tonight, this was his show.

All eyes, except Walters's, were on the screen, viewing a spectacle both horrifying in image and implication. The gaping maw of a railroad tunnel spat out the Olympian, a thundering locomotive. Smoke and steam poured from its mighty stack, sparks shot from the track, and the shriek of a whistle whined through a desolate Montana valley.

One by one, train cars emerged from the tunnel. The first five held passengers, then came a pair of box cars, and finally, tank cars, with the word "HELIUM" painted on the side.

The locomotive roared onto a 180-foot-high trestle bridge that stretched across Custer Creek Canyon like a spider web made of steel.

Suddenly, an explosion shook the trestles. The bridge crumbled as if made of matchsticks. With a wailing shriek of its whistle, like a dying scream, the train plunged into the chasm. Almost simultaneously, the cars carrying the helium cracked open, releasing the liquid to the open air, where hundreds of tons of the valuable substance immediately disappeared into the atmosphere.

As the train dropped into the canyon like a bizarre, reticulated snake, Myerson shifted his heavy girth and muttered through his soggy cigar, "The Montana Line crash ..."

"I still say that crash was an accident," injected Gyrakos. "A flash flood weakened the bridge...."

"Then who the hell took this movie?" Walters turned to Buckhurst. "What did Hoover's boys find out?"

Buckhurst answered coldly and precisely. "The footage was taken with a wide-angle lense from a low-flying aircraft of unknown type and origin flying approximately twelve hundred feet above the train with an airspeed of sixty knots. None of the survivors reported hearing or seeing an aircraft at any time before, during, or after the crash.

"I considered the possibility that the aircraft had dropped a bomb on the train and had several forensic experts in my lab check the film frame by frame. The first explosion was on the bridge, the next two on the train, though the helium itself, of course, could not explode. It leads me to believe that they were set off by some type of remote control—perhaps activated from the aircraft or somewhere nearby—or even by the train itself—a pressure mine on the tracks, a trip timer with a fuse, or any of a dozen other ways. It's impossible to tell at this time."

The images on the screen changed suddenly, pulling back the men's attention.

This time, the scene was of a distant factory in a desert. Several experimental-type fighter planes sat on a nearby airstrip. A high security fence surrounded the entire complex. At one security post, three guards could be seen idly chatting in the midday sun. All appeared calm and orderly.

And then—

A massive explosion ripped through the factory, sending chunks of steel, airplanes, men, and cement-block wall upward in a growing, smoke-filled tower of debris. Moments later, the shock waves from the massive explosion knocked the guards off their feet, soon shaking even the camera itself, as evidenced by the jittery movement of the image. Then, only spiraling smoke and raining debris filled the screen.

Buckhurst knew what his colleagues' questions would be. "The footage was taken with a tele-photo lens from the Lone Steer Cafe, an abandoned structure approximately one thousand yards from the northern perimeter fence of Westron Aircraft—"

"You mean what used to be Westron Aircraft," grunted Gyrakos, the joker.

Eyeing him disapprovingly, Buckhurst continued, "The destruction was total. More then sixteen hundred cubic feet of ground composition was displaced. The resulting crater was approximately seventeen feet deep and fifty feet in diameter at the surface."

"Those guys didn't have a chance," mumbled Halloran, his silver coin shining in the light as he flicked it faster and faster.

"Any aircraft seen in the area?" asked Walters.

"Not that's been reported so far," Buckhurst replied, coughing slightly and glancing irritably at Myerson and his eternal cigar. "Once again, we believe that the bomb was activated by remote control. Shortly before the explosion occurred, one of the guards along the northern fence remembered seeing a brown Ford pickup truck pull into the Lone Steer Cafe with steam pouring out of its engine. The driver climbed out, lifted the hood, and appeared to be making some repairs to the steaming engine. It was at this time that the explosion occurred. Several minutes later, the driver, seemingly terror-stricken, jumped into the truck and fled."

"Did he get a make on the guy?" demanded Myerson.

"No," replied Buckhurst. "The driver was too far away for the guard to identify. But two days later, the burned-out remains of a truck fitting the description was found in the desert forty miles from the factory. A clean white sheet of paper was on the charred seat inside the cab, and embossed on it was the symbol you'll find black-and-white glossy prints of in the folders in front of you."

Leafing through his folder, Myerson found the desired print. He pulled it out and studied the symbol.

"It is the symbol Omega," continued Buckhurst. "Experts on these things have been unable to attach it to any known organization."

"What does it mean?" demanded Halloran.

"The end."

Myerson snorted. "The end of what?"

"Just 'the end,' " Buckhurst said with an edge of finality. "There were no words, no demands, only the symbol. As for the truck itself, the license plates and engine serial numbers had been removed."

"Untraceable?" queried Myerson, snubbing out his cigar.

"Thus far. What my men found even stranger was that there was no sign of anyone or anything leaving the wreck, though there'd been no wind or rain for days. The sand was smooth, blank. No foot or tire prints to be seen anywhere nearby." Buckhurst raised his hand as a signal for the projectionist to continue.

"Sounds like your boys have had their hands full," remarked Walters, his attention again shifting to the screen.

This time it was a more familiar image—the dirigible *Hindenburg*, the pride of the German airship fleet, slowly settling to its mooring-mast at Lakehurst, New Jersey. The film was being shot by someone standing in the crowd on the ground. Suddenly, the blurred image of a woman's large hat filled the screen.

As the shot was brought into focus, the intricate beadwork design encircling the hat came into focus. The design was the same Omega symbol found in the pickup. Her 'message' delivered, the well-dressed woman disappeared back into the crowd, her face hidden by the large hat bearing the symbol. The film shifted its focus back to the Hindenburg, just in time to see it burst into flames. Slowly the inferno spread, engulfing the huge ship as it fell, fatally stricken, to the ground.

"Just after the disaster, we questioned the ground crew and the people who had been waiting for arriving passengers." Buckhurst's voice was clinical in its detachment. "There were several people taking motion pictures of the landing. We've checked all of them out—they're all legit. Besides, none of them had cameras nearly sophisticated enough for this film. We believe that someone hidden in a service vehicle parked in the area took the motion picture—same method as was used at the Westron Factory."

"The cause?" asked Gyrakos, though his tone said he already knew the answer.

"After examining the film, we once again believe it was a bomb, planted in the *Hindenburg* before its departure from Frankfurt. The device probably exploded near one of the rear gas bags of the ship. It wouldn't take much—hydrogen's so combustible the littlest spark would set it off."

Walters asked Buckhurst, "What do the Germans think?"

"I sent them the information on the other disasters and we're still waiting for their experts to give us their opinions. Off the record, they appear to be as confused as we are, but, see-ing all the enemies they've been creating lately, I'm sure they have ideas of their own...."

A figure slowly superimposed itself over the image of the flaming Hindenburg. The figure wore a hood over its head. The only features of the face visible through the mask were a pair of cold eyes and lips, whose skin was parched and cracked. The Omega symbol found in the burned-out truck and seen at the *Hindenburg* disaster was seen once more—now affixed to the center of the cloth hood. An evenly measured, sinister voice began to speak as the airship continued to burn.

"Gentlemen, what you have just witnessed is only a sample of the disasters that I, the Masque, am capable of causing. They are but a hint of the horrors that will befall the United States and other countries if my demands are not met.

"My present demands are as follows: First, weapons research and production at the Taylor, McVickers, Bearings, and Thompson plants will be stopped immediately.

"Second, 'Operation Seahawk'—the naval exercise scheduled to take place in the Caribbean next month—will be canceled.

"Third, all work and research relating to the *Essex* and *Atlanta* class warships will be discontinued immediately.

"Fourth and finally, for the time being, the Naval Research Laboratory will be disbanded. All its scientists and personnel will be filtered back into civilian life."

After a pause, the sinister figure continued, "We can strike anywhere at any time. You and your armies are powerless to stop us. My demands, like my disasters, are easy to understand. You have one week to respond. If you intend to comply, I'll expect to see a red flare glowing over the Treasury Building in Washington, D.C., precisely at midnight on October 20. Failure to do so will set off disasters of even greater magnitude.

"Do not test my patience, gentlemen—"

Halloran turned to Buckhurst. "This is the fifth time we've seen this. That's enough."

Buckhurst turned and signaled the projectionist in the back of the room. "That'll be all for tonight, thank you." The projector ground to a halt as the lights came back up in the smoke-filled room.

Several of the men, blinking in the sudden light, looked at the large wall clock in the corner of the room. The time was 11:35 p.m.

Buckhurst puffed on his pipe, bringing a reddened glow to the cherry tobacco. "I wish I had better news, but as you can see, thus far we haven't come up with anything of much use."

"What about the clown in the hooded mask?" demanded Gyrakos with a gruff Bogart tone.

"Nothing. We've had linguistics experts, trying to detect a regional ac-

cent or something, but there's nothing. We even sent film samples to all the major development labs, hoping they could help us trace it to the processor. Again nothing."

Buckhurst turned to Myerson. "What did the Attorney General say?"

Myerson, stuffing papers back into his folder, said, "He talked to the President himself. Roosevelt refuses to budge. Under no circumstances will he compromise our national security and give in to the demands. They view the problem as ours, and they expect results!"

Halloran looked at the clock, watching as the final moments ticked by. "Well, then it looks like we're going to have to ride out the storm."

Gyrakos shifted nervously in his seat. "The deadline expires in fifteen minutes." Standing suddenly, he walked to a window and opened it. In the far distance the lights atop the Treasury Building glowed and somewhere beyond that glowed the eyes of a fiend, waiting for a signal that would never come.

From behind them came a voice.

"You are fools to underestimate the danger the United States is in. Yet you would also be fools to submit to it."

VOICE FROM THE SHADOWS

Gyrakos spun around. Standing directly behind him was the projectionist, a nondescript, middle-aged man with a receding hairline and rumpled clothing.

"When we need a projectionist's advice, we'll ask for it," snarled Myerson, glancing at the man irritably. "Meanwhile, you're through for tonight. Just get the hell out—"

But Gyrakos made an abrupt cutting motion with his hand. "Wait a minute. Something about this guy's not right," he said evenly. "Look at his eyes."

Every man in the room turned his attention on the projectionist, who was nodding and smiling grimly, letting his gaze sweep over them in turn. He held no weapon—unless it was that strange, intense look in his eyes.

"Mr. Walters, move your hand away from your pocket, or I'll be forced to kill you."

Walters did as he was told. The others instinctively placed their hands on the table, attesting to their lack of weapons. The air of danger in the room was palpable.

The projectionist continued speaking. "I am Agent 13. You all have heard of me, and you all have different opinions of me. Some are accurate, others are not, but whatever you think of me or my motives, have no doubt that I am your ally against the Masque."

The Agent, with extensive files on these men, knew what each was thinking.

Buckhurst (and thereby the FBI) had no evidence to prove the Agent's existence; therefore, the Assistant Director believed 13 did not exist. But Buckhurst was, of course, willing to listen, filing everything away in his head to report to J. Edgar.

Walters, whose overheard words

at the Fischer demonstration had led the Agent to this meeting, regarded Agent 13 with an icy calm, perhaps looking for the flaw within the Agent that would permit him to disprove 13's existence and shuffle him out of the deck.

Myerson had once asked his underworld leads to give him the scoop on Agent 13 and had come up dry. He concluded that the Midnight Avenger was most likely a dangerous paranoid, who must be humored.

Gyrakos, who was born in a land of ancient legends and myths and who had heard vague tales of the Brotherhood, was a sympathetic listener.

Halloran studied the man as if he were a bug under a microscope. He'd seen every type of flapper and scammer on the street before . . . but something about this bird was different.

It was Walters, though, who got down to business. "What do you know about the Masque?"

"Too little, save that he belongs to the Brotherhood. "

Gyrakos nodded, with the smug look of one in the know. This irritated Myerson.

"What the hell is 'the Brotherhood'?" he snapped.

"There isn't time to go into the checkered, labyrinthine history of the Brotherhood," responded Agent 13, "but it has existed since the ancient kingdom of Lemuria. In the past, it guided mankind along the paths of good. Unfortunately, as the film dem-

onstrated, this is true no longer. Unless immediate steps are taken, time is short for civilization."

"Oh, bullhockey!" Halloran snorted. "Call the guards."

Removing a special set of gloves he wore to avoid leaving fingerprints, Agent 13 lifted up his hand. "What do you see on my palm?"

"This is ridiculous!" Halloran snarled angrily.

"Shut up, Jack." said Buckhurst coolly. "We see nothing. What is your point?"

In answer, Agent 13 reached into his vest pocket and withdrew the Seer Stone. Tossing it across to Buckhurst, he held up his palm.

"Now look at it," Agent 13 said. Buckhurst, peering through the stone, saw the number 13 and the Omega symbol—the same symbol as adorned the Masque's hood.

"This doesn't prove anything," Halloran said, sneering, "except that you're probably one of the them—"

"I *was* one of them," 13 responded coolly. "That is why they fear me and why you should listen to me. But, now, silence, for time is short. Already, the Brotherhood has tightened its fingers around Germany, Italy, Russia, and Japan. You want proof? Look at this." As he spoke, he threw photographs down on the table.

One after another, the men seated there lifted the pictures, studying them intently. There were photographs of documents, with attached translations from the German, giving figures indicating massive rearmaments. There were photos of secret U-boat factories in Sweden, blueprints of new tanks and rockets, plans for a hidden rocket base at a place called Peenemunde, photos of the training of fighter pilots in sham "Aero sports clubs," and, finally, meticulously detailed plans for global conquest.

"Is this stuff real?" spat out Gyrakos, knowing that, if it was, Hitler was in violation of every treaty Germany had ever signed. "This means war!"

"Yes," answered 13 to both questions.

"Where did you get these?" asked Myerson.

"I cannot, of course, divulge that, but if you check the figures and the locations mentioned, you'll find them correct."

"What are these?" Walters asked, pointing to another stack of photos 13 dropped on the desk.

Halloran picked them up.

There was a picture of Adolf Hitler with his high command. A picture of Mussolini in Ethiopia, a picture of Tojo aboard a Japanese carrier, a picture of Stalin in a darkened room.

And in each of the shots, one face was circled—that of the German officer 13 had killed in Istanbul. Always in the background, always shadowed, always slightly different, but recognizable just the same.

"His name was Colonel Reinhardt

Schmidt of the SS. Until recently, this man was one of the Brotherhood's primary operatives."

"You said 'was.' Have they deactivated him?" asked Buckhurst, his scientist's voice implying neither belief nor disbelief, simply the need for information.

"No. I did," the Agent responded. "As you see, the Brotherhood now has each of these countries in its grasp. And the Hand Sinister is reaching toward the throat of America. In this nation lies mankind's last, best hope. In other countries, these criminals need only sway a few men, but here, they must sway public opinion. Hence— terrorism. We must stand united. Only with this,"

he said, holding up the Seer Stone, "do we have a chance of removing the cancer that has already infected the nation."

As the others watched the Agent, the clock began to chime. It was a cold, terrifying moment, and all the men went silent. When the last bell sounded, Myerson was the first to speak. "The ball's in his court."

Even through his disguise, a strange look could be seen to cross 13's face—a look of stunned realization as he saw, instantaneously and clearly, the subtlety of the Masque's plan.

"Hit the ground!" he shouted as he dove to the floor. But his understanding came too late. Before the crime fighters could move, a hail of machine-gun fire turned the penthouse windows into jagged shrapnel....

Four assassins, wearing black masks and dark suits, burst through the windows into the room, spraying lead death.

Bullets hit Buckhurst from both sides, spinning his chair wildly around and dumping his body into the fireplace. Gyrakos jumped to his feet, only to be drilled to the ground by a bullet. Halloran tried to duck under the table, but a single shotgun blast shattered the wood. He looked up, stung, only to have a second blast take off his head.

Myerson tried to jump across the table to safety but was hit in the back with a shot that sent him sliding across the conference table like a giant broom, mopping up the papers and ashtrays on the way.

Walters ran for the door. A shot rang out. He slipped in a pool of Buckhurst's blood, fell to the floor, and did not get up.

Crouched in the corner of the room, Agent 13 drew a .45 and started firing his special high impact bullets. The killers leaped for the windows as his shots gouged walls and shattered timbers. Their Thompsons turned on 13. He pulled his hat over his face.

It seemed a stupid, futile gesture—the hopeless, instinctive action of a desperate man. One of the assassins even laughed as the machine guns blew 13's body about the room like a piece of litter.

Then, as quickly as the noise had come, came the silence. One of the assassins grabbed the Seer Stone from the floor where it had fallen from Buckhurst's lifeless hand. Drawing out a small spray canister, he squirted a liquid substance onto the photographs. They began to smoke and, within instants, were nothing more than gray ash. As he did this, another assassin produced a grappling hook and, stepping out the window, hurled it upward. The two other assassins warily backed to the window, firing a shot here and there into a twitching body.

There was the sound of a grappling hook striking the roofs top ledge and the soft sound of bodies padding up the side of the building.

AFTER THE ASSASSINS

Agent 13 groaned softly. His body convulsed in pain. Silver spots swam before his vision. His eardrums, numbed by the horrible cackle of the machine guns, screamed in harmony with sirens howling in the distance.

Throbbing pain told 13 that the murderous lead rounds had struck him in numerous places. What he didn't know was if his protective, bullet-proof garb had held. 13 felt the floor below him. There was no blood. The knowledge was of slight comfort as he fought off the darkness that threatened to enshroud him.

Painfully, the Agent pulled himself up, having no time to marvel at the thin material, barely heavier than wool, that had saved his life. The dumpy-looking coat and hat had stopped the slugs from ripping him to shreds.

A glance at Buckhurst's lifeless hand told 13 that the assassins had acquired an unexpected bonus—the Seer Stone. He had to get it back!

Ignoring the pain of cracked ribs and deep bruises, he softly repeated an ancient mantra he had been taught in childhood. With the repeated utterance of a single word, vibrations in the body, generated by the brain, wrapped 13 in a soothing cloud of internal consciousness. Waves of energy coursed through his body, and the pain subsided. Such was the power of the Agent's meditations.

Such was the power of the Brotherhood's teachings.

Returning to the material world, the Agent heard the insistent whine of distant sirens coming closer. Moving across the room, he quickly surveyed the massacre scene. Buckhurst lay in a twisted heap with his head in the cold fireplace. Assistant Attorney General Myerson lay across the table, his head hanging over the edge, dripping blood to the floor like a tap with a broken washer. The remains of Gy-rakos, which the assassins must have used for target practice, were scattered about like so many old rags.

From somewhere in the room, though, 13 heard what he thought was a soft moan. But he could not determine which of the victims it came from. An expert at first aid, the Agent had a hard decision to make—should he save the wounded man, or pursue the assassins, who, even now, were slipping away across the rooftop? The sirens screamed louder. Long ago, 13 had become a master of hard choices.

Agent 13 was a battered sight as he jammed a new clip into his pistol, threw off the bullet-proof coat that would have hampered his dexterity, and climbed out the window to a narrow marble ledge. The shadows of the assassins could be seen swinging from one rooftop to another with the aid of their grappling hooks.

Seven stories below him, a fleet of police cars raced toward the building.

He had to get to the next rooftop. 13's eyes scanned the dirt-encrusted brick wall of the opposite building, looking for a ledge. There was none, and he cursed the lack of a grappling hook. Then, he spied a damp flag, dangling from the top of a flagpole twenty feet below him.

It was an impossible jump, of course. But Agent13 had learned long ago that there are no impossibilities, merely improbabilities. Dashing

along the ledge with a speed and dexterity usually reserved for professional gymnasts, he leaped out and down toward the flag.

For a moment of ice, he hung frozen in the air. He missed the pole, but then his hand caught the fabric of the flag. There was a sharp ripping sound as the worn fabric tore....

Then it stopped. The Agent's life hung precariously by the tattered strands of Old Glory. Peering into the night, he scanned the lines of the rooftops but could see no trace of the assassins in the velvety fog.

Closing his eyes, the Agent blocked out the insistent whine of police sirens, the view of the ground still far beneath him, the sound of the strands of fabric slowly parting. His mind's energy sought one thing only—the assassins.

Using a technique he had learned from the Brotherhood, he concentrated on absorbing the energy of those he pursued into his own being. As a result, their shadowy forms appeared on his closed eyelids. Concentrating on these distant shadows, without opening his eyes, Agent 13 took careful aim. His gun let out a loud roar, and ... in the distance, probably on the rooftop of the elegant apartment building next door... he heard the thud of his bullet striking a human body. He saw a sudden burst of light as the assassin's body burst into flames, and cremated itself from within

Jindas! The Brotherhood's killers!

The Serpentine Assassins. Hidden in life. Burned in death.

Suddenly, the Agent was pierced by a sterile, white searchlight.

"Freeze!" an amplified voice shouted from below. Agent 13 twisted, looking down. A score of police marksmen targeted him from the open parking lot, crouching behind their cars. Without his bullet-proof jacket, he would be torn to shreds by their bullets.

"Don't shoot!" he shouted back in the projectionist's voice, dropping his gun to the pavement. "I am a government employee! The assassins are escaping!" he cried, pointing into the distance.

"No tricks, buster. Move and we'll drill ya!" returned a voice from below.

The Agent was trapped. Holding on to the flag, he peered into the gloom, cursing, as the assassins escaped. But there was no help for it. Now he had to keep up his role of the projectionist.

He remembered his training at the Shrine-how he'd been taught to hang motionless from a tree limb for over twelve hours. Those lessons had saved his life many times in the past. But he was impersonating the projectionist, who, without 13's special training, probably couldn't last more than another few moments.

Down on the street, the marksmen still held him in their sights as ambulances screamed up to the scene and attendants tumbled out with stretchers for the dead and wounded.

"Help!" 13 shouted. "Jeez! Get me off of here!"

Near the base of the flagpole, a window opened. The heads of several policemen appeared, staring upward.

"I can't hold on!" 13 babbled.

"Just take it easy, don't panic!" one cop ordered in panic-stricken tones.

The heads disappeared. Apparently someone with authority had arrived. A graying head appeared, and world-weary eyes stared up at the dangling Agent.

"How'll we get him down, sir?" one cop asked breathlessly.

"Lower the damn flag!" snarled the grizzled old captain.

Grabbing the ropes, the cops pulled and, accompanied by the squeaking of winches, they hauled in Agent 13, clinging to Old Glory.

"How the hell did you get out there?" the old captain asked.

"I dunno!" 13 stammered. "Adrenaline, maybe. Like little old ladies liftin' cars offa kids."

Suddenly, the milling, uniformed police officers in the room parted like the Dead Sea, and out stepped a man dressed in a plain gray suit and tie and a battered fedora.

"Detective LaMonica," the man said in a bored voice, flipping out a well-worn wallet, flipping it open, then flipping it shut all in a blur of movement.

One look at LaMonica, and Agent 13 knew he was nobody's fool. The man's keen, hawklike eyes surveyed the Agent.

"Cuff him," he said matter-of-factly to two nearby uniformed cops.

The officers quickly obeyed, slapping bracelets on the disguised Agent's wrists as LaMonica stepped over to the window ledge and peered up at the flagpole.

"Hey!" 13 protested. "What's with the rough stuff? I'm innocent! The guys that did this are getting away!" Standing behind LaMonica, Agent 13 began to talk rapidly, as though tense and keyed up.

"I-I was showing a film, top secret stuff, and then there was glass all over the place and flying bullets...."

"Yeah?" LaMonica said noncomittally. Turning around, LaMonica eyed 13.

"You got an ID, mister, or just a mouth?" LaMonica asked.

"Of course I got an ID. But how'm I supposed to get to it?"

With a lazy gesture, LaMonica brought forward a cop, who proceeded to frisk 13 quickly and efficiently. Pulling the Agent's wallet from his pants, the cop handed it to LaMonica.

LaMonica studied an official government security card.

"Howard Richardson," he read aloud.

"That's me. Member of the union since '32," said 13.

"Union rules require you to carry a .45, do they?" LaMonica asked, holding up Agent 13's gun, wrapped in a handkerchief.

"That's Halloran's gun! I defended him with my life and—"

"Get a lot of exercise in the projection booth, do yah?" LaMonica continued conversationally.

"What? Exercise?"

"Since when does a wheezy old guy like you dash across a ledge and make a jump like that?"

"I told yah, I didn't know what I was doing. I just—"

"And I got a witness who said you fired a shot. Since when does a guy hanging for dear life from a flag got the time or the nerve to go takin' pot shots over rooftops? Plus he says you started some sort of fire-"

"I'm a veteran. Three times decorated in the Great Wa—" the Agent began indignantly as LaMonica stepped once again to the window and stared out at the street.

"Stash it," LaMonica said. Looking back, he smiled. "Walters is still alive. We'll see if he recognizes you."

Looking out the window, 13 saw a stretcher being carried from the main door of the large marble building. Unlike the others, the face of its occupant wasn't covered. Kent Walters, the National Security Advisor, had miraculously survived the carnage.

"Take 'im out," LaMonica said to two cops. "Where's Doulson?"

"Just coming out of the building now, sir," reported a cop, who was watching out the window. "Good.

Let's go."

Agent 13 was led out into the drizzle, where he stood and watched as LaMonica spoke to a fat, balding man—apparently Doulson, another detective at the scene. He'd just come down with the critically injured Walters. "Whaddya get out of him?" asked LaMonica. "Not much except that four men entered the room through the windows and sprayed the place." "Professionals." Doulson shrugged. "Sure." "Did he get a make on them?" "No, they wore masks. What about him?" Doulson looked at 13.

"Claims he was the projectionist. Can Walters talk?" "Give it a try. They got him pretty doped up." LaMonica led the way to the ambulance, which was blowing blue plumes of exhaust, waiting to vanish into the night. Two men were loading the stretcher bearing Walters inside, under close supervision of a doctor.

"Hold it a minute, boys," LaMonica said, flipping out his badge.

"This man is in extremely grave condition!" the doctor snapped.

LaMonica gave him a look that said some things were more important than a man's life right now— information being one of them. The doctor, used to cops, mumbled, "O.K., but make it quick."

"Mr. Walters, I am Detective LaMonica. This gentleman claims to be from your department. Could you identify him? It's extremely urgent."

Walters rolled his glassy eyes. "Of course," he responded in a weak voice.

LaMonica led Agent 13 to the open ambulance. The National Security Advisor's eyes cleared for a moment as he evaluated him.

Would Walters betray him? Was the man able to think clearly? Quickly, Agent 13 began to talk in his projectionist voice, hoping Walters picked up on the hint.

"Mr. Walters, I thought you'd had it!" he said breathlessly. "I chased the thugs to the roof, and took a couple of shots, but—"

"Shut up," said LaMonica, shoving the Agent forward. "Do you know this man, Mr. Walters?"

Walters looked at Agent 13 for a long moment, then said weakly. "He is ... our projectionist."

"That's all, dectective!" said the doctor, elbowing them aside.

It took all of 13's training to keep him from exhaling a sigh of relief. As the orderlies slammed the doors of the ambulance shut, 13 turned to LaMonica, who was still regarding him with a keen look.

"There's still somethin' I don't like about you, pal. Let's say we go down to the station and have a little chat— you being a material witness and all."

"The cuffs?" 13 asked, raising his shackled hands.

"All right, uncuff him," LaMonica growled, "but keep your eyes on him," he told the uniforms who accompanied them.

Agent 13 shook his wrists to get his circulation going, smiling inwardly as LaMonica and his men headed for a squad car.

The Agent relaxed. His escape would be simple. All was going well. Walters had come through for him. He'd be after the assassins again within moments.

One of the uniforms opened the back door of the cop sedan and shoved the Agent inside. As the door was about to slam, 13 heard a shout from the distance and looked up. Something was going on, but the Agent couldn't see what. One of the cops stood between him and the action.

Then, the uniform looked down at 13, grinned, pulled out his pistol, and held it to 13's head. In doing so, he moved out of the way, letting 13 get a look at what was happening. What 13 saw sent a jolt of horror through him. As if seeing his own reflection in a mirror, the Agent saw the two cops escorting the real projectionist, who was swaying on his feet and looking slightly drowsy from the knockout gas 13 had administered before the meeting.

For what might have been the first time in centuries, LaMonica's stoic face broke into a wide grin. "Well, whaddya know. I got twin projectionists."

In all of his years of pursuing the Brotherhood, the Agent had never been caught quite so flat-footed. Cursing himself, he sank back into the seat. If he had killed the projectionist instead of simply knocking him out, this wouldn't have happened.

He could never let them take him in. Even if he told them who he really was, they'd never believe him. And after that, it would only be minutes before the Brotherhood, with its many eyes and ears, would eliminate him.

"Sergeant, cuff 'em both," said LaMonica, climbing into the squad car. "I don't know what's going on here, but we'll find out soon enough."

WHO STALKS THE NIGHT?

In his first battle with the Brotherhood after escaping their grasp years ago, Agent 13 had been cornered on a small island ferry that shuttled passengers from Manila to Zamboanga. The Brotherhood's agents had closed in on him in the boiler room. Trapped, 13 did the only thing he could—set fire to the ship. He survived, but the explosion set off by the fire sent the ship to the bottom and killed seventeen innocent people.

Standing among the flotsam washed up on the tropical shoreline, 13 felt deep sorrow . . . but no regret. He knew that if his fight against the Invisible Empire were to fail, millions would suffer death, or worse—live out their lives in slavery.

As a man without a country, Agent 13 had to become a law unto himself. Thus, on that beach, he swore to his Code of Death. This code allowed for killing in only three circumstances:

First, when the victim was a member of the Brotherhood. Second, when the victim was in league with the Brotherhood. And third, when Agent 13's life mission was threatened.

Agent 13 sighed. By threatening his mission, these D.C. cops had signed their own death warrants.

As the squad car rolled past the Washington Monument, 13 was sandwiched in the back seat between Detective LaMonica and a massive lieutenant who smelled of cologne and garlic. The real projectionist was in the other squad car. The Agent contemplated numerous escape strategies, finally settling upon one.

Using the skills of a Houdini, he noiselessly slipped his hands out of his handcuffs and activated a ring he wore on his left hand. The real projectionist wore a similiar ring, only his didn't turn into a lethal weapon.

Then, 13 rehearsed in his mind injecting LaMonica with the ring's poison, then delivering a swift and fatal jab to Cologne and Garlic.

Slipping his hands inside the dead officers' coats, he could draw both guns and dispatch the two uniforms in the front seat before they knew what hit them. He only had to wait for the police car to come to a stop at a traffic light.

A couple blocks ahead, the light turned yellow. As the squad car slowed, Agent 13 relaxed his muscles and then, like a cat, tensed them. He was ready to strike, when the driver's window shattered and he was staring at the headless body of the driver.

Razor-sharp shards of glass flew about the car, shredding the other cop in the front seat. Agent 13 was sprayed with blood.

LaMonica raised his weapon and lunged forward to fire, but the window next to him exploded. He slumped forward as Agent 13 dove for the floor. Cologne and Garlic failed to move in time, and his own blood joined the sprayed blood of others. He tried feebly to crawl out of his door. Death whistled his tune, and he was blown down the street like a leaf in the wind.

Agent 13 crouched on the floor, but screaming bullets turned the interior of the Ford into a hurricane of shrapnel. Bits of glass and lead tore the upholstery to lint and flesh to pulp. The horn began to wail as the driver's mangled corpse fell on it.

The squad car roared out of control, the dead driver's foot jammed on the accelerator.

Agent 13's only protection was the body of Detective LaMonica, which had toppled over on top of him.

Suddenly, the car slammed into something hard and came to an abrupt stop. There was the sound of breaking glass. Shoving LaMonica's bleeding body off him, Agent 13 cautiously raised his head and looked out the gaping hole that had been the windshield. He saw through the steam rising from the hood that the squad car had crashed through the display window of a meat market. Glancing out the car's back window, 13 saw the killing car screech to a halt behind them and two assassins jump out. The Agent caught the glassy glint of their eyes and confirmed his own suspicions. Jindas.

He searched for LaMonica's gun but couldn't find it. He couldn't reach the guns in the front seat without exposing himself to the Jindas. One was already approaching the smoking wreck of the squad car while his partner covered him, ready to I spray molten death on anything that moved.

The Agent slumped in his seat, playing dead as a glassy-eyed Jinda came to the window. Much to | his surprise, the enemy did not study any of the bodies. He simply gave the blood-spattered interior a quick once-over, then drew a grenade from his coat.

Agent 13 had no way of knowing if the assassins were after him specifically, or whether they were simply engaged in a janitorial clean-up. As the Jinda prepared to pull the pin on the grenade, 13 made his move. Leaping across the sprawled body of LaMonica, he grabbed the door handle.

But the battered handle came off in his hand. Now the Jinda studied him directly, a sinister smile on his face as he grasped the grenade's pin.

Out of the corner of his eye, Agent 13 caught a glimpse of movement. The other Jinda was raising his gun. Agent 13 recognized it, and his heart sank. A Browning Automatic. If he did manage to make it outside the car, the BAR's bullets would rip him to shreds.

The Jinda pulled the pin. 13 had ten seconds. Everything went into slow motion as the Agent tensed to leap through the window at the Jinda.

The move would put him in the sights of the other assassin's BAR. But if he was to die, his mission unfulfilled, then he wanted to go down fighting, his hands clenched in death around the assassin's throat.

Then, from a completely new direction, 13 heard the rumbling cracks of machine-gun fire.

TRAIL OF TORMENT

Maggie Darr's life had always been inextricably connected to crime. She grew up on the South Side of Chicago during Prohibition. It was a wild and violent era. Her own father was shot dead right on the family's front doorstep.

Some said he had it coming to him. Maggie never really knew for sure. Even as an adult, Maggie would be jolted from bed by the remembered sounds of shots and screams.

Life was tough for a while, but when Maggie was twelve, her mother remarried. Maggie's stepfather was an Irish Alderman named McGarrity, who always seemed to have a great wad of greenbacks. Things took a turn for the better.

When she was sixteen, Maggie was sent to a private girls' prep school located between the mansions of Kenilworth and the factories of Chicago. Respected by educators, it was also a feeding ground for the young bachelors of Chicago, who cruised around it like sharks on patrol.

Jimmy Lasatti's gray-and-white convertible looked like a shark. And when he saw the tall, shapely, blonde girl coming out of class, he went into a frenzy. At first she was terse with him. appearing uninterested, as a well-brought-up young lady should. But the shark smelled blood— the blood of loneliness.

Jimmy's gambling uncle had taught him that the longer you stay with a bet, the more likely it is to pay off. Jimmy took this philosophy into amorous relations, wooing Maggie in a dizzying, fairytale manner that made her the envy of her schoolmates. The cars, the yachts, and the parties overwhelmed the young girl, making her feel as if she had stumbled upon a golden garden in the midst of the dust bowl.

Maggie was deaf to her parents' pleas that "he might not be safe." Jimmy said he was in the export business. That was good enough for Maggie.

One night Jimmy took her to Como Inn, the finest and most romantic Italian restaurant in Chicago. After a leisurely dinner of pasta and Chianti, he popped the question, presenting her with a diamond ring. Maggie, wide-eyed, had no trouble coming up with "yes."

Several bottles of champagne later, they left Como, entwined in each other's arms. The valet brought Jimmy's DeSoto to the front. As they got in, Jimmy found a .45 shoved in his ear. A frog-voiced thug gave him driving instructions.

Whirling around to see, Maggie's fear turned to revulsion. The thug in the back seat had hideously distorted features that resembled candle drippings much more than a nose, eyes, and a mouth. Purplish skin surrounded hideously misshapen, bulging eyes and a drooping hole of a mouth that could never close all the way. His nose barely projected beyond the contours of his face, and his ears were small lumps of butter melting off a hairless scalp.

Maggie started to scream, but the thug, who she would later know as "Waxface," punched her. Revulsion turned to rage. No one had ever dared strike Maggie Darr before. She screamed and kept on screaming. The thug hit her again and kept on hitting

her. Before long, Maggie was out cold.

When she came to, her wrists were cuffed together and she was hanging by the handcuffs from a hook in a meat locker, surrounded by bloody sides of beef. She had been stripped to her underwear, and her skin was blue from the cold. Her screams got attention. A large wooden door flew open and a pin-striped thug stepped through.

"Let me down!" she shrieked.

Beyond the thug, Maggie could see a man she knew from pictures in the Daily News—Lucky Milano. Lit by a bright, overhead light, Lucky was a dapper sight. Medium height, he wore a crisp blue suit with a flower at the lapel and was surrounded by a squad of torpedoes the Navy would be proud to own.

For the moment, Lucky wasn't paying any attention to Maggie, however. He and his boys were standing in a circle, staring at something Maggie couldn't see.

But the thug at the door walked toward Maggie. Suddenly conscious of her partial nakedness, Maggie eyed the man whose face was shadowed by his fedora. As he drew closer, she saw that it was Waxface. She gagged. His hideously contorted mouth grinned at the sight of her horror.

Suddenly, she heard a loud, pain-filled scream. Looking into the other room, Maggie could now see what was in the center of that pin-striped circle—Jimmy, tied to a chair. The cause of his hideous yell was Lucky Milano stubbing out a cigar in his eye! Maggie retched.

"I'll talk! I'll talk!" Jimmy shrieked. Maggie could then hear the low rumble of his voice and even occasionally make out words. Then there were blood-curdling, muffled shouts....

Then silence.... And Maggie knew it was over. Despair, pain, and fear joined forces to put her mind on hold.

Some time later, a commotion brought Maggie back to reality, and she found Lucky, without a wrinkle in his pin-stripe, staring at her. She trembled like a small, trapped animal.

"Sorry, broad, but you were in the wrong place at the wrong time. Your friend Jimmy squealed big before Fats erased him. Now, toots, we gotta zap you before some tin star tips us over.

"She's all yours, Jacky," Lucky said, and his triggerman lifted his gun. "Nothin' personal," Lucky said, shrugging.

Maggie stared down the barrel of the gun. The darkness inside there would transport her to eternal darkness or to heaven or to hell. She didn't know which. But as she realized that the horror was about to end, a cooling veil fell over her. She grew calm. Many who stare eyeball to eyeball with death have known that calmness.

She would, in later weeks, remember that moment and long for it passionately.

As Jacky Red started to squeeze the trigger, Waxface spoke up. "Hey, Lucky. Remember, after I got sizzled by that acid, you said you owed me? You said that one time, just one time I could ask for something."

Maggie looked at the hideous, melted face, splotched with horrible colors, an eyeball bulging out of its dripping socket, and retched.

She knew what he was going to say, and he did.

"I want her."

Maggie's heart stopped for an instant. Though the bullet in Jacky Red's gun was never fired, she died there, hanging from the meat hook.

Lucky shrugged again. "Sure thing, Waxface. But I get to be the first to kiss the bride."

Walking over, he put his hands on her naked torso, fondling the curves. Then Lucky kissed Maggie, cruelly, brutally.

Maggie did not spit in his face. She did not scream. She did not kiss him. She just looked at him. Stepping back, Lucky eyed her and for just a moment, his mock revelry stopped. Looking into her eyes, he saw death.

Hands bound, Maggie was thrown into the back of a limo by Waxface and a thug named Bucky Wold, a smiling guy, missing his front teeth. They drove her to Waxface's flat.

"Yer different from them others," Bucky said to Maggie as he helped haul her inside. "Usually dames yell and kick a lot when we feed 'em to Waxface."

"I won't kick until I know you'll feel it."

Once in Waxface's basement, Maggie's leg was manacled to a steam pipe. Waxface dismissed Wold, who leered at Maggie before leaving her. "I'm waiting for your kick," he mocked.

Maggie didn't say a word. She just looked back at him. Bucky shuddered and abruptly turned away. He had just stared into the grave.

Moments later, Waxface poured cologne all over himself, then walked over to stand in front of Maggie. Opening his mouth, he exposed his melted lower gums and chin bone in a hideous attempt at a smile. He only drooled.

For weeks without number, Maggie was manacled to a ten-foot-chain in Waxface's basement. The chain extended to a bathroom, a chair, and a bed, where she was the captive victim of Wax-face's lechery and beatings. Days melted into nights in the living hell of the dark basement, while Maggie racked her brain for a means of escape. Finally, she figured one out.

Man has a nearly infinite capacity for self-delusion. Maggie forced herself, during each degrading assault, first, to indicate that she found some pleasure in it, then to praise him for his prowess and amatory skills.

"So your face is a bit of a mess," she'd whisper throatily. "You got a way with women any guy would envy. I'll bet I'm the first to see it."

Waxface was suspicious at first, but eventually, he began to believe her. Because he wanted to.

One night, Maggie suggested that they have a little drink to "get them in the mood." Waxface drank and drank and drank. Maggie pretended to keep up.

Almost dead drunk, Waxface dropped the bottle and reached for her. Snatching the bottle up from the floor, Maggie smashed it over the man's head as hard as she could.

It shattered. Blood mingled with rot-gut whiskey, both of them spilling down over his body. Leaping on the bed, he crawled after Maggie. As he drew closer, Maggie reached out and grabbed Waxface's lighter from a table. Flicking it, she drew a small blue flame and touched it to his whiskey-soaked clothing.

The grotesque thug burst into flames. His screams echoed off the cold, concrete walls of the basement. A ball of fire, he rolled around the floor, trying desperately to put out the flames. Instead, he spread them everywhere.

The bed caught, and Maggie, still shackled, put it out. Finally, Waxface managed to extinguish the flames. Amazingly, the man still lived. Rasping for air, he crawled toward her.

"Help me!" he gasped.

Maggie eyed the begging, pathetic face. Wax-face collapsed. She didn't know whether he was alive or dead. She reached for the key chain that he wore around his neck. It was hot and burned her hand, but Maggie couldn't feel a thing. Numbly, she started to lift it off over his head.

Suddenly, Waxface's horrible face jerked up. His twisted, contorted hands reached for her throat. With a strength born of hatred, he began to squeeze Maggie's life from her body.

As blackness descended on her, Maggie's frantically searching hand clasped the broken bottle. Swinging it viciously, she jammed the razor-sharp, jagged edges straight into the man's neck.

Waxface groaned and died.

She shoved the blood-soaked dead weight off her. As she retrieved the key, Maggie felt nothing. She was numb. She turned the key in the shackle, heard a click, and watched the lock fall open.

For long moments, she just stared down at her leg. Then it sank in—she was free!

Her mind raced as she planned how to disappear. But then Maggie caught a glimpse of herself in the mirror. The face was smeared with blood and soot, black and blue with bruises, her lips split from Waxface's previous beatings.

She knew then that she had another option-she could carry out the revenge she had vowed.

Dressing in the clothes she had been wearing on that fateful night with Jimmy, Maggie went to the garage and found what she had hoped to find—a two-gallon drum of gasoline. She took it back into the house.

Spreading the incendiary fluid all over, she left the large container in the basement to explode. She pulled Waxface's wallet from his pants, took the money in it, tucked the money into her blouse, then set the flames with his ID.

The flames spread so quickly that Maggie herself barely escaped before the gas can exploded. The fire was so complete that it took the police days to identify Waxface from the charred teeth.

When Lucky heard about the fire, he only shrugged, figuring the big dolt had just gotten sloppy. He didn't spend two seconds wondering about Maggie. He should have.

Knowing that Chicago wouldn't be safe until Lucky and his gang were dead, Maggie headed north. With part of Waxface's money, she purchased a pistol and enough bullets to learn how to use it. With the rest, she rented a lakeside cabin in Wisconsin. Here she practiced target shooting, day in and day out.

When she was good, she went hunting.

The first of Lucky's gang to see her again was Bucky Wold, the low-life scum with the toothless smile. She caught him on Oak Street.

"Bucky," she said.

He turned.

"I'm kicking."

The last thing Bucky ever saw was

the flash.

Jacky Red, Lucky's triggerman, was getting a shave and a shine when the phone rang. The barber came back from the call to find the gasping Jacky gripping at his slit throat, trying to hold back the gushing blood. He might as well have been trying to stop the flow of the St. Lawrence River with a family of beavers.

The last words he heard were, "Nothin' personal."

For Fats Milligan's. bachelor party, the boys rented an old speakeasy. After the movies were over, a giant cake rolled out. As Fats drooled, a curvacious woman wearing nothing but a smile popped out. For a moment, she just stood there in her birthday suit, then she disappeared back into the cake to a torrent of cat-calls. An instant later, she reappeared cradling a Thompson Model 21 machine gun. Fats froze in horror, trying to place her. She held back, watching his eyes, waiting for that split second when they flashed, "I know you." Then, she pulled the trigger, giving him and the others a one-way ticket to oblivion.

Only one name remained on her list—Lucky Milano.

Seeing his men dropping around him, Lucky began to get cautious. Being the tough that he was, he wasn't about to pack up his business interests and hoof it to New York, even though that might have been a wise move... considering.

Instead, he hired new bodyguards.

The new thugs were heavily armed and protected Lucky well. His boys knew they could deal with any situation their boss might find himself in. Only one place worried them—that was the small neighborhood church just outside of Cicero that Lucky had attended since the day of his baptism.

Lucky liked the masses and he liked going to confession. It made him feel better, he would tell his boys. That was O.K. by them. What they disapproved of was the fact that Lucky did not allow them to enter the church with their heavy artillery. He told them it was "disrespectful."

So they would wait outside in the limos while a muscle or two, packing concealed palm heaters, entered the House of God and stood "respectfully" by the entry doors.

It was an ice-cold Saturday in April. March had come in like a lion and never left. Milano was feeling bad because the things he had to confess were piling up.

When Lucky entered the church that afternoon, he paid no attention at all to an old man in the balcony, tuning the pipe organ. Nor did he notice several old Italian women saying their penance in the back pews. He only glanced at a new priest, who had been introduced to him as Father McNulty; the good father was going about his chore of lighting the altar candles.

Lucky felt confident, knowing that his muscle was behind him in the doorway. Glancing back, he could see the thugs standing there like eagles on a rocky crag.

Lucky walked toward the enclosed confessionals in the rear of the church. There were six pine doors, side by side, recessed into the wall—two for the priests and four for the sinners. The priests would sit in the second and fifth compartments, alternately absolving the guilty first on one side, then the other. Small red lights above each of the doors informed new arrivals which of the compartments were occupied and which were free.

On the Saturdays before Easter and Christmas, the church would be packed with people wanting to confess their sins. All the lights above the doors would be lit and long lines would snake through the back of the church.

That afternoon, there were only two lights on— those above the first and second doors. The one priest on duty in the second booth was confessing someone behind the first door. Lucky walked to the third door and entered the narrow enclosure. He closed the door and knelt on the padded kneeler, awaiting his turn with the confessor.

Maggie, for her part, had tailed Lucky for weeks looking for the flaw in his protection. After several aborted attempts, she realized that the church was her only opportunity. She knew God would understand.

Noticing Lucky's fondness for the act of confession, she devised a plan. She studied the neighborhood church and its procedures, and she learned that, unless there was a holiday, only one priest would be confessing, and he always sat behind the second door.

When old Father Ponzo entered the booth that afternoon, Maggie was the first to seek forgiveness. Kneeling in the first booth, she confessed all that she had done to Lucky's men over the last several months and why. Father Ponzo said he would have to pull major strings, but, with massive amounts of prayer, she would be forgiven.

When Maggie withdrew from the confessional, she left behind a large rock perched on the kneeler. As a result, the light above the first pine door never went off. Someone just arriving would see that the first booth was occupied and head for the third door.

Sitting in the church pew near the altar, Maggie began to recite her prayers for forgiveness. When the two old women behind her left, she sneaked back to the confessionals and quietly entered the fourth door. By not kneeling on the kneeler, she didn't activate the light outside, and no one was aware of her presence.

Turning, she faced the rear wall of the third booth and silently removed the ornamental fiber wall tiles. Then she ripped out the thick soundproofing tiles until all that separated her from the sinner in the next booth were the thin wall tiles of the third booth. These, she left undisturbed and in place.

Maggie had long ago decided that

a bullet in Lucky's forehead was too kind, too quick. He had caused her months of untold suffering and humiliation. Her life had been changed forever. No, she had something special in store for Mr. Milano when he entered the third confessional.

From beneath her jacket, Maggie Darr produced a large Bowie knife with a twelve-inch hunting blade. Everything prepared, she leaned against the side wall and waited.

When Lucky arrived, he entered what appeared to be the only available confessional booth and knelt on the prayer cushion. Lucky's luck had just run out.

Maggie allowed him to say, "Bless me, Father, for I have sinned—" before she jammed the knife through the thin panel behind him. But he was leaning a little farther forward than she expected, and the knife didn't go all the way in. Impaled, he screamed and twisted as she tried to finish the job. Hearing his yells, his two sidewinders were already on their feet, pulling out their shooters as they ran to the rear of the church.

Maggie knew she had only a moment left. She didn't care about her own death, but she wanted to make sure she took that scum, Milano, with her. Thrusting her hand farther through the tile, she drove the knife deeper and watched as Lucky squirmed like an eel on a spear. Gathering all her strength, she jerked the blade sideways. The movement of the blade severed Lucky's spine. He collapsed to the floor of the booth, a lifeless mass of flesh.

Satisfied, she stepped out of the confessional, her gun before her, prepared to sell her life dearly. But, before she could fire, two shots rang out. The thugs dropped to the floor, guns sliding away from lifeless hands. Startled, Maggie whirled to face her savior.

Father McNulty!

At least, the man was dressed as a priest, but no priest Maggie ever knew carried a repeater beneath his vestments! Before she could speak, though, he spun and looked into the confessional. A flow of blood met his shoes. Lucky Milano was cutting a hard bargain with Saint Peter.

"They heard the shots outside," he said, grabbing the confused Maggie and pulling her along. "They'll be after us."

Together, they disappeared into the city.

SANCTUARY

"Father McNulty" shoved the confused Maggie Darr inside a dark gray Packard. They sped away from the church as the wail of police sirens split the air behind them.

Huddling in the front seat, staring sightlessly at the lights flashing past, Maggie Darr was in a state of numb shock. Having prepared herself for death, it was unnerving to find herself still alive.

She'd been counting on death to end this pain in her heart, she realized. Her motive for living-revenge—was gone. What was left?

The driver, this strange priest, didn't appear to have any answers. He didn't have any questions either. In fact, he ignored her and just drove.

Finally, though, after they'd apparently been driving aimlessly for thirty minutes, ducking in and out of alleys and crisscrossing the same streets, Maggie said dully, "Drop me any-where."

"No," the priest said. "You're too hot."

Maggie shrugged and leaned back.

Soon they pulled up at a seedy-looking hotel somewhere south of the Loop.

"Oh, so this is your game, 'Father'?" Maggie said with a sneer.

The priest didn't answer. Getting out on the driver's side, he walked around to Maggie's door and opened it. When she didn't move, he reached in and dragged her out. He didn't hurt her, his touch was firm but not rough. Maggie considered putting up a fuss. One look in the man's eyes, however, changed her mind.

Why? It was a question she often asked herself later but never answered. Maybe, in that moment, her heart knew more than her brain.

The priest led her inside the hotel. The sleepy desk clerk looked up and smiled.

"Another one, Father?"

"Yes, Sam," the priest answered softly. "This poor child has agreed to give up her life of sin and follow the ways of our Lord. The usual."

"Certainly, Father," the man said respectfully, shoving over the register book. "Room 13."

Maggie craned her neck to see the signature. It read simply, "Father McNulty."

Upstairs, the priest opened the door to a room at the front. Stepping inside, Maggie saw—to her surprise—that it was clean, comfortably furnished, and more like someone's living room than a hotel room in this shabby part of town. But then, she saw the windows were barred. Crossing quickly, she found she couldn't open them.

Whirling angrily around, she found the priest watching her with a faint smile on his face. "Those are to keep people out, not keep you in." He glanced around. "The room is yours for as long as you want it, Maggie Darr."

She started. "How did you know—"

"Let's say I hear a lot in the confessional," the priest said wryly. "To continue, the room is yours for as long as you want. There're new clothes in the closet. If you're hungry, call the desk. They'll send something up."

All Maggie's suspicions returned. "Yeah? And what's the charge, 'Father'?"

"Not what you might expect." The priest's smile widened. He reached over and handed the startled Maggie the key to the room. "Leave whenever you want. But I'd suggest you at least stay the night. You could use the sleep."

He turned to go.

"Wait!" Maggie cried in confusion. "I— Who are you? Why are you doing this? I don't—"

The priest was already out the door. "Just get some sleep, kid. There's a bottle of bourbon in the drawer under the phone. If you decide to stick around, I'll see you again. If not, good luck." Giving a wry grin, he added, "And may God go with you, my daughter."

For a moment, Maggie stood, lost and alone, in the middle of the quiet room. Then, in sudden resolve, she went to the door and locked it, sliding the chain in place. He was right. She was exhausted. This place was a hell of a lot better than the dump she lived in. She could always leave in the morning.

Finding the bottle of bourbon, Maggie Darr drank a toast to life.

Maggie Darr didn't leave in the morning. She didn't leave the following morning, either. She didn't know why. The room was quiet. There were some good books lying around. The clothes fit. The food was edible. No one bothered her.

But she found herself listening to footsteps in the hall, waiting for that firm, even tread she'd been hearing in her dreams.

It came—one night. But not as she'd expected.

Maggie was half-asleep, listening to the radio reports about the growing tension in Europe when there came a knock on her door.

Her heart leaped. "Father McNulty?" she called out, her shaking hand on the chain.

"Yes, my child," came the soft voice of the priest. "I've come to see if you are well."

"Please, come in, Father!" Maggie cried eagerly, undoing the lock and flinging open the door. "I—"

She stopped, surprised at her enthusiasm. Father McNulty walked into the room, then—suddenly, without a sound—crumpled to the floor.

Maggie gasped. Closing the door, she knelt beside the priest. Then she noticed a large wet bloodstain that had been invisible on the black cloth of his robes. She was about to run for the phone, when the priest's hand closed around hers.

"No," he said. "Don't call anyone. Too dangerous. The bullet's entered between the fourth and fifth rib. You can get it out."

"Me? Are you crazy? Do I look like a damned surgeon?" Maggie demanded in anguish. "Look, you're bleeding like a stuck hog. Let me—"

"I said no," the priest said in a matter-of-fact voice. "You can do it, Maggie. You can do anything, if you have

to. I'm counting on you, Maggie." His voice failed. "Maggie ... Darr ..."

He lost consciousness again.

Helplessly, Maggie stared at the priest. Then, she noticed something odd. His face—it was phony! Now that she looked at it closely, she could see the clever make-up job. Reaching out a trembling hand, Maggie peeled away Father McNulty. The face beneath was handsome—incredibly handsome. But, even unconscious, it was cold, cold and ruthless. Then Maggie remembered the look in the man's eyes when he'd rescued her. There had been warmth, understanding. And it was because of that look that she had stayed.

And, because of that look, she would stay-always.

Her lips pressed together firmly, Maggie picked up the phone. "Sam," she said to the man on the front desk, "I know this sounds kinda odd, but I need the sharpest kitchen knife you got—"

ASHES TO ASHES

When Agent 13 arrived at the meeting of the National Security Council earlier that night, it was Maggie who had driven him there through the dark streets of Washington, D.C. He told her to wait in the shadows for his return, keeping an eye out for anything suspicious. Unfortunately, the Jindas—expert assassins and masters of stealth—had escaped her attentive watch, as they had escaped the notice of various FBI and Secret Service agents who had also been lurking about outside.

The noise of the massacre, however, had not.

The sound of sirens filled the night by the time Maggie reached the blood-spattered meeting room. Her heart in her throat, she quickly examined the bodies, then sighed in relief. 13 was not among them.

She heard a moan and saw movement from a body. Stepping over to help him, she heard thudding shoe leather pounding up the stairs. The wounded man would have help soon enough.

Maggie fled down a fire exit, reaching the street only moments before the building was completely sealed off. Someone standing on the sidewalk beside her gave a shout and pointed upward. Maggie followed their awed gaze. High above, bathed in the police searchlight, hanging by a shredded flag, was the disguised Agent 13.

Maggie swore under her breath as the police stormed into the building. Within minutes, he was in their custody, handcuffed, and on his way to the station.

Hurrying back to her car, she waited for the squad car bearing 13 to turn the corner, then she followed at a safe distance, hoping for the Agent to make his move.

Suddenly, the tires of a black Hudson screeched around the corner, cutting her off, nearly sending her crashing into a line of parked cars. Fighting the wheel, she regained control and tore after the Hudson, sensing trouble as it closed in on the squad car.

Her instincts were good. All hell broke loose. The spitting flames of gatters began to talk. Bullets tore through metal, and the squad car swerved out of control, its driver dead.

Horrified, Maggie watched as the squad car slammed through the glass of the meat market. She saw the assassins' car pull up behind it and two men get out, one approaching the car for the "coup de grace," the other covering his pal.

Maggie reacted quickly. She didn't know whether 13 was dead or alive. It didn't matter, not now. If he was dead, she'd avenge him. If he was alive... Steering with her knee, Maggie reached down and unsheathed her Thompson Model 21 submachine gun. Jamming a fresh drum-clip into its base, she roared past, firing out the window just as the Jinda was pulling the pin on the grenade. The gunshots Agent 13 heard came from Maggie in her white roadster Lagoda, blasting away with her Thompson.

The Jinda with the grenade was struck by several bullets simultaneously. As he died, his body burst into flames. The grenade rolled from his hands into the gutter. 13 dove back into the car, throwing his hands over his head.

The second Jinda whirled, turning his armor-piercing gun on Maggie. But he wasn't quick enough. Maggie spattered him with half a dozen shots before bringing the car to a skidding stop just as the grenade went off, showering the area with deadly fragments.

Maggie instinctively ducked as the shower of metal rained down. When the smoke cleared, she turned and looked back at the second assassin, ready to finish him off if necessary. Only a pile of black ashes remained.

Suddenly, she heard the engine of the assassins' Hudson start up. A hired thug, who had been crouched down in the driver's seat of the killing car, snapped into action, sliding the car into first gear and peeling away. Maggie spun her gun around but couldn't get a clean burst off in time.

Even as the grenade exploded, Agent 13 was reaching over the front seat. Grabbing LaMoni-ca's .38, he dove through the squad car's shattered rear window and landed on the street.

Taking careful aim, he fired a single shot. At first he thought he'd missed, but when the thug's Hudson plowed into a street lamp instead of making the turn, the Agent knew he'd hit his target.

Tossing the gun back into the squad car, he turned to Maggie, who was staring at the burning corpse of the Jinda she had shot.

"What is that thing?" she asked in

disgust, looking up at 13.

"A Jinda of the Serpentine Assassins."

"What's that when it's home?"
The Agent was running over to the wrecked Hudson. "The cops'll be here any minute! Get back in the car—I'll explain later!"

Steam hissed from the Hudson's smashed radiator as the Agent flung open the car door. Out fell the gangster, a bullet hole through his neck. Pulling the corpse from the seat, 13 quickly rifled through the thug's pockets. He found the two items he needed—a blood-drenched, snakeskin wallet and the Seer Stone.

Maggie pulled the roadster up beside him as the wail of police sirens could be heard approaching from the distance. "C'mon!" she shouted.

The Agent didn't respond. He couldn't leave. Not yet.

13's concentration was focused on the corpse before him. Pulling back its eyelids, he discovered that the deceased had brown eyes. Then he touched the face. His fingers carefully moved over every inch of it, memorizing the contours, the bone structure, the skin textures, the blemishes, warts, and moles. The face of this thug was his key to the next locked door of the mystery.

Maggie fingered the Thompson again; the sirens seemed as though they were just about to scream around the street corner. But if Agent 13 was going to assume the identity of the

dead man, he had to perform one last grisly chore.

Lifting the corpse by the shoulders, he dragged it to a manhole. Grabbing a crowbar from the sedan, he pried off the heavy iron cover, then slid the corpse through the gaping hole. A splash sounded as the corpse fell into the swiftly moving drainage waters. He replaced the cover, concealing the gangster's body forever in a grave beneath the capital's streets.

Maggie slid over as the Agent hurried to the car. His driving skills were exceptional. She relaxed— they'd soon be far away. Then, suddenly, they heard a loud groan. Turning around, they saw Lieutenant LaMonica crawling through the debris-strewn street from the open door of the destroyed squad car.

"How could anyone have survived that?" Maggie gasped.

"He's tough. And good," the Agent responded, easing up on the clutch of the Lagoda.

Twenty-four hours later, Police Detective Kelly LaMonica regained consciousness in room 211 of George Washington University Hospital. He was told that he was the only officer to survive the terrible massacre. When the police arrived on the scene, they had found him unconscious but wearing a unique kind of bandaging—unlike any the doctor had ever seen—which had staunched the flow of blood.

"Whoever did that saved your life, Detective," said the doctor. "You would have bled to death in the middle of the street before help arrived, i Funny that whoever did it didn't stay around. You don't remember anything, do you?"

But LaMonica didn't even remember the gun battle. He proceeded to demand the official reports.

Slumped back against his pillow, LaMonica's thoughts went to the "projectionist" who shared the back seat of the squad car for those few j minutes—his strange prisoner, whose body was never found.

He glanced at the report of the real projectionist. The man remembered walking into the building with the film under his arm, then nothing-The next thing he knew, "some cop" was jostling him up inside a utility closet. The lump on the man's head and a check on his background seemed to confirm the story.

While the detective was thinking about this, an orderly came into the room, bearing a bouquet of white roses. LaMonica raised his eyebrows.

"Wrong room," he said with a grin. "You must want the redhead down the corridor—"

"Not unless her name's Detective LaMonica," said the orderly, setting the flowers down on the table beside his hospital bed.

"Who're they from?" LaMonica asked, astonished.

"Dunno, there's no note. Odd number, too— thirteen. Never heard of anyone sendin' thirteen roses. Did you?"

"No," murmured LaMonica. But even as the orderly left the room and the scent of the roses sweetened the air, LaMonica remembered the rumors, the idle talk around the station, of a man who was fighting some sort of weird organization that no one else had ever heard of....

One day, Agent 13 would want the favor returned.

TICKETS TO DOOM

The blast of a distant locomotive echoed from the darkness as the sleek, white Lagoda streaked through the streets of the warehouse district.

The Agent handled the rosewood wheel of the roadster with the finesse of a Le Mans driver. Sitting in the seat beside him, Maggie examined the contents of the snakeskin wallet.

"Guy's name was Michael Carson," she said. "You want this cash?" she asked, holding up a large wad of greenbacks.

13 gave no reply. Shrugging, Maggie stuffed the green into her pocket. "Must have been a lot more where this came from. Because this dame sure wouldn't have hung around if there wasn't."

She held up the tinted photograph of a bottle blonde with bright red lipstick, drawn-on eyebrows, and too much mascara. The Agent made a mental note of the photo.

"Hey—get a load of this. The bum had tickets to the opera!"

"Opera?"

Maggie flashed the tickets. "Wagner's *Tristan and.* . . and something. Here's a playbill about it. 'Featuring international star, China White.

Maggie, happening to glance at the Agent, was startled to see his face muscles tense, the color disappear and slowly return. She stared at him, but, just as she was about to make some remark, the odd look vanished. She wasn't even sure she had seen it.

As there was nothing else in the wallet, Maggie changed the subject. "Tell me about those guys back there, the ones that burst into flames."

"The Serpentine Assassins—a secret cult of ruthless killers. Some believe they come from Burma, others say Siam. Whatever the case, they style themselves as 'artists of death.' Their organization had disappeared for several hundred years until it was resurrected by the Brotherhood.

"They have a hierarchy, whose membership has multiple levels and purposes. The one you saw back there was a Jinda-Hai. That means Bat Assassin. They slip in at night and strike like bats. Jinda-Hai are the lowest in the order, completely expendable. Once the mission begins, they have a life expectancy of twelve hours."

"But why'd they burn up?"

"Before their missions, they are mesmerized through an ancient process. They lose all volition and then are made to drink mantha, an Eastern serum that causes their bodies to burst into flames upon death."

"How?"

"When the physical body experiences the transformation referred to as 'death,' strong chemicals are naturally released throughout the body. The combination of these chemicals and the mantha causes a combustible reaction that consumes the corpse and—"

She finished for him, "—leaves nothing left to identify at the scene of the crime."

"Exactly."

"Sounds like a hard way to make a living." Maggie shook her head. Then she had a sudden thought. "What about Carson? He didn't burn."

"He was the pointer."

"What do you mean?"

"A common thug who has probably never heard of the Brotherhood. He was contracted to deliver the mesmerized Jindas to their targets.

"Pointers are offered a lot for the mission because they usually don't survive to collect. If something goes wrong, they're expendable, plus—if they're caught—the pointer's past criminal record will lead the police to believe that it was a mob hit—and they won't look any further."

"And what about that weird-looking rock you took off him?"

"A Seer Stone. Perhaps the most valuable thing the Brotherhood could have hoped to find tonight. Ironically, they didn't know they had it."

"I don't follow."

"Carson took it from Buckhurst's hand on a hunch. Just a hood, unable to resist a jewel.... Probably figured to fence it or see if his employers might be interested. Sort of a bonus for him. He would never, of course, realize the full value of what he had accidentally stumbled across. His employers would recognize it, though."

Agent 13 fell silent. Maggie, glancing at him, sighed and settled back in her seat, watching the passing nightscape and wondering what they were getting themselves into this time.

"Isolde," said Agent 13 suddenly.

"What?" Maggie started.

"Isolde. The opera— *Tristan and Isolde*."

"Oh." Maggie shrugged and turned to look back out the window. But there was that strange expression on 13's face again

The Lagoda pulled into an abandoned alleyway, its headlights flashing on a large freight door. The Agent emerged from the car and activated the hydraulic gate. Moments later, they had parked and entered a large freight elevator.

13 operated the ordinary-looking controls that guided the device to the twelfth floor. After a pause, he took it to the fourteenth floor, and then he did something to the controls that the manufacturer had never intended, causing a special gear to kick in. The elevator slowed to a stop, then descended to another floor—a floor that wasn't supposed to be there—the thirteenth.

As a secret panel at the rear of the elevator slid open, they stepped into what appeared to be the waiting room of a corporation that had gone bankrupt in the Depression. Two couches stood against one wall. In between them was an end table adorned with copies of the *Saturday Evening Post* from 1932. In the center of the room was a tired, wooden desk. Above the desk, a calendar for the year 1934 hung from a hook next to a broken sign that read "Grogan Export." Across from the desk was a door with the words "Office of the President" stenciled on the glass.

This was, in reality, a decoy set up by 13. In the unlikely event that anyone would figure out how to work the elevator controls, all they would find as they emerged through the secret panel was this sad scene. If they persisted in being curious, anyone attempting to go through the "President" door would discover that its lock was frozen, the glass was unbreakable, and the door was unbelievably difficult to force.

The only entrance to Agent 13's sanctum was gained by swinging open what appeared to be a plain, ordinary cement pillar. Agent 13 did this and stepped into the darkness beyond.

13 flicked on the light, automatically scanning the room to make certain all was as it should be.

Though it was only one of the Agent's many secret lairs, the Washington sanctum was a complete crime-fighting headquarters. A target range extended the full length of the room. The wall on one side of the range was filled with weapons ranging from automatic rifles to swords to blow-guns. The wall opposite held a small but amazingly comprehensive library.

Beyond the rows of books, barely visible from the secret door, was a clutter of machinery. The blade of an autogyro jutted out of the shadows. Next to it was a diving suit complete with shiny brass helmet. Beyond that was a small but well-outfitted chemistry lab and a great oak table laden with books, maps, charts, and a huge globe.

Of particular significance was a large wall map on which 13 had traced several circles. For years, he had been searching for the fabled Shrine—the place where he'd been taken blind-folded as a child. The place from which, as a young man, he'd been cast out to die after he'd discovered their heinous secrets. The secret place that was the heart of the Brotherhood.

Below the map was a small gymnasium and, opposite it, Agent 13's disguise atelier.

Tables filled with make-up lined the walls. Hundreds of wigs perched upon faceless heads. Racks and racks of clothing stood in the center of the room. The ghosts of hundreds of people lived— ghosts that Agent 13 invested with life.

Maggie, entering beside 13, looked at him to say something but saw the Agent's eyelids flutter. Instantly, she reached into her purse and drew her revolver. Something was wrong.

Without warning, the room turned into a combat zone. Crackling explosions hammered at their ears. Shrieking missiles streaked about in wild, unpredictable patterns.

Half-blinded by the bursting light, Agent 13 and his beautiful counterpart hit the floor.

Shielding her eyes from the fiery brilliance, Maggie scanned the room, looking for the source of the attack. Raising her gun, she was about to see if she could smoke anything out when Agent 13 knocked the gun from her hand.

Standing up, he stepped into the barrage, ignoring Maggie's scream of alarm. The streaking projectiles bounced off him like Ping-Pong balls.

"Fireworks!" Maggie muttered, disgusted.

Though generally soft spoken, the Agent could command a bellowing voice. "Ray!" he shouted over the barrage.

A figure loomed beside Maggie, reaching for her gun. Instinctively, she spun and threw a lethal Savate kick at it. A hand of steel caught her foot in mid-air, nearly sending her toppling over.

"Maggie, meet Ray Furnow," 13 said.

Holding her foot, snickering, was a man of Asian extraction, whose age might have been anywhere from twenty to sixty. He grinned at her with a slightly stupid expression that was belied by cold, calculating eyes.

"You said he was dead," Maggie said, jerking her foot away. "Killed in a knife fight in Bangkok."

"I thought he was," the Agent responded.

"Foolja agin, podner," Ray said, smiling, in the voice of a cowpoke. Then, in his best bad Charlie Chan, "Number Nine Wife chase me down. Had to take powder before forced to drink powder."

Agent 13 stepped over to Ray and examined a small pellet the Oriental held in his right hand.

"I call it 'Fourth of July in a Marble,'" Ray said.

"The propellant?" Agent 13 asked.

Ray grinned. "You maybe forget about that so minor incident in Saigon?"

"Maybe." 13 sounded noncomittal. Ray shrugged. "Cobalt, C-140, dragon's tooth, and ginseng."

"Ginseng? That's real scientific," Maggie said sarcastically.

"Keeps it in air longer," Ray said. Producing a ring, he held it up. "I've put disk into ring you wear on your finger. Use if problem occur."

13 peered at the ring. A small Chinese coin was mounted in the center. Ray pointed to a tiny raised edge. "Push here and the fireworks begin."

"I already wear a ring, sometimes two," the Agent said.

Ray looked at him, puzzled for a moment. Then he grinned in understanding, making the motion of burning a number onto someone's forehead.

"I will make it into cuff links."

13 smiled a rare smile as he pocketed the ring anyway. When his hand came out of the pocket, it was holding the Seer Stone.

"I need a copy. Can one be made from glass?" 13 asked, handing the stone to Ray.

The Oriental pulled a loupe from his pocket and studied the stone with an expert eye. "Have never seen jewel like this. How soon you need?"

"Tomorrow."

Ray breathed a sigh of relief. "Tonight problem, tomorrow no problem."

Maggie eyed the little man. Something about him didn't play real. Something? Nothing about him played real!

"Nothing about me is real," Ray responded.

She looked up with a start. "You didn't tell me he could read minds!" Maggie said accusingly to the Agent.

13 didn't answer—he was walking to the atelier. Ray and Maggie followed. Glancing at Maggie, Furnow smiled.

"When man is trying to keep away from fifteen wives and ninety-four children, man must not only read minds but have a sixth sense," he said.

Then, gesturing toward 13, he added, "Tell me about the case that furrows his brow."

"An American scientist with a horrible new weapon, a burning dirigible, an exploding train, a building blowing up, a man with a mask making an ultimatum, a clock striking midnight, and a room full of dead lawmen. How does that sound?" Maggie said glibly.

"America in grave danger," Ray Furnow pronounced.

"Brilliant deduction," Maggie snapped. "Why would someone go to all that trouble to threaten America?"

"Maybe person *wants* America," Ray said, then shrugged again. "Although, if I wanted to take over America, I would just shoot President."

Sitting down in a chair before a table filled with supplies, the Agent muttered, "Ray's psychic abilities are matched only by his ignorance and lack of common sense."

"So I gathered from the wives and kids." Maggie laughed.

"What is the matter with that plan?" Ray asked.

Maggie took the bait. "Because you'd have to shoot the Vice President, too."

"So, I kill him, too. Then who takes over?"

"Whoever's next in line. I forget. Speaker of the House, maybe. Or else the President Pro Tem of the Senate, Secretary of State, National Security Advisor.... I don't know." Maggie shrugged.

Ray yawned. "A lot of killing. Most boring. Maybe I would find another way. What if I—"

While Maggie and Ray discussed ways to take over America, Agent 13 calculated his plan of attack. 13's only link to the Brotherhood's plot was Carson's opera tickets for the following evening at the Met. The dead Carson didn't seem like the type to be interested in Wagner unless he had a reason ... like payment.

And there was something else, another reason for 13 to attend the opera ... a reason more personal than he would care to admit.

13 drove the memories from his mind.

He had a night and a day to perfect their disguises. He had to concentrate, he had to be exact, for the slightest deviation could spell death for all of them.

Lost in concentration, the agent stared up at the "faces" of past disguises that looked down at him from upper shelves—a silent audience. Near him, large boxes overflowed with eyelashes, false beards, mustaches, and hair pieces of all colors and textures. Jars containing warts, moles, and even birthmarks sat like goods at the market.

Looking into the mirror, the Agent began peeling away his disguise of the projectionist. For just a brief moment—not noticed by either Maggie or Ray Furnow, who were disputing constitutional questions—the real face of Agent 13 could be seen. It was that of a surprisingly handsome man in his late thirties with intense, light eyes.

Staring into the mirror, the Agent silently plotted his disguise strategy.

He must build "bones" to match the cheek bones of the man he had killed. Then he would apply a layer of wrinkled latex—a second skin used to simulate the flesh of others. Finally, he would match the facial hair and the pigmentation, all reproducing the vivid image his mind retained from his brief study of the dead thug.

Tomorrow night, the Agent's face would be gone, and the face of a dead man would come back to life. And, after that, he would transform Maggie into the blonde floozy whose picture Carson carried so proudly.

THE SIREN'S SCREAM

A jagged streak of lighting flashed through the darkness of New York's skyline, lighting the opera house as if the gods were taking photographs. Below the brooding structure, late patrons stepped quickly from limousines, racing up the steps of the Met as servants hurried to keep pace with large umbrellas, protecting their employers from the driving rain.

Inside the ornate structure, the well-dressed men and women were led to their seats. Presenting his tickets to an usher, Carson and his blonde girlfriend, Crystal Murdow, were taken to an exclusive box that afforded an excellent view of both the stage and the audience.

Both acting their roles, Agent 13 as Carson appeared highly uncomfortable in his obviously rented tuxedo, while Maggie—in a sequined, low-cut gown and a garishly colored feather boa-accepted the disapprov-ing stares of the women with gum-smacking aplomb.

"Geez, Mickie, it looks like a flower bed, don't it? See, the ladies in their fancy dresses are the flow-ers and you men are the dirt? Get it, Mickie? The dirt!" She laughed rau-cously as Carson regarded her with pride and admiration.

But Maggie's laughter was forced, all part of the act. For Maggie knew that somewhere in this gaily appoint-ed room was a deep evil. Somewhere was a force that had wrought disaster after disaster. Where would it strike next?

Maggie felt naked and exposed in the elegant box seat. Anyone in the opera house could pick them off. Holding tightly to Carson's arm, Maggie played his woman for all it was worth. It was a role she enjoyed. But Maggie knew that the admiring smile the Agent beamed upon her was not for her eyes but for whatever unseen eyes were observing them.

"Mr. Carson?" a voice said suddenly.

Maggie started, whirling in alarm. Standing behind them was an usher holding a tray.

"Yeah?" Carson replied coolly.

The usher held the tray out. Resting in the middle was a large envelope with the name—Mickie Carson—written on it. Languidly, 13 lifted it from the tray.

"Uh, hey, wait a half a sec, pal," he said as the usher started to leave.

"Sir?" the usher replied, turning and looking down his nose.

"I got a letter to deliver to the person who gave you this envelope."

"I'm sorry, sir, but I'm afraid I don't know where it came from. The central office asked me to deliver it, and they're now closed."

"Don't worry. Just take the note, they'll find you." The Agent slapped a sealed envelope into the usher's hand, along with a twenty dollar bill.

"Whatever you wish, sir," the usher replied as he left, with double his night's usual wages.

Carson turned to Crystal. "Honey, flash around that rock I gave ya."

"You know I'm not dat kinda girl. Do I got to?" Maggie cooed, smacking her gum.

"Do it for me, babe."

The disguised Maggie relented, lifting the Seer Stone from between her breasts where it hung from a golden chain. Then, like a B-girl showing off a new gift, she flashed it about for ail-particularly those unseen eyes—to see.

This was the bait. In the letter 13 gave to the usher, he explained how he—Carson—had taken the strange jewel from the dead Buckhurst's hand. It looked valuable. He was interested in selling it, if the price was right. He knew some other fences who would be interested in it, of course, but he was an honorable guy. He always believed in giving first right to his employer.

The theater lights dimmed and darkness curtained the opera house in a shroud that felt sinister to 13 and Maggie.

The prelude to Wagner's *Ttistan and Isolde* softly wooed the great hall in an emotional yearning, a tenderness, and an unrestrained outpouring of love's declaration. Agent 13, whose life was devoid of the form of sentimentality that such music brings, could only marvel at the mathematical symmetry of the sound—the balance of notes against notes, of instruments against instruments, the soft, mournful sigh of the violin with the dark foreshadowing of the drums, the expectant horns and the brooding oboes.

As the music played, Agent 13 tried to make order out of the strange and twisted plot being played out by the Hand Sinister. A Zeppelin in flames, a train tumbling over a bridge, an aircraft factory exploding, and, finally, Dr. Fischer. How were they related and how did the Masque fit into it all? What did this impossible ultimatum have to do with it? Where would the hand of death strike next?

As Wagner first lulled him and then bombarded him, 13 suddenly realized that the answer was all around him.

Isolated from the rest of the symphony, the music of any individual instrument can be flat, meaningless. But in concert with the other instruments, it becomes an integral part of a moving story painted upon a vast and beautiful canvas.

Likewise, any single crime of the Brotherhood's was in itself meaningless. But 13 knew that the Hand Sinister built his plots upon repeating themes to be played by a vast array of instruments. Each operative's part was small. Each plot was built upon another, all moving toward a grand finale.

The Masque was the conductor of the Hand Sinister's composition. The Masque's ultimatum was the overture. It was up to the Agent to figure it out before the crescendo of doom thundered the voices of mankind to silence. Within the Masque's seemingly unrelated crimes was a melody that bound them together—a repeating theme that should give him the clue to the conclusion.

13 was jolted back to the real orchestra as the curtain parted. The music of the instruments slowly gave way to a chorus of voices, and then a single voice rose above them, its purity and sweetness suddenly commanding the opera house.

Almost unconsciously, Agent 13 sat forward in his seat, his wandering attention captured.

Maggie Darr's attention was captured, too—by 13's strange reaction. Raising her opera glasses, Maggie looked at the woman. She was Isolde ... and she was striking. Even beneath Isolde's blonde wig, the woman's dark beauty smoldered like a flame, the somber medieval-style gown floated about her like smoke.

Maggie glanced at the program. Of course, China White. Maggie's eyes went once more to Agent 13. His attention was completely riveted upon the woman. Maggie suddenly remembered 13's odd reaction to the name in the car.

"She is stunning!" Maggie whispered to her companion. He made no response. His heart and soul were, it seemed, wrapped up in that beautiful figure upon the stage. Seeing his face—and knowing that the expression on it was *his* expression— not Mickie Carson's—a pit opened in Maggie's stomach and all her hopes and fears seemed to drop into it.

Agent 13 was in a world of another place in another time: *Moonlight in a scented garden. She floated, dreamlike, above the glowing sand. His*

*heart pounded, ached. Against hers.
Pounding.*
*Gardenia and night jasmine tickled
the sir As he drifted into the abyss of
her eyes.*

And he might have disappeared
forever had it not been for—

Suddenly aware of another presence in the opera box, Agent 13
crashed out of his trance and whirled
around, prepared to strike. But it was
only the usher again, holding a silver
tray.

The usher was apologetic for having startled him. "Excuse me, sir. I
am so sorry to have disturbed you. I
have been asked to deliver these."

Agent 13 carefully lifted two items
from the tray. One was a boutonniere
consisting of an ivory-white rose
surrounded by delicate silver lace,
the other was heavy linen notepaper
of the same color. Tearing it open,
Agent 13 found a printed invitation
to attend a "private party" that night
at the Brown Rat. A single phrase
was scrawled at the bottom—"After
the performance."

They were biting.

BELOW THE BROWN RAT

Shortly after the end of World War I, a group of self-appointed guardians of public morals bonded together to pass the Prohibition Act. For almost fourteen years, the unpopular and unenforceable law remained on the books, producing more organized crime than sobriety.

Finally, in 1933, it was repealed by the 21st Amendment. But the damage had been done—cities were catacombed with illegal speakeasies, and a nearly indestructible system of organized crime controlled large segments of American life.

The legalization of alcohol was bad news for the crime bosses. Now, instead of having to simply pay off the cops, they had to compete with legitimate businessmen. Strong-arm tactics, protection rackets, arson, and knee-cappings were enough to take care of these minor annoyances, but what was to be done with the real es-

tate and the underground apparatus that had kept the mob going for so long?

Thus, the innocently naughty speakeasies turned into opium dens, smuggling warehouses, slaving docks, and brothels. And some, like the Brown Rat, were all of the above.

A dark, dockside joint near Chinatown, the Brown Rat was an open secret among the police, celebrities, and politicos of New York City. Cops knew better than to bust the place unexpectedly because they might come face to face with their bosses. Therefore, when it was necessary to appear to be cracking down on the Brown Rat, the police would stage a carefully choreographed raid on the establishment, string up a petty crook and a couple of illegals, and shut the place down for good measure.

The papers ate it up, the public slept easier at night, and two weeks later, the Brown Rat would open up with a new paint job and stage show.

13 thought about this as the sedan plowed through the rain-drenched streets. Capably driven by Ray Furnow, 13's assistant, the car wound its way from the Metropolitan Opera House among the back streets and alleyways of Chinatown. Still acting their parts, 13 and Maggie sat together in the back seat. They had been going over their plans, but, since the Agent was uncertain what to expect, there wasn't much they could discuss. So, they sat back and listened to Ray Furnow.

Ray's complaints practically drowned out the hum of the rented DeSoto limo he was driving.

"Wives all over the place—like fire-breathing dragons! Find another chauffeur, friend," Ray had said at first.

But 13 insisted on bringing him along.

The Agent knew the value of having a well-connected Oriental like Ray with them. If there was trouble, and they had to take refuge in the neighborhood, Ray could help open the doors of the suspicious, close-knit society.

Patiently, 13 had explained all this earlier to Ray, who shook his head adamantly.

"No, forget. I hear the patter of too many little feet-After a moment, 13 said, "Uh, Ray, about that incident in Singapore—"

"What time do I bring the car around, boss?"

As for Maggie, it was logical for Carson to take Crystal with him to a party. She looked like a fun-loving girl in the photograph they'd found in Carson's wallet, to say nothing of the fact that Carson probably enjoyed showing her off. Beyond "Carson's" reasons, 13 appreciated Maggie's keen mind and her ability to uncover information. He also welcomed the added firepower of Maggie's gun. If things got sticky, he could depend on her. They made a good team.

Posing as Carson's driver, Ray pulled the DeSoto into the Brown Rat's parking lot, which was jammed with cars and waiting drivers. The expensive limos attested to the fact that the night's party was a big do.

"Out of the pan and into the steamer," Maggie mumbled as a valet opened her car door and helped her out.

"If we're not back in one hour, leave," 13 muttered to Ray as he climbed from the car.

The white rose attached to his lapel, the disguised Agent 13, with Maggie clinging to his arm, stepped into the elegant Chinese restaurant. Patrons could be seen dining romantically in front of large windows that overlooked the river. The lights of New York's skyline reflected off the waters like millions of heavenly stars, while large freighters slowly plied the river, bound for distant, exotic ports.

"Two for dinner?" inquired the maitre 'd' in a welcoming tone.

"We're here for the party," responded 13 in his best Big-Man-about-Town tones, while Maggie broke out her compact, making final make-up adjustments.

"Party?" asked the maitre 'd' vaguely.

13 passed the man his invitation. One look at the card told the maitre 'd' that the low-life before him was legit.

"Your name?" He sounded faintly disgusted.

"Carson, Michael Carson."

Maggie, pouting, nudged him in the ribs.

"Oh, and this is my friend, Crystal Murdow," Carson said nonchalantly.

"How yah doin'?" she cooed, holding out her hand to be kissed.

The maitre 'd' ignored her hand, quickly turned, and summoned a nearby waiter with a snap of his fingers.

"Mr. Chen, please take Mr. Carson and his— uh—companion to table 12B."

"Please follow me." The Oriental waiter led them past several rows of round tables and candlelit booths, occupied by various members of the elite elite and the shady elite.

Expecting glitter and noisemakers, Maggie was startled when the waiter led them through a small doorway into a smaller room. Here he gestured to a quiet, lonely booth.

"Some party," Crystal whined to Mickie Carson as she took her seat.

"It'll be O.K., babe," Mickie said with crude, bluff confidence, though it was obvious to the waiter that the hood was just as nonplussed as his girlfriend.

"Enjoy yourselves," Mr. Chen said, bowing and leaving the room.

Left alone, the two sat in silence for a moment, lost in their own thoughts. Then Maggie Darr turned to Agent 13. "Tell me, who is—"

13 shook his head. "I'll tell you later what you need to know about China White." Maggie gasped. "You read my mind!"

"It was not as mystical as you presume. I've been watching you. Your hand brushed across your heart, telling me that if you were thinking of amorous affairs. You opened your mouth to speak, but, an instant later, your hand brushed across your lips, symbolically shutting them. This, added to your obvious curiosity at the opera house—"

"Curiosity! I didn't ask you a word in the opera house!" Maggie whispered defensively. Then she realized that his attention had gone to a Japanese print hanging on the wall across from the booth.

"We're being watched!" he said to Maggie softly.

Maggie followed his gaze in time to see a shadowy shape pass behind the print.

"It's a screen," 13 began, when, suddenly, the table between them began to hum and rise! Instinctively, Maggie grabbed for her purse containing her pistol, only to feel Agent 13's hand closing over her own. Then she realized that the booth was, in fact, a cleverly disguised elevator. The table wasn't rising, they were descending!

The moisture in the air and the massive, steel-plated walls told 13 that they were going down beneath river level, probably into one of the deep channels.

After several seconds, the booth slowed to a stop. Large doors carved with elaborate Chinese characters faced them on one side. The doors parted, revealing the most exotic Persian cabaret in the Western world.

The room was thick with the stench of palpable evil. The smell of burning hemp greeted their nostrils, as the wild wails of swing music stung their ears. Half-dressed "harem girls" swooned about a large stage, while gold-digging floozies seduced their men at surrounding tables, always with an eye to their next sugarpops.

"Isn't that Senator Fra—" Maggie whispered, but the. Agent silenced her with a look.

"Don't use names in here," he said coolly.

Behind them, a laughing couple stepped into the ingenious elevator they had just left. The ornate doors closed, carrying them back to the street-level restaurant above.

A large man with a pencil-thin mustache approached.

"Your names?"

"Michael Carson and Crystal Murdow."

Maggie smiled as the man checked a clipboard with a long list of names.

"Very good, Mr. Carson." he replied.

13 and Maggie started to enter the room, when suddenly the mustached man reached out and stopped him. "We ask that you check in any firearms you or the lady might be carrying." He pointed to a small room that looked like a police armory. "We provide the protection here."

"No problem." 13 didn't want trouble. He had other forms of protection, equally as deadly.

"Ooooh, imagine me packin' a rod, Mickie?" Crystal giggled with a cute little shiver.

"Gives me the chills, babe." Carson laughed. But 13 grinned as he followed Maggie to the gun checkroom. He knew that she wasn't about to part with her pistol. Ever since the days of Lucky and his gang, the pistol had become a part of her.

13 gave his .45 to the man behind the counter and was given a claim check for its return. He could feel the eyes of the mustached man watching his every move. As he went back out into the crowded room, 13 noticed that there seemed to be a lot of eyes watching the newcomers. One man especially was looking intently at the white rose on 13's lapel. He gestured to a buxom, long-legged tobacco girl,

who was wearing nothing but a sign-board that advertised Pyramid cigarettes.

"If we're separated, you know what to do?" 13 said softly to Maggie.

"Sure, babe," she said, grinning at him.

The cigarette girl swayed across the room on her high heels, coming to a stop in front of Agent 13. "Mister Carson, would you follow me, please?"

"Anywhere you wanna go, sugar!" Carson leered.

"Mickie!" squealed Crystal, grabbing Carson by the jacket.

The cigarette girl smiled at the gangster's blonde bit of fluff. "Not you, I'm afraid, honey. Don't worry, I'll take real good care of your boyfriend."

"And I'll take real good care of your eyes, you little—" Crystal started forward, her painted red nails glistening. Carson caught hold of her.

"I gotta do some business, Crystal baby. Here's a fiver," he said, pressing a bill into her hands. "Grab yourself some hooch. Daddy'll be back before you see the bottom of two glasses." Turning, he followed the woman's naked back through the glittering crowd.

Not breaking character, Maggie rolled her eyes, sucked in her cheeks in a pout and then flounced off toward the bar. She was stopped halfway across the room by a pair of hands closing over her shoulders. Turning, she saw a tall thug in an ill-fitting tuxedo and with a black patch over one eye.

"Watch your meat hooks," she said, shrugging his hands off her shoulders.

"Carson's fluffs got some spit. I like that!" he said, turning to a pair of the strangest-looking torpedoes Maggie'd ever seen. They were dressed like characters out of Sinbad the Sailor with colorful silk suits, huge jeweled turbans, and scimitars at their waists. But it wasn't so much their costumes that startled Maggie—it was the weird look in their eyes. They stared straight ahead, seemingly completely oblivious to what was going on around them.

The thug in the tux, meanwhile, eyed Maggie. "My hands go where they want to go, sister, and no one stops them," he said, allowing his fingers, as if by accident, to brush across her breasts.

For a moment, Maggie was back in Waxface's room. Disgust and rage overwhelmed her, nearly making her choke. She came to herself to find her hand actually opening her purse for her pistol. This was no time to make a scene. In fact, this was just what she'd been hoping to be able to run across— some hood who might have some information.

And so, instead of pulling out her gun and shooting the fellow down on the spot, Maggie Darr smiled up at him and fluttered her mascaraed eyelashes.

"Oooooh, so strong!" she cooed.

The hood tumbled.

"Say, since your buddy's takin' off, why don't we talk for a moment?"

Maggie glanced over to see Agent 13, led by the cigarette girl, vanish into the liquid crowd that swirled around and finally engulfed him. "Sure," she said coyly. "What'cha wanna talk about?"

His greasy face, cigar breath, and sweaty, meaty hands drew close to her. A wave of revulsion washed over her, followed by the strong desire for her Thompson submachine gun.

"Whaddaya say we talk about a drink, you and me," the thug said.

DARK GREETINGS

13 watched as the cigarette girl shut the heavy door behind them, abruptly silencing the music and chatter from the party room. Carefully locking the door, the girl moved forward again, walking straight toward a blank wall. Pushing on the molding, she stepped aside as the wall swung open, revealing a stairwell on the other side.

A ruse within a ruse, thought 13 as he followed the girl down the clanging iron steps. A distinct odor of water reminded 13 that they were below the river. Looking at the steel-plate walls, 13 envisioned the massive pressure of water these walls had been designed to hold back. It was an ideal hideout, safe from prying eyes and ears.

Quickly, 13 planned what he would say when he met the person who snapped at his bait of the Seer Stone. He knew it would be a member of the Brotherhood, but who? A name came to mind. How would he react when they were face to face? Just seeing her from a distance tonight, looking even more beautiful than she had looked when—

Coldly, 13 put those memories out of his mind. He forced himself to concentrate on her as she existed now, not in the twilight of their past. Was she involved with the Masque? Was she herself the Masque?

If it was China waiting below, would she be likely to know Carson? 13 figured not. Carson was a pointer, nothing more. If he hadn't just happened to pick up the Seer Stone, he would probably have been either paid off by now—or dead. Probably no one in the upper echelons of the Brotherhood had ever seen the hood face to face.

They would only know Michael Carson by his mission, which the disguised Agent felt comfortable handling. They probably wouldn't even notice any change in the Agent's voice. Fluent in twenty-six languages, including Sanskrit, Agent 13 was also a master of speech and voice control, including ventriloquism. He could imitate anyone's voice perfectly—once he'd heard it. Unfortunately, Carson had been beyond speech when they'd met.

At the bottom of the staircase, the girl opened a large set of sealed, inlaid doors and gestured for him to enter. He immediately noticed a flickering light that seemed to dance out of the chamber beyond.

As 13 stepped through the doorway, he was bathed in a shimmering green light. The shivering cigarette girl closed the door behind him, leaving him alone, or so he thought.

Two walls of the enormous room were constructed of thick, fourteen-foot-high, plate-glass windows bound by reinforced bands of copper. Their banded construction and reinforced steel held back the massive sea on the other side, while permitting an unobstructed look at the underwater kingdom.

Large, submerged lights illuminated the plankton that filled the waters and covered the pylons supporting the Brown Rat. It was the plankton, an abundant micro-organism, that gave the underwater light its greenish hue. The almost invisible growth at the base of the ocean food chain thrived in the artificial light and drew in the larger creatures that feasted on it.

The final receiver in the late-night food chain was the great white shark, whose never-ending appetite was often rewarded by the smaller feeder fish hovering about the plankton. One of the great sharks was there now, gulping down its prey, its skin glowing green in the weird light. Agent 13 found its presence symbolic and amusing.

The room's furnishings consisted of a pair of high-backed, black, lacquered chairs and large black marble desk. The severe pieces were massive and cold. To the left of the desk, two sealed doorways led through an iron plate wall. A large mirror with a golden frame hung in the center of the metallic wall—the only touch of humanity in the otherwise spartan chamber.

The sea was the real focus of the room, the sea with its constant movement, turmoil, and never-ending life or death struggle for survival....

"Welcome, Mr. Carson," said a woman's voice.

13 turned, remembering—as Carson—to give a start of surprise. In reality, 13 was surprised. Even with his acute sense of hearing, he had not heard the woman arrive, which made him suspect that the voice belonged to the one person he knew to be equally well-trained in the arts of silence and stealth. Looking in the direction from which the voice had come, he saw—framed by the graceful wings of a stingray drifting in the water behind her—China White.

Though she was now simply if elegantly dressed, her appearance was no less dramatic than it had been on the Wagnerian stage. The undulating lines of the green light's reflection in the water caressed her high cheekbones, her deep blue eyes glowed like a cat's, and the gleam of her perfect teeth slashed through the darkness like a knife in the sunlight.

"Jesus, yah scared me half to death. How'd you get in here?" Carson asked.

"I'll ask the questions," China replied flatly.

"However you wanna do it, sugar."

Although 13 had never met Carson in life, 1 knew the type—a rude, cocky tough, who wouldn't take any lip from "some dame." Carson would believe he was the man in control.

13 knew the truth, however—China White was deadly. Trained by the Brotherhood in the arts seduction, she was like a spider enticing the powerful into her web of lust and deceit, then devouring them whole. Watching her as she contemplated Carson, 13 could see her considering how best to handle this imbecile. And his mind went back...

A moonlit night at the Shrine. Two young people in love. Thrust together by the Brotherhood sinister forces, they were to view each other as lessons, objects in a grand plot so twisted that neither could understand. Love was never supposed to have happened. But something went wrong.

China drew near him. "I understand

that y have something of ours you wish to return."

"No, no, babe. You misunderstand, I might have something of *mine* I might consider *selling*."

"I see."

"So let's talk price."

"Let's."

"Now, the way I figure, with the market for stones the way it is...."

A low sinister chuckle slowly echoed from the area near the desk. A blinding bank of arc lamps switched on. Everything whited out. It was as if someone had torn off the roof and dropped the blaring noonday sun inside.

"What's goin' on here!"

Shielding his eyes from the glaring lamps, the agent instantly became aware of the cold pressure of a gun barrel at his back.

"What's this?" he snarled. "What's with the big lights and gat in my back? Call off the wiper or the deal's off!"

"But you wanted to talk price, Mr. Carson. Let's start with your life. What is it worth?

"Less than yours when I get outta here, sister!" Carson sneered.

"If you get out of here, Mr. Carson....*If*."

13 had expected this. The pure tone in China's voice was one of disdain.

"Now, let's start at the beginning. Please give me a full account of last night's activities."

"You're not getting anything, you little bit—"

A sharp blow to the kidneys doubled 13 over. As he fell, he caught a glimpse of the hard butt of a pistol before a jagged bolt of pain shot through his neck.

"You must learn some manners, Mr. Carson."

China's cool, beautiful voice was the last thing 13 heard as he slipped into unconsciousness.

The next thing the Agent knew, he was on his knees staring at the rug. He tried to open his eyes, but all he could see were bright flashes of throbbing pain. All he could hear was the sound of heavy breathing from somewhere above him.

13's arms were pulled out from under him, slamming his head against the floor. He tried to move his arms, but they were held fast by a strong pair of hands. Then he felt cold metal on his wrists, hear a click and a snap, and realized that he had been handcuffed. Ansett 32 Police Restrainers, from the feel. They would would be no match for his talents once he regained his strength and bearings. He got up and looked around the room. It was then that he got his first clear look at China's assistant.

The man was a giant, towering well over nine feet tall. Carson was appalled at the sight, but 13 was only slightly surprised. For he had seen these enormous creatures before, back in his days with the Brotherhood.

The giant was a member of a nearly extinct race called the Nephilim, or the Sons of Nephilim, as referred to in the Book of Genesis. They were the result of a genetic breeding experiment conducted by the brotherhood during the reign of the Lemurians, thousands of years ago.

With the fall of the mighty Lemurian culture, civilization in the known world collapsed, and anarchy prevailed.

The Brotherhood sought a quick way to unify the world once again. Thus they created the Nephilim, men of undisputed power and strength. So impressed were the pagans that soon the giants of Nephilim were worshipped as gods.

Forming their own communities, the Nephilim flourished, while always remaining in the service of the Brotherhood. But, unfortunately, because they were so different, the Nephilim made convenient scapegoats. Everything from plagues to earthquakes were blamed on them, and soon the people who had at one time worshupped these peaceful creaturesbegan to attack them.

The Nephilim fought valiantly under the leadership of Og, the last of the great kings of Bashan. But it was to no avail, for even though they were superior in strength, they were greatly outnumbered. On the run, they fled to the only safe haven they knew – the Shrine of the Brotherhood.

During their flight, they were hunted across two continents. Many were taken prisoner. Turned into slaves, they were pressed into guard duties in palaces from Luxor to Memnon. Their children were thrown into armies where they once again distinguished themselves as great warriors and leaders.

There was Goliath, the champion of the Philistines, who was slain by David; Gabbaras, who was captured after a heated battle and brought in shackles to Rome after Emperor Claudius's Arabian victories; Idusio and Secundilla, who, assigned to protect the Sallustian Gardens from Augustus Caesar's legions, were slain after a three-day siege and had their remains dragged through the streets.

The few that managed to reach the Brotherhood continued in the loyal service for years to come, never to be seen in the public eye again. At the Shrine, their new duties ranged from patrol of the secluded mountain passes to protecting the most sacred of relics—
the Crystals of Uru.

The mystic Crystals date to an unknown time before the Lemurians. Contained within them are the truths and knowledge upon which the Brotherhood is based. No one person is in possession of all the knowledge they contain. A complete understanding of their content is rumored to cause physical death, for only when one is free of the constraints presented by a physical existence can one be free to explore the subtleties of truth. Thus, the knowledge of the Crystals was divided into a triad of equal leadership called the Aukhu.

One of the triad was Tog, a leader whose age was believed to equal that of the Crystals themselves. He was the holder of the spiritual realm. Itsu, a direct descendant of the Lemurians, was the keeper of the political affairs, guiding the world with his unseen agents. And lastly, there was Nof. The keeper of the sciences, he was careful in releasing the great secrets at a pace that could be safely assimilated by the general population. He knew of the great disasters which could unfold by "too much, too soon, too quickly."

It was the giant Sarius, with his gifted sense of perception and understanding, who first came to realize the evil intent of Itsu, the keeper of the world's affairs, and his followers. It was Sarius who noticed Itsu accessing the Crystals of Tog and Nof—a direct contradiction to the laws of Uru.

Sarius alerted others, but the alarm came too late. Itsu and his conspirators had already sunk their talons deeply into the heart of the organization. Those who resisted were slain. When it was over, the physical beings of Nof and Tog and Sarius had died, leaving Itsu as the leader of the Aukhu. He was to be known by a new name—the Hand Sinister.

Unhampered, he carefully absorbed as much from the Crystals as he could, without risking his own self-destruction. What little was left in the Crystals would remain unknown, for the Hand Sinister trusted no one.

The power shift complete, the Brotherhood moved onto a new and darker path, whose ultimate purpose was to gain an active, rather then a passive, control of the planet. He, the undying Itsu, would be the earth's new supreme leader.

The giants of the Nephilim, having been part of the resistance against Itsu, expected death to come quickly. Unfortunately for them, they were spared. The Hand Sinister had a new use for these colossal men.

Their tasks would be to invoke fear and terror among the general populace wherever needed. Knowing that they would resist such service, the Hand Sinister ordered the giants' minds to be forcibly altered through mind probes, hypnosis, and—in extreme cases—lobotomies.

Agent 13 knew that the Titan who towered over him was a descendant of these fabled men. The dullness in his eyes and the scar on his forehead told 13 that the man had been forcibly altered.

As the giant bent over him, 13 coolly assessed the huge man, looking for the fault, the point to strike at if and when the occasion arose.

"Search him," China's voice commanded.

The giant spun the shackled Agent over like a steak on a grill. 13 offered a token resistance.

"Hey! Nobody pads me!"

The giant found the object of his search—the Seer Stone. With a grunt of pleasure, he held it up proudly, his smile revealing a mutilated tongue.

Taking the pendant from the immense hand of her assistant, China examined the stone for a moment, then peered through it, studying her own palm.

"A fake," she said, tossing the stone to the floor.

"How dumb do you think I am?" Carson snarled groggily. "Think I'd bring it here so you and Stilts could wrestle it outta me? What kinda palooka yah take me for?"

"Show me his palms," China commanded.

Without a moment's delay, the giant spun 13 over on his belly and forced open the Agent's manacled, clenched fists.

Slowly China approached him, pulling her own Seer Stone from between her smooth, shapely breasts.

"Hey, what is this? You wanna see if my hands're clean or what?" Carson demanded, looking at China with a puzzled expression.

China ignored him. Lifting his hands, she gazed at the palms through the Stone. Her thoughts were visible on her face. First, a hungry kind of hope in her eyes. Then, disappointment, a faint regret. Finally, her eyes went back to ice blue.

13 snatched his hands away from hers. "Nobody does this to Michael Carson! Nobody!"

JAWS OF HORROR

China White turned away from the thug who was trying to blackmail her. Had she really expected to see the tattoo of the number that had at one time meant so much to her life?

Like the rest of the Brotherhood's top-level operatives, China White had heard the details of the murdered agents and theft of the Seer Stone in Istanbul. She had heard how the number 13 had been branded into the corpses' foreheads.

China shivered. Always before, the Brother hood had been the hunters, never the hunted. But now they were the victims, and the man tracking them had been trained in their tactics and knew the organization well. Agent 13—the fallen angel, the Lucifer who fled from the Brotherhood so that he could strike back with a vengeance. He was dangerous, and he had to be stopped. But to China White, he was something more.

The Seer Stone Carson had brought was a copy and a good one. It could only have been made from the Istanbul stone. So her conclusion that he might have been 13 in disguise was reasonable. But—did she really believe that the Agent would Walk right into her den? No, of course not. But then, this Carson must be tied to 13 somehow.

13 knew that there were several Seer Stones in existence. All top Brotherhood agents carried them. Certainly the Masque would have one. Therefore, he had prepared for the possibility of what had just occurred. Before leaving his lair in Washington D.C., 13 had applied a special new elastic imitation flesh over his hand. Identical to flesh in every way, it successfully hid his tell-tale tattoo of the Brotherhood. Then he had attached the fake Seer Stone Ray produced to the golden chain of the original. Fi-

nally, he'd hidden the real Seer Stone in a place that was known only to him, certain that the Brotherhood dared not kill him until they had regained possession of the stone.

"Help him up," China commanded the giant. "Show Mr. Carson to a proper seat."

No sooner had she uttered the commands than 13 felt the massive hands of the giant tightening around his waist. Suddenly his body was lifted from the cold floor and dumped into one of the black lacquer chairs in front of China's desk.

"That's better. Now, how 'bout these bracelets?"

"Soon, Mr. Carson. First, I'd like to ask you some questions."

"Listen, toots, I got somethin' you and Stilts here want pretty bad. Now, I'm not happy, you're not happy. I want money, you want the rock. It sounds like a pretty simple deal to me, and judging by the look of the place, you can certainly afford the price. So, if you're done with the rustle, then we can get down to business."

China was silent, staring into the water. 13 had leisure to study her.

Time had only made her more beautiful. None of the brutal intrigue that surrounded her had left its mark. The sound of a buzzer suddenly disturbed the tranquillity.

China reached behind her desk and brought a telephone receiver to her ear. "Yes?"

13 watched her face, trying to deduce what was being said by the voice on the other end. But China's face remained smooth and cold.

"I see," she said into the mouthpiece after listening several moments. "Proceed with your plan." With that, she hung up the receiver.

Picking up the fake Seer Stone, she said, "Again, how did you get this?"

"I made it from the original."

"And where's the original?"

Carson grinned. "I gotta spell it out?"

China looked at him, bored.

"We agree on a price," Carson said as though talking to a stupid child. "You hand me the money. I tell you where the rock is."

"Tell me how you came by the original."

Carson sighed. "Jeez! All right, if it's so damn important. We was waitin' to strike. I was lookin' inside the room and seen this film fellow standing up, holding the rock out and startin' to talk 'bout secret societies and stuff. I was thinkin' 'what a wacko.' Then he goes into this long hurrah about invisible tattoos and whatnot. I tell ya, the guy was full of more hot air than a weather balloon. Anyway, we let 'em gab till the clock started dingin', then we turned the room into stringed beef, just like we was told. When it was all over, I grabbed the rock. It looked like it might'a been worth something. And that's the story."

"Was he killed in the attack?" China asked, her voice losing some of its coolness. "Who? The palooka with the flapping jaw?" China nodded.

"The only people who left that room were measured for boxes."

"Are you sure?"

"When the guy's lying in blood, you look in his eye and see nothin' but milkshake spillin' out,

"Have you ever seen sharks in a feeding frenzy?" China's voice sounded as if she were giving a disinterested lecture.

"No! And I've had enough of you and your fancy threats. Now you either make the deal or you don't, but if I don't go walkin' outta here in five minutes, my boys are comin' in to get me!"

"Your boys?" China remarked coolly.

"That's right, sugar! Fifty of 'em, coming here to tear this place apart."

The great white struck at a slab of descending beef and bone, whipping it from side to side in its viselike jaws. Several other great whites shot out of the water's darkness, looking for similar treats.

"Lovely creatures," China remarked as she watched. "Nature's most perfect feeding machines. Their evolution has changed little in ten million years."

Carson made a feeble attempt to rise from his seat, but the giant grabbed the Agent's shoulders with his massive hands, forcing him down.

"Stay, Mr Carson. I'm sure this will be a show that you'll enjoy." China

turned to her assistant. "Please give our guest a better view."

The giant picked up the Agent and the chair, easily carrying them both to the nearby window.

Outside the glass plates, more sharks arrived, darting through the bloody water and lights in a frenzied dance of death. The windows buckled and shook as the creatures slammed against them in turmoil. Then there was a huge surge of water against the glass. A huge black object drifted downward.

"Why, here comes one of your boys to the rescue now!" China mocked.

Agent 13 watched in horror as the object entered the realm of artificial light. It was his rented DeSoto! The vehicle came to a gentle stop on the sandy bottom near the windows. Trapped inside the auto, gasping and struggling for the final breaths from a diminishing air pocket, was the terrified Ray Furnow.

The Agent knew Ray had two choices—he could either suffocate when the air ran out, or he could take his chance with the great white sharks by leaving the car and breaking for the surface.

China was watching him closely.

"I don't think the others will be coming, do you?" she asked.

13 didn't reply. His mind raced through his options. Getting out of the handcuffs presented little problem. What occupied him more was figuring out a way to get to Ray before it

was too late.

China turned from the window and slowly approached him. "Now, why don't you tell me who you are and who you really work for?"

The giant's grip tightened on his shoulders. 13 swallowed hard. The masquerade was over. Even if China believed he wasn't Agent 13, she also knew he wasn't Carson. And if they knew about Ray, they also knew about Maggie....

13 was alone and without a gun. His poison ring and heel dagger would be of little use against the hybrid giant, whose immense size would dilute and slow the potency of the poisons. But it didn't matter. There were other, more effective, "tools" available to him.

His mind raced backward in time to his days at the Shrine, to the training sessions when he'd had to defend himself against ten armed attackers at once. There was no room for error—to have failed Would have meant death. The Brotherhood Wasn't interested in agents of lesser abilities. But 13 had survived and excelled. He was their best.

Agent 13 relaxed. His joints and muscles became pliable. His hands slid free of the handcuffs like a knife sliding out of warm butter. He grasped the freed manacles in his hands. His years of training had taught him how to turn any object into a lethal weapon.

The giant's enormous height forced him to bend over as he held the Agent firmly in the chair. Knowing that the giant's weight was slightly displaced, the Agent threw his own shoulders into dislocation, causing the giant to fall forward, slightly off balance. It was all that was needed. During the split second the giant struggled to regain his leverage, 13 broke free. Snapping his shoulders back into place, the Agent spun to face his towering opponent.

He quickly thrust upward with the serrated edge of the handcuffs. The makeshift weapon tore through the giant's clothing and entered his abdomen just below his sternum. The giant, caught off guard, let out a low, painful gasp as 13 continued to jam the lethal instrument up toward his heart. The giant swung at his tormentor. The blow drove the Agent across the cold iron floor.

The giant howled in pain as he grabbed at the handcuffs dangling from his chest cavity. Spinning and twisting around the room out of control, he looked like a trout trying to free itself from a fisherman's hook.

13 pulled himself back to his feet. Out of the corner of his eye, he could see China reaching behind her desk and pulling out a pistol. Its distinctive shape told him it was a long-barreled Mauser. She leveled and fired as the Agent leaped for the nearest shield he could find—the giant.

The shot missed, but only because of the Agent's catlike reflexes. The slug slammed into the plate glass holding back the sea. A small bullet impact hole appeared in the surface of the window. The tremendous weight of the water caused the sea water to jet into the room in a stinging, pencil-thin stream.

China fired twice more. One flashed over the Agent's shoulder, the other hit the giant in the thigh. The man twisted in confusion as he swung again at the Agent and missed.

Apparently, the giant was expendable, for China fired again—this time right at the giant, hitting him in the hand. He fled backward, clutching his hand and howling in pain while trying to avoid the gunshots. The Agent stayed close to him. Dimly figuring that 13 was responsible for his problems, the giant swung at him again with his deadly, hammerlike fists. The Agent dived out of the way, landing beneath the stream of water being forced through the bullet hole.

China held her fire for fear of hitting the window again. The giant saw his chance. Rage built within him as he lunged at the fallen Agent. Suddenly his feet slipped on the wet floor and the giant's enormous bulk slammed head first into the window. The plate buckled under the force. A screeching sound suddenly filled the chamber.

Everyone in the room stared at the window, which had a new six-foot crack from the bullet hole to the lower corner. Small tricklets of water first seeped, then jetted through the crack.

The faltering giant pushed himself up slowly from the floor, putting his mangled, blood-drenched hand against the window for support.

A fifteen-foot shark, seeing the motion, lunged at the window with its thrashing jaws. The shark's impact sent another crack screeching through the glass pane. Small, growing streams of sea water began to shoot out along the length of the two cracks, but the strong metal bands held the glass in place. Frustrated, the massive shark circled back into the darkness. Finer cracks suddenly appeared as the window started to give way.

There was sudden movement in the room. Agent 13 looked over at China White, only to catch a fleeting glimpse of her as she escaped through a revolving wall panel behind her desk. The giant, it appeared, had an instinct for survival. Forgetting about the Agent, he ran to the doors, hoping for an exit, but they were sealed and locked. Even his great strength couldn't force them open.

The chamber echoed with the moaning of the buckling window as needle shards of splintering glass shot from the cracks. 13 ran to the panel through which China had disappeared. It was secure and refused to budge. Turning, he slammed his body's full weight against the mirror. It was solid as a wall. 13 looked back at the cracked window. The giant was there, futilely holding his massive hands against the glass, hoping to keep the cracking plates in place. Blood and jetting water were everywhere.

Then something swam into view. The giant looked beyond his crimson hands, beyond the plated glass, and into the massive sea that he was attempting to hold back. He glimpsed his fate. A huge great white shark moved from the inky blackness like a torpedo. The monster's grisly jaws opened wide as its speed increased. Its cold, dead eyes locked onto the giant's bleeding form as it sped toward the window.

The giant backed away in horror, trying to retreat to the back of the room. Seeing what was bound to happen, 13 leaped onto China's desk, jumping from there up to the ceiling, where he grabbed hold of an iron beam just as the shark, driven wild by rage, crashed into the window.

The metal bands buckled, and the pane shattered. The tremendous pressure of the water shot into the room, carrying the shark directly at the giant like a rocket riding the airstream. Striking the giant in the back, the shark's massive serrated teeth dug deeply into his flesh as the pressure slammed them against the opposite wall.

The door the Agent had entered burst away, blown off its hinges by the powerful pressure. The waters rushed up the stairwell in an inverted whirlpool of destruction.

The shark, sucked by the water from its hold on the giant, was sent spinning and thrashing. The giant held on to a wall beam for support as the water gushed inward. But even his great strength gave way. He was sucked down, toward the staircase, fighting and struggling.

Suddenly the rushing waters grew calm; having filled the room to the window and door-frame level, an equalized pressure had been obtained. An eerie silence settled over the room, broken only by the rhythmic, dying surges of the water.

13 lay along the iron ceiling beam, breathing from a large pocket of trapped air. The ceiling light beside him flickered its last moments as 13 watched the giant who refused to die pull himself from the depths to share the pocket of air. The giant's respite was short-lived, however.

With the water calm, the great white moved in to claim his prize.

The waters churned and boiled a frothy red as the two giants spun and twisted in a match for survival. But the human giant had been injured too many times, and the world he was fighting in belonged to the shark.

Try as he might, the massive man couldn't break the beast's iron grip. With a final gasp, he was dragged down for the last time.

13 realized he had to get of there, fast! The shark would take a few minutes to devour the giant, then it would look for its next snack. And there was still Ray, somewhere out there. It was only a matter of moments until Ray's air supply was exhausted, if it wasn't

already. And Maggie— what sinister fate had she met in his absence?

He carefully slid along the upper beam. Positioning himself so that he was directly above the shattered window, he began concentrating on lowering his breathing rate, thereby reducing his need for air. Using such techniques would permit him to remain under water for up to three minutes. He glanced about for the sharks. They still appeared to be feasting in the far corner. With great resolve, 13 took his last breath and gently slid into the chilling waters.

The water tasted of blood and death. He swam in slow, evenly measured strokes, trying not to attract the attention of the feeding beasts.

The blurry image of the sunken DeSoto loomed in the distance. 13 fought against the strong tidal currents that snaked between the large pylons and threatened to carry him out to sea.

Seconds counted and his progress slowed to a near stop. He fought down the urge to break for the surface. Only after an incredible effort was he able to reach the car. He was too late.

Ray was gone. Only a pilot fish, who seemed to have laid claim to the new home, was to be found in the car. The Agent didn't have time to carry on a search for his trusted assistant— or what was left of him. His lungs screamed for air, his head began to burn. Soon, the sharks would be returning to the business of eating.

Lungs bursting, Agent 13 swam upward toward the surface....

DANCE IN THE DELUGE

While Agent 13 went to his fateful meeting with China White, Maggie Darr studied the slobbering thug beside her at the mahogany bar like a panther eyeing game from a tree branch.

Somehow, the one-eyed slickster seemed familiar to her.

"What's your monicker?" she asked.

"Jack Spade, on account that I only got one eye, like the Jack of Spades," he said, jamming his cigar into his lips and sticking his hand out.

Maggie shook hands with him. The name meant nothing to her. He moved closer, the smell of gin on his breath.

"Say, yer a real good looker." Spade leered. "Yer wasted on Carson, dollface." A sudden thought seemed to cross his mind. He said, grinning, "I'll bet you look great in a swim suit. What would you say to an ocean voyage?"

Leaning close, he tried to put his hand around Maggie's waist. She coyly slipped out.

"What was that about an ocean voyage?" she said, backing up slightly.

"It's a job on the *Normandie V* he said.

Maggie raised her eyebrows. "A 'job'?" she said, sneering. "You gotta work for a ride?"

"You don't call it work, not on the biggest, classiest ship sailin' the ocean. I'm runnin' cards outta a suite. It's easy pickin's, the tub's packed with Mainliners and other high-muckity-mucks. Hell, the Babe's gonna be on the ship, along with a few Astors and Vanderbilts. Heck, China's even gonna make the scene."

"China White?"

"Only one I know of."

"Is that so?" Maggie asked with interest. "I tell ya, any flimflammer can make a killin'." He winked. "Maybe even you...."

"Yah think so?" Maggie smacked

her gum.

"The ship don't sail till Tuesday." Jack Spade reached into his pocket and produced a ticket folder for passage on the *Normandie*. "I got two tickets, First Class."

Moving closer, he slipped the tickets into her hand for inspection.

"I'm lookin' for a good dish to help me pull 'em in, if ya know what I mean."

He placed his hand on the inside of her thigh and patted it twice.

Maggie hauled off and slapped Spade across the face. "Whaddya take me for? I ain't no floozie, I'll tell you that!"

"Easy, babe," Jack said soothingly. "You don't have to do nothin' but meet the softs in the bar, feel 'em out, drop a coupla hooks, then reel 'em into the room for the game."

"What's in it for me?" Maggie asked, holding up a cigarette at the long end of a diamond-studded holder for Spade to light.

"Ten percent of the take," he said.

"I don't know ... . There's Mickie...."

"What's there to know? It's like shootin' fish in a barrel. I'm tellin' you, it's the easiest money you'll ever see. As for Mickie, he's a loser. China'U take care a him."

"Oh, yeah?" Maggie asked casually. "What does that mean?"

"Never you mind, sweets. Just don't worry about the clod, that's all."

Maggie froze, wondering what Spade meant. Somehow, she had to find out what was going on!

Maggie's attention was drawn to a pair of doors at the far end of the crowded, smoke-filled room. Three large thugs from the establishment were working their way through the crowd, checking out the women one by one. Somehow, Maggie had a feeling they weren't looking for dates for the evening. They seemed particularly interested in blondes. Turning around, she fired a dirty look at the fat drinker who sat next to her.

"Ya gettin' an earful, Mack?" she said coldly. Flouncing off her bar seat angrily, she looked at Spade. "Ya think we could go somewhere more private?"

Spade's eyes lit up. "No problem!" He signaled to the bartender.

The attentive bartender—an older, balding man with a whiskey-reddened nose—was quick to respond. "Another round, Mister Spade?"

"Got any rooms, Barney?"

"Three left."

"Gimme your best, and tab it."

"Whatever you say, Mister Spade." The bartender signaled to a nearby waiter. "Show Mister Spade and his friend to the Sheik's Tent."

The waiter quickly led them through the crowd to a hallway in the back of the establishment. Maggie looked back at the thugs, who continued to search the crowd. She hadn't been seen.

Jack caught one of her nervous

glances.

"Still worried about your friend?" He sneered.

"What 'friend'?" she said, taking Jack's arm.

He laughed raucously.

Several closed doors led off the hallway. The Waiter opened one of them and parted a heavy curtain, then stood back.

"You're gonna love this place!" Jack informed her as he entered the room.

Maggie paused. It was like walking into the Arabian Nights. The walls were covered in Persian tapestries, the floors in rich, hand-woven rugs. Large, overstuffed pillows covered low couches that encircled the room. In the center was a large, circular, brass-hammered table, on which sat a tall water pipe with multiple hoses. The room was perfumed with exotic incense ... and something else—the smell of hashish.

Maggie entered the room to find a man, attired in Turkish Scimiteer clothing, standing at attention in the corner.

"I thought this was private," she said to Jack, pouting.

"Part of the show. Here to serve." Jack smiled and pulled Maggie down on the couch beside him. "Besides, the guy's a mute. He ain't goin' be repeatin' nothin' we say to nobody."

"He makes me nervous." Maggie sniffed. "Tell him to cart out."

"Relax."

Jack snapped his fingers. The Scimiteer produced a bottle of champagne and held it out. With his other hand, he flashed his sword. The cork popped like a gunshot and bounced off the ceiling as a tall plume of champagne flew across the room, dousing the table.

The Scimiteer quickly sheathed his blade and bent down to pick up a pair of champagne glasses. In an instant, he caught the flowing wine in the glass and presented it to Maggie Darr.

Giggling in pretended delight, Maggie took the glass. As she did so, however, she looked directly into the Scimiteer's eyes. Startled, she saw there a disturbing mixture—numbness, distance, evil. Was he a Jinda? Or just a hood? Or maybe nothing, just her imagination? He turned away, going back to his post by the wall.

Turning back to Jack, Maggie raised her glass and smiled.

Jack smiled, too—a devilish, wolfish smile.

Maggie couldn't be sure whether the Scimiteer had seen her pour the first two glasses of champagne into the fern by the big velvet pillow she was leaning against while the gangster wrapped his arm around her. But he couldn't have missed the third time, for she leaned over at an awkward angle, hoping Spade felt as if she were caressing him, while she was, in reality, dumping the drink.

Spade slipped his hand up the long slit of Maggie's skirt.

Her knee came up and caught him in the chin, causing him to bite his tongue.

"Oops, sorry, accident," she said sweetly.

Spade glared at her, wiping blood from his chin. "Listen, blondie, there's a lot more where you came from. If you're not gonna play the game, you're gonna get hurt!" He pulled at her hair to remind her who was who, but it flew off in his hand. Spade stared at the wig for a moment in shock, then began to roar with laughter.

"Your hair's as phony as you are! But I'll betcha there's parts of you that are real!" With that, he grabbed the front of her gown.

Not wanting to break cover, Maggie shouted, glancing over at the Scimiteer. "Help me!"

As if made of wood, he stood, staring silently ahead, apparently having seen it all before.

Bracing her foot against Spade's chest, she shoved him backward. His clutching fingers tore her gown to her waist as he slammed back against the pillows, propelled by her foot.

A grim laugh came from his blood-stained teeth. "I love watching 'em squirm!" he said to nobody in particular.

Then, his single eye flashed as Maggie jumped to her feet. "Wait," he said, gasping. "That red hair! I seen you before!"

In a cold moment of recognition, Maggie realized why he had looked familiar. On the night of Fats Milligan's bachelor party, when she had popped up from the cake with the grease gun, he had been one of the faces in the crowd.

As she raked the room, she caught him in the eye. He crawled away. She was about to dust him, but he begged for his life, holding one hand over his bleeding eye. Since he wasn't part of Lucky's gang, Maggie had been merciful.

Now, she regretted it. Lucky's gang had come back to haunt her.

Maggie dove for her purse as the gangster dove for her. He grabbed her ankle.

"You marked me!" Spade said, spitting blood from his mouth. "I done nothing and you whanged me in the eye!"

"You were in the wrong crowd," she said with a husky voice, kicking her foot in a try to break free.

"That still don't call for this!" he said. Still hanging on to her firmly with one hand, with the other he pulled away his eye patch to reveal a ghastly purple socket where an eye should have been. Then, he drew a buck knife.

"I'll show you what it is to be mutilated!" he roared, dragging Maggie toward him.

The hell with her cover. It was blown anyhow. Her hand had hold of her purse. Ceasing her struggles, Maggie pretended to be weak with fear, letting Spade pull her toward him.

"I know it doesn't count for much," Maggie began babbling, to keep him occupied as her hand fished around inside her purse. "But I had a score to settle with Milligan."

"Oh, yeah?" He ran the flat of the knife blade up over her arm. "Yeah. We-we had a badger game going."

He laughed.

Maggie continued, talking feverishly. "I'd lead 'em into the room, start showin' 'em a good time, and he catches the whole thing on film."

"Pretty cheap scam, even for Fats."

"Cheap, yeah, but safe. Most of 'em were married and didn't want to have hotel room stuff
come up."

Damn! Her gun wasn't there! It must have spilled out onto the floor during their struggle. Her fingers felt around. Her gun was out of reach. But an atomizer of perfume wasn't.

Jack Spade glared down at her. "That don't explain rakin' a room, sister!"

Swinging her hand up, Maggie sprayed her perfume into Spade's one good eye.

Spade let out a loud shriek and grabbed for his burning eye. Using the training Agent 13 had taught her, Maggie jammed his elbows upward with one hand while she struck him in the Adam's apple with the other. Then she wriggled off the couch and dove for her pistol.

Spade gagged and recoiled, giving

Maggie time to jump to her feet, her gun leveled, her eyes on both Spade and the still-unmoving Scimiteer.

"Take it easy and no one gets hurt," she said.

She was backing for the door when, suddenly, it opened, and what appeared to be a pin-stripe wall stepped in.

"Going somewhere, sweetie?" the harsh voice said as huge arms grabbed her from behind.

Pin-stripe started to squeeze. Maggie still held the gun, but she couldn't move it. Her upper arms and chest were being slowly caved in.

Jack Spade struggled to his feet.

"You've done your last damage, dame!"

Ripping the gun out of her hand, Spade slapped her across the mouth. Then he turned to the impassive Scimiteer.

"Go get Rudy. He's got a corpse to deal with."

The mute Scimiteer left the room.

The odds were suddenly better. Spade let out a loud groan as Maggie's foot kicked him square in the solar plexus, knocking his breath out. The gun flew up in the air as he stumbled.

In the same flash of movement, Maggie's foot came down hard, her pump heel burying deep into Pin-stripe's instep.

"Bitch!" he screamed, as he momentarily eased his grip. Maggie spun and twisted free, grabbing her gun up as it hit the floor.

Pin-stripe's hand disappeared into his jacket and a gun appeared in a flash of silver. But he was too slow. Maggie's finger closed over her trigger. A shot rang out, and Pin-stripe stood stupidly as a third eye opened in his forehead.

Jack Spade crawled toward her, shouting for help. Ignoring him, Maggie ran through a door and found herself on the dance floor of the club. Spade's voice rang out. Two thugs lunged for her when, suddenly, Maggie heard a loud crack.

A door burst open, and water cascaded into the room. The dance floor was caught in the flash flood. Scrambling up onto a piano, Maggie jumped for a chandelier as the waters swirled beneath her.

The room went dark. Screams were drowned out in the rushing torrents of water. The tidal wave overflowed the stage and splashed against the far wall. Clinging to the chandelier, Maggie saw people clamoring up on top of the mirrored stage while water swirled around them.

There was nowhere for her to go, apparently. Desperate, her arms throbbing with the strain, Maggie reached up to the ceiling above her and felt around. Suddenly she gasped in relief. There, within reach of the chandelier, was a ceiling vent!

Climbing the chain of the chandelier, Maggie reached the ceiling vent. Using her earring as a screwdriver,

she unscrewed the cover and, with a strength born of desperation, pulled herself wearily up into the ventilation pipe.

She leaned back against the shaft, her legs straightened to hold her in place as she tried to catch her breath and ease the pain in her arms.

Where was 13? She didn't dare think about it. She had to keep going. She didn't have much time—it wouldn't be long before the whole building collapsed.

Propelling herself up the ventilation shaft, Maggie reached the main floor of the Brown Rat. Most of the patrons had guessed something was wrong, though no one knew yet what it was. The bartenders were working frantically to clear the building. No one noticed as Maggie kicked out the grillwork. A moment later, she was free.

Outside the Brown Rat, a river of fleeing people emptied into a sea of onlookers. Maggie glanced at the parking lot. Their car was gone! A quick search of the crowd revealed no sign of either 13 or Ray.

Then, Maggie saw some of China White's thugs studying the crowd. Could they still be searching for her? She didn't dare hang around.

Sliding away, she disappeared into the shadows.

DEATH WAITS ALONE

A flurry of stars flickered over the Imperial Palace Hotel. By night, lit only by the ambient light of stars and moon, it seemed a regal structure. But when the hard light of day fell upon it, revealing its peeling paint, cracking cement, and broken windows, the hotel gave away her age.

When the Imperial Palace in New York was built, Grover Cleveland inhabited the White House. It had been a fine establishment, catering to the rich and famous of Europe and America alike. But her glory was not to last. Years of disinterested management ran it into the ground, and the Depression reduced the once grand dame to destitution.

By 1937, the hotel crawled with those dregs of society who could afford a dollar a night and did not mind erratic heating, testy plumbing, the skittering rodent, or the occasional ghost here and there.

For everyone knew the hotel was haunted.

In 1886, when the hotel was in her glory, a terrible incident had occurred in it. Harold Stanton, a California railroad magnate, ran into financial troubles and came east to persuade bankers to prop him up. Armed with dozens of letters of introduction, Stanton traipsed up and down Wall Street, trying to interest bankers in his plan to create the largest railroad monopoly in North America.

At first, his plan stirred great interest, but rumors about his financial woes reached the East coast. The warm greetings became chilly rebuffs. Dinner invitations became unreturned messages. Still Stanton persisted, but eventually the magnate's funds ran out.

In the depths of winter, he fell behind on his hotel bill. Claiming that he was awaiting an overdue check from

California, Stanton was allowed an extension. When the second due date came, the manager sadly, respectfully, and dutifully informed Stanton that he would have to vacate his rooms on the following morning.

As the sun rose, bellboys, maids, manager, and clerk eagerly awaited Stanton's appearance, filled with morbid curiosity to know what a man who had dropped from the height above them to destitution below them would have to say for himself.

By 11:00 a.m., Stanton had not graced the lobby, and the manager—a meek, timid man-ordered a chambermaid to enter his apartment and remind him of his departure time.

Fearful of losing her job, she had no choice but to obey. When a knock on the door received no answer, she entered the room with a passkey. She came upon a sight that would torment her for years to come. Stanton hung from the chandelier in his suite.

Irony fell upon irony. The friends who had never sent Stanton the money he needed in life lavished it upon his funeral, hoping to ease their guilt.

Once news of his suicide was made public, telegrams poured in. The magnate's funeral was the highlight of New York's social season. Meanwhile, New York society quickly turned upon the "heartless" hotel. The manager went into isolation and eventually died in his own hotel under mysterious circumstances. The Imperial was rumored to be hexed.

In a weak effort to make amends, Myron Hartford, the owner of the hotel, arranged to have the room where Stanton died sealed off, vowing that it would remain unoccupied forever.

Though the taint of the incident hung over the hotel for a long time (and may well have been a contributing factor to its subsequent fall from grace), the incident that caused it had been forgotten. Still boarded up, the cursed room itself was avoided by even the most hardened vagrant.

13, however, found the reports about the incident during one of his many searches through the newspaper morgue. He had used this method to discover other hideouts and secret rooms, searching through old records for abandoned buildings, sealed-off rooms, houses tied up in lost wills and estates.

After an investigation of the old hotel, he knew that the location would be perfect for a lair. He was able to devise a swinging brick wall that would permit him entrance into the sealed room from the neighboring flophouse.

The room became one of three bases for Agent 13's New York operations. The hotel's location afforded 13 access to the seedier sections of the city.

Maggie Darr stared through the small window of the dark room, watching the sleeping city. Though she was both warm and dry, she was still wrapped in blankets, and her hands trembled.

She had been waiting for Agent 13

for hours now. It was their agreed meeting spot in case their plans went awry.

The room was just the same as when it had been sealed years before. It looked expensive, old and dusty. 13 had no use for the comfort of the plush red-velvet couches and chairs. The only sign of his presence was a large corner filled with his weapons, files, and disguises.

As the minutes ticked slowly, agonizingly by, Maggie tore her gaze from the darkness outside, looking at his things as if she could will him back. What would she do if he failed to return? Her heart felt the distant murmur of pain.

Hours passed. Day dawned. She listened for his footstep, but it didn't come and there was no word from him. She knew that, if he were alive, he would have contacted her somehow. No, he was dead. She would have to accept that. Ray must be dead, too.

Maggie slumped on the couch, wrapped in the blanket. What should she do? Where could she go? A sudden draft wafted into the room as floor boards creaked.

Maggie leaped to her feet.

"You!" she cried, startled.

It was 13—cold, alone, and alive.

"Good, you're here," he said without emotion.

Maggie, nonplussed at this casual response, came to a halt just as she had been about to fling her arms around him. Something in his face told her this would be highly unwelcome. Gulping, Maggie managed to shrug.

"Sure," she said in her best Crystal-the-floozie voice. "I'm here. Whaddya expect?"

If he caught her sarcasm, 13 let it pass without comment. Unable to keep from breathing a trembling sigh of relief, Maggie hurried to help the Agent remove his wet clothes. He normally would have rebuked her teasingly for such fussing over him, but this time he didn't say a word. His face was a blank, even beneath its mask.

Maggie went colder than 13. Something had happened to him, something that had affected him deeply. Was it his encounter with China White? She couldn't bring herself to ask. She couldn't make herself say that name. Maybe that wasn't it at all. Maybe it was something else.

"Ray?" she asked gently.

"Either dead or fleeing from his wives, I don't know—" 13 said coldly.

Maggie swallowed, chilled by the coolness of his response. Would he have reacted the same way if it were Ray asking about her disappearance? she wondered bleakly.

Moodily, 13 threw on a dressing gown she handed to him. He seemed preoccupied, worried.

"I learned that China White is sailing on the *Normandie*," Maggie said brightly, hoping for a reaction that might lift him from the gloom.

It worked.

"Where did you hear that?"

"Some greaseball at the Rat said that she was going to be on the ship," Maggie said, pleased to see him liven up.

"That's it!" 13 cried. And, just as the water had gushed through the broken window pane, Agent 13 began to pour forth a torrent of words, talking so fast that Maggie had trouble following his tale.

13 told her of his meeting with China White, even alluding to the moments they had shared years ago, though he did not go into these in detail.

He told her of his fruitless five-hour search of the bay for some sign of Ray's body. It was only after dawn that he had called off his search and returned to the lair. But first, he did one last thing. He had stopped in a phone booth to call Benny the Eye, who was still busy tailing Dr. Fischer.

"Some foreign-looking types with German accents met with Fischer last night at his place," Benny reported. "The bug I planted worked perfectly. The Nazis are all hot for this Lightning Gun of his, and they want to see a demonstration. They're talkin' big bucks. More'n this prof 11 see in a lifetime of teachin' losers. They gave him a ticket—First Class—"

"For the *Normandie*!" Maggie cried triumphantly.

13 nodded. Suddenly it was beginning to make sense, the pieces were falling together. The Brotherhood wanted Fischer, that much was plain. The next disaster? What more horrible incident than to destroy the wealthiest, most lavish luxury liner the world had ever known—especially since it would be loaded with celebrities. 13 saw the simplicity of the plan. Hundreds, thousands might die. And, in the confusion, who would miss Dr. Fischer? He would be presumed dead.

13 swore in frustration. He saw the elements of the plan, but how to stop it?

There was always the alternative of killing Fischer, but he didn't have time. The Normandie sailed tomorrow. He would have to take his grim business aboard the ship. But would killing Fischer stop the disaster? Not likely. And how would he get onto the Normandie anyhow? At this late date, it would be impossible to get tickets. 13 considered his options carefully. He'd have to call in more than a few favors....

"What are you grinning that idiotic smile for?" he snapped at Maggie irritably. "Don't you realize how serious—" 13 stopped.

"Two tickets ... on the *Normandie*," Maggie Darr said smoothly, holding them up. "First Class."

VESSEL OF LIGHT

Between the years 1912 and 1929, the French ruled the seas of luxury passenger liner service with three ships—the *France*, launched in 1912; the *Paris*, launched in 1921; and the *lie de France*, launched in 1927. With these ships, the French dominated the lucrative and ever-growing market of transatlantic service.

The year 1928 had been a banner year for the line. During that year, they transported over ninety thousand passengers, and receipts exceeded a billion francs, with over half coming from its New York service alone. Other countries, seeing the potential for profit, took notice and entered the growing marketplace.

Germany tossed her hat into the ring in 1929 with the launchings of the *Bremen* and the *Europa*. Modern, quicker, and larger, the ships sliced into the French Line's profits, England commissioned work on a new liner to be called the *Queen Mary*. The French were losing their market.

France needed a new ship. Work began on the vessel that would become the largest, fastest, and most luxurious vessel ever to sail the seas. Her name—SS *Normandie*.

One thousand twenty-nine feet in length, the *Normandie* was capable of attaining a speed well over thirty-two knots. She weighed as much as several Eiffel Towers and, if stood on her bow measured taller than the Empire State Building. She could carry two thousand passengers—eight hundred and fifty of them in First Class.

But she was not only functional, she was beautiful as well. Artwork by Dupas, Dunand, Jouve, and Gernez adorned her corridors. The tables were set with crystal by Rene Lalique, silver by Puiforcat. The elegant furniture and tapestries were by Gaudissart. Journalists called the *Normandie*

"The Eighth Wonder of the World," "The Vessel of Light," "The Floating Versailles," and the "Messenger of Peace."

"Messenger of Peace..." It could be a "Messenger of Death...."

It was a busy afternoon at the French Line pier in New York Harbor. Cars, limos, and cabs queued up, waiting to unload their passengers. Baggage handlers pushed heavily laden carts past the bow of the great ship.

Standing atop the gangway was Night Watch Officer Renard, a dashing Frenchman in his mid-thirties, who had the distinction of being known as a "Ladies' Man." Conscious of his swarthy good looks and the fine fit of his Paris-tailored uniform, Renard smiled effusively at the boarding passengers—informing them of the meticulous service they could expect to receive.

Standing near the First Class gangway, Renard reveled in the reflected glory of the illustrious people walking past him. It was the cream of 1937 society—Mr. and Mrs. Douglas Fairbanks (taking a European vacation while attending the opening of his new film in Paris); Mr. William C. Bullitt, the U.S. Ambassador (returning to France after his latest briefing on the "German situation"); the famous Vogue model, Mile. Delamarre, and her fawning "escort," Michael Richardson, a wealthy American industrialist. Behind them came such diverse notables as Cary Grant; the

Maharajah Manikya of Tripura; the painter, Salvador Dali; the author, Antoine de Saint-Exupery. The Normandie had become "the only way to cross."

Officer Renard considered himself a master of human nature. For many, this was an amusing hobby. For Renard, it was a career. Being the officer of the night watch, he was able to gain a great deal by knowing who was willing to pay what for what or who was lonely for his company in the wee, small hours.

Renard had spent many pleasant nights comforting newly divorced movie actresses, young starlets seeking time away from aged producer husbands, new brides who married for money and begged for affection. Renard had pocketed many, many dollars from men who traded love for money as well as those who traded in poker chips. Renard enjoyed his job, especially the fringe benefits.

So, Renard kept an eagle eye on all boarding passengers, classifying them, slotting them in his mind, making a running commentary on each.

"Young wife, jewels, old husband. Mmmm. She will be needing company, I have no doubt. And that so very chic gentleman is a gambler, and not an honest one. Perhaps, one of Jack Spade's friends. I think I shall have to raise the price on Monsieur Spade."

And so on. His attentive eye caught sight of a wrinkled-looking man hovering around the baggage loading area, making a nuisance of himself.

"Be careful with that!" he was shouting as a huge crate was being swung aboard. "Are you certain those ropes are secure? Gently, man, gently! Twenty years of my life are in that crate!"

"Humpf!" Renard sniffed. "Le Professor. I wonder what is in the crate? Books, undoubtedly. I will get nothing from him. I am surprised he could come up with the price of a ticket."

"Excuse me," a voice said, bringing Renard's attention back to the gangway. "Could you tell us where our state rooms are?"

Renard turned to eye one sad sack of a man. From the looks of his face, one of his parents had been a weasel, and his glasses were as thick as the windows on Al Capone's limousine.

"The name, monsieur?" said Renard, looking over his passenger list.

"Plotkin, Hiram Plotkin," said the man.

Renard glanced at his list, but, at the same time, he managed to ogle Plotkin's wife.

What a beauty! A strawberry blonde, ripe for the picking. But she appeared pale and depressed, glancing often at her husband with a wistful look.

Finding Plotkin on the list, Renard raised his eyebrows, then examined his tickets.

How could this frumpy weasel ever come up with the francs to go First Class? Renard wondered. Maybe he was one of those eccentrics who had invented a better mousetrap or something. It was obvious that Strawberry Blonde had married him for his money, then quickly realized that it wasn't enough.

"Is this your first time aboard ship, Monsieur Plotkin?" Renard asked with oily politeness.

"Yes," mumbled Plotkin nervously.

"It's our second honeymoon," said Mrs. Plotkin in a soft voice.

More like a last-ditch attempt to save a dying marriage, thought Renard, already slotting Mrs. Plotkin into his schedule.

Renard bowed. "You are fortunate above most men, Monsieur Plotkin," he murmured, looking meaningfully at Strawberry Blonde.

Mrs. Plotkin blushed. Plotkin only scowled.

Renard turned to a cabin boy hovering nearby, "Ronzo, show Monsieur and Madame Plotkin to Suite 36."

Renard turned back to the Plotkins. "My name is Officer Renard. I am the night watch officer on the promenade deck. If I can be of any service, please let me know...

Strawberry Blonde took note. "Thank you for your kindness," she said, offering him her hand, then smiling with pleasure as he kissed it elaborately. Renard smiled as the two walked away. He felt sorry for the weasel, but in the same thought, he looked forward to the comfort he might be able to supply the clearly deprived Mrs. Plotkin.

The cabin boy and the Plotkins had vanished, leaving Renard in a blissful reverie, when the sound of applause from the wharf caused him to snap to attention. Looking down, Renard beheld the most beautiful woman he had ever seen. Wrapped in expensive sable, her sultry features were enhanced by the twilight.

Pausing dramatically before boarding, she waved to her admirers and the photo-bugs, then turned and regally ascended the gangway. She looked up at Renard. Their eyes met. He felt a tingle up his spine and a soft burn in his stomach. Taking her hand to help her, he was lost in a beautiful dream. For a wild moment, they were drinking a champagne toast on a baroque balcony in Monte Carlo. They were stepping off the running board of a cream-colored Hispano-Suiza, waving at an opening-night audience. For just a moment, he stood in the light— the light of flashbulbs, flood lights, marquee lights.

Then China White, ethereal, beautiful, perfumed, elegant, drifted on past him, a gaggle of reporters hot on her heels. Her expensive fragrance tantalized his nose in the passing breeze. Renard wanted her.

Someone else on board the *Normandie* also a special interest in China White. Hearing noise of the approaching crowd, Hiram Plotkin turned to see what all the excitement was about. At the sight of the gorgeous woman, Plotkin's bucktoothed mouth dropped open and his weasel eyes bulged through the coke-bottle specs, anyone getting a close look at him, however, would have been have been chilled by the look of intelligence light, intense eyes; an intelligence that belied absentminded, bumpkin guise. But nobody noticed, for all eyes were on China White.

Nobody noticed, that is, except the straw blonde.

"Come on, Hiram," she said, poking him.

"Leave me alone!" he snapped, and there was an edge to his voice that chilled Maggie Looking at the disguised Agent 13, Maggie wondered how much of that rapt, enchanted look he gave the beautiful China White had been act

The cabin boy, realizing that other tips getting away while he wasted time, said "This way, sir!" and hurried on down the corridor.

It was the first time Maggie had ever been on an ocean liner. She was awed by its size. The already walked for what seemed like miles to reach their staterooms. With fourteen different levels, the Normandie was a floating city of steel. She tried to imagine what it would take to sink this mighty ship. It seemed impossible. Surely, they'd made a mistake! Nothing could harm wonder of technology—nothing! Even as the thought crossed her mind, she realized others must have must have said the same thing the day they boarded the Titanic....

Maggie would soon have been lost in the maze of corridors had not Agent 13 made her spend last night memorizing the ship's layout. 13 also knew the number of officers, crew, the procedures above deck and below, as well as the locations of the bridge, the captain's quarters, the radio rooms.

Above all, he knew every detail about China White—her concert schedule, where her suite was located, even where she had insisted they park the limousine she had brought on board.

As Maggie looked around in pleased, naive wonder at their elegant surroundings, 13's eye was drawn to a theater marquee. China's name leaped out at him. China White, Appearing Tbnight, in Concert.

13 stared at the marquee, feeling frustrated. What could she be up to? China was such a visible personality, she would be foolish to attempt any kidnapping or overt action on her own. Her role, therefore, was that of the conductor of this grim concerto, but where was her orchestra? Who were the players? Where was the music? As he walked past Normandie's elegant theater, 13's eyes were drawn to the two ancient masks carved in the entry doors. They seemed to echo his confusion.

Comedy, tragedy. Life, death. Lover, enemy.

He examined the variables.

China knew the where, the when, and the how.

13 knew China.

Somehow, he had to be the sour note in her deadly symphony. And the only thing he could do was to try to force her hand, to make her afraid, to make her wonder. Backed into a corner, she might grow careless, she might make a mistake.

13 smiled grimly. The performances transpiring on board ship that night would be far more elaborate than anything being performed on stage.

GRIM ASSIGNMENTS

The cabin boy opened the suite door, proudly standing back for them to enter.

Maggie looked around, marveling at the beauty of the decor. The furniture was made of rich cherry wood; the lighting was soft, indirect; velvet upholestry covered the chairs; and a bouquet of lilies stood on her night table.

"Oh, Hiram! It's wonderful!" she said.

"I'm glad you're pleased" he responded flatly, glancing about the room with only technical interest.

Had it been a different time, Maggie might have been able to enjoy the plush opulence. But this mission and the danger they were in consumed her thoughts. Looking at Agent 13, thinking back to her glimpse of the ravishing China White, Maggie realized with a sinking heart that the danger she feared was not a danger made up

solely of hot, spitting lead.

The cabin boy began to open up their luggage, so that he might hang their clothing in the closet.

"That won't be necessary," said Plotkin, pressing a five spot into the boy's hand.

"Thank you, sir. Dinner will be served starting at eight in the Grand Lounge. I suggest reservations. I would be happy to make them for you, if you wish."

"We'll handle them ourselves, thank you."

"As you wish. In the drawer here, you will find a book containing lists of all events scheduled for the passage, as well as all the services offered. My name is Ronzo. Should you need me, just dial room service. Is there anything else I can do for you?"

"No, we want to be alone right now."

"Very well, sir."

Maggie listened as the sounds of the cabin boy's footsteps receded.

"What do you think?" she asked 13 finally.

13 did not answer. He was checking over the room and, from the frown on his disguised face, he didn't like what he saw.

He had requested an inner cabin, but none was available at such late notice. So they'd had to make do with the room reserved by the late, unlamented Jack Spade. Apparently Spade enjoyed a cabin with lots of light. As a result, 13 had two large portholes to contend with. These looked directly out on the upper deck. Though the curtains could be shut, nothing could stop the spray of machine gun fire. The walls were paper-thin, the locks easily picked.

Agent 13 switched on the radio, and the strains of "In the Mood" filled the room. This, he hoped, would make their conversation harder to discern for the casual eavesdropper.

13 reached into his case and pulled out several photo enlargements of Dr. Fischer, taken both at the Lightning Gun's demonstration and by Benny the Eye. He held them out to Maggie.

"Fischer," he said.

Taking them from his hands, Maggie gave them a quick once-over.

"Study him," 13 admonished. "He's traveling alone. Staying in Suite 48, right down the hall from us. Spade was probably supposed to keep an eye on him."

"Fischer looks a worse weasel than you!" Maggie laughed.

13 shook his head. "Appearances are deceiving. Within that ingenuous head are stored some of the most sensitive military secrets in the world."

"Could of fooled me."

"I want you to follow him. Don't let him out of your sight. According to Benny, he's not partial to lipstick on the collar, but he might be vulnerable to tears on the shoulder. Keep up the act that we're not getting along...."

"If you say so." Maggie shrugged. "But I still don't see how they plan to kidnap a man on the open sea!"

"Put no crime past the Brotherhood. Assume no feat is beyond them. Unless I am terribly wrong, they do not intend to let the *Normandie* drop anchor at Le Havre."

"O.K. I watch Fischer. Meanwhile, what will you be doing?" Maggie asked. But she already knew the answer.

"Watching China White."

Maggie smiled wryly. "Of course," she muttered.

Hearing the sarcastic tone in her voice, 13 looked up quickly. "Whatever the plot might be, rest assured that she's behind it."

"And how many are behind her?"

"There's no way to tell, but I believe it's reasonable to assume that she's not acting alone."

"Is she the Masque?" Maggie asked hesitantly.

13 thought for a moment. It was a

question that had drifted through his own mind like leaves in a windstorm. The evidence all seemed to say yes, yet something wouldn't let him believe it. Something kept wanting to hold on to the memories of innocence and love that they had shared years ago. But people change....

"I believe so," he said finally, his voice flattened.

"So what can we do?" Maggie asked, feeling helpless. "Just watch Fischer? Just watch her? That isn't much—"

"Time is my enemy, her ally. Whatever the Brotherhood has planned, they are operating on a crucial time schedule. I've got to force China's hand, try to upset that time schedule if I can. To do this, I must risk everything. If I fail, responsibility for the safety of hundreds of thousands of lives will fall upon your shoulders."

Maggie's eyes opened wide. She swallowed. "What—what does that mean?"

"Under no circumstances are you to allow the Brotherhood to escape with Fischer. Kill him if necessary."

"And what about China White?" Maggie asked softly. "Will you kill her?"

"If necessary."

Ignoring Maggie's look of disbelief, 13 sat down resolutely before the large mirror and began to strip off the make-up that had turned him into the innocuous Mr. Plotkin.

As he did so, he wondered—he

had killed so many without a qualm. But—could he kill her?

Fearful that China White might try to kidnap the scientist and smuggle him off the ship even before it departed, Maggie stayed out on the top deck, close to Fischer, until the gangway was pulled up.

Dr. Fischer was among the throng packed on the deck, but he was not part of it. Everyone else was waving and tossing gay spirals of colored paper down into the cheering crowd below. But the professor was staring dully at the shore, looking worried and preoccupied.

"No wonder!" muttered Maggie grimly. "Thinking about selling out your own country to the Nazis! How much are they paying you, Judas?"

The *Normandie* blew her powerful horn, a final salute of farewell to the skyscrapers of New York. The city responded with a synchronized din of auto horns and cheers as the huge ship slipped slowly backward into the Hudson River. Turning, it then made for the waiting Atlantic and, five days later, the shores of France. One by one, the escort of small yachts and planes were left behind until the Normandie was alone, the mighty queen of the swirling seas.

The salty breeze of the Atlantic filled Maggie's lungs as she drew a deep breath. There was no longer any turning back, she thought, watching the skyline of New York grow small. The passing waters looked cold and deep, covering unmarked graves. The mighty Normandie suddenly looked very small and vulnerable when compared to the vastness of the restless sea.

Fischer abruptly left the deck. Following him, Maggie saw him safely ensconced in his cabin. Then she returned to her own to report that there was, as far as she could see, no one the least bit interested in Fischer. But Agent 13 was gone.

Sighing, Maggie propped the door open slightly, so that she could hear and see if anyone either came to or left Fischer's cabin. Then she started to change for dinner. Everything was so peaceful. For a fleeting moment, Maggie questioned the Agent's hypothesis, hoping he was wrong.

GATHERING GLOOM

Dinner was like a splendid dream that night for the passengers dining in the *Normandie's* First Class dining room. Two hundred and eighty-two feet long, the room was capable of seating over seven hundred diners under the beneficent gaze of Athena Parthenos, Greek goddess of protection, whose thirteen-foot-tall statue stood watch over the room. The walls of the great hall were adorned with Labouret's glass slabs that rose twenty-eight feet up to the richly coffered ceiling. The "miraculous grotto," as it was termed, was lit by startling sixteen-foot sconces decorating the walls, as well as by crystal towers of light that rose in the room's center.

The dining room was a floating four-star restaurant. Since the price of the food was included in the crossing price, diners could eat themselves into oblivion on *Jambon d'York* or *Le Caneton a L'Orange*. The ladies put their diets aside when tempted with the delicacies of sweet Patisserie and Glaces, prepared in mysterious ways, to which only the French were privy.

Watch Officer Renard stood on the grand stairway that flowed into the hall, his uniform starched stiff and spotless. He scanned the busy tables carefully, then he saw her. She was not hard to find, her raven hair a beacon of darkness amid the glitter.

China White sat at a table surrounded by admirers—the entertaining Maharajah on one side, a handsome, well-known German actor on the other. It would be tough for Renard, but he liked challenges—he wasn't about to let this one slip away.

He watched her dine, entranced by her grace and elegance. Mozart's *Eine Kleine Nachtmuzik* filled the air.

As the dessert remains were taken up, Cuban cigars were lit. Courvoisier and Benedictine were served. The diners rose from their tables, many heading for the Grill Room for its wild swing dancing. But, for the more romantic couples, it was the Grand Lounge. Here they could sip life at a slower, more elegant pace, dancing to the music of seductive strings that lulled them into oneness.

Renard observed China White as she drifted from the table like an elfin spirit, her pearls and elegant Chanel gown enhanced by the beauty of her satinlike flesh. Her courtiers stood up, offering escort. She shook her head, leaving them behind as she walked toward the Grand Lounge alone. It was Renard's moment. He closed in carefully. Little did he realize, but the hunter was also being hunted.

Few rooms in history have been as elegant as the Grand Lounge of the *Normandie*. Modeled after the Hall of Mirrors at Versailles, it sparkled like an elegant jewel within a crystal box.

Four large glass reliefs by Dupas, each measuring twenty-one feet high by forty-nine feet wide, adorned the gold and silver gilt hall. Its ceiling rose thirty-one feet from the dance floor; tall rectangular windows, five on either side, opened to the "green pastures" of the passing waters. What space was left was filled by elegant mirrors.

Without knowing it, those in the Grand Lounge that night saw something only a chosen few had seen in twelve years. Yet the only ones to no-tice were a pair of young newlyweds.

"Who is that man? I don't recall seeing him embark," the young bride asked, eyeing a tall, handsome man dressed in a tuxedo.

"And I shouldn't be sorry to see him disembark," the groom responded, turning his young wife away, not knowing that he was one of the few ever to have seen Agent 13's true face.

It was a face unlike any other nature has chiseled. At once stunning and unremarkable, each line and curve of the face was perfect. His cheek bones were neither low nor high, his eyes were neither blue nor brown, his mouth was neither large nor small, his teeth were neither straight nor crooked. It was the perfect base on which to construct the many identities he adopted—a canvas that accepted any hue.

Yet, guiding the face was a strength of character and a charisma rarely found, a strength that showed through and could have acted as a magnet to beautiful women or theater fans or political backers, had he chosen those lines of life. But Fate had arranged differently....

13's lack of disguise was purposeful. Other than Maggie Darr, there was only one person on board tonight who would recognize his real face. Recognize it and, hopefully, be startled enough by the recognition to act rashly.

Keeping near China White, Agent 13 watched in amusement as Renard made his move.

As China floated through the Grand Lounge, Renard swooped down on her like a hawk, intercepting her only paces from the dance floor. Renard had charm, there was no denying the fact, 13 thought. China smiled and laughed at Renard's quick torrent of well-rehearsed words.

Bowing, the suave French officer indicated the dance floor. A moment later Renard's strong hands encircled China's slim waist. Clad in a skintight black gown, she flowed effortlessly across the floor like a dark angel, Renard guiding her gracefully. Agent 13 watched and waited.

While others danced in the Grand Lounge, Maggie Darr spent a bored evening trailing the professor. She wasn't finding it difficult to keep an eye on Dr. David Fischer. After a hurried dinner, he immediately set out for the Winter Garden Room, located near the bow of the ship. Entering the room, he sat down in a wicker chair, sipped sherry, and began to study a sheaf of papers.

"Boy, some fun evening this is gonna be!" Maggie thought, slipping into the room after Fischer was settled.

Filled with examples of prize French horticulture, the lushly planted Winter Garden Room gave an unparalleled view of the windswept seas. It was peaceful, uncrowded, suited to those who preferred the quieter pleasures of shipboard.

Trying to keep from thinking about the fun and excitement going on in the Grand Lounge this evening, Maggie sat down at a table nearby, pretending to read an account of Dame Penelope Hat-ford's trip up the Nile.

But her eyes covertly surveyed the room.

Soft lights fell upon a curved marbled bar that jutted out from the wall like the prow of a sleek ship. Everything in the room was done in peachy mauves, greens, and whites—gentle earth colors asking to go unnoticed amid the lilies, roses, and palms.

There were several other people in the room. In one corner, a man with a thin mustache played a baby grand piano. Fingers dancing across the ivory keyboards, he was responding to the requests of several young men sporting cream-colored blazers adorned with the Harvard emblem.

Of the other men in the room, Maggie knew one by sight, having read about him numerous times in the newspapers. His name was Nat Spencer, but he was commonly known as "the man in the iron coffin." A millionaire inventor, he had been stricken with infantile paralysis several years ago and was now forced to continue existence lying on his back in an iron lung. Only his head stuck out from the coffin-like device. Since he could not move, several small mirrors had been mounted to afford him views of the surrounding area.

Nat had refused to give in to his affliction, however. Possessed of a wry, witty sense of humor, he was a much sought-after addition to any party. With the help of two constant attendants, he went everywhere, did everything. Tonight, Nat and his "lung" rested on a wheeled cart near a table. Under the watchful gaze of a streamlined deco goddess holding a light in her hand, Nat was taking on a distinguished-looking older man in a high-stakes game of backgammon.

Other than these people, however, the room was nearly deserted. Occasionally a beautifully gowned woman and a tuxedoed man would drift in, apparently hoping to find a more "discreet" place aboard the crowded ship. Seeing them gaze into each other's eyes, watching their hands twine about each other's waists, Maggie sighed. This ship seemed to be stirring long-suppressed yearnings.

Her occasional glances about the room, however, had not gone unnoticed. They met with a surprising result. Looking back to check on Dr. Fischer, she was startled to see him staring at her!

His face twisted into a scowl. Hurling his papers down, he rose from his seat and moved directly toward her!

A red, angry face leaned into Maggie's. Crooked teeth, too tightly packed together for the small mouth, spat out words.

"You have been following me, young woman, and I don't like it!"

Blast the man! Setting her book aside, Maggie looked up at him in as-tonishment. "Excuse me?"

"There's no excuse! Either this situation ends immediately or I shall report you to the captain."

"I believe that you've mistaken me for someone else," Maggie said politely.

"Don't be impertinent, young lady! You've been following me all day and now I can't even drink my sherry in peace. Who are you working for?" he demanded. "The FBI?"

Maggie glanced around. He was creating a scene. The Harvard men were watching now with attentive interest, and even the older backgammon player looked up. Nat in the iron lung was watching through his mirror.

She was suddenly angry. Damn Fischer anyhow! Probably feeling guilty, and too weak and nervous to deal with it.

Coldly, Maggie rose to her feet. She would have to bluff her way out. "My name, sir, is Mrs. Hiram Plotkin, Hiram Plotkin the Third. My husband is presently taking a nap in our stateroom. If you don't quit bothering me, I'll get him, and I don't think he will take kindly to your accusations."

Dr. Fischer stared at her a moment, then—to Maggie's amazement—his face went gray. Mumbling something, he turned away, running a trembling hand through his hair.

Impulsively, feeling truly sorry for the man, Maggie reached out her hand. "Please, don't go," she said sincerely. "Look, I didn't mean that about getting my husband. He probably wouldn't care anyway. Say, are you sick or something? You don't look good. Can I help?"

Fischer looked around. "I'm sorry I bothered you," he said with a sigh. "I've been under a lot of pressure lately and I—"

Smiling, Maggie encouraged him to talk.

"I'm Dr. David Fischer," he said with belated grace, "and I would like to apologize."

"Accepted," she replied, shaking his hand.

"Would you join me in a cognac?"

She smiled. "I would."

Seeing that apparently there wasn't going to be any more action of interest, the Harvard boys, shrugging, went back to their piano. The backgammon players returned to their game.

Maggie took a seat with Dr. Fischer. The attractive young woman proved a sympathetic listener, and soon, before he quite realized it, Dr. Fischer was pouring his heart out to her.

"The demonstration of the Lightning Gun was an astounding success!" he said. "I thought for certain that the Army would be crawling to me on their hands and knees. All I needed was a grant! That's all. Two days later—I got a letter." Fischer shook his head. "The State Department says that, although the Armed Services see the 'potential' of such a device as this Lightning Gun, they aren't interested in developing it at the present time!"

"But why?" asked Maggie curiously. "If it's as good as you say—"

"Oh, it's good!" Fischer said, tearing his hair in frustration. "But they're locked into technology rooted in the past. They want guns that fire real bullets, not light. I'm a toy-maker, a tinkerer. They don't begin to comprehend the power I can harness and direct!"

13 comprehends, Maggie thought uneasily. He knows this gun's deadly potential—and so does the Brotherhood! Unconsciously, her hand went to her purse.

"Twenty years of work and grants down the drain!" Fischer's head sank into his hands. "My colleagues pitied me... pitied me."

He tossed back another Cognac. How many was that, Maggie wondered—his fourth? And he probably wasn't accustomed to drinking. . . . She ought to try to get him out of here.

"But then," he said in a loud whisper, "I got a call. A scientist, very big name. Happened to be German. They're interested."

"Who?" prompted Maggie.

"The United European Defense Company. They want me to bring my gun to France for more detailed study."

Maggie frowned. Seeing her look, Fischer squirmed uncomfortably. "Oh, I know what you're thinking. I thought the same thing. That madman Hitler isn't far away. And the scientist I spoke to was German. But he swore to me that he hated the Nazis. What could I do? I agreed.

"Then"—his voice dropped—"I noticed I was being watched, followed! A paper boy on a corner, a cab driver, a man with one leg—everywhere I went, someone was behind me. But who? The Army—after they'd turned me down? The Nazis? The French? I thought it would stop on the boat, but it's started again! I've seen a man hanging around my cabin. I'm frightened! And I have nowhere to go, nowhere to turn." His head in his hands, he began to weep.

Maggie shifted uneasily. She was only supposed to keep an eye on Fischer—now it looked like he might fall apart at the seams! She needed 13, needed him badly. But where was he?

WALTZ OF THE SPIDER

"I give you my word, beautiful lady," Renard said, looking deep into China's eyes, "you are as safe aboard this ship as you would be in your own bed. Our course takes us near no icebergs. Our radio man is in constant contact with the shore. Even in the unlikely event of a mishap—"

"I know it is silly of me to be so frightened of the ocean." China White performed the amazing trick of making her voice vulnerable and sultry at the same time. "And you are very reassuring. So, these men in the radio room, they are in constant communication with the shore? What would they do if some terrible disaster were to occur...."

Renard was enchanted with her. Smiling down into those deep, dark blue eyes, he was just about to describe in elaborate detail the workings of the radio room when he felt a hand tap him lightly on the shoulder.

"May I cut in?" said a baritone voice.

Renard turned, barely able to conceal his outrage. How dare anyone interrupt him, an officer of this ship! He would brush the person off, politely but firmly. Then his eyes met the eyes of the stranger's, and Renard suddenly had second thoughts. The man's eyes were animal-like, with no trace of emotion in them. Renard had seen eyes like that only once before—in a Parisian zoo-They had belonged to a black panther.

The stranger's gaze went to Renard's dancing partner.

Startled, Renard turned to look at her as well. China White was staring at the stranger as though he truly could be a black panther! She didn't say a word, she didn't gasp or start. But she was affected by the stranger, that was certain. Her skin was pale, her eyes wide and shimmering with a radiant luster, her lips slightly parted.

Renard stepped aside. Who was this man? the officer wondered as he walked from the dance floor. He certainly would have recognized such a striking face! Perhaps the man was from the tourist class ... Looking around the Lounge quickly, Renard saw Purser Andre Damour standing near the staircase, observing the gala. He would ask him. Damour never forgot a face.

China White looked at the man before her. She said nothing. What could be said when life stopped and then spun backward? Her heartbeat quickened. She stared into his eyes. Reaching up, she touched his cheek. She breathed his scent. The man was older, wiser, darker. But it was him.

The orchestra played *Tales of the Vienna Woods.*

"Touch me and wake me," she said to him.

He held out his hand. She took it.

Her hands tingled as the pulse from his hand echoed through her, beckoning for a union of two rhythms so much alike but separated for so long.

He held her, transporting them both to another place, another time.

The world disappeared around her. She had often dreamed of this moment with longing and with dread. She was suddenly unsure of herself, remembering days of lost innocence and purity, days of a wondrous, splendid love....

Why had he come back now? Her soul cried in agony. Why now? The moment before the storm.

"You're alive," she whispered, pressing her cheek into his shoulder.

"Disappointed?"

"Relieved."

They drifted across the dance floor, his strong arms holding her effortlessly. She pressed herself against him. The threads of her gown couldn't hold back the passions she felt surging through her, passions she had felt for this man long ago. Could those moments be relived?

"I heard you were dead."

"Did it matter to you?"

"Yes! Oh, yes!" she admitted, her arms tightening around him.

Her words stung 13 with a thousand barbs. Was she playing him for the fool? Or was she telling the truth? And if the truth, what then? Only torment perhaps...

"Once upon a time" was a long time ago...

Seventeen years old. Walking among the high arches and pillars of the Shrine on a moonlit night, he had glimpsed the truth, and in so doing, saw the dark heart of the Brotherhood. The horror was revealed, a dream shattered. Suddenly he realized that he had been trained for a life of evil!

For long months, he concealed his knowledge. But, of course, they found out—as they find out everything. He was a threat. They tried to silence him forever, but he had learned their les-

sons well, and he escaped.

She was the girl he loved. He would leave, but he would take her with him.

His heart pounded as they embraced secretly beneath the canopied trees. "They tried to km me," he told her. "Soon, they will come for you. We must escape, tonight."

Young, frightened, unsure, they held each other in the shadowed moonlight. Their urgent whispers forged a path to the future.

"I'll meet you in the garden when the moon disappears behind the peaks," she promised.

She never came.

Instead, agents of the Brotherhood arrived, but they were late. Too late to catch 13. Hunted, he left her behind, his love poisoned by the knowledge that she had betrayed him. Never to see her again until now....

The unspoken question came to his mind, the question that he had carried with him since his day of flight. "Why did you do it?" he asked. "Why did you tell them where to find me?"

As if she had been waiting for that question, she answered it with a burst of words. "They were waiting for me when I returned to the cloister! I tried to lie, but it was no use! They knew—everything!"

Her head bowed. "You know what they were capable of doing. I held out as long as I could...."

He didn't answer, only held her more tightly. Finally, however, he said harshly. "Then why did you stay? After what I told you?"

"I stayed because the alternative was death." Her voice was flat, emotionless.

"Come with me now! Together we can—"

China put her hand to his mouth. She knew what he was going to say, and it was useless. The Brotherhood was too strong. It was only a matter of time before they caught up with him and crushed him.

"Please, don't! These events have a life of their own. Neither of us has the power to stop what will occur."

"And what are 'these events'?"

China White shook her lovely head. "We've both traveled down many dark roads since then."

"Turn back," he whispered.

"It is too late."

An instant later, he felt a slight movement of her hand at his shoulder and glanced into the mirror of her eyes. A waiter melted back into the crowd. But, 13 noticed, this waiter was not waiting tables. He was doing nothing but watching them. And he kept one hand in his pocket.

13 smiled grimly. "How many more of your friends are aboard?"

"I don't know what you are talking about."

Looking down at China, 13 could almost see her mind working. He smiled again. She was in a strange predicament. As long as he was with her, no harm could come to him. A man suddenly dropping dead in her arms would attract the attention of the world. But, if she let him leave, he would melt into the crowd, assuming one of his many disguises.

So, he was not surprised to see her beautiful face turn up to his or to hear her whisper seductively, "The Brotherhood would welcome your return." She tempted his ear with the warmth and lightness of her breath. "I could arrange it."

"I'd sooner pass through the gates of hell."

"Listen to reason," she said, pressing against his chest. "You are alone against an organization that has existed thousands of years!"

"An organization that has become as rotten as a corpse."

"Definitions will reverse, history will change. The Brotherhood is strong! Soon they will rule this planet under one law, one goverment."

"How many innocent people must die first? Ten, twenty, a million?"

"It doesn't matter! The petty squabbles that have kept man a slave to himself will be broken. the end result will be a lasting peace!"

"The peace of slavery!"

"Your struggle is futile and you will die!"

"Then that is my fate. As you said, people dying doesn't matter to you. Know this, China, I am sworn against the Brotherhood and all who stand for it."

She looked into his eyes. "Including me?"

He didn't answer.

"Miss White?" a voice implored.

A frantic steward had hurried onto the dance floor and was now hovering near.

"Excuse me, Miss White. I was told to remind you—your curtain is in fifteen minutes."

"Thank you, I'll be right there."

The steward stood off to the side and waited, obviously having received instructions to come back with Miss White or not come back.

"Will you be at my performance?" The dark blue eyes looked up at him.

13 smiled. "What do you think?"

"I can't guarantee your safety unless you escort me."

13 scanned the area. The entire room seemed to be filled with eyes watching them. Whether it was because of China's beauty and celebrity or because the eyes belonged to agents of the Brotherhood, he had no way of knowing.

China waited, smiling confidently, certain of what his answer must be.

"Another time, perhaps" He had made his decision years ago and there vas no turning back. To walk with her was to wall into darkness.

Disappointment and a brief flicker of anger marred her lovely face for an instant. She looked at him long and intently, as though seeing his face for the last time and waiting to memorize it. "I tried to save you," she said. "Remember that."

Then, in a barely audible voice, "I

love you. I always have."

She kissed his cheek. Her warm, soft lips sent sparks through him. Then, gracefully, she turned and walked away.

The moment China White left the room, her agents began to close in. 13 could see them sidling across the dance floor, eager to get to him. China must have given them some sort of sign.

Coolly, Agent 13 walked slowly and with nonchalant grace from the dance floor. He wasn't concerned because, in effect, the cavalry was riding to his rescue. On second thought, you might say it was the French Foreign Legion. Sure enough, here came Officer Renard and the purser. He had noticed them, waiting like jackals for China White to leave. It would never do to make a scene before her. But now she was gone, and they were swooping in for the kill.

"Excuse me, monsieur," Renard said arrogantly, putting his hand on 13's lapel.

"Yes, what is it?" the Agent said brusquely, brushing the officer's hand away.

"Purser Damour would like a word with you," Renard said.

A uniformed purser stepped forward and held out his open hand. "I would like to see your cabin key, monsieur."

"Is there a problem?" 13 glowered.

"We sincerely hope not, monsieur." The purser's tone insisted that there most certainly was.

13 glanced around nervously, fingering his tie like a petty crook caught in a scam. What he was really looking for were China's agents. They had stopped in their tracks, glaring at Renard and the purser, waiting for them to leave.

13 searched his pockets and patted his jacket once, then shrugged.

"I guess I must have left it back in my room. Damn! Now I'm locked out! Can one of you let me in with a passkey?"

"Which is your cabin, monsieur?" The purser sneered. He had heard this one before.

"Twenty-eight D"

"Twenty-eight D?" Snorting. "I'm afraid there is no such cabin."

"Well, it's been a long night, hasn't it, Officer, uh—?" 13 strained to read his name tag.

"Renard, Officer Renard."

"And I don't believe we caught your name," the purser said.

"Fredericks, J.C. Fredericks." The purser promptly pulled out a passenger list and gave it the once-over.

"You are not listed as a passenger, Monsieur Fredericks."

"What do you mean—'not listed'?"

"It means that unless you have forgotten your name as well as your key, monsieur, you are a stowaway."

"How dare you!" 13 snarled, outraged. Several people turned to gaze at him with interest.

Renard grabbed him firmly by the arm. "I suggest that we take a walk down to Security, Monsieur Fredericks."

"I didn't pay good money to be treated like this!" 13 yelled. Now everyone in the immediate vicinity could see and hear him, which was precisely what he wanted. The more attention he attracted, the greater the risk China's agents Would take in trying to get to him.

"This won't take long," the purser said.

"I'll sue! You'll be hearing from my lawyer!" 13 shouted as they hustled him out of the hall.

13 smiled grimly, catching a glimpse of the disconcerted faces of China's agents as the purser dragged him—still protesting—past them. They glowered at him, powerless.

Once in the safety of the foyer, Renard gave 13 a quick frisk. He halted at 13's inner coat pocket. Reaching in, he pulled out a deck of cards.

"A card man, eh?"

"Are they marked?" asked the purser.

"Probably."

"Those are your own cards from the Smoking Room! I'll have your jobs for this!" 13 snarled. "I demand to see the captain!"

"He will undoubtedly be delighted to see you, too, I am certain." Ignoring his threats, the purser turned to Renard. "Can you handle him, or do you need help?"

"No one's going to handle anybody," 13 muttered.

Renard looked at the card sharp in disgust and said something in French. The purser smiled.

"Let me know what you find out. He may be working with friends."

Renard tugged on 13's arm. "Let's go."

13 allowed Renard to pull him down the corridor. Glancing back, he saw two of China's agents in the doorway.

Lifting his hand, 13 made a quick sign to them—as though warning them away. Renard took note immediately.

"Ah, ha!" he said triumphantly, whirling to look at the agents. "So, you are working with someone. Purser—"

But the purser was already in hot pursuit. China's agents, looking extremely startled, were trying to melt back into the crowd.

Grinning to himself, 13 allowed Renard to drag him off.

FISH IN THE NET

The more Maggie was around Dr. Fischer, the more pity she felt for the nerve-shattered man. He was obviously caught up in a maelstrom of events he didn't understand.

"I've made a horrible mistake," Fischer blubbered. "I need to get to the authorities—"

A waiter with slicked-back hair suddenly appeared at their table. "Would you care for another cognac?"

"Yes, and one for the lady as well," Fischer mumbled without looking up. The waiter wrote down the order and left.

"Is he one of the men who's been following you?" whispered Maggie.

Fischer looked up blankly. "I don't know."

"The hem on his pants is an inch too short and his shoes weren't regulation. He left your empty glass on the table. He wrote down an order any waiter worth his salt could remember. Plus he smelled like gasoline and his hands were heavily calloused and smudged with grease. I don't know who he is, but he sure isn't a waiter."

Suddenly she heard the click of a pistol's hammer behind her.

"If it ain't Sherlock Holmes," a voice hissed.

Dr. Fischer's mouth sagged open. Maggie whirled. A man was standing behind them. His bald head resembled a cue ball, and he wore a tuxedo that looked two sizes too large. Walking around the table, he jabbed a heavy pistol into the professor's spine.

"By God," Fischer moaned, "I'll report—"

"You won't do no reportin' to nobody, pal. You're comin' with us." Cue Ball nodded to the "waiter," who went to check on the exit door.

Leaning down to speak into Maggie's ear, Cue Ball mouthed, "Just keep nice and quiet, Duchess. I got others around. Yah start squawkin' and they'll drill yah."

"Don't hurt me, please!" Maggie whimpered, cringing, even as her hand went to her purse.

Cue Ball turned back to Fischer, who seemed drained of life. "Now get up, doc. We're gonna walk outta here nice an' slow."

"Iron Lung" Nat and his friend, so interested in Fischer before, now seemed completely engrossed in their game. The music being generated by the Harvard boys was loud enough to drown out anything, except maybe a gunshot.

The fake waiter, standing at the door, motioned that the coast was clear. Cue Ball gripped Fischer's coat, pulling him to his feet. "Move it."

Fischer rose like a zombie and staggered out of the room. Cue Ball looked as if he were just helping a man who had had too much to drink.

Maggie took another quick look around. Cue Ball had said there were others, but it could be a bluff. At any rate, Maggie didn't have much choice. Fischer was obviously incapable of doing anything to help himself. Making up her mind, Maggie's hand dove into her purse.

"Look out! She's gotta gun!"

Maggie fired.

The screaming slug slammed into Cue Ball's shoulder with a sickening thud. The impact spun him around. Rage contorted his face. Glaring at her, he raised his pistol.

Maggie fired again. This time the spinning lead found its mark, tearing through his throat and out the portside window.

Suddenly, it seemed, gunfire came from everywhere. Using Fischer as a shield, the "waiter" was backing out the door. Maggie hesitated. 13 had told her to kill Fischer. But how could she shoot that poor man whose only sin was being a genius ahead of his time?

As another bullet tore an arm off a Winged Victory statue behind her, Maggie hit the floor shoulder-first and rolled. That bullet had come from a different direction! Crawling to the cover of a large marble planter, she turned to see Nat's aide with a shrieking gat in his hand. And, behind him, she saw the iron lung fly open. The fake Nat crawled out, a machine gun in his hand!

Maggie risked a quick glimpse at Fischer. The waiter was dragging him out the door. But Maggie had other, more pressing problems. Nat swung the chattering automatic around. Keeping her head low, Maggie raised her pistol and fired. The bullet sent him spinning back into his iron coffin—forever. His finger tightened in death around the trigger. The machine gun's wild staccato riddled the ceiling like swiss cheese and sent the gangly aide diving for safety.

Two more shots came at Maggie from yet another direction—the bartender!

The flowers above her shredded like confetti. Maggie's pistol barked, striking the mirror behind him and blowing an etched Phoenix to smithereens, but not harming the bartender. Nat's aide had regained his feet and was shooting with renewed coolness.

Maggie was trapped, caught in a crossfire of deadly lead. Chipping sounds told her the planter she was using as cover was slowly disappearing.

Hearing a yelp of terror, Maggie spun and fired. Her bullet thwacked into the splintered door frame. But it was too late. The waiter and Fischer had disappeared.

Maggie tried to get up to follow, but another bullet went zinging past her ear. She was helpless. Cursing herself for letting Fischer get away, she peered up over the planter, firing blindly at her attackers. But then her gun clicked empty.

Spitting a clip out of her gun and jamming a new one in, Maggie noticed that, suddenly, everything was quiet. She risked raising her head just in time to see the bartender scuttle out a service door. Her glance went to the iron lung. A plump arm dangled over the side, dripping blood into a crimson puddle. The aide and the other backgammon player were gone. Stunned, her ears ringing, Maggie sat back, dazed but in one piece.

Someone shouted. Then there was the clamoring of the Harvard boys pulling themselves out from behind the piano where they'd taken refuge. One of them grabbed a ship phone.

"Get me Security! There's been a shooting!" he said in a shaking voice. People jammed in the doorway, pointing and yelling. The Harvard boys came running over to Maggie. Hurriedly stashing her gun in her purse, hoping they hadn't seen it, Maggie sank back into the corner, sobbing and wailing.

"You all right?" asked one of the Harvard men, dropping down beside her.

"It was terrible," Maggie moaned. "They just came from nowhere! They almost sh-sh-shot me."

"Who?" demanded a man in the uniform of an Army colonel, dropping to her other side.

"Gangsters! And they took my David...." She wept bitterly.

"Which way'd they go, ma'am?" asked a burly Texan.

Maggie pointed weakly to the service door behind the bar.

What followed amazed even Maggie Darr. It seemed as if every man in the room pulled a pistol, ready for pursuit. This wasn't at all what she had expected. She had to go after the kidnappers and either kill Fischer or rescue him. But when she tried to get up, one of the Harvard boys held

The Texan, checking the chamber on his pearl-handled Colt .45, was already bounding out the service door, followed by the Army colonel and several Harvard boys. More people were beginning to crowd in the door-way. Maggie had to get out of here!

Slumping back, she let her eyes roll in her head. "Water!" she murmured.

"Water! She's going to faint!" cried the Harvard boy at her feet. Leaping up in a panic, he ran for the bar. That was Maggie's chance. Scrambling to her feet, she drew her gun. "Get out of my way," she said coldly, glaring at the shocked people in the doorway. "They've got my David, and I'm go-ing after them!"

"She's gone mad!" wailed a fat woman in the doorway.

"That's right, sister," Maggie said grimly, walking forward. "Now I'm going to tell you once more...."

People melted from the doorway. Maggie darted through, catching a glimpse from the corner of her eye of the ship's security officers dashing down the corridor.

Pressed up against the side of a bulkhead, Maggie watched as the se-curity officers dashed inside the Win-ter Garden Room. Good. They'd be kept busy in there for a while, sorting out all the stories. What with the cow-boy and the soldier wandering around with guns, they probably wouldn't come after Maggie just yet.

Satisfied, she hurried down the cor-ridor.

Outside the immediate area sur-rounding the Winter Garden Room, the rest of the ship was quiet. Most people were either dancing, drinking, or sleeping off the effects of one or the other. The corridors were empty. The few people Maggie passed ap-peared totally unaware that a blazing gun battle had just been waged a few hundred feet away. It wasn't surpris-ing when one considered the sheer size of the ship with its fourteen dif-ferent decks and sophisticated sound-proofing.

Maggie longed to find 13, but there wasn't time, even if she had known what his present disguise looked like. Fischer was her responsibility, any-way, and she'd failed. Running down the corridors, glancing into open doorways, Maggie thought of report-ing to 13 that she'd failed. Her face flushed.

She had to find Fischer! But how? Her muscles aching, her lungs burn-ing, Maggie stopped to rest and make herself think calmly. She couldn't waste time dashing around the ship aimlessly. It could take weeks to search every room. He could be any-where. Then—

Gasoline! She suddenly remem-bered. The waiter who had escaped with Fischer had grease-smudged hands and smelled like gasoline!

"The garage!" she said to herself. Checking the clip on her pistol, she headed for an elevator.

LIGHTS OUT FOR THE LADY'S MAN

Watch Officer Renard dragged "Mr. Fredericks" through the corridor.

"This isn't the way to the bridge," the Agent mumbled.

"No," said Renard coldly. "The captain is a most busy man. We will see him later. First, you and I have a score to settle."

Renard hauled 13 through a bulk-head door to the Promenade Deck, now deserted at night. "Your dancing days are over, my friend." Flinging the Agent up against the railing, Renard took a swing—and connected with nothing but air.

"*Mon Dieu!* What the—" He gasped.

Renard never knew what hit him. Suddenly, he was flying through the air. The cold iron of a beam sent him dribbling to the deck as his world whited out.

Agent 13 looked at his watch— the time was 11:45. China's concert would end at midnight. Even if she had been informed that 13 had escaped her agents, she would be able to do nothing until she had finished her concert. That left 13 precious time.

An elderly couple strolled by, arm in arm in the moonlight. They looked at the crumpled officer and the Agent.

"Food poisioning," the Agent said in a worried tone.

The couple shook their heads in sympathy but moved on quickly, not wanting to get involved.

13 quickly heaved the unconscious Renard into one of the lifeboats. A moment later, he re-emerged, dressed in Renard's slightly rumpled uniform. By stuffing several small pieces of cotton in his upper and lower gums and slicking back his hair, 13 managed to transform himself into a passable member of the French crew. With a crew of over thirteen hundred, 13 felt little fear in being unveiled as an

imposter.

Hurrying along the deck until he reached the Terrace Deck cabins, he peered through the curtained windows of the Rouen Suite. The rooms were lavishly decorated with black lacquered furniture and freshly cut lilies in crystal vases. A baby grand stood in the center of a living room.

But there was no movement.

13 pressed his ear against the chilled, smooth pane of glass. There was silence. Satisfied that the suite was empty, he entered the corridor and approached the door. He listened again... still no sounds. Easily picking the lock, he entered.

Normally reserved for Marlene Dietrich, the Rouen Suite had been given over to another star of equal brightness—China White.

13 padded softly through the empty rooms, searching for a clue that might reveal China's plans. Opening her closet, he quickly went through her designer gowns. Her fragrance lingered on the fragile silks, making him remember. ... Angrily, he shook his head. There was no time for that now!

Frustrated, 13 shut the door. To all appearances, China was just what she claimed to be—an international operatic star on her way to a series of European engagements.

13 turned his attention to a black lacquered deskin her bedroom. In a drawer, he found a leather portfolio containing booking dates around the Continent. Paris, London, Rome, Milan, Berlin-all the capitals in Europe would have the opportunity of paying China White homage. Her booking agent had booked her in the finest hotels the cities could offer, and her date book showed a full schedule of dinner engagements.

Maybe I'm wrong, 13 thought. Maybe the Brotherhood has no intention of destroying the Normandie. Maybe they just want Fischer.

No! 13 clenched his fist. Every fiber of his being told him he was on the right track.

He could see the Masque's plans as clearly as if he had drawn them up himself. Destroy the *Normandie*, destroy the most beautiful ship afloat, kill thousands, including some of the world's most popular, beloved celebrities—and it would create a world-wide incident. Pressure would be brought to bear on America from every corner of the globe. She would be forced to give in to the Masque's demands....

Suddenly, something caught 13's attention.

Scrawled at the bottom of a page, as though China had dashed it off on the first thing at hand, was a notation, 46° 14' N x 59° 22' W.

To the untrained observer, it was a meaningless mathematical jumble. But to a sailor, it indicated in degrees and minutes of latitude and longitude an exact position in the sea.

13 went cold. The area pinpointed by the coordinates was in the North

Atlantic Drift, a point in the currents which—if he calculated correctly—the Normandie, with her steaming speed of 30.2 knots, would be passing in less then fifteen minutes! Was it a point of meeting—or a tomb?

13 had to act immediately. The sleeping ship had to be roused.

Spying a new electric fire alarm on the wall, 13 pulled it.

Nothing happened!

He grabbed the ship phone. The line was dead!

"Sabotage!" he muttered.

"Well, well, well. Miss White sure had you figured right, buddy."

Throaty laughter suddenly filled the cabin. 13 spun around to see two thugs from the Grand Lounge standing in the open doorway—the cold blue steel of their pistols zeroed in on his heart.

"Looks like we caught ourselves a fish," said a short, skinny thug with a misshapen nose.

"Lookin' for somethin', officer?" His friend, who looked like a prize fighter, laughed. He had a massive lower jaw and a spudlike growth on his balding head.

"Somethin' to write your will with maybe?" commented the skinny one.

13 gave them an indignant glance. "I was delivering flowers to Miss White—"

"Stash it," said Spud, cocking his handgun.

"We search him now or when he's dead?" The skinny one grinned.

"Dead."

"Bon Voyage, skipper." They raised their pistols. Suddenly, the room exploded with thundering crackles and flying particles.

It was as if twenty guns had opened up at once. Glowing fragments whizzed and ricocheted through the room as 13 activated the special fireworks cufflink Ray Furnow had designed for him.

"We're surrounded!" yelled Spud, diving beneath the couch for cover, while the skinny guy turned, trying to avoid the fire.

The Agent sprang at the skinny one like a leopard, hitting him on the bridge of his nose. Bone and cartilage gave way as he gave a throaty, inarticulate cry and collapsed.

13 grabbed the pistol and spun around. He wanted the other one alive. Searching the smoke-filled room, he saw a glimmer of iron—the barrel of a gun sticking out from behind a nearby couch. He kicked. A fat hand turned to jelly from the bone-crushing impact. The gun flew across the carpet.

"I want answers!" 13 demanded, pulling the thug out in the open and shoving the barrel of the .38 into his nose.

"Go take a—"

13 gripped Spud's smashed hand. Sometimes, the threat of a bullet wasn't enough.

Schooled by the Brotherhood in the months before he got away, 13 knew the various pressure points on the body and he knew just how to put them to the most effective use. ...

With just a flick of his wrist, the Agent sent overwhelming waves of anguish through Spud's central nervous system. 13 knew from grim experience what the hood was feeling—everything in his body would suddenly turn to white-hot searing pain. Even the roots of his own hair would feel like crimson nails being driven through his scalp.

"What's going to happen?"

"This—this tub's going down," Spud moaned.

"How?" demanded the Agent.

Suddenly, a shot cracked through the room. The bullet thudded into the skull of the thug, spraying 13 with blood and brains. Flinging the body to the floor, the Agent whirled around in time to see a fleeting shadow pass the window.

He looked at his watch. The minutes were ticking by. "This tub's going down..."

Agent 13 hurried down the outer Promenade Deck to the central telegraph office. He jerked open the door, and his nostrils were stung by the stench of burning rubber and smoldering death.

The radio operator, a fresh bullet wound in his temple, was slumped over a blood-splattered radio table, his finger still frozen on the touch pad. Two other officers, in red-speckled whites, lay motionless behind a smashed transformer. 13 ran back out the door.

There would be no S O S from the *Normandie*.

13 dashed up a staircase leading to the Sun-deck. Leaping the stairs in fours, he passed an elderly couple he vaguely remembered seeing on the dance floor.

Making a grab at the white-uniformed 13, the man mumbled, "Pardon me, Mon' Capitan, but our phones don't—" 13 was gone before he could finish, hearing the man mutter, "Typical French," as he ran past.

13 sprinted along the upper deck, the cold sea air whipping at him. Passing the smoke stack, he hurried to the stairwell, was down in two leaps, and jerked open the door to the bridge telegraph room. It was the same scene repeated. Five men dead, all the equipment destroyed.

Adrenaline pulsed through his system as he hurried past the carnage to the bridge. It was empty, cold, and deserted. The sea winds howled freely through the broken windows that had been raked and shattered with machine-gun fire.

Three officers lay dead across the white, grilled metal of the steering platform. An acidic yellow smoke drifted slowly from the shattered equipment like a spectral reaper coming to lay claim to the deceased.

The only hint of life came from the frantic voice of the engineer. Down below in the engine rooms, he was shouting into the tube, demanding confirmation of the strange orders he had received to stop the engines.

"Disregard the command!" 13 shouted. "And get someone up here to steer this thing!"

"What? Who is this?" the voice from below yelled.

"Everyone here has been killed! The ship is in danger! Send an S O S, if you can."

"Who is this?"

"A friend." 13 replaced the tube. Pilotless, the *Normandie* steamed on into the misty night. 13 hurried out to the deck. The sounds of music and laughter echoed from a distant deck, while the silhouettes of embracing lovers could been seen near the bow. Even the waters and gusting winds had calmed, as if granting the doomed ship a moment of respectful silence.

It was ironic. Before him, he could see passengers and crew, drinking and partying the night away. Behind him lay the bullet-riddled corpses of the people responsible for their safety.

Suddenly, the night air carried the faint, incessant drone of an aircraft engine! 13's heart leaped.

He scanned the moonlit skies, searching for the source. Nothing. Yet the droning grew louder.

Then he saw it—not in the skies, but in the frigid, calm waters—a sleek, black shape skimming rapidly over the water's surface on pontoons, approaching at a speed of over one hundred miles an hour!

"A Flying Mosquito Boat!" 13 mut-

tered grimly. He could see the torpedoes resting beneath the fuselage of the sleek prototype airboat.

The Masque's plot was now all too clear.

WHEELS OF FURY

A suave officer was more than happy to give the vibrant strawberry blonde directions to the garage. As the elevator she was riding stopped at C-Deck, Maggie left it cautiously, not knowing what to expect. The gun was back in her purse, but she had the latch open. All she saw was the closed post office and a photo studio.

Continuing past, Maggie came to an iron stairwell that led to the other five decks below.

Her high heels softly clanged on the black metal steps as she descended into the garage on the D-Deck. The gleam of night security lights shone on the highly polished hoods of expensive limos and sports roadsters.

A sudden chill wind whipped through her shimmering gown. Maggie smelled sea water.

Strange, she thought, picturing what she could remember of Agent 13's plans for the ship. There was no access to the open deck this far below the main decks! Walking around a support wall, Maggie came to another staircase. The sea wind blew much stronger here. Maggie drew her pistol and descended silently.

Reaching the greasy deck, she stumbled over a body—a mechanic, dead. Then, suddenly, she heard the hum of a freight elevator and, above that, the din of an aircraft engine.

Retreating into the shadow of a '36 Rolls, Maggie watched as a freight elevator brought a large crate up from below. Several men in cheap, well-worn suits maneuvered the crate off the elevator loaded it onto a dolly, and then rolled it along the center aisle to the chamber beyond.

They wheeled the crate right past her hiding place. Maggie stared at the crate intently as it went by. A label, plastered to the side, was clearly visible—"Dr. David Fischer." The Lightning Gun!

Where was 13? Maggie wondered as she followed the sinister figures through the growing pall of darkness. She didn't have to worry about making noise. The heavy crate rumbled over the concrete and metal floor as they shoved it hurriedly along. The wind grew stronger. Sneaking around a bulkhead, Maggie finally saw its source. The auto embarkation doors were open! Ducking behind a Cadillac, she studied the scene. Moored in the waters beside the liner was the strangest-looking airplane Maggie had ever seen. The teardrop-shaped fuselage of the sleek black craft was well above the water, supported by two pontoons affixed to struts on the craft's underbelly. It had no wings, yet it was moving at an incredibly fast speed.

The forward section of the fuselage—the pilot's compartment—was a clear Plexiglas dome. A 35-millimeter cannon protruded from its nose. A large pusher propeller provided the craft with the propulsion needed to keep up with the Norman-die's 30-knot speed.

An airboat, a seaplane? What was this thing? Maggie couldn't tell, and she didn't really care. Only one thing was clear—its purpose.

She watched as the figures transferred a large, ruglike bundle along pulley lines they had rigged up to an open cargo door in the craft. They were having a difficult time due to the choppiness of the seas.

A figure stepped into the light, issuing orders, and the bundle finally reached the plane safely. Dressed in a black leather flight suit, the figure turned and gave orders to prepare the crate for transfer. Her face came into the light. China White! Maggie fought back the urge to unload a full clip of lead.

Then Maggie's gaze saw something move behind the beautiful woman. There, bathed in the harsh glare of a bare light bulb, stood Dr. Fischer.

Clearly a broken man, he huddled in a corner. No one paid the least bit of attention to him. If he had any guts, Maggie thought angrily, he could escape. But he just stood there, a dull, vacant look in his eyes. Her hand tightened around the grip of her gun. He'd just signed his own death warrant.

Maggie continued to scan the scene anxiously. China White was here. Surely 13 must then be here, too. But if so, where? He could be one of the men loading the crate into the plane. He could be one of those thugs standing next to China White. Or, he might be dead....

Maggie didn't know, and she couldn't count on finding him. She had her mission. But there were seven of them, she saw, counting hurriedly, and only one of her. What could she do?

Peering at the thugs and China through the window of the Cadillac that she was using as cover, Maggie suddenly had her answer—the keys of the Caddy were in the ignition!

She mentally put her "targets" into priorities. Fischer and his Lightning Gun came out on top.

Quietly, she opened the car door. The handle made a loud click, but she doubted if anyone could hear it, not over the sounds of the surf and the whirring propeller.

Sliding into the seat, Maggie started the quiet engine. No one noticed the small plume of exhaust that rose from the tailpipe. Backing the car out of the stall, she braked and brought it around. The crate with the Lightning Gun lined up nicely with the Caddy's hood ornament, she thought as she slammed the pedal to the floor.

By the time the thugs saw the Cadillac, Maggie had its speed up to over thirty miles per hour. Shouts and curses rippled through their ranks as one of them—the waiter from the bar—whirled around with a Thompson, pointing it at the vehicle hurtling toward them. The staccato of his kicking barrel lit the garage in a flash of flame.

Maggie gripped the wheel tightly, not letting up as hot blasts of lead tore the Cadillac's body to shreds. The needle on the speedometer showed forty, forty-five, then fifty miles an hour!

More pistols were drawn and shots fired. The windshield splintered into a thousand fragments. But Maggie, ducking down behind the wheel, drove on, ignoring the hundreds of pinpoint wounds. Her eyes burned like coals in the darkness as bullets slapped through the leather seat around her.

Faster and faster she drove, her foot frozen on the pedal. Her mind flashed to other places, other events. Time took on a quality of slow motion as images of people she had once known flashed before her.

She saw Jimmy, the man she had once loved, who died at the hands of Lucky's gang, then 13, a man of mystery, who had rekindled the flame of passion she believed extinguished forever. Was this death, she wondered, speeding closer and closer... ?

Splintering wood and snapping shards of metal and glass showered down upon her like rain. The Cadillac bounced and lifted into the air as it thundered into the crate containing Dr. Fischer's Lightning Gun.

Sparks and smoke trailed from the undercarriage as the Cadillac plowed through the remains of the death device, plus two thugs who had failed to leap out of the way at the last minute.

A moment later, Maggie opened her eyes. She was alive. Then the fumes of spilling gas tickled her nostrils. Grabbing her pistol, she kicked open the battered door and rolled to the ground, preferring to meet the thugs' curtain of lead than to roast alive in a '37 Caddy.

Battered and bruised, Maggie

dragged herself through the oil and grime of the garage floor as a series of jarring explosions buckled the steel deck. A wave of heat and concussion blasted her. Shielding herself from the blazing inferno, Maggie looked back. She could just barely make out the ruins of the Lightning Gun and the Caddy amidst the flame and smoke.

Beside her, she heard a low moan. Turning to look, she saw Fischer, huddled motionless several paces away, staring at his flaming gun in horror. Staggering to her feet, Maggie saw China's men scrambling around the burning gun—trying to save it from the all-consuming flames.

Seeing them occupied—at least for the moment—Maggie lurched over to the professor. A glazed look filled Fischer's eyes. She shook him, but there was no response beyond that moaning sound. Drugged! she thought. Raising her gun, she aimed it at him. Then shook her head. No, she couldn't kill him. Not yet. Not as long as they had a chance.

Grabbing Fischer by the coat collar, Maggie dragged him to an alcove. Suddenly, the gunmen saw them. Bullets ratatated off the steel walls like rain dancing on a tin roof. Maggie crouched low and fired twice in rapid succession. One of her bullets bit into the arm of an advancing thug, as two others returned her fire.

The hot blasts of their lead kissed her hair as she fired twice more and missed. Only two shots left. She was trapped.

The three uninjured henchmen must have had the same thought. They now advanced with reckless abandon, the blackened muzzles of their tommy guns glistening by the light of the still-blazing Caddy.

Maggie looked down at the catatonic Dr. Fischer beside her. She had no choice. At least, she knew he wouldn't suffer. Drugged as he was, he'd never know what hit him. Aiming, she gritted her teeth and prepared to carry out her assignment.

IRON FIST OF DEATH

Agent 13 clutched the lifeboat's railing with one hand. In the other, he held the pearl handle of a Colt .45. Assisting him from above, operating the winch to lower the lifeboat, stood the burly Texan, the Army colonel, and several cheering Harvard boys.

Directly below him, he could see the startled face of the Mosquito's pilot staring up at him, cursing. 13 fired into the craft. The window was bullet-proof, but not the alloy skin of the craft. Other bullets hailed down on it as the Army colonel opened up.

13 could see the embarkation door on the Normandie now. There was a blazing fire there, along with the blackened skeletons of a car and what looked like Fischer's Lightning Gun. Good, 13 smiled grimly. Maggie had done her job well.

But he couldn't take time to wonder how or where Maggie was. He could see the pilot yelling at someone on board the *Normandie*. Reading his lips, 13 knew the pilot was shouting that he would have to get out of there or risk being blown out of the water.

Several thugs appeared at the embarkation door, tommy guns trained on 13. The Agent aimed the .45 carefully and fired. A thug slumped forward and fell into the water.

The pilot throttled up and motioned to someone on board as his men prepared to cut away from the pulley lines holding them to the *Normandie*. A figure clad in black leather grabbed hold of a wheeled device and slid across the pulley lines from the Normandie to the Mosquito with the grace and daring of a circus performer. Bullets from above pinged the waters around the fast-moving shape.

But it was 13's shot, and he knew it. He took a cold, deadly bead on the target, applying slow pressure to the trigger. Suddenly he saw a flash of raven black hair. China White! Something screamed from deep inside him, but the impulse commanding his finger to fire had already been sent from his brain.

13 twitched his shoulder. It was all he had time for, but it pulled back his shot. His bullet missed her by inches.

China looked back at him briefly, her eyes cool, her face beautiful. She smiled.

With a strange kind of fascination, 13 watched as she slid through the cargo door in the craft.

Shaking his head, as though to break a spell, 13 turned his attention back to the *Normandie*. One of the thugs was attempting to grab hold of the line while the other two were struggling with each other behind.

13 was taking aim when suddenly the line fell away from the airboat. Staring in horror, the thugs realized that they were being left behind. Their hoarse protests were answered by the Mosquito's barking machine guns. China had no intentions of leaving her men behind ... alive.

The Mosquito turned, heading out to sea. Beneath its belly hung the torpedoes.

The Agent counted the seconds left before his motorized lifeboat could reach the waves, before he could set off in pursuit of the airboat.

Suddenly, 13 became aware of two other figures standing in the *Normandie's* open embarkation door. One was Dr. Fischer—he saw the man

shake his head groggily. The other figure was Maggie Darr. The Agent watched as Maggie raised her gun. He looked to see her target—China White.

Standing in the open cargo hatch of the airboat, China White looked up at Maggie. The blonde eyed the sultry, raven-haired adversary and coolly aimed her weapon.

"Don't shoot!" shouted Agent 13.

Did Maggie hear him and ignore him? Or was she unable to hear his voice over the roar of the aircraft engines? 13 never knew. Maggie fired her last two shots at China White.

The first shot missed, but the second found its mark. China's body jerked back hard, sliding back into the blackness of the craft's interior.

13 shrieked out something incoherent. Maggie, dropping the spent pistol to the debris-covered deck, stared up at 13 in shock, her strawberry blonde hair whipping around her face in the wind.

But then 13 felt the splash of water beneath the hull of his frail craft. He had no more time to waste. Signaling to the men up top to release him, he started the motor.

13 knew the lifeboat's speed was no match for the Mosquito's. But he'd been fighting the odds all along.

13 was familiar with the prototype airboat. He knew that the Mosquito would never be able to take off from the surface of the water until after it had discharged its two 1,200-pound

torpedoes. It would need a long approach toward the Norman-die in order to assure itself of enough airspeed for lift.

13 watched and listened as the swift craft skimmed along the surface and disappeared toward the shimmering, moonlit horizon.

He silenced his motor and stared at the black waters, listening for the prop sounds—the noises that would tell him the trajectory of the craft and, ultimately, of the torpedoes' approach.

It was a strange silence. Only the lapping of the chilling waters could be heard beneath his hull. 13 and this frail lifeboat were all that stood between the torpedoes' explosive warheads and the Normandie, a quarter of a mile away.

He glanced back at the great ship. Her lights shimmered peacefully off the waters in painted streaks. The only clue to the tragedies that had struck this night was a small fire seen through the still-open embarkation door.

Agent 13 looked at the sky. The night was clear. The Milky Way, with its millions of stars, streaked across the chilled night's air like the stroke of a paint brush wielded by the hand of God.

Then 13 heard it. It made a buzzing sound at first, like the insect it was named for, but that quickly grew louder. 13's trained eyes spotted the diminutive shape coming out of the north. Firing up the lifeboat's motor

again, he set his course, a bearing that would deliberately take him on a collision course with the Mosquito!

It was his only chance—to slam into the craft before its torpedoes could hit the water.

13 throttled the engine as hard as he could, hoping that by the time the pilot saw the low profile of his craft it would be too late.

The deadly Mosquito approached, its propeller giving a screaming whine of death. Closer and closer it came . . . 2000 yards . . . 1500 yards . . . 1000 yards. It kept coming, straight ahead. They hadn't seen him yet. Then he saw a flash of flame from its nose, and, a quarter of a second later, he heard the explosion. The 37-millimeter nose cannon.

No sooner did the thought register, than the bow of his launch exploded in a splintering ruin. A direct hit.

But it was too late for the Mosquito! It had built up so much speed that it couldn't avoid the sinking lifeboat, not without doing a nose dive into the sea! Quickly, the pilot launched the torpedoes, then, relieved of their weight, pulled the plane up in a climbing turn.

The plane nosed up toward the moon. 13 spared no time looking at it as it roared by, almost knocking him overboard, as he stared into the sea, into death, watching the bubbling wakes of the torpedoes close in on his craft.

DEAD IN THE WATER

A large crowd of pensive crew and passengers stood on the Main Deck, their eyes trained on the iky blackness to the north. Maggie, still standing near the open embarkation door, couldn't see them. Behind her, various medical personnel and assistants were trying to save some of the wounded. She was dimly aware of someone leading Dr. Fischer away.

The night suddenly turned into a horrifying day as two bright orange bursts of light flared from the ocean.

BLAA-BLAAAAM!

The concussions of the two simultaneous explosions hit Maggie an almost physical blow. Above her, she could hear the sounds of cheering.

"He did it!" whooped a voice with a Texas accent.

The Mosquito roared out of the blackness, thundering up over the stacks of the Normandie. Maggie heard gunfire—apparently the Army colonel was shooting at the plane. But he must have missed—Maggie could hear the engine of the plane drone on.

"Nazis!" shouted a voice.

A solicitous officer appeared beside her. "Please, my dear, allow me to assist you—"

Glancing at him, Maggie's eyes focused on one thing—his binoculars. Reaching out, she grabbed hold of them and jerked them away with a force that nearly strangled the man. Ignoring his cry of protest, Maggie lifted the powerful binoculars to her eyes.

Her hands shaking so that she could barely focus, Maggie scanned the waters where the torpedoes had exploded. She could see clearly the oil and the burning wreckage of the lifeboat.

Then, slowly, as she still stood there, the fire died. Darkness fell.

Maggie Darr stared out to sea, tears running unheeded down her face.

There was no trace of Agent 13.

A kindly hand patted her shoulder. "I'm afraid no one could have survived that explosion, my dear," said the officer gently.

Maggie was overwhelmed at that moment by how much she loved the man who had sacrificed himself to save the thousands aboard the *Normandie*.

She had saved Dr. Fischer, and 13 had thwarted the Brotherhood's plan to perpetrate another disaster. But, oh the cost had been dear!

Then Maggie heard screams from the deck above.

"U-boats!" cried someone. "The Nazis are everywhere! Head for the lifeboats."

"*Sacre Bleu!* What imaginings!" swore the officer. Leaving Maggie, he headed for the Main Deck. But panic soon seized the ship. People were sighting submarines, destroyers, even icebergs. But Maggie knew the danger was over.

Later, there would be an investigation. It would produce no solid answers. All that was known was that many had died and two passengers had strangely disappeared—China White, for whom the world mourned, and a meek, mousy little man named Hiram Plotkin.

Maggie stood on the windswept deck, her hands gripping the railing as she stared at the now-silent, cold, black sea. Tears welled in her eyes, as the sea winds reddened her cheeks and blew back her hair.

After a moment of silence, she whispered, "Good-bye."

The world fell out of focus.

She dried her eyes.

Then, placing her handkerchief in her purse, she caressed the cold metal of her gun.

She would carry on, somehow trying to ease her grief with vengeance.

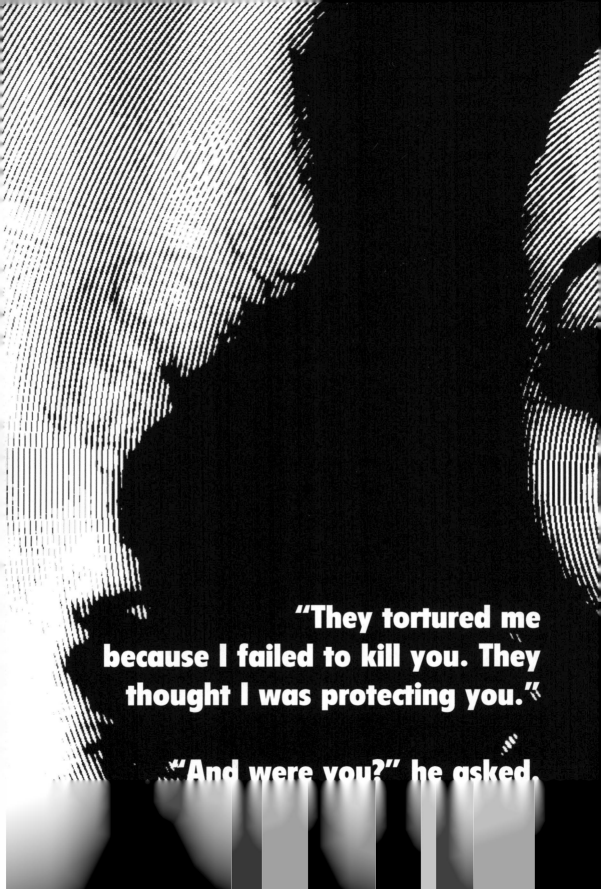

"They tortured me because I failed to kill you. They thought I was protecting you."

"And were you?" he asked.

WHO IS AGENT 13?

In 1907, a gifted child was kidnapped and taken to a place known as "the Shrine," the ultra-secret headquarters of the sinister "Brotherhood." The child's real name was erased, and he was given the number 13. As memories of his parents faded, he was trained in the arts of power. An exemplary student, he seemed destined to become a great agent of the Brotherhood. Instead, 13 learned the true nature of the Brotherhood, and fled.

Thus began a deadly cat-and-mouse game between Agent 13 and the Brotherhood.

The Brotherhood has existed since the dawn of civilization. For millennia, it guided mankind down "the bright path." But then Itsu, the Hand Sinister, seized power and converted light to darkness. Now, in the 1930s, the Brotherhood lusts for global dominance and intends to throw the world into a debilitating war to gain it.
Only Agent 13 stands in their way.

A midnight avenger, Agent 13 is a master of disguise, an invisible operator, and a ruthless destroyer of evil-committed to toppling the Brotherhood through any means. And the Brotherhood fears him, for many of the members have been discovered dead, with the number 13 branded into their foreheads.

Essentially a loner working through a network of informants, Agent 13 has come to trust Maggie Darr, the only person who has seen his real face. Daring and beautiful, Maggie looks as good with a Thompson submachine gun as with a smile. She and 13 are allies, not lovers, but were Agent 13's lifelong mission any less compelling, things might be different....

PREVIOUSLY

In 1937, a sinister hooded figure, known only as the Masque, sends the President of the United States film clips of three disasters—the destruction of a train carrying carloads of helium, an explosion and fire at the Westron aircraft factory, and the destruction of the German airship, the *Hindenburg*.

Unless the United States is prepared to meet his demands to begin military disarmament, the Masque threatens even more terrorist attacks. The President, of course, refuses to allow America to be blackmailed. In retaliation, the Masque sends a band of Serpentine Assassins to slaughter everyone present at a meeting of the National Security Council. There are only two survivors-Kent Walters, National Security Advisor, and Agent 13.

Agent 13 sees a terrible pattern in these disasters. The Masque, he believes, is a member of the secret, powerful organization known as the Brotherhood. And, if that is true, then these disasters and the Masque's demands are all part of a much larger scheme for total world domination!

Aware that another disaster of major proportion is imminent, 13 and his beautiful associate, Maggie Darr, work to thwart the Masque's plans. The mystery is further complicated by the Brotherhood's sudden interest in Dr. David Fischer, developer of a unique and powerful weapon known as the Lightning Gun.

When the Lightning Gun, Dr. Fischer, and a host of celebrities—including the beautiful Brotherhood agent, China White—board the luxurious liner, the *Normandie,* 13 believes he knows where the next disaster will strike.

It is up to him to stop it ...

AGENT 13

CHAPTER II

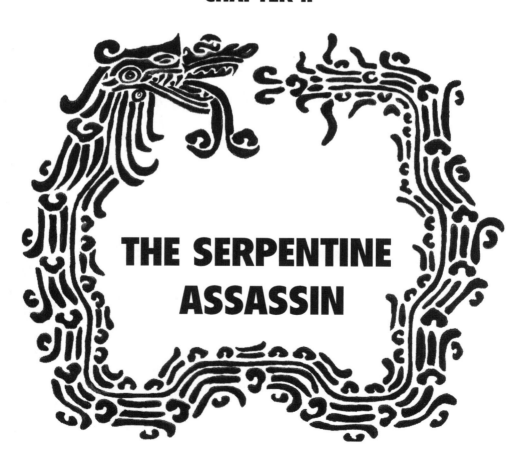

THE SERPENTINE ASSASSIN

EYES OF CRIMSON

1937. A sea lane two hundred miles off the coast of Newfoundland.

The midnight waters of the Atlantic were cold and serene, reflecting the full moon that cut like a beacon through the crystal blackness.

Suddenly, the throb of churning engine screws filled the night as the tall, crimson bow of the SS *Normandie*, the pride of the French liners, sliced through the black waters.

While Europe stood on the brink of an armed conflict that threatened to tear apart the world, the *Normandie* offered a temporary, elegantly appointed haven of peace to those who could afford her.

From a distance that night, the *Normandie* was truly a wonder to behold—one thousand twenty-nine feet in length, fourteen decks high—she was a floating palace of twinkling light. A closer look, however, revealed that something was wrong ...

terribly wrong!

The bars aboard ship were crowded, but no one was celebrating. Rather, they were talking in hushed, sad, or angry tones about the great tragedies they'd been witness to that night.

Security officers were posted around the ship, scrutinizing the passengers closely, for no one knew whether those responsible for tonight's bloody carnage were still on board or if they had all escaped on that mysterious airboat.

On the bridge, grieving, shocked crew members were removing the bodies of their captain and his officers from the bullet-ridden command center of the great ship. Another group was doing the same with the men who had been in the radio room—a room with all its equipment now smashed and blood-spattered.

With most of her officers dead and her radio equipment destroyed, the

Normandie had no choice but to turn back to New York. The investigation of just what happened had already begun on board. Also sealed off was the garage, where still more bodies lay—bodies of the thugs who had been in on this operation and who had been shot down by escaping comrades.

The fire that had raged in the garage had been brought under control, but too late to save what was rumored to be the prototype of a new and devastating weapon developed by one Dr. David Fischer. Dr. Fischer himself, it seemed, had narrowly escaped with his life. Drugged and only partially aware of what was going on, he had given a rather incoherent account of Nazis trying to kidnap him and his gun.

One person could have told the confused investigators the whole story of the strange, sinister figure behind this near-disaster—the hooded figure known as the Masque, who had engineered this horror in an attempt to blackmail America into meeting his demands. One person, who was—even now—still standing on the deck, staring back out into the dark sea at a tiny pinpoint of flame on the horizon. That spot of flame marked the burning wreckage of a lifeboat—and it marked the burning pain in Maggie Darr's heart.

For out there, in the cold, black waters, had perished the man Maggie loved, Agent 13.

Maggie might have stood there for hours, staring back at the spot of flame that gradually disappeared over the horizon. But the Texan, who had loaned Agent 13 his pearl-handled Colt .45, discovered her standing there.

"Say, little lady, what's this?" he drawled, true concern in his voice. Maggie's blood-stained, grease-smeared evening gown clung to her body. Her long, strawberry blonde hair whipped in the wind of the ship's motion. She was shivering violently, her lips blue.

Grabbing a blanket from a deck chair, the Texan wrapped it around Maggie's shoulders.

"Yer Mrs. Plotkin, ain't ya, little lady?" the Texan said awkwardly. "I heard your husband was—er—lost in the stampede, so to speak. I'm real sorry, ma'am. But, look, standin' here ain't gonna bring him back. Let me take you back to your cabin. The doc'll fix you up somethin' to help you sleep...."

No, thought Maggie wearily, this won't bring him back. Nothing can bring him back. But at least I'll avenge him. At least I'll keep fighting!

Maggie straightened up and gave the Texan a strained smile.

"Thank you," she said in a toneless voice, "you are very kind. I'll take your advice. I'll go back to my cabin. Thank you."

"You sure I can't help you?" the Texan asked.

"No, thank you," Maggie said wearily. "I—I'd rather be alone right now." Seeing the Texan look doubtful, Maggie added, "I'm all right, truly."

The Texan touched the brim of his Stetson. "Glad to be of help, ma'am. Again, I'm right sorry about yer husband, Mrs. Plotkin."

Mrs. Plotkin. Maggie sighed. Would she have to keep up that charade the rest of the voyage? And what about when they arrived in New York? No. There'd be too many questions. It would come out that Hiram Plotkin had never existed.

Trying to think, Maggie made her way below decks. She had been with Agent 13 long enough to know about disguises. Mrs. Plotkin would disappear along with her husband. Give them another little mystery to ponder....

As Maggie moved along the silent corridors to her cabin, the cabin that would seem so empty now, she passed cabin 48. The number registered in her weary brain. 48. Stopping, she stared at it, trying to remember. . ..

Of course! Dr. Fischer! It was *his* cabin number. Agent 13 had given her a mission—to watch Fischer. She had been successful in preventing China White and the Brotherhood from kidnapping him. She had also managed to destroy his prototype weapon—the Lightning Gun.

Maggie recalled her last glimpse of Fischer. The ship's doctor had been leading the dazed, drugged man away. Had they taken him to the infirmary?

Or back to his cabin?

"I ought to check on him," Maggie said to herself with a sigh. But she was tired, so very tired. She only wanted to get to her room, alone.

"But I promised him. ..."

She knocked softly on the door. "Dr. Fischer?" she called out.

"Who's there?" asked a frightened voice.

"It's me, Mrs.—uh—Plotkin. Remember? We talked in the Winter Garden Room?" she said lamely, wondering how much Fischer remembered about the attempted kidnapping.

There was a moment's silence, then the door opened a crack. Fischer peered out. Maggie was shocked. The man looked terrible! His face was gray and haggard, and it barely resembled the face of the man she had rescued. His eyes still had that glazed expression of someone shaking off the effects of a drug. That must explain why even his voice sounded different, Maggie thought.

"I'm sorry to disturb you," Maggie said gently. "I just wanted to be sure you're all right—"

"Come in," Fischer said, his eyes darting nervously down the corridor. "This has been a horrible ordeal! My nerves are shattered...."

Mumbling, running his hands through his graying hair, Fischer turned from the door. Maggie followed him inside.

He turned and shouted, "Shut the door!" Hurtling past her, he slammed and locked it.

Maggie, alarmed at Fischer's distraught state, suggested, "You really should be in the infirmary." She went to the phone. "Let me call—"

"No!" He knocked the phone from her hand.

Seeing her startled expression, he said, "I'm sorry. I—I didn't mean to be so abrupt. It's just... I'm so frightened!" He looked at her pleadingly. "You're the only one I can trust!"

"Dr. Fischer," Maggie said firmly, "I really believe you are safe now. You should go to bed—"

"Oh, but first I have to thank you for saving me!" Dr. Fischer said in a trembling voice. "I have money! Lots of money! Let me give you—"

"Really, Dr. Fischer," Maggie said with a sigh, "that's not necessary—"
Fischer's hand went to his inside coat pocket.

"Yes, it is!" he said. Then, suddenly, his voice changed. "Believe me—it is—very necessary!"

Fischer's eyes gleamed strangely as he stared intently at Maggie. His body no longer trembled, and the expression on his face grew hard.

"What the—" Maggie began, then stared in horrified fascination as Dr. Fischer's hand emerged from his coat pocket, holding a .38.

FIRES OF FREEDOM

"Dr. Fischer! Are you crazy?" Maggie gasped, watching as the gun, seemingly in slow motion, swung around until it was aimed at her head. "I'm not going to hurt you! I'm not one of them!"

The man didn't answer. Maggie looked into his eyes and saw the glazed, insane stare... Fischer's ordeal had driven him over the edge.

Backing up, Maggie grabbed for the only thing within reach—the telephone. Picking up the entire instrument, she threw it at the professor with all her strength. The gun fired just as the phone slammed into his hand, sending the shot wild and the gun from his hand.

Maggie reached for her own gun inside her purse, then remembered it was empty. She had used her last bullet on the escaping China White.

She dove for Fischer's weapon. Sliding on her stomach across the floor, Maggie grabbed the gun and pulled it toward her. But the professor jumped on top of her, pinning her hand and the gun it held beneath her body. Sitting on her buttocks, he wrapped the telephone cord around her neck and began to twist.

Desperately, Maggie fought to free herself and the hand with the gun. But the scientist was strong, incredibly strong for such a frail-looking man. The phone cord cut into her windpipe, slowly choking the life from her body.

Maggie saw bursts of light and pain. For a brief instant, she thought about giving up, to join 13 in that far-off realm....

But something in Maggie refused to surrender. Even as she was beginning to lose consciousness, she remembered an old trick 13 had taught her. She went limp, letting her body fall flaccid. Her head slumped forward. She ceased to struggle.

Fischer quit twisting the cord. Maggie held her breath. Still crouched on top of her prone body, the scientist sat back. With his weight shifted to her legs, Maggie could raise up enough to free her gun hand. Fischer made another lunge for her as he felt her body move, but it was too late. In a sudden, rapid motion, Maggie twisted onto her side.

She raised the gun and fired, point blank....

Dr. Fischer's head exploded in blood and brains and bits of bone. His body, still on top of Mag gie, began to convulse.

Fighting back her horror, Maggie pushed the headless corpse off her. Then she realized that the body was growing rapidly hotter! She leaped out of the way just as the corpse burst into flames!

Agent 13's words came back to her. "They are called Jindas, or Serpentine Assassins—the Brotherhood's legendary killers. Before they go out to kill, they drink *mantha*—an ancient drug that causes the body to burst into flame when it mixes with the chemicals of death."

No trace of the Brotherhood's assassins would remain—even after death. As the last pieces of "Dr. Fischer" burned away, so, too, did Maggie's illusions about the success of her mission to keep Dr. Fischer out of the hands of the Brotherhood.

The Dr. Fischer who had boarded the *Normandie* had been real, Maggie was certain. During the gun battle, China White had apparently substituted her assassin for the real Dr. Fischer. Maggie now remembered the lumpy, ruglike bundle she had seen being transferred to the airboat.

The Brotherhood thought of everything, Maggie realized grimly. If the torpedoes Agent 13 had stopped had sunk the *Normandie*, the disappearance of Dr. Fischer would have never been questioned. But if their plan failed, if there were survivors—the "fake" Dr. Fischer would remain on board for everyone to see. And Maggie Darr would be silenced forever.

Opening the door, Maggie staggered out into the hall, coughing with the smoke.

"FIRE!" a voice in the corridor screamed.

Dully, Maggie looked back. The body was gone, but the room was filled with smoke. The rug was afire and the flames had spread to the drapes.

Someone grabbed Maggie, pulling her out of the way. The corridor outside the room was quickly filling with smoke and sleepy-eyed passengers.

"Get water!" yelled another voice, and immediately pandemonium broke out.

Fleeing the scene before anyone could ask questions, Maggie crept to the upper deck, heading for the one place she was certain she would be undisturbed—China White's suite. Already, baskets of flowers stood outside the door, gifts of mourning for the beautiful opera singer who had mysteriously vanished during the disaster.

No one had seen the black-leather-suited woman board the airboat—no one except Maggie Darr.

Glancing up and down the darkened corridor and finding it empty, Maggie picked the lock and entered the elegant Rouen Suite. Closing the door behind her, she locked it securely. She would wait out the voyage here. Maggie didn't dare turn on a light, but she didn't need one. Lying on the satin-sheeted bed, she stared up into the darkness.

So, the Brotherhood had succeeded at least partially in their diabolical scheme. Though they hadn't managed to destroy the *Normandie*—a disaster that would have had world-wide repercussions—they had kidnapped Dr. Fischer. That they wanted him for his Lightning Gun was certain. But why? What did they intend to do with it? And how did it tie into the other disasters and the Masque's outrageous demands on America.

Something had to be done.

As she had stared at Agent 13's funeral pyre, she had sworn vengeance. Somehow she had to expose the Brotherhood, tell someone about Dr. Fischer. But what would she say to the authorities? As quickly as she wove together the strands of a persuasive story, it unraveled of its own improbability.

What evidence did she really have? Certainly there were witnesses aboard the Normandie to the gunplay and the presence of the airboat as it dropped its torpedoes. But what did it all prove?

That a crime had taken place? Of course.

That criminal masterminds were at work? Not necessarily. Everyone was blaming the Nazis!

That there was a secret 'Brotherhood' trying to take control of the world?

Maggie shook her head wearily and began to cry. They were tears of grief, tears of frustration.

Even in failure, the Brotherhood had succeeded in masking its very existence.

For the first time, Maggie Darr felt the depth of the frustration that Agent 13 must have known.

Gradually, she cried herself empty. But, as she drifted into sleep, Maggie Darr made a pledge.

"Wherever you are, beloved," she murmured, "I swear to you that I will never cease fighting them! Somehow—I'll make someone listen...."

HANDS OF LIFE

The prototype Mosquito airboat had left the *Normandie* far behind. Aboard the strange craft, the pilot was cursing about their failure to destroy the ship. In the cargo hold, the drugged Dr. Fischer lay wrapped in a rug.

Near him, leaning back against the metal fuselage of the Mosquito, her sultry beauty evident even in the moonlit darkness, China White was staring out into the night with unseeing eyes.

One of the crew members knelt beside her, clumsily trying to bandage her bleeding shoulder where Maggie Darr's bullet had penetrated.

"Leave me alone!" China murmured viciously.

Still she stared straight ahead, as though listening to a voice only she could hear. Then, abruptly, she rose and made her way forward.

"Turn the airboat around," she commanded.

"What?" The astonished pilot looked up at her. "Are you nut—"

"I said turn it around!" China White hissed.

The pilot stared into her eyes. "Sure thing," he muttered, feeling a chill shake his body.

The fires of the floating wreckage slowly burned out and darkness descended on the ocean. To the semiconscious figure who clung to one of the larger fragments of wood, death was closer than morning.

Dreamily, he imagined what it would be like to die on top of this bit of wood. His body would bake in the sun. The flesh that had once been Agent 13 would slowly wither and dry.

Suddenly, a harsh white light hit him a palpable blow. Spray washed over him as a roaring sound struck his ears. The waves became larger, threatening to topple him back into the sea forever. 13 hung on to the splintering wood with his last remaining strength.

Then hands were pulling him upward, lifting him into something cold, black. He was encased in metal. He saw faces—eyes and voices blurred in a flurry of images. Moments later, he felt a sharp stinging pain in his arm, and though he tried to resist, he drifted into blackness.

"Will he survive?" China asked coldly.

"I doubt it," the crewman muttered, standing up and replacing the syringe in the first aid kit. "That morphine'U ease his pain, but we need to get him to a doctor pronto!"

"Then do so," China White said, her voice carefully devoid of all trace of emotion.

Biting her lip against the pain, China forced her rapidly numbing hand to scrawl out the location of a hidden airfield near America's eastern coastline. This done, and the crewman on his way to deliver her note to the pilot, China White leaned back again.

Her face carefully expressionless, she reached out and gently stroked the wet hair back from Agent 13's pale face.

The sound of the props reached full throttle as the airboat slowly lifted off the frigid waters. Rising effortlessly, the Mosquito disappeared, unseen, into the night.

DARK MEDITATIONS

Itsu's throne room had been hacked from the mountain thousands of centuries ago, practically at the dawn of human history. Its cavernous expanse dwarfed all who stood within it.

The high throne rose two hundred feet from the center, with hundreds of steps leading up to it. Status among those who served Itsu was revealed by how high they were allowed to ascend the great marble stairway that led to the black onyx throne. None but Itsu set foot upon the final twenty golden stairs that led from the top landing to the throne. For the moment, none save one figure in the robe of a Bishop stood upon the stairway at all.

It was from this vantage point, two hundred feet above the nave of his dark cathedral, that Itsu, the Hand Sinister, meditated upon the *Normandie* mission. Though his agents had failed to destroy the vessel and his beloved nightingale had been wounded, his master plan could still proceed.

In fact, things had worked out better than the Hand Sinister had dared hope. For he had just heard of the probable capture of the one man in the world who came close to proving a threat to him—Agent 13. But was it really Agent 13, or was it—as had happened many times before—a false report? More than once, 13 had disguised others to resemble him, even as he disguised himself to resemble others. There was only one proof—the tattoo of the number 13 upon the palm of his hand. All agents of the Brotherhood bore similar marks, which only death and the decomposition of the flesh would erase.

The tattoo could be seen in only one way-through a Seer Stone. The Hand Sinister would have to wait for this to be confirmed.

Even as he sat motionless upon his throne, the Hand Sinister projected his consciousness onto another plane. Many times before, he had detected actions of Agent 13 in the astral realm, but had been unable to thwart the Agent, whose spiritual aura was unusually strong.

Now, however, when he detected the Agent's aura, he sensed it changing. Dividing. The two halves of the same entity were moving independently. This unique occurrence puzzled the Hand Sinister.

Nevertheless, he wasn't surprised when he spotted a red-robed minion dashing up the steps to stand on the second landing far beneath him.

"We have confirmation." The servant gasped for breath. "It is he—Tredekka!"

"What evidence?" growled the Bishop.

"China White confirms his identity. . ."

"Bah!" the Bishop started to argue. "Who can tell without the Seer Stone?"

Itsu smiled.

"She can tell," he murmured.

MIDNIGHT ECHOES

The Mosquito dropped out of the sky just as the sun was beginning to peak over the horizon.

Skimming along the glassy waters near the Virgina shore, the airboat coasted to a landing, then the airboat turned and cruised toward the large building built partially in the water. Huge doors beneath the structure opened up, swallowing the moving airboat like a whale consuming a fish.

A sign on the building read "Sea Breeze Fish Cannery."
As the airboat taxied to a stop against a stone pier, men dashed forward to help and, before many minutes had elapsed, stretchers carrying three people had emerged from the plane. One was Dr. Fischer, still unconscious. That stretcher was taken to hidden quarters far below the cannery. The other two stretchers were carried to the infirmary where Dr. Colbert Winslow waited. To America, he was a renowned surgeon. To the Brotherhood, Winslow was one of them.

Less than an hour earlier, Winslow had received one of the cryptic phone calls he had come to know so well in his double life. Hastily jumping out of bed, he drove through the night to the cannery's infirmary.

Two patients awaited him. One, he was astonished to see, was the beautiful opera singer, China White. Weak from loss of blood from a shoulder wound, she had lapsed into unconsciousness. But, after a quick examination, Winslow discovered that her situation was not life-threatening.

The same could not be said of his other patient, a man whose face was unknown to the doctor. Checking his patient who, even unconscious, was being closely guarded by two huge thugs, Winslow marveled that the man was still alive.

"This man needs to be in a hospital!" Winslow barked. "He has multiple fractures, undoubtedly internal bleeding. He's suffering from shock and exposure...."

"Just patch him up, doc," growled one of the thugs. "We'll take care of the rest."

Shrugging, Winslow did as he was told, then turned his attention to China White. Carefully, he removed the bullet from her beautiful shoulder, thinking—as he did so—what a pity it was that such lovely skin would be scarred for life.

"She'll be fully recovered in a couple of days," Winslow told the guards, who nodded silently. "I'm going to make one last plea that you let me take this man to a hospital."

The guards shook their heads silently.

Winslow shrugged, packed his medical bag, and set off for home. The less he knew about this, the better he'd sleep.

As China emerged from the anaesthetic, a disheveled-looking young man picked up a phone, gave a brief report, then hung up.

"What happened to the man we brought in?" China muttered drowsily.

The young man, who had been hastily pulled off guard duty in the tunnels below the fish cannery, shrugged.

"We boxed him an hour ago."

"He's . . . dead?" asked China White, shocked into full consciousness.

"Looked that way to me, lady. Stiff as a board." Then, he shook his head. "Though," he added thoughtfully, "with all the strange stuff I seen around this place lately—" Suddenly,

the hood's voice changed. He began to shake and clutch at his throat.

China stared at him, startled at first. Then she recognized what was happening—the brainwashing. The young hood had been wagging his tongue too freely. Now he was getting tied up by it. The hood's face turned purple as he flopped onto the floor, gagging and gasping for air.

What a nuisance, thought China irritably, looking around for a bell to push to have someone come fetch him. Maybe it was only his first offense and he would come out of it. If it wasn't, he would die, choking on his own tongue.

A wave of sadness swept across China. Not for the gagging hood, but for Agent 13. Even she had come to believe he was immortal. And there was something more—a feeling deep inside her that even the passing of time couldn't subdue.

Pausing, she listened for his voice— that spiritual voice that had spoken to her on the plane, making her return to the wreckage of the lifeboat. But that voice was silent.

Something left her then, as a pleasant dream leaves upon wakening. No matter how hard she tried to fall back asleep, she knew that dream would never come again.

She was empty.

The orderly suddenly slumped into the corner, limp, silent. He was either unconscious or dead.

THE INVISIBLE GUARD

Crowds thronged the French Line pier in New York as the passengers from the *Normandie* disembarked. Applause clattered over the water as reporters crowded around, chucking questions at anyone who would answer.

"Where's the guy who piloted the lifeboat?" demanded one reporter, crowding the Texan.

"Mind you don't step on man boots, boy," the Texan growled, eyeing the man irritably. "What do you mean, where is he? Probably bein* awarded a medal by St. Peter 'bout now "

"What about this Mrs. Plotkin? Has she disembarked yet?" another asked.

"I believe she has been in seclusion," said the Texan. "And, if they're smart, they'll keep her away from you coyotes!" Shrugging, the reporters hurried off after another victim.

The authorities, too, were interested in Mrs. Plotkin. In vain, the harassed security officers aboard ship insisted they hadn't seen her. No one had seen her since the disaster. The authorities began to search the ship cabin by cabin.

A small, wrinkled, old Chinese man in dark, wire-rimmed glasses on his thin, bald head stood on the edge of the crowd, peering at all who disembarked intently. "That daughter of mine," he muttered to anyone within earshot. "Always the last to leave. Probably lost her luggage. . . ." His fingers bedecked with several jeweled rings, tapped impatiently on a metal railing. No one gave the old man a second glance.

If they had, they would have noticed that his eyes behind the glasses were much younger than his face. They would also have noticed that he was scrutinizing the face of every passenger who walked down the ramp.

Finally, his fingers ceased their tapping. The old man smiled. His eyes were focused on a middle-aged woman descending the ramp alone. Her hair was gray, her dress was gray, her life was probably gray—the kind of woman who passes through life unnoticed. She was the woman he was looking for—conspicuous by being inconspicuous.

He shadowed the woman closely, his own movements and presence as unobtrusive as hers. His smile broadened as his suspicions were confirmed by the woman leaving the terminal without so much as a piece of luggage.

The woman stepped toward the crowded cabstand and tentatively raised her hand at the passing cabs, but the drivers ignored her.

Sidling next to the gray woman, the old man took off his hat and rubbed his bald head with a handkerchief. The rings on his fingers flashed in the sunlight. An out-of-service cab suddenly went back on call. Pulling over to the curb in front of the woman, the driver opened the door. Startled, the woman stepped back, carefully scrutinizing the driver.

A young Chinese man with a warm, infectious smile, the driver jumped out of the cab. "You get in, lady," he said, respectfully taking her arm. "Not good, you stand in cold like this." Talking volubly, the young Chinese assisted the woman into the cab quite before she knew what was happening. Bystanders who had been wait-

ing longer glared at her, but she just locked the door and settled back into the seat.

The Chinese boy jumped into the cab and sped off. Replacing his hat, the old man pulled a newspaper from the pocket of his overcoat and appeared to be reading. But his eyes were scanning the nearby area.

Suddenly, he focused on a middle-aged newsstand attendant hurrying toward a double-parked Hudson and jumping in. He saw the man point at the cab as it pulled into traffic.

The old man raised his ringed hand in a quick gesture. A beat-up, rusted DeSoto leaped out of its parking place like a rampaging bull, swerving directly in front of the Hudson.

The Hudson tried to avoid the DeSoto, but it was too late. There was a shattering crash. The Hudson broadsided the DeSoto so hard that it lifted the car up on two wheels. Glass flew everywhere.

The driver of the DeSoto, an ancient Chinese man, jumped out and began waving his hands and babbling angrily. The slightly damaged Hudson backed up, trying to get past the DeSoto, only to be boxed in by the honking cars behind it.

The Hudson stopped, trapped.

Suddenly there was the sound of a siren, and lights flashed on the roof of a squad car stuck eight cars back.

The newsstand attendant and two thugs jumped from the Hudson and dashed wildly away as the police battled their way forward.

When the police finally arrived, they looked helplessly at the two driverless cars, while the symphony of blasting horns played around them.

Smiling with satisfaction, the old Chinese man melted into the crowd.

"Where to, lady?" the driver asked Maggie.

"Just drive around awhile, young man," Maggie said in her best "frumpy" voice. "And please let me know if anyone's following us."

"Following you, lady?" the Chinese boy asked in astonishment.

"My husband's so jealous!" Maggie simpered, patting her gray wig.

"Okey dokey, lady," the Chinese boy said, hiding his grin.

Leaning back in the seat, Maggie was too preoccupied with her own thoughts to notice the skill with which the young man dodged in and out of side streets and took practiced advantage of gaps in traffic.

"No one follow, lady," he finally said. Maggie started. "Oh, well, take me to Grand Central Station then, please," she said.

Reaching the cathedral-like train station, Maggie paid the driver and watched as he pulled away. Then she entered the station. Occasionally she peered surreptitiously behind her but didn't notice anyone taking an unusual amount of interest in her. In fact, no one seemed to take any interest in her whatsoever!

No one, that is, except a small Chi-

nese urchin who was begging for pennies. Maggie purchased her ticket, then walked to the appropriate track. The dark-haired child followed closely behind, dodging with ease in and out of the crowd.

The child watched as Maggie boarded the train, then ran back to the crowded station area.

"Starlight Express," he said in Chinese to an old man waiting for him there, "to Washington...."

JOURNEY TO DARKNESS

The grieving couple stood in the rain, watching as the casket was loaded aboard the airplane.

"Our only son," sobbed the woman, her face hidden by a thick black veil.

"He'll be glad to get back home," said the man, patting her on the shoulder.

Within moments, the coffin was airborne. Inside it, the unconscious Agent 13 was in his most bizarre disguise—one he would never see; he was disguised as a corpse, with two of the Brotherhood's trusted agents as his "parents."

So powerful was the drug the Brotherhood injected periodically into Agent 13 during the journey that it slowed his heart beat to only twice per minute. He breathed only once per hour.

Thus the air in his sealed casket lasted him for days, and even the skilled eyes of a doctor might fail to see the glimmer of life that existed behind the mask of death.

Twice the casket was opened and checked by border guards as it moved across international boundaries where caskets had been used for smuggling. But on both occasions the guards found only what was claimed by the grieving family—the battered body of their handsome son.

On one occasion, the "family" thought they were being followed. To shake off pursuit, the body was buried under the watchful eyes of a priest. But, before the spades had patted the last clods into place, the casket was being hauled down through secret passages built beneath this cemetery long ago for just such fake burials.

Thus, there was no way that any investigator, no matter how diligent or clever, could have followed the path of the corpse from America to its final destination.

After a ten-day journey covering thousands of miles, the unconscious Agent 13 arrived at the mysterious, cloud-shrouded Shrine.

He was taken to a dark, vaulted chamber, There, several grim figures in monks' cowls, their shadowy forms almost indistinguishable from each other, hovered over the unconscious man. Their faces, normally cold and expressionless, gleamed with strange, sinister smiles as they looked through the Seer Stone. Agent 13 had come home.

"I'm not dead" was his first clear thought. If he were dead, his soul would have been liberated. But he knew that it was still chained inside his body. He tried to open his eyes, but his lids would not move. He tried to clench his fists, but his muscles failed to obey. Agent 13 was paralyzed. Where was he? What had happened?

Then he discovered that he could hear and understand people talking around him.

"When was he last given the serum?" The voice hissed like wind whistling through a cave.

"Two nights ago."

"Then soon he should be able to hear me."

"Perhaps he can hear you now."

"He has caused me much displeasure, yet I do not want to destroy him. It will be better to see him destroy himself—and all that he cares for. See that it is done."

13 heard the words. The cold, hissing tones seemed familiar... a long time ago. Then the horror suddenly registered—it was Itsu! The Hand Sinister! He was back at the Shrine!

His mind tried to retrace events. His last remembered thoughts were that at least the *Normandie* would live. The Mosquito plane . . . the torpedoes screaming toward the great liner. He maneuvered the frail lifeboat into their path. The moment before impact, he dived into the frigid waters, swimming deep, deep. Then the explosions, then pain, then nothing....

He drifted away again....

Moments, maybe days, later, 13 felt his first physical sensation since the Normandie disaster. He felt a pair of fingers upon his eyelids. They were cold and dry, more like bone than flesh.

Desperately, fearful of what he would see, 13 tried to keep his eyes closed, but hands pried the lids open. He stared into a skull! Dark, rotting eyes stared down at him.
Itsu!

The lipless mouth spoke in a hoarse whisper. "Forget not my face... It is life.. It is death.... It is all!"

Suddenly 13's eyelids closed and he was plunged back into darkness, his very soul shuddering with horror.

It was the face of his nightmares, implanted when he was a child and first brought to the Shrine. He had heard the words then, as well. They were etched on a holy wall erected deep inside him and taken as faith. For though he had fought and won many battles with the Brotherhood, he had never questioned what the skull had whispered, "Life ... death ... all!"

Never questioned it, because he knew it to be true!

SEARCHING FOR PIECES

Washington, D.C.

The lights glimmered brightly over the sleeping city. Somewhere high above a street in the warehouse district, a faint shadow paced past a window, lost in thought.

A twisting smoke plume drifted from the glowing cigarette in Maggie Darr's fingers as she absently eyed the distant Capitol dome.

The almost dark room she stood in was Agent 13's Washington lair, one of several that existed on the 13th floors of abandoned buildings— non-existent 13th floors. The room was jammed with make-up materials, mechanical devices, information.

Maggie recalled the last time she had been in the cluttered lair. 13 had been one of the few to have survived the Brotherhood's attack on the National Security Council meeting where they had slaughtered the nation's top lawmen... only to fall prey to the Jinda assassins. Maggie had managed to save him from brutal death. But then they had sailed on the *Normandie*....

Upon her return to Washington, Maggie found she could not walk into 13's lair. The things in there were his things. His presence was still alive in those rooms. Maggie rented a small motel room where she kept to herself... and thought.

Locked in seclusion, Maggie gave way to her grief. Then, one morning, she woke up and knew everything would be all right. She could go on. She *must* go on—for his sake.

Now.staring at the illuminated Capitol from the window of 13's lair, Maggie felt the ghost of 13 everywhere, calling her to pick up the flag and continue. She remembered others who had died in his service—the Oriental named Ray Furnow, a strange man who had helped the Agent with many of his inventions. Doc Kendall, the white-haired man who was tailing one of the Brotherhood's agents when he was sliced in two in a "trucking accident." Freddie Dey, Willie Peck, and "Dogs" Kelly. . . . Someday, she knew, the name of Maggie Darr would be added to the list.

She repeated the names over and over in her mind, like an ancient mantra. And, almost unconsciously, she began to pick up the investigation where Agent 13 had left off.

Her first thoughts were of Dr. Fischer. She was the only one to know he had been kidnapped. She ought to report it someone—but who? Who would believe her? Time and again she picked up the phone to call the police—only to put it down again. Finally, she realized she needed more to go on. And it was up to her to find it.

She reviewed what she knew about the events that had occurred prior to the *Normandie*'s sailing. Somehow, they all tied together. Agent 13 had always told her that the Brotherhood plotted their campaigns the way a composer writes a symphony. There is always a repeating motif.

So she recalled everything 13 had told her about the filmed ultimatum delivered to Washington. In that film, a shrouded Brotherhood agent calling himself "the Masque" had threatened disaster after disaster if the United States did not comply with his demands—demands that would virtually cripple the Armed Services.

To back his powerful threats, the Masque had shown film clips of three disasters. First, a train trestle blowing up, sending passenger cars and some helium tank cars tumbling to a fiery end in the canyon below. Then, an armaments factory went skyward in a fiery blaze that destroyed an entire new generation of fighter planes. Finally, the *Hindenburg*— pride of the German dirigibles—exploded while docking at Lakehurst. A film clip of the *Normandie* would undoubtedly have been the next to be shown— were it not for Agent 13's sacrifice.

All of the disasters might have been attributed to other causes were it not for two facts. First, the films of the disasters themselves could have been taken only by ultra-sophisticated camera equipment specially positioned to catch the events on film, and, second, the Masque made sure that his sinister, secret symbol appeared on the film made at every disaster—the Omega and the Star.

The same symbol used by the Brotherhood.

Maggie replayed the disasters in her mind. Allegedly, these crimes were all committed to demonstrate the Masque's power over America, but 13 had been convinced that there was something more to them.

If China White had indeed been the Masque, as Agent 13 had supposed, would her death bring an end to their plots? Maggie doubted it. But there was always the possibility that China

White wasn't the Masque. 13 had suspected her, but he hadn't been certain. If not her, then who?

Maggie pored over stacks of papers, clippings, and photographs. A lot of it was research into Dr. Fischer, inventor of the Lightning Gun. Here, too, were the papers Agent 13 had removed from the briefcase of SS Colonel Reinhardt Schmidt, papers showing the Brotherhood's plan to participate in a test of the gun.

A photograph taken during that test suddenly caught Maggie's attention. The test had been conducted for the United States Army when Fischer was trying to raise money to fund his weapon's development.

13, having discovered the Brotherhood's interest in the gun, attended the test firing disguised as a reporter, camera in hand.

The test was a success—the small cannon completely destroyed an old steel tank—but the U.S. Goverment didn't bite. Others did, however, and one interested party paid Fischer's passage to Europe aboard the *Normandie*, making certain that he was on the right ship at the right time.

She carefully studied the photographs of the test. Somewhere was a clue, somewhere an answer—there was General Hunter Braddock, the aging head of the Joint Chiefs of Staff; Fischer; Colonel Joseph Pack, head of the Army's weapons development; Kent Walters, head of the National Security Agency. ...

Kent Walters! Suddenly it clicked. With the exception of Agent 13, Walters was the only survivor of the Jindas' attack on the meeting in Washington where the Masque's filmed threats had been revealed. But it was also at that meeting that Agent 13 had exposed his identity in an effort to stress the seriousness of the threats!

Walters knew who 13 was, he knew that 13 was on their side. Walters had, in fact, even protected 13's identity when the police had arrested the Agent! Walters would understand the terrible danger they faced! Walters would be the one to tell about Dr. Fischer!

At last, she had something to do, something to think about. Perhaps—even someone to help.

SENTENCE PRONOUNCED

The first sensation Agent 13 felt was a slight tingling. Starting in his chest, it spread slowly outward. It was a strange sensation, as if he were being reborn. Soon his heart rate increased, slowly at first. Thirty times a minute, then forty, finally—normal—sixty-eight beats.

The tingling spread throughout his body. As it did, he wasn't Agent 13. He was a small boy. His subconscious suddenly came to vivid life. . ..

A weather-beaten wagon creaked down a rutted jungle road, spoked wheels turning, bumping.

He sat in the back of the wagon, playing with his tin soldiers. He was angry because he couldn't get them to stand up—the wagon was shaking too much. Angrily, he looked up at the two men and a woman sitting on the seat of the wagon. One man was the driver, but the other wore the black suit and white collar of a missionary.

At his cry of protest, the woman turned and smiled at him. Cheered and comforted by her smile, he forgot his anger. She said something to the missionary, causing him to turn around too. Suddenly, an icy chill ran down the Agent's spine. He recognized the man and the woman— his father and mother!

Slowly, 13 began to hear sounds in his vision. First, the rustling in the jungle, then the whizzing of arrows through the air. He heard a scream and saw his father fall over sideways, an arrow stuck through his neck. It was his mother screaming. She reached back for him. . . .

Everything was wrong! His father's eyes were open and staring. Blood was all over his black suit. The child's mother tried to pick him up to protect him with her own body from the hail of arrows. But he was ripped from her soft arms by stronger hands.

As he was lifted, wailing, through the air, he turned his head to strike out at whatever it was that was hurting him. What he saw made him recoil in horror—the dead-white face of a Puljani warrior! The man's lips were painted bright red, and jagged lines streaked down the cheeks.

His mother's screams stopped suddenly as strange hands carried the boy swiftly into the jungle. The world became a blur of green.

Soon, many miles up the path, they reached a small village. There, the warrior entered a bamboo shack and dumped the boy on the ground in front of a man of indeterminate race with a face as smooth as polished stone.

"The preacher's son?" the Strange One asked. The Puljani responded quickly in a native dialect, bowing many times.

Apparently the Strange One was satisfied, for he motioned to a crate of rifles on the floor beside him. Grinning, the painted warrior lifted the box and carried it out.

The boy crouched on the floor, watching. With a syringe in his hand, the Strange One came forward and grabbed his arm. There was a sting....

It was then that the veil fell upon the Agent.

A soft bell tinkled in the distance and the Agent felt a twinge of hunger. As if waking from a night's sleep rather than from a drug-induced coma, the Agent opened his eyes. He was in a small room, nearly as old as time. It had been carved from stone. A jagged slit of light sliced through his chamber. As 13 looked away from the radiance, he realized he had known, even in his coma.

He had returned to the Shrine.

The bell rang, and he was a boy again, this time older, responding to the call for breakfast. For just a moment, he felt the twinge of a deep inner peace that he'd forgotten. He waited, his heart pounding, to be joined by his love, China White....But she never came.

She had betrayed him.

Escaping the Shrine, escaping the evil he had discovered at its core, 13 fled, hunted and pursued like a wild beast. But, because of the training he'd received at the Shrine, he survived his trainer's best efforts to kill him.

Slowly, 13's eyes adjusted to the light. He peered out of the thin crack in the rock wall.

For a moment, 13 thought about escape, then smiled grimly. The Brotherhood would never let him go a second time. He briefly considered suicide, but that would be conceding defeat. He could not do that.

On unsteady legs, 13 hobbled to a door bolted into the rock. He tried the handle. It was open. As he suspected, they would not lock him in. Their prisons were far too subtle for that.

Stepping through the door, his eyes

fell upon the sparse, yet rich symbolism of the Cloistered Garden. Composed of nothing but rocks, it was—nonetheless—of surpassing beauty. For each rock was of a different size, a different shape, a different color. And, to the trained eye, each shape, size, color had a meaning. The interrelationship of all formed the harmony of the whole.

Looking down, 13 saw the shape of peace. It could not exist if it were not outlined by the shape for war, which itself could not exist were it not for greed and aggression, these two balanced by charity and restraint.

It was the garden of his childhood, yet it looked different to him now than it had then. It was as if the forces of Itsu had been disturbing the rocks, shifting the geometries, the way he had shifted the philosophy of the Brotherhood itself.

"Tredekka!" a voice thundered.

13 turned, hearing himself called by a name he hadn't heard in twenty-one years.

Spinning around, he stared into the dark, cold eyes of the Jinda-dii, the legendary High Priest of Serpentine Assassins. It was a familiar face, for the Jinda-dii had been his mentor long ago. It was the Jinda-dii who had indoctrinated 13 into the Brotherhood, teaching him the principles upon which all was based.

The Jinda-dii still possessed the face of a kindly mentor and wise sage—except for the eyes.

The Agent's expression did not change, even as mentally he reeled under the impact of memory and emotion. But the Jinda-dii instantly read the complexities of the Agent's emotions. He knew, at that moment, that the rumors were true. 13 had discovered "the Dark Truths." Those that went against everything—supposedly—he had been taught as a youth. Too late, he saw that his very soul had been twisted into the soul of a power-hungry fanatic. Too late? No, it had not been too late for 13. He had, after all, escaped.

"Jinda-dii," 13 said calmly in the Brotherhood's ancient language, "I assume it is no accident that we meet here."

"Long ago, Tredekka, I taught you that there is no such thing as an accident," the Jinda-dii responded, smiling a non-smile, then bowing.

"Then there is purpose in the fact that I am still alive," the Agent concluded.

"There is purpose to all...."

"What is this purpose?"

"Because you are an initiate of the Brotherhood, there can be no subterfuge between us. It will be up to you. If you want truths, I shall tell them. If you want lies, I shall create them. The decision is yours and absolute."

Heads/Tails. Yin/Yang. White/Black.

There could, of course, be no doubt. "I want truth," 13 said firmly.

The Jinda-dii smiled slightly. "Of

course you do, Tredekka. It was ever your shortcoming. Very well. You have been sentenced to the Serpentine Assassins. You will swear obedience to a Pagan Afterlife. You will drink the mantha, the oil of fire. When you die, the oil of fire will erupt in flame and consume you, leaving only ashes and a sooted air as testimony of your existence."

The Agent listened calmly. There was nothing he could say. There was nothing he could do. His mentor watched him calmly accept this horrible fate with pride, mingled with sorrow. The Jinda-dii had bitterly opposed this sentence. He felt like an architect watching a building he had spent years designing and perfecting being torn down before his eyes. 13 had been his favorite pupil, his most glowing success, his most horrible failure. Thus, he understood the necessity of the sentence. Thus the Jinda-dii would carry it out.

The blue eyes of the Agent and the dark eyes of the Jinda-dii looked deeply into each other. There was no emotion, both were well trained to conceal such things. But there was understanding. Agent 13 knew there would be no escape....

FRESH CLUES

A smartly dressed young woman ascended the granite steps of Bethesda Naval Hospital.

"May I help you?" asked a bulldog-like nurse who manned the reception desk as grimly as if it were the Maginot Line.

"Yes, please. I'm Kimberly Wirth, with the *New England Journal*." She flashed a press badge. "I'm here to see Kent Walters."

The nurse studied the woman closely. She was attractive and well-proportioned, her strawberry blonde hair was tied smartly in a bun, and her eyes flashed with a keen intelligence. She certainly *looked* like a reporter.

"Is he expecting you?" the nurse barked.

"Yes," the young woman replied, somewhat impatiently. "I'm certain my editor cleared it."

Reluctantly, the nurse lifted the phone. "This is reception. There's a Miss Wirth of the *New England Journal* here, claiming to have an appointment with Mr. Walters."

She paused, then, "Very well," she said in disappointed tones. She turned back to Miss Wirth. "You may go up—he's on seven."

"Thank you."

Inside the elevator, Maggie quickly went over her disguise. Long ago, Agent 13 had forged fake press credentials for Kimberly Wirth. This wasn't the first time she had gone after a story. Having been well versed in writing skills at the expensive private school she had attended in Chicago, Maggie discovered she had a real knack for reporting, At 13's suggestion, she had constructed a more solid cover by working up some genuine stories, and several had been published.

So, the name Kimberly Wirth wasn't unknown in journalistic circles. Phone calls to a few editors with hints that she had an interesting angle on the "Washington Massacre" won her a brief interview with Kent Walters, the National Security Advisor who had been one of only two survivors of the slaughter that had killed the nation's top law officials. Agent 13 had been the other.

Arriving on the seventh floor of the big military hospital, which was also used by important government officials, Kimberly Wirth showed her ID and press badge to several guards. She was then searched for weapons by a female officer. Finally, reluctantly, Kent Walters's aides let her see his doctor, who stressed that she must do nothing to upset the Advisor. Maggie promised and was at last permitted to enter Walters's room.

With her very first sight of the official, Maggie was impressed. Kent Walters was as handsome as the papers had made him out to be. Clad in a red satin smoking jacket, he was sitting up in his bed, going over a pile of reports. He looked up and smiled.

"Miss Wirth?"

"It's a pleasure to meet you, Mr. Walters. Thank you for seeing me." Maggie stepped forward to shake his hand.

"The pleasure is mine, my dear." He smiled warmly. "I was expecting some guy in a battered fedora and ready to devour me like a barracuda. Instead, I'm being interviewed by an angel!"

"Don't be so sure!" Maggie said, laughing. She had heard that Walters was quite a ladies' man; she might be able to take advantage of that.

"Please excuse me if I don't get up," he said in slightly mocking tones. He gestured toward the heavy bandages on his legs as if they were mere nuisances.

"Of course," Maggie said, her voice unconsciously softening with compassion.

"But you may tell your readers that I'll be up in no time," he said.

"Sounds like a good quote for my story," Maggie replied, making a note. "And just what is your story?"

"I want the exclusive on what really happened the night of the Security Council meeting."

Walters smiled again, only this time it was the smile he used for the press. "You're a little late— you can read the story in any paper."

Maggie raised one eyebrow. "You know, I haven't read one single article yet that mentions the Masque, his link to the Montana train accident or the Westron and *Hindenburg* disasters, or of the involvement of the Brotherhood, or a man known as Agent 13."

The smile on Walters's face vanished. With a visible effort, he regained his affability. "Someone has been filling your head with fairy tales, my dear. I'd be curious to know who."

Maggie was suddenly all business. "That's not important. Let's just say that I know." Maggie paused, then went on. "I'm not really here as a reporter, Mr. Walters. I'm here to give you some important information."

Walters sneered slightly. "Of course. And what is to be the price? A thousand dollars? Two?"

"Your help," Maggie replied coolly.

Walters blinked, then frowned, caught off guard. "Very well. What is your information?"

His voice was now colder.

"Dr. David Fischer has been captured by the Brotherhood," Maggie said.

Leaning back on his pillows, Walters shrugged. "Provided I even acknowledge that I know of this 'Brotherhood's' existence, why should it matter to me whether they have this Dr. Fischer or not?"

"Please don't play games, Mr. Walters," Maggie said sternly. "Time is running out. You are interested in Dr. Fischer because he is the developer of the Lightning Gun—a weapon you and General Braddock saw demonstrated in October, only one day before the massacre at your headquarters."

Walters stared at her thoughtfully. Finally, he sighed and said, "Very well. You seem to know all the answers. Perhaps you can give me a few. How sure are you about Fischer?"

"Very sure." Maggie turned abruptly toward the door. She thought she'd heard someone coming. Lowering her voice, she said, "They took him off the *Normandie*, just before trying to blow it up—"

A sudden thought struck her.

"What else?" Walters urged. "Uh"—Maggie was jolted back to her surroundings. "Oh, yes. I believe I know the identity of the Masque.

What's more, she *may* be dead."

"She?" he asked, startled.

"The opera singer, China White."

Maggie had expected scorn at this statement. But Walters only looked grave.

As if reading her thoughts, he said, "No, that information does not particularly surprise me. We have noticed that she is often in the company of the powerful, those 'in the know,' so to speak. In fact, General Braddock was once involved with her." He was silent for a moment, then glanced up at her and nonchalantly asked, "By the way, what do you know of this Agent 13?"

Maggie was about to give a glib reply when the door to the room suddenly flew open.

"Eet ist time vor dinner, Mr. Valters," boomed a voice with a thick German accent.

Startled, Maggie turned to see a large nurse glaring at her from the doorway. The woman's face was odd—it was ugly, but a strange sort of ugliness. Nothing matched. Glowing eyes were contrasted with a pale, splotched complexion. Cracked, chapped lips split over remarkably pretty, pearly teeth. The nurse's hair was gray, her face wrinkled, but her hands looked soft.

"You vill haf to leaf, Miss Virth."

"Dinner can wait, Miss Stahlberg," Walters said coldly. "Miss Wirth can stay the allotted time."

"Really, Mr. Valters—"

"I said she can stay," Walters said in the voice that even Roosevelt had come to know meant "no argument."

With a muttered remark in German, the nurse left the room, shutting the door behind her.

"Do you have any political plans for '39?" Maggie asked Walters loudly, all the while jotting down a note on her pad.

Walters began a long-winded, canned speech, during which he read what Maggie handed him.

That woman is wearing a disguise!

Walters looked at her quizzically. Maggie nodded emphatically.

I'll have her checked out, Walters wrote back. *About Fischer, have you told anyone else this information?*

Maggie shook her head.

Walters wrote again, still continuing to speak on his future political career.

Don't. I have no idea who I can trust anymore.

What can I do? Maggie wrote.

Suddenly they both looked at each other. The heavy footsteps of the German nurse could be heard, finally walking away from the door.

Meet with Braddock and find out what you can, He might be involved. But be careful! If Braddock is the Masque—he's very dangerous!

Shouldn't one of your people do that?

I told you! I can't trust anyone!

What if he won't see me?

Walters leaned over to whisper,

"Then my office will issue you the necessary clearance. I wish I could do more, but I'm stuck in this damn bed, And I'm afraid that without any solid evidence concerning this 'Brotherhood' organization.... Well, you can imagine what the President's reaction would be."

"What if I could get proof?" Maggie whispered.

Before Walters could reply, the door was thrown open with a crash. The Advisor glared angrily at the nurse, but Miss Stahlberg was armed and ready for him.

"Miss Virth, your fifteen minutes is up!" With a commanding gesture worthy of an opera, she ordered Maggie out.

Walters gave Maggie a rueful, little-boy look. "I can't fight doctor's orders. Sorry. I look forward to reading your article."

Maggie stood up. "You'll be the first to see it, Mr. Walters!" She clutched her notebook to her like a reporter with a scoop.

As Maggie turned to leave, she saw the nurse's eyes go to her notepad, then to Walters, who had nonchalantly spread his blanket over the notepad he had been using.

The nurse glared at Maggie and, for a moment, Maggie wished she had her pistol. But, since she couldn't fire a gun at this strange woman, she fired a phony smile instead, then walked out.

CEREMONY OF FALSE HOPE

Agent 13 was locked in a small, cold, empty room painted stark white. It had no window exits, other than the small door he'd been fc to crawl through. It had no feature of any that his eyes could grasp.

He had no idea how long he'd been in the unnervingly featureless room when there was a crackling sound behind him. Whirling, 13 that the far wall of the small room was on *fire!*

13 ran to the small cell door and pounded on it. But—even as he did so—he knew it was a futile gesture. No one would come.

The flames grew in intensity, though there nothing in the room to feed them. He huddled by the far wall, then it, too, exploded into flame. Then the third wall, and the fourth— unt cringed in the center of the small room, the place not ablaze.

Walls of heat seared him. The flames flared from all sides, send-ing the stench of burning flesh—his own!—to his nose. He pleaded to consciousness, to end the excruciating pain his own innate strength kept him aware, thi screaming in horror, as the flames spread ove body. He saw his skin bubble and char, slough off his raw arms in sheets.

The white-hot flames engulfed his legs, carbonizing them until there was nothing left but burned bits of bone.

He could no longer hear his own screams....

Suddenly—silence. Gentle, cooling wind ...

13 was back in the subdued light of his stone chamber. The Jinda-dii sat cross-legged next to him, regarding him calmly.

"You see, Tredekka, the ultimate terror is inside your own mind."

13 looked at his arms and legs, then lay back, gasping with relief. Mental torture. The Jinda-dii was an expert at

it. He was, after all, the designer of the Helmet of Truth—a diabolical device 13 remembered from his youth—and from just a few days before, at China White's "office" beneath a New York dive, the Brown Rat.

The Helmet of Truth could reproduce electrically what the Jinda-dii could produce with his own extraordinary mental powers.

Agent 13 felt savage rage well up inside of him. But he quickly repressed the urge to kill his tormentor. The Jinda-dii was the highest of the Serpentine Assassins. He would know what 13 was thinking and could instantly send the Agent on yet another journey to the unspeakable hell of Primal Fear.

"You still have a high tolerance for fire, Tredekka," the Jinda-dii was remarking with detached interest. "I remember that, from your childhood. But there are, of course, three other Primal Fears."

As the Agent looked into the Jinda-dii's face, a hideous transformation began. The teacher's skin turned brown and scaly, his eyes became dark slits, his eyeteeth lengthened into fangs. The hissing reptilian head swayed, its tongue flickering out.

His heart pounding, 13 slowly pulled his legs into a crouching position and crept backward, away from the pallet. Then, behind him, he heard another hissing sound.

13 peered back over his shoulder. He was surrounded by cobras! King cobras, the most intelligent and deadliest reptiles in the world! Their hoods spread, the snakes were ready to strike. Slowly, the slithering reptiles closed in on their target, their great, scaly bodies undulating toward him in hypnotic motions.

The Agent knew how to catch a cobra—lure it into striking at one of your hands, then grab it by the neck with the other.

Simple in principle, difficult in practice.

The first serpent struck, narrowly missing the Agent. He grabbed its head as it lunged past. The creature hissed horribly as the Agent crushed its skull with his bare hands, then threw the lifeless corpse away with a shudder.

The second serpent closed in.

Agent 13 had a sudden flash of perception. This is an illusion! He'd been hypnotized again!

13 stood stock still in the snake-filled chamber, an almost sneering smile of condescension on his lips. He was in control now. He would not again fall prey to an illusion!

Then he felt a whoosh of air like a whip streaking past, the sharp sting of two fangs entering the flesh of his leg. Pain shot through his body. His muscles contracted in convulsive spasms. He couldn't breathe.

13 saw an arrow whiz toward the cobra's hideous head as it reared back to strike again. Then the snake twisted and writhed in the throes of death.

Through the pain of his own approaching death, 13 saw the blurry images of three robed acolytes removing the other cobras with forked sticks.

An instant later, the Jinda-dii slammed him to the ground and injected antivenon into him.

13 heard the Jinda-dii murmur, "You must learn to distinguish illusion from reality, Tre-dekka," as he slowly faded into unconsciousness.

When Agent 13 awoke, his first sensation was remembered pain in his leg from two small puncture wounds. Looking up, he saw—of course—the ever-present Jinda-dii.

"You thought you were safe in the realms of illusion, did you not, Tredekka? Perhaps you are. Did you ever stop to think of that? Perhaps I am nothing more than illusion—perhaps this Shrine, everything ..."

"Then perhaps I will surrender," 13 said wearily. "I will die, then it will not matter."

"No, Tredekka, you will not surrender as long as there is a single ray of hope. It is not in your nature to do so. And as long as you live, you shall see that ray. I will make certain of it. Therefore you will be mine for as long as I want. You will not be killed, nor will you die by your own hand. But, I can assure you, you *will* be broken!"

13 closed his eyes. He could do nothing now but wait.

The Jinda-dii made a sweeping ges-

ture to the ground on which 13's pallet rested.

Sitting up the Agent looked around. It was familiar. It was the scented garden.

His heart ached. Long years ago, he had stood in this garden with the woman he loved—China White. Tredekka was the only name he knew then, and she was Carmarron. As the flowers in the exotic garden bloomed, so too did their love. But then he had discovered the "Truths." He learned of the central dark core of the Brotherhood. He learned that everything he had been taught to believe was a lie.

For long months, he kept his new knowledge a secret from his mentor. He continued to advance in his studies. Believing him to be one of them, they taught him the arts of torture and assassination. They taught him the arts he would someday use against them.

Always, he watched for his chance to escape. And then it came. But he could not go without her. And so, here, in this scented garden, he and his beloved Carmarron made plans to flee together.

Then, "Wait for me here," she whispered. "I must get my things. Then I will return."

His love for her overrode his good sense and very nearly cost his life. He counted the minutes, knowing how long it would take her. Then he began to grow uneasy. She was late. ... .

Still he did not leave. He could not

go without her. Only when the figures in black—the assassins—appeared did 13 admit to himself that, yes, she had betrayed him. He lingered a moment longer, secretly hoping to die—death seemed so much easier than to live knowing she had given him to them.

But, 13 already knew his mission, and her betrayal just confirmed it. It was to destroy the Brotherhood and everything it stood for.

Agent 13 ducked away in the dark and fled into the snow-covered mountains surrounding the Shrine. Hours turned into days as he trudged through the white landscape. Then a blizzard closed in, and it took all of his skill to survive. But finally, even his will to continue eroded. Lying in a snowbank where he fell, he wrapped himself in illusory warmth and gave himself up to sleep.

His dream was one of great horror. He saw Itsu, the evil divider and slayer of Tog and Nof. He saw the Triad that controlled the Brotherhood of good destroyed, but he also saw hope....

The dream shifted. He was in a sunny villa in Sicily. His body had been completely healed of its frostbite. His mind was clear. Standing over him was a grinning man with Chinese features. The man who had saved his life more than once. The man whose body had long ago been torn apart by sharks. Ray Furnow....

The dream shifted again. Or was it a dream? Was it reality? He was back at the Shrine.

And then, China White appeared, bearing a pot of tea. She set it between the Jindi-dii and 13. Moving with elegant grace in her silken kimono, she knelt down beside them to pour the tea.

Agent 13 stared at her, breathless with longing. This was how he had remembered Carmarron— young, innocent, beautiful.... Their hands touched under the transparent china cup. She looked into his eyes, and he knew that nothing had ever changed between them.

As she rose and began to walk away, 13 found himself rising, too, but, after a quick, shrewd glance from the Jinda-dii, he sat back down.

"Life goes in circles," the Agent remarked, sipping the perfumed tea.

"It is the ceremony of false hope," the Jinda-dii replied. "In the last minute, I have reminded you of the one great pleasure in your life. A pleasure that could still be yours...."

"What do you mean?" Despite himself, 13 could not keep a catch from his voice.

The Jinda-dii smiled. "Ah, there you see, Tre-dekka? You hope—still! It is impossible to torture one who has no hope."

Suddenly, it was dark—totally, absolutely dark. There was no sound, no wind, no light—only blackness. 13 felt the floor beneath his feet. It was curved upward slightly, as if he were standing in the bottom of a giant bowl. Its texture was smooth, cold, and hard to his touch—polished marble or perhaps metal.

Then he had another sensation—that he was not alone. Something was with him in the darkness, something evil. It was silent. . . waiting.

He sniffed the air. There was no smell. Reaching out with his senses, he tested the space around him. There were no vibrations, save for his own. Yet something told him he was being stalked in the darkness.

A chill shook him. He fought to get a grip on himself, knowing well what this was—the test of the Primal Fear of Darkness.

Something leaped at him!

He lashed out at the blackness—

—nothing.

There it was, behind him!

He lashed in another direction—

—nothing.

He began to move. . . .

Suddenly he was slammed to the floor by a powerful, clawlike object. Its stench was bestial, nauseating. He struck in its direction—

—nothing.

He felt a warm, sticky substance running down his face. He tasted it. Blood.

Frantically, 13 whirled about the blackness searching for anything. Even the horrid monster of his imaginings would have been welcome compared to this nothingness. And then the feeling of being watched

passed. He was alone. Absolutely alone in the blackness. This is madness, he thought suddenly, coldly.

Feeling his way along the floor, he began to investigate the room. Following the floor carefully, he concluded that the room was indeed circular. He discovered that he could crawl perhaps thirty yards in each direction before the upward pitching of the bowl-like enclosure became too steep.

Suddenly he felt "it" again. Its fetid odor approached like a cloud of death. It seemed to be searching. ... 13 lay flat on the curved surface, trying to be a less obvious target. But then—out of nowhere—it attacked. Grabbing his arm, it yanked with a sudden, violent force.

13 screamed in agony as his bone was snapped from its socket—cartilage and muscle tore, while tendons snapped like rubber bands. The "thing" disappeared into the darkness, carrying with it 13's left arm as a sort of gruesome trophy.

13 went into shock. The blood flowed from his mangled shoulder. Ripping his clothes, he hastily constructed a rude tourniquet to stem the flow of blood. Then he stumbled downward. ...

And came to hole in the surface.

13 fought against the mists of darkness closing over him. He felt about the edge with his hand. A hole cut in the floor, about four feet in diameter. He put his hand in the hole. He could feel no bottom. He yelled down into

hole. Seconds ticked by, then he heard a faint echo. But it was so faint, so distant. Did it come from his own mind?

This was a way out—but would it lead only to death? Wasn't he bound to die anyway? What did it matter? Hope came the voice of his master. Hope.

Minutes ticked by. He waited, trembling in fear. The bleeding stopped. The pain in his arm had vanished. But he didn't notice.

Nothing was real to him. Nothing but the darkness around him and the hole .. .

The Primal Fears. He had faced three of them— fire, reptiles, and darkness. There was one more— falling.

13 could sit in the darkness forever or he could ease himself into the hole, into the next unknown plane of existence.

Then he felt "it" again, coming back for him. He didn't move, there was no use.

A slimy, fetid clawed hand caressed him, tor menting him, prolonging the inevitable. He struck at the empty air as its rotted breath filled his nostrils. It was everywhere, nowhere. It began to suffocate him with its nearness. He couldn't breathe.   .

Crawling slowly to the edge of hole, he hesitated. Then, suddenly, he couldn't stand it any longer. The horror was too ghastly. He let go, slid ing through the hole...

As he plummeted into the darkness, he realized that it didn't matter if it was illusion or reality. He had made the decision for death.

He had surrendered.

A scream rose from deep inside of him as he fell, a scream of pain and anguish.

From somewhere deep in the nothingness came echoing laughter. "He is mine! He is mine!"

FURTIVE MOMENTS

The desk lamp shown brightly on the blueprints for Dr. Fischer's Lightning Gun. The light reflecting off the blue diagrams bathed the darkened area in cold, sinister hues.

China White stood in front of the massive desk. Beyond the bright beam of the lamp, she couldn't see to make out any details of the hooded figure who sat before her. She could only see his eyes, when he looked up at her.

"The capture of Agent 13 was worth the minor failure in the matter of the *Normandie*. And, you did bring Dr. Fischer in as well," the Masque said. His eyes gazed at the woman who stood before him. She was so incredibly beautiful....

"Remarkable how quickly you recovered from your wound," he added softly, his gaze lingering on her left shoulder.

"The miracles of medicine," China responded coolly, smiling slightly at the lust in the eyes that stared at her. So—even the Masque was human. That bit of information might prove valuable someday. "It's ironic that he thought I was the Masque when he died."

"Died?" The Masque's eyes glittered. "You haven't been kept informed—13 is very much alive."

"Alive?" China's composure wavered.

"He's been returned to the Shrine."

China stared speechlessly at the seated figure. He was amused to see that she was so distraught. So she was still emotionally involved with this man. She would have to be returned to the Shrine for "re-education" after this mission.

"There are those who believe you are dead as well," China said coldly, aware that she had revealed too much of her inner feelings. Deep inside, she

feared this man as she feared few others.

Behind his hood, the Masque
smiled. "Soon, the entire world will
know that I am very much alive." His
eyes returned to the blueprints again.

China said nothing. She stood mo-
tionlessly, hoping he would say something more about 13 but not daring to
ask.

"That is all," the Masque murmured,
without looking up.

Turning, China walked, somewhat
unsteadily, from the room.

Finishing with the diagram, the
Masque glanced at the first draft of
a script he had written. Clearing his
throat, disguising his voice, he began
to read the text from his second—and
final— ultimatum. This one had to
play well, for an entire nation would
eventually hear it—after the investigation into the latest disaster....

BACK IN THE FOLD

The Jinda-dii saw the strange irony of the scene being played out before him. Two men sat facing each other, staring into each other's eyes. One was Itsu, the Hand Sinister. The other was Agent 13. One possessed the decomposing face of death. The other, the bloom of life. But the living face was dead, devoid of will. While the dying face was very much alive.

The Hand Sinister suddenly turned his bright, black eyes upon the Jinda-dii. "I read your thoughts, my friend. You are right, this body is dying once more. Shortly, I shall be transported for *Juvita-ta*. But that will happen only when it is safe ... or when it is absolutely necessary."

The Jinda-dii bowed. His thoughts had betrayed him and caused an embarrassment.

There was no movement or sound from Agent 13.

"As for this one," Itsu continued.

"His gaze is dull. Is he ours?"

"Completely."

The Jinda-dii looked at the man who had once been known as Agent 13. His face was sunken and sallow. Though completely well and undamaged—the loss of the arm had been illusion, nothing more—in his eyes was the look of a man who has surrendered. Gone was the spirit, the fight, the defiance. Gone was any trace of the Mlidnight Avenger.

He was Tredekka.

The Jinda-dii was overwhelmed with sadness. Though proud of his success—hadn't he broken the best agent the Brotherhood had ever aroduced?—he couldn't help but contrast the magnificent specimen this man had been upon arrival with the dull-eyed wretch who sat before them.

Itsu had no such qualms. "Will he carry out my mission?"

"Yes. He will carry out any mission.

He has consumed the *mantha*," the
Jindi-dii answered.

"Good." Itsu turned to Agent 13.
"Look at me, Tredekka." The man's
eyes raised reluctantly to the leathery
skull before him. "Your mission is to
slay the woman who was your companion, your associate, your friend.
She is getting much too inquisitive.
She is too near the truth." Itsu smiled.
"When the deed is done, Tredekka,
you will wake up. In your normal
mind, you will behold the terrible act
you committed."

Tredekka nodded.

Itsu turned back to the Jindi-dii.
"You have power over him?"

"Yes."

"Even in his normal mind?"

"No matter where he is, what he is
doing— when I call, he will obey,"
the Jinda-dii said with pride.

Itsu nodded in satisfaction. "After
he has suffered to the fullest," the
Hand Sinister said, "we will call him
back to our service."

WORDS TO SQUIRM BY

As Maggie Darr had suspected, her reporter ruse didn't work when she attempted to gain access to General Braddock. As a result, she was forced to turn to Kent Walters's agency, who supplied her at his orders with the necessary papers.

But the young man who handed her the phony identification papers for Sara Sheldon, investigator for the National Security Council, made it painfully clear to her that she was operating on her own. If anything went wrong, Kent Walters would deny ever having heard of her. Even the National Security Council wasn't in the habit of intimidating high-ranking generals.

In the days that followed, Maggie did her research, trying to find out as much about the disasters and General Hunter Braddock as she could. In particular, she was checking up on the quick flash of insight she'd experienced when talking to Kent Walters in the hospital. As she had expected, disturbing patterns began to emerge. Not so much with the general, but with the disasters themselves.

At the Montana train crash disaster, for example, Maggie discovered through persistent phone calls and research, that there had originally been five helium-carrying tank cars attached to the train behind the passenger cars. Only two showed up in the Masque's film. Only two had been found in the wreckage.

There were also three people missing whose bodies were never found, though all were believed to have been consumed in the fire that followed the collapse of the trestle into the canyon. One of the missing was Dr. Richard Taylor, a physicist, noted for his work in helium and other lighter-than-air gases.

Odd, thought Maggie—Dr. Fischer disappears on board the *Normandie* in the midst of what might have been a disaster. This Dr. Taylor vanishes in the train disaster....

Quickly, she turned to the list of those killed in the Westron factory explosion and in the crash of the *Hindenburg*. Sure enough, the names of several scientists were on both lists. In each case, no remains had been discovered. That could have been explained by the resulting fires, of course. But might there have been another reason? Had anything else disappeared in these disasters, its loss carefully concealed, as appeared to have happened to the missing helium cars?

As Maggie reached for the phone to contact Kent Walters with her new suspicions, she reflected that undoubtedly General Braddock— China White's sometime escort—could shed additional light on the subject.

"General Braddock," the officious-looking female investigator began, "you have the option of reporting honestly to me here, in this informal inquiry, or being summoned officially to appear before the full board...."

"Inquiry into what?" the gray-haired Braddock *** p 60 or so. demanded.

"Inquiry into the Westron factory incident. I must warn you that if you are brought before the board, it will damage your record, regardless of the outcome. We have enough evidence—"

General Braddock leaned back in his chair, eyeing Maggie angrily.

"Who the hell do you think you are, barging in here and threatening me?" Maggie steeled herself. She was bluffing, and if she didn't play her cards just right, she would spend the next twenty years behind bars. Or worse. She recalled Walters's words to her in the hospital—*if Braddock is the Masque—he's very dangerous!*

"I'm with the National Security Council," Maggie said, "and with the backing of the highest authority—the very highest, General—I am conducting an investigation into the Westron factory explosion and other related events. Information has implicated you, General Braddock."

"Balderdash! What kind of information?"

"*I'm* the one conducting the investigation here, sir. But I will say it is substantial, otherwise I wouldn't be here."

"I'll give you five minutes, Miss Sheldon," Braddock growled, "then get out. As for Kent Walters, you can tell that bastard that he doesn't frighten—"

"Certain 'objects' were discovered missing after the Westron explosion. You failed to mention these 'objects' in your report of the incident."

Braddock's already red face went splotchy, with patchy circles of white in his heavy cheeks. He glared at Maggie without answering.

Maggie glanced inside a file folder, then referred back to the pad of paper in her hand.

"One of the projects Westron was working on was the development of a new, secret fighter plane. Several prototypes had been built. These outperformed anything the Germans have in the air. After the explosion, no trace of the plans or the prototypes were discovered in any of the wreckage. The Westron people were told that, in the interests of national security, they were to keep their mouths shut. Now, however, they have become convinced that it is in the best interests of national security to talk.

"What do you believe happened to those planes, General?" Maggie asked coolly.

Braddock swallowed. He looked deflated, like a balloon that has lost its air. "I'm sure your boss has drawn his own conclusions, but I suspect sabotage."

"But no trace of the planes was found. Don't you mean they were stolen?"

"No comment," Braddock muttered.

"Why didn't your report mention that?"

"Because it's a radical theory, damn it!" Braddock exploded. "How the hell do you steal thirteen damn airplanes? We have no evidence, no suspects. The last thing we wanted was a witch hunt. What with this talk of weird characters in masks—"

"Surely that wasn't the only reason," Maggie said, eyeing him sternly.

Braddock shifted in his seat. "Well... there had been problems with securi-

ty at Westron. Suggestions had been made that things needed beefing up a bit." "Who made these suggestions?"

"Hoover at the FBI. His boys are always coming by and telling us how to run our operation. They're annoying as hell."

"So what was done to tighten up security?"

"I made my recommendations," Braddock blustered. "I assumed the matter would handled."

"Was it?"

"I can assure you that those responsible have
been—"

"In fact, they weren't," Maggie interrupted firmly. "How did the explosion affect the project?"

"It set us back only a year. At the most."

"I see." Maggie pondered as she made her notes. The General was obviously guilty of gross incompetence, but whether of anything more remained open. He seemed to be admitting this all very freely—almost too freely. . . .

Glancing up, Maggie noticed a framed picture of a woman and two girls, presumably his wife and daughters, hanging on the wall behind him. By all reports, he was a happily married man.

"Tell me, General Braddock, are you an opera lover?"

Looking startled at this abrupt change of subject, Braddock snorted. "That screeching and yowling?

Fat women in plate armor carrying spears?"

"Then how is it that you have been covertly meeting the noted operatic soprano, China White?"

Braddock's face went from splotchy to livid. "Th-that's a personal matter!" He rose to his feet. "You are stepping beyond your bounds, Miss Whoever-you-are! Tell your boss that. Any further questions concerning Westron, I will answer at your damn inquiry. But I will not be strong-armed or black-mailed by Walters or anyone else. Now Set out."

"But, General—"

"That is *all*, Miss." The General turned and scowled out the window.

Maggie gathered up her papers and left. Was his behavior due to the fact that she had discovered a tawdry little affair or was it because of something else?...

The pieces were slowly fitting together.

THE SERPENTINE ASSASSIN

Everything was familiar to Tre-dekka. Even the street felt familiar beneath his worn shoes.

It had been a long journey from the Shrine, one that had taken him thousands of miles, across countless borders. He remembered little about the first stages—they had kept him drugged. There were none who knew how to reach the Shrine. Few who knew how to find their way back once they had been there. Tredekka knew that this wonderful secret would be given to him, however—as soon as he had completed his mission.

But, for now he was back in Washington, walking through the streets that he knew so well, even though they were in a life that he recalled as something that happened to someone else. The garish colors of neon splashing across the damp walls and pavements—once this had given him some small enjoyment, he recalled. Once

he had found time, even among his larger concerns, to appreciate such things. But no longer.

Everything was now categorized into four classes. Those that would help him to commit the murder, those that were of neutral relevance, those that might interfere with his mission, and those that might actively hinder him if he were not careful. Nothing else mattered.

Mentally, he rehearsed the murder he was about to commit. It would be simple. He knew his victim and he knew her habits. Simple and savage. Yes, savage. Very savage. His place in the highest circle of the Serpentine Assassins— the *Jinda-Gol* —would then be assured.

He would need proof, something that would show the Jinda-dii that he had acted without passion, without mercy. Tredekka smiled. He knew what that proof would be. He would bring the Jinda-dii the woman's head. That, as nothing else, would prove his unquestioned loyalty. He would, once again, be recognized as their best. His would be the example for those beneath him to follow.

And there were many beneath him. Very like the sacred stairs that led one up to Itsu, the Hand Sinister, there were stairs leading to the Jinda-dii, the head of the Serpentine Assassins.

At the very bottom, not even really upon the stairs, were the *Jinda-Hai.* Hauled from the streets that were their homes, these wretches would do anything for money, drugs, liquor, or a combination of all. Typically, they would make quick brutal hits that appeared to be robberies or actions in a gang war. They were expendable. If a Jinda-Hai returned alive from his mission, it was a bonus.

Above the Jinda-Hai were the *Jinda-Nuul.* Their expertise was death in the night. They were poisoners—adept with ancient powders that caused heart attacks, viruses that would be transmitted in drinking goblets, and small, venomous creatures that would work their way into warm beds.

Above the Jinda-Nuul were the *Jinda-Gaan*— masters of persuasive killing. Practioners of brutal torture and ritual mutilation, they caused deaths that were meant to be examples to others and so the killings were done in such a way as to gain as much publicity as possible. The theory behind this was that a single, effectively executed murder could stem or spark an entire revolution, start or prevent a war, bring law or chaos to a fledgling society.

At the apex were the *Jinda-Gol.* Well practiced in the arts of the other Jinda, the Jinda-Gol had a repertoire all their own. They were masters of deception and disguise. Able to change their appearance radically, they could murder with impunity, knowing that no eyewitness would ever be able to identify them.

Tredekka had been raised as a Jinda-Gol. This had given him the skills that made him such a deadly enemy as Agent 13. His abilities to melt into society and assume other identities had frustrated the Brotherhood's plans dozens of times.

Tredekka's capture and "re-education" had caused many of the Brotherhood's agents throughout the world to breathe a sigh of relief. Once again he was in their fold. Once again he was on a mission of their calling. . . .

Tredekka stood silently in mist-filled air of the winter night. Before him was the warehouse, the end of the journey that pulled him halfway across the world. A few feet and a few minutes away, his mission would be complete.

He began to walk briskly toward it.

Inside the warehouse, Agent 13's Washington lair, Maggie Darr sat at 13's old desk, poring over her notes. Her meeting with Braddock had yielded some interesting facts about not only the general, but also the Westron disaster itself.

Braddock had definitely been guilty of a cover-up, but the question was why. Was it to save his face or was it because of direct involvement with the Brotherhood?

And China White? Was the General just a worried man caught in an affair that could wreck his marriage? Was he a minion of China's? Was he her boss?

Maggie knew that there was one way to tell for sure whether or not Braddock was a Brotherhood agent. That was with the Seer Stone—the ancient stone that Agent 13 had stolen months earlier from the dead hands of a Brotherhood agent in Istanbul.

Its purpose was identification. Every top-ranking Brotherhood agent had an invisible tattoo branded on his palm. This tattoo was a number contained within the Brotherhood's symbol, "Omega"—meaning "the end." The tattoos were invisible to every known detection device except one—the Seer Stone. It was the only device that would absolutely confirm a person's membership in the secret, ancient organization.

The knowledge that Agent 13 was in possession of one of the stones had come as a severe blow to j the Brotherhood. Thus, Agent 13 had hidden it carefully, telling no one—not even Maggie— where it was.

If only I could find it, Maggie thought longingly. Then, somehow, I could find a way to check Brad-dock. It would yield the "proof she needed of Braddock's complicity to bring to Walters!

The phone rang.

Maggie answered, not saying a word—as had been Agent 13's habit.

"Miss Wirth, the National Security Advisor says to tell you that we have received a new filmed threat from the Masque. It is being examined by our department and the FBI. There will be a high-level meeting in two nights at Walters's country estate to discuss it. Please plan to attend."

"Yes, of course," said Maggie.

"Next, Mr. Walters has asked me to relay the information that there is a survivor of the *Hindenburg* disaster you might be interested in questioning regarding your theory—"

"Where?"

Giving her the hospital and the room number, the impersonal male voice clicked off.

Walters was starting an investigation of Braddock, she knew. But he was dubious about its outcome. Braddock was a long-time friend not only of FDR's but of J. Edgar Hoover's as well. Without absolute proof, Walters emphasized, their investigation of the popular general would be squelched instantly.

Hanging up the phone, Maggie stood for a moment, lost in her thoughts. Suddenly, she jumped and whirled about.

"Who's there?" she called out.

There was no answer. Of course not! She was in a well-protected room in an abandoned warehouse on a floor that didn't exist! How could there be anybody here? Shrugging, scolding herself for her irrational fears, she sat down.

But she couldn't shake the feeling. She was being watched—she knew it!

She had known it for weeks. The feeling had been especially strong when she had gone to interview Walters at Bethesda. She had experienced it once again while returning from her interview with Braddock. 13 had taught her the art of recognizing and losing a tail.

She tried all the tricks—stopping to look in store windows, going in a building and exiting through the back, even climbing out a restroom window. But she never saw anyone, and the feeling was always there. Now, here it was, haunting her in the supposed safety of 13's secret lair.

Then she heard the whine of the warehouse's freight elevator. Someone was coming up!

Maggie glanced at her watch. Someone coming to an abandoned warehouse at 1:36 a.m.? Her heart leaped as she scrambled to the back room and grabbed her Thompson submachine gun from the rack.

Maggie knew that the Agent had built escape passages into the lair, but she had never had reason to find out where they were. She had to wait and,

if necessary, shoot her way out.

Heart pounding, she heard the elevator stop at the fourteenth floor—the floor above the lair. Then, she heard the special gear being manipulated, the gear that no one on earth knew about! It dropped the elevator down to the unmarked thirteenth floor! There was no time to reach the elevator doors and be ready as they opened for whoever it was. Better to find a safe and hidden spot inside the lair itself. See who it was first.

Maggie quickly switched off the lights, taking refuge behind a large wooden desk in the chemistry lab. Anyone coming through the secret entrance would be silouetted by the light from the fake office by the elevator.

She was the one with the advantage, Maggie knew. But fear of the unknown intruder began to well inside her. Her palms began to sweat, and her fingers fumbled as she fitted the steel drumload into the bottom of gun. The click of it being secured eased her fright a bit, but not much. She leveled the gun at the doorway.

The elevator doors slid open. The floor boards creaked slightly as someone stepped from the elevator into the fake office.

Maggie's finger poised on the trigger.

Wood creaked in the anteroom of the lair— someone walking across the floor. She started to tense her finger, aiming at the doorway ...

Nothing happened.

For several heartbeats, she sat there, gritting her teeth, trying to keep her hands steady.

Then, the secret door to 13's sanctum flew open.

She almost fired, but 13's disciplined training told her—find out who it is, why they're here, if possible.

She waited for someone to step into the light.

But as abruptly as the door had opened, it closed again! She could see no one. Nobody had entered!

Then she heard the elevator start again! This time going back up to the fourteenth floor!

But why? Was it being sent up by the same person, to deliberately throw her off guard? Had someone come and—thinking the room empty-left?

Slowly, ever so slowly, the elevator reached the floor above and stopped, giving its usual recognizable clatter of machinery.

Breathing a sigh of relief, Maggie lowered her Thompson.

Then, a man stepped into the light glowing hrough the anteroom door. His head turned slowly as he looked around. She jerked her gun up again.

"Maggie?" the man's voice called. He raised his hands. "Don't shoot."

Maggie froze, not believing her ears. It couldn't be! He was dead beneath the Atlantic! No one could have survived that explosion, not even him!

"Maggie? I know you're here."

What could she do? The Brother-hood had tricked her before. What better way than this? But his voice. Having been around 13—a master of deception—she knew how difficult it was to mimic a voice... and this was perfect! It had to be him! But how?

Tears flooded her eyes. She had accepted his death, absorbed the pain she never wanted to experience again. And now he stood before her.

She had to know.

Rising to her feet, Maggie reached out to flip on the lights, her Thompson cradled and ready to send whoever-he-was to the afterlife for good....

"Maggie!" he said as he moved toward her, arms outstretched.

It *was* him! She was one of the few to have seen his real face and this was it! Or else it was a clever disguise....

"Stay where you are and keep your hands where I can see them," Maggie commanded, ignoring the tears that rolled down her cheeks.

"Good girl," he said approvingly. He stopped. Then, hands in the air, he turned and walked slowly over to the bookshelves.

"What are you doing?" Maggie demanded.

"Settling your nerves," he replied as he pulled an old book out from the upper shelf.

Keeping his movements slow and deliberate, both hands visible at all times, he opened the book, letting her see inside. The book was fake! It was really a box. Inside, glittering like a priceless gem, was the green Seer

Stone.

13—was it he?—lifted out the Seer Stone and placed it on the desk. Then he backed away so that Maggie could get to it.

She walked over and picked up the stone. She held it to her eye, gazing through it at the palm of his right hand, which he displayed for her.

13!

Even if the Brotherhood had faked the tattoo on a bogus agent, only the real Agent 13 would have known where the Seer Stone was hidden.

Dropping the Thompson, Maggie ran into his arms, sobbing, as the tension, the fear, the loneliness ran from her.

"I'm sorry!" She buried her face into his shoulder while holding him tightly. It wasn't proper— the display of open affection for him was a clear violation of all of the unspoken rules he had forged in their alliance. But the man she loved was back from the dead!

She rested in his embrace as his strong arms wrapped around her, tightening in a passionate hug.

They kept tightening.

"Hey," Maggie teased, squirming, "you don't know your own strength—"

She looked into his eyes—and realized something was terribly wrong! His eyes were glare ice, cold, pitiless.

His grip tightened.

"No!" Maggie gasped in horror, struggling for breath.

She kicked, twisted, and fought, but none of her movements had any effect on his trained, killing embrace.

She felt the air being squeezed from her lungs. Her body tingled, not with passion, but with death. She was growing weak. The room began to spin, and darkness closed in. His steely expression, cold and murderous, was her last sight.

THE DEAD RETURN

When his victim had ceased moving for several moments, the Serpentine Assassin relaxed his grip. Holding the carcass of his prey, he felt her neck for a pulse.

There wasn't one. Good.

He let go of the corpse. She slid from his arms to the floor, landing like a pile of rags. He pulled out a sharp knife from his pocket and knelt down beside her.

Suddenly, a dark veil lifted within him.

The essence of who he was flooded back into Tredekka as if a dam had broken somewhere in his soul. He looked down at the corpse....

"Maggie?" he whispered in agony.

Her vacant eyes stared sightlessly at the ceiling. She had died a brutal death. She appeared to have been crushed!

13 looked at the knife he held in hands. He began to shake, torn by horror and confusion.

Looking around, he saw that he was in his Washington lair. But how did he get here? Frantically, he sorted through his memories—the last thing he remembered was piloting the lifeboat from the *Normandie* into the path of the torpedoes. ...

Or was it? He seemed to remember perfume, a soft voice, dark, sultry eyes, hands pulling him from the water....

Then he knew! The Brotherhood! China had rescued him and given him to the evil organization he sought so hard to destroy! And they had turned him into a murderer!

Frantically, 13 tried all the lifesaving techniques he knew to restore Maggie to life. Again and again he felt for a pulse, to no avail. He put his ear to her cold lips, but there was no breath. Finally, in grim silence, he closed her beautiful eyes forever.

The Brotherhood had claimed another life, this time that of his most trusted assistant. Assistant? Who was he kidding? he asked himself bitterly, gently gathering the limp body into his arms and holding her close. How often had he longed to do this when she had been warm and alive, but he had forced himself to think only of his mission.

13 remembered the first time he had met her, how he had saved her from mobsters' bullets inside a church after she had avenged the death of her young fiance by killing one of their kingpins. He remembered the years she had helped him in his crusade againt the Brotherhood. She loved him, trusted him, and what had he done?

Killed her in the most horrible way possible-crushing her to death in his arms.

"Please forgive me, Maggie!" he whispered, bending his head to kiss her one last time. Then, he saw something—a small sliver, a tiny needle-little more than a thorn—protruding from behind Maggie's ear. The Agent knew what it was.

A blow dart.

A hand touched his shoulder. 13 froze. His eyes went to the hand. It was adorned with jeweled rings. Raising his eyes, he looked into the face of an old man. At least it seemed to be an old man. Or maybe not. The man's features were Asian. His age might have been somewhere between forty

and sixty. His eyes were those of a sage.

"Ray Furnow!" the Agent gasped. "You're alive?"

"It seem everybody think everybody dead around here," Ray said, nodding at Maggie's lifeless body. "We all think you dead, but Brotherhood bring you back to life as Serpentine Assassin."

Taking a small vial of brownish liquid from his pocket, he handed it to the Agent.

"You drink."

"What is it?"

"Too long to explain. But it counteracts oil of fire that you have been made to drink."

The Agent downed the foul-tasting liquid.

"I watch Maggie for many weeks now," Ray continued, "ever since she come off boat. She not know, of course. But I had thought you or someone else might come looking for her and the Seer Stone."

"Then why did you let me do this to her?" 13 asked angrily.

"The only way to bring you out of the hypnotic trance was to make you believe she is dead."

"*Believe* she is dead ..." 13 echoed softly.

"I know well the ways of Hand Sinister and Jinda-dii. I know Serpentine spell lifted when you kill woman you love."

"Why?"

"You feel more for others then yourself. Pain and sorrow much greater, as you can see. He wants to punish you, wants you to hurt very badly. You be easier for him to get next time."

Ray Furnow knelt beside Maggie. "But you must be careful, for until you die and go to next plane or the Jinda-dii dies, he will be able to control you."

Ray pulled the tiny dart from Maggie's neck. Holding it up to the Agent, he said, "Laced with powerful drug, makes person seem dead. Only use small amount. She come 'round soon. She have one hell of a hangover, though."

Agent 13 was silent for a while, staring at Maggie thoughtfully. Then, he glanced at Ray.

"What did you mean—'next time' and 'control me'? How?"

"Many ways possible, but particulars not known. Rest assured, my friend, the Jinda-dii has key to your soul. It buried deep in your brain." He shrugged. "Maybe a gesture, a word.... You will become Serpentine Assassin again!"

"Am I—" "—safe now?"

Standing up, Ray pulled the Agent to a small square cut into the wall. It was actually a window that looked like a normal brick from the outside. Ray pointed to the deserted street below. There, in the middle of the pavement, were two black patches of ash.

"Jindas," said 13.

"Yes. Sons of fifth wife make certain followers cease to follow. Contained within Jindas was most probably key to bring you back to Shrine."

Agent 13 looked curiously at his old friend. "Who are you?"

Ray grinned. "You know who I am. Balding Chinese man on the run from many wives—"

Agent 13 snorted. "Can it! Even that accent's phony! You know more about the Brotherhood than anybody—even me. Join me for good! Help me fight them!"

"The more you understand, the more you will understand," Ray said. "Did not Jinda-dii say that?" He shrugged again. "If not, he should."

"This is serious—"

Ray's grin vanished. "So am I, my friend. I no more capable of direct acts of aggression than Hand Sinister capable of direct acts of kindness. 11 save lives. I do not take them. I can make shields for you. But I cannot make spears. I can make fireworks. But not guns."

"But the Jindas on the street?" The Agent gestured. "Fireworks didn't kill them!"

"The work of my sons, who have sworn themselves to protect me. They are effective, but they are not the deadly assassins the Brotherhood has produced.

"A day shall come, my friend, when you will understand the reason for what occurs. For now, you must remember that you are the bridge, and in you lies our hope. Your solitude builds strength. Strength you will need on final day."

Ray knelt beside Maggie. "For now, take this as a sign that I am with you in other ways."

Ray's hand touched Maggie's neck in strange, gentle motions. Slowly, she began to move. Her eyes opened. Looking up, she saw 13....

A wave of horror, fear, and rage contorted her face as she leaped up. "Maggie—"

13 took a step nearer, only to be knocked from his feet by a flying spin kick. Lifting her foot, Maggie was about to smash it down onto his neck when he reached out, caught her ankle, and flipped her back to the floor.

"Ah, see," said a laughing voice, "I tell you, she have terrible hangover...."

13 couldn't answer Ray. He had his hands full. Grabbing hold of Maggie, he tried to pin her arms to her sides.

"Maggie! Stop! I can explain—"

She bit him.

He loosened his grip inadvertently, and she twisted away, staggering to her feet. He ran after her, caught her, and finally, exhausted, she sagged limply in his arms.

"I won't hurt you," he said softly. "Believe me!"

"Then let me go!"

"I'm going to let you go. But you have to relax."

"I'm relaxed." Maggie caught her breath with a sob.

He let go of her.

Instantly, she lunged for her Thomp-son.

He didn't stop her.

Grabbing the gun, she spun around and trained it on him.

"Now I want answers!"

"Ray, explain it to her," the Agent said calmly.

No answer.

"Ray?" 13 looked over at where Ray had been standing.

"What kind of trick is this?" Maggie sneered. "Ray Furnow's dead! Shark bait! You should remember! He died trying to save you—"

"Ray!" 13 yelled.

There was no reply. Looking around, 13 saw the room was empty except for the two of them.

"Well, then, I guess I'll have to explain it to you myself. Do you mind if I sit down?"

Maggie kept the Thompson leveled. Smiling at her, Agent 13 sat down. "You've no idea how great you look right now, Maggie Darr," he said softly. "Now, the last thing I remember was being dragged, half-dead, into an airboat...."

"And so," he concluded, looking at her earnestly, "there is every possibility that I might turn into a Serpentine Assassin again—at any time. I might try to kill you again. Can you live with that?"

He sighed, looking down at his strong hands. "If not, I'll understand. You can leave now, go somewhere where I can't reach you. I'll never bother you again."

Maggie had, long ago, laid down her machine gun. Now, in answer, she rose and walked up to him . . . and into his arms.

The lamps burned late in the lair that night as Maggie Darr told Agent 13 of her investigations into the disasters.

"The newspapers reported China White dead. She hasn't been seen—"

"She isn't dead," 13 said, his tone strained. Maggie—watching him closely—noticed this and sighed. "I remember seeing blood. You wounded her, when you shot her from the ship, but only in her shoulder."

Maggie changed the subject. "The Masque has issued a new ultimatum. There's a high-level meeting at Kent Walters's house day after tomorrow. I got a call from his office earlier tonight."

"I'll go there," he said. "You go to the hospital and interview that *Hindenburg* survivor."

Sighing wearily, Maggie laid her aching head on the table. "This is all so dark, so foggy!" she said. "Do we have a chance?"

"Hope, that's all we have," said Agent 13, wondering why that one word should give him a sudden shivering sensation.

GRIM REPORTS

On the first landing below the golden stairs that led to Itsu's towering throne in the Shrine, the Jinda-dii knelt. Raising a sharp dagger high in the air, he cried out, "The penalty for my failure is death!"

There was no answer from above. Bowing, the Jinda-dii put the dagger to his abdomen, preparing to disembowel himself.

The Hand Sinister heard his servant's words but paid no attention to them. His eyes were locked on the cathode image of the Masque that showed on the immense screen that hovered in the air above him.

"Do not worry, your Holiness," the Masque was saying. "Our plans are too far advanced for Agent 13 to be any threat to us. In fact, we might be able to use him."

"Your thoughts are clear to me," the Hand Sinister said. "I am pleased. Continue."

Itsu made a ritual sign. The Masque returned the gesture. Then the black and white picture swirled away.

The Jinda-dii had been waiting for this moment to rip his stomach open. Itsu's attention was now fixed upon him. The Jinda-dii ordered his arms to drive the dagger deep into his stomach. His arms, blocked by an outside force, refused to obey the order.

"Suicide is the act of a coward," the Hand Sinister said.

The Jinda-dii looked up at the being who held sway even over his own body. He tried to respond, but, as his hands were frozen, so too was his tongue.

"You may well die a hideous, screaming death," Itsu continued, "but it will not be by your own hand." The Hand Sinister gestured. "Go now. Continue your duties until you are summoned. Carry with you the knowledge that your work was good, but mighty forces interceded to save the Agent."

With that, the Jinda-dii's muscles went limp. The dagger clattered to the floor, as did he.

Moments later, he gained full control of himself and began his long trek down the staircase. Death might have been preferable, thought the Jinda-dii, than to have to live on under the spectre of failure.

THIRTY-SIX HOURS TO DOOMSDAY

It was well for the law enforcement agencies that Agent 13 had not turned his superior talents to criminality. As it was, he was able to penetrate Kent Walters's heavily guarded house with only two things—Senator Tom Hanover's face and ID card.

Several years ago, Senator Hanover had faced complete and total ruin. Compromising photographs arrived in the mail, showing him engaged with several young women in certain recreational activities that neither his wife nor his public would condone. These photos would be sent to the papers and his family unless Hanover agreed to vote a certain way on matters of defense.

Hanover was innocent. It wasn't him in the pictures—it was a man disguised as him. But he knew no one would ever believe him. After all, politicians were notoriously corrupt. Yet, he was an honest man. He could

no more sell his vote than he could sell his soul. Alone, without anyone to turn to, Hanover took a gun out of his desk drawer and contemplated it thoughtfully. One bullet in the head and he would never live to learn if he might ever be tempted to give in.

Then a man had stepped into his office through a door the senator had thought was locked. He was a strange man with a nondescript face but intense, penetrating eyes.

"Put the gun away, Senator," he said. "If you've got the guts, we can fight them—you and I."

And thus Tom Hanover met Agent 13, and thus began a terrifying race against time through some of the worst parts of New York City that ended in the capture and conviction of a local mobster with ties to War Department contracts. Hanover's reputation was saved. Indeed, he became a hero when his part in the daring capture was revealed.

But he had learned enough to know—as did Agent 13—that this hood was but a pawn in a bigger game. And so Tom Hanover became one of 13's most loyal associates in his fight against the Brotherhood. When 13 learned that Hanover had received an invitation to Kent Walters's top-level meeting, he had called the senator and asked to assume Hanover's identity. The senator had been only too pleased to comply.

The police officer at the door was apologetic. "I am sorry, Senator Hanover, but because of certain extraordinary circumstances, we have been ordered to frisk everyone for weapons."

"What circumstances?" the Agent asked casually, submitting to the search gracefully. The cop did his job well. It would have taken an expert, however, to discover the cigarette lighter that turned into a small pistol with explosive bullets.

"Sorry, sir. I can't discuss it."

"Sure!" Agent 13 shrugged, but he was uneasy. This seemed an extraordinary precaution, when everyone here tonight was here by invitation only.

"Thank you, Senator Hanover," the cop said, motioning him on into the foyer of Walters's home. As more uniformed officers took his overcoat, 13 looked around, absorbing his surroundings. Walters's country house was both tasteful and lavish, he noticed.

Though the Agent's disguise came so near to perfection that even Tom Hanover's own family might not have recognized him, 13 had not had time to perfect the little gestures, facial expressions, the hundred other things that made up Tom Hanover. Therefore, he had to avoid contact with anyone who might know Tom intimately.

As the other guests filed through a corridor to the large study where the meeting was to be held, Agent 13 stayed at a table in the living room, apparently absorbed in a number of files.

"Tom, my boy!" a voice shouted.

Agent 13 looked up. The speaker's face was soft, his face fat and jowly. His eyebrows were raised in an expression of perpetual surprise, and his mouth hung half-open, awaiting Hanover's response, giving him a dull-witted look that contrasted with his keen, intelligent eyes.

He was Chester Hallet, one of the men who had helped Tom Hanover rise in his political career.

Agent 13 sensed danger. What on earth was Hallet—purely a behind-the-scenes farmer politican—doing at a meeting to discuss national security? Rarely was the Agent caught unprepared, but he had never questioned Tom Hanover concerning Chester Hallet. 13 made a casual response, hoping to gather information as well as keep his conversation to a minimum.

"Chester! I never expected to see you here!" The Agent awaited a response, hoping Hallet would explain his presence.

But Hallet only looked at him shrewdly. "Figured *you'd* know—if anyone! C'mon, Tom. Don't play it close! What's the reason behind all this?"

13 hesitated, making it appear as if he was considering whether or not to reveal his information. Suddenly, they were interrupted.

"Excuse me, gentlemen," a police officer said. "But the meeting is about to commence."

Nodding to Hallet, Agent 13 rose to his feet.

"Guess we'll all find out soon enough," he said with a short Hanover laugh as he walked into the large study that had hastily been converted into a screening and lecture room.

Looking at the group gathered there, however, 13 wondered himself—why had all these diverse people been invited? There were highly placed government officials mingling with pig farmers like Hallet. There were top lawmen rubbing shoulders with military brass. 13 was growing more and more uneasy. He knew that if the Masque wanted this whole group of people dead— dead they'd be, in a matter of minutes.

There was nothing he could do but find a seat in one of the chairs lined up before a lectern. Behind the lectern

was a movie screen.

When all were seated, the ambient voices hushed as the door on the far side of the room opened and the Kent Walters, National Security Advisor, entered. He was seated in a wheelchair, pushed by a young, muscular attendant. Though the recently wounded official was doing his best to appear on the mend, 13 noted that a doctor and a nurse hovered at a discreet distance.

The fifty or so guests gave Walters a round of respectful applause. A weaker man, having escaped death by a hair's breadth, would have gone on leave of absence or even resigned. But Walters kept going, seemingly filled with a new resolve.

"Gentlemen, let me begin by assuring all of you that I appreciate your coming tonight. We have done everything in our power to provide the best security available for all of you." An uncomfortable silence blanketed the room. "And, in an effort to minimize the risk, we will keep this meeting short. We'll start with the screening."

As the lights in the room went out, the loud whirr of a projector tickled the air.

The crisp gray lines of a small battle cruiser— the *USS Trent*—appeared against the darker gray of the ocean and sky. It remained in their view for several moments, then the camera shifted its angle to show an incredible-looking weapon. While many faces present registered skepticism, even amazement, at the sight of the weird contraption, Agent 13 stared at it grimly, recognizing it easily—Dr. Fischer's Lightning Gun!

13 gritted his teeth. The Brotherhood had constructed the full-size version of the device much faster than he had expected! Even as he watched, the Lightning Gun fired. The *Trent* exploded in a ball of flame.

At that moment, a hooded face appeared on the screen, superimposed against the burning ship. Whispers of surprise rustled through the room among those who had not seen the Masque before. The enigmatic figure spoke.

"Again I have perpetrated disaster. Will you continue to ignore my demands? Oh, I know you are searching for me. But you have been for weeks, with nothing to show for your best efforts! Fools! Do you think you will be more successful this time? You don't even know who I am! You don't know where I am! And, you do not have one single lead!"

No one moved, everyone in the room apparently transfixed by the mysterious shrouded face on the screen.

"No, you do not have any clue as to who I am. Maybe you have seen me on the street. Maybe some of you even know me! But what must concern you now is this question: where am I going to strike next? I think, by this time, you accept that I can strike wherever and whenever I choose.

"I assure you that it will be in your best interests to give in to my demands. As you have seen, I am willing to kill for my cause. Are you willing to die for yours? Are you willing to sacrifice your sons, your daughters? Are the voters who control your destinies willing?"

The baiting voice was silent for a moment. Then, in a quiet tone, almost tender, the Masque continued. "Sometimes, it takes men of great strength to admit defeat. I ask that you show that strength tonight. I do not want to kill more."

Many of those in the room, 13 among them, looked around uneasily. As if reading their minds, the Masque went on in an amused tone. "Do not worry. You need not fear an attack upon your meeting. It is my belief that you men present here, and you alone, can advise President Roosevelt to listen to reason.

"And now—my warning: During the State of the Union Address on Tuesday night, your President will announce that he will immediately dismantle all aggressive weapons in the United States, or I will unleash a horror upon this nation the magnitude of which has never been seen before!"

The film end flapped and the projector's bright light glared on the screen. The room lights came on. At first, there was silence, then a low rumble of muffled conversation began. A tall, thin man with grayish skin, gray hair, and silver wire-rimmed glasses stepped up behind the lectern.

13 didn't recognize this man, who spoke with a thick, German accent. "Before ve get on with this meeting, ve vill be taking one precaution. Ve vill be checking your fingerprints before you are allowed to leave."

The murmur in the crowd turned to outrage.

"First searched by cops," muttered one, "now this! Do they think one of us is this Masque?"

"Who are you?" A challenging voice called to the speaker.

"I am Dr. Arthur Eisenstaadt, Department of Forensics—"

"Take your brownshirt tactics back to Germany. We don't have any use for them here!"

There was scattered applause. The combination of the terrible threat, plus the nervousness of everyone in the room was apparently finding an outlet. Seeing things getting rapidly out of hand, Kent Walters wheeled his chair to the front.

Picking up a gavel, the pale government official pounded on the lectern with remarkable strength for a man so frail. Those in the room slowly fell silent.

"Yes, Senator Hanover?" Kent Walters said coldly as the disguised Agent 13 rose to his feet.

"Mr. Advisor, it will take hours to analyze every fingerprint in the room! Surely you don't suspect one of us of being the Masque? Everybody here knows everybody else. I say that each of us vouches for everyone in the room he knows!"

There was a muttering of approval. Then the crowd was silenced once more by the insistent hammering of the gavel.

"Silence!" Walters glared at them sternly. "There is one element to the assassination attempt at my agency's headquarters that was intentionally left out of the newspaper reports. One other person was present in that room. One other person survived—Agent 13."

The room buzzed—incredulous, curious, disbelieving, dubious, scornful. So that's it, thought 13 grimly.

"What's that got to do with us?" cried out one.

Walters went on. "As you may have heard, the Agent is a master of disguise. He could very well have taken on the appearance of any man in this room. In our first encounter with him, he drugged the GS-7 projectionist and took his place. I believe he is in this room right now. And if he is, he knows something—something vital about this case. We want to talk him—now!"

Agent 13 frowned. What was Walters*s game? He knew that 13 was trying to help them with the case—he had implied so to Maggie. He knew 13 wasn't involved in the assassinations. Why was he trying to nail him?

"Tom Hanover" stood up again. "Why are you after this Agent 13?" asked the disguised Agent 13. "Aren't there more important things we should be doing?"

"Because it is my belief that Agent 13 is the Masque," said Kent Walters.

Agent 13 sat down. Not often in his lifetime had he been stunned, but this new twist had taken him completely by surprise.

"Bear in mind that I have no evidence that Agent 13 really is the Masque," added Walters. "But, as I said, I believe he possesses valuable information that he has not passed on to us. So let me lay down a challenge to him, if he is indeed in the room with us"—the National Security Advisor's eyes scanned the crowd—"Agent 13, come forward, and I personally offer you immunity from all prosecution. If you are indeed aligned with the forces of good, then you are in good company in this room. Step forward that we might know you."

13 knew now that no one would protest being fingerprinted. He could have been prepared for this situation by matching Hanover's prints by any of a hundred techniques, but he had not foreseen this drastic turn of events. One by one, he eliminated each idea he had.

Walters sighed. "Let it not be said that I did not give Agent 13 adequate opportunity to ally himself with us. We can only assume, therefore, that he is against us. And, if he is in this room, we will capture him!"

With that, two efficient-looking Army lieutenants stepped up and gestured to the crowd to form a line from the front desk, extending past windows overlooking a beautifully manicured garden. Agent 13 stood next to a grumbling Hallet.

13 had to get out of here! Precious time would be lost while he endeavored to explain to the authorities who he was and what he knew. His freedom was the only chance these people had against the Masque!

He hoped he could escape without killing anyone, but 13 had long ago sworn his Code of Death—if his mission was imperiled, he would kill if necessary for the greater good.

Reaching into his pocket, the Agent felt the solid weight of an expensive cigarette lighter—a real lighter, not the gun. Unscrewing the fuel reservoir of the lighter, 13 pulled it out as he brushed up against a beautiful curtain. Then 13 "accidentally" allowed a thin stream of the fluid to dribble down the fabric. Glancing around, he made certain no one was looking at him. Hallet was scoffing with the Secretary of State over the proceedings. He didn't believe any of it—not this Masque, not this Agent 13.

Good. No one was paying any attention to him. 13 pulled out a pack of cigarettes and proceeded to light one.

Inhaling deeply a couple of times, he then bent down to adjust his shoelace. Swiftly placing the cigarette next to the dampened curtain, he stood back up. The line had advanced forward by several feet. Casually, Agent 13 moved away from the curtain. He had calculated that it would take about one minute for the fabric to catch.

The line moved slowly. Agent 13 glanced at his watch. His eyes caught a small stream of smoke curling up from the curtain. One man, near the window, sniffed, frowning. He looked around

"Fire!"

Within seconds, the chemically-treated curtain material had burst into flames! The flames spread quickly. As everyone in the room reacted to the fire, 13 ducked back against the wall and inserted one end of a bent paper-clip into an empty electrical socket. Again checking to see that no one was watching him, he jammed the other end in with an abrupt flick of the back of his hand. Sparks flew. The lights in the room went out.

In a high, shrill, panic-stricken, Tom Hanover voice, Agent 13 shouted, "My God! It's the Masque! We're trapped!"

Drawing his lighter-gun, 13 fired several shots into the air. That was all that was necessary. Within seconds, everyone was shouting "The Masque! Another massacre! Burned alive!"

In vain, Kent Walters pounded his gavel and yelled for calm. In vain the guards endeavored to stop the surge of terrified men that rolled over them to the door.

Within moments, all was over. The only sounds that could be heard were outside Kent Walters's house—the calls for chauffeurs, the slamming of car doors, the roaring of engines and the shouts of the policemen who were searching the grounds for assassins that didn't exist.

The fire was quickly brought under control, Kent Walters was helped back to his bed and given a sedative after the excitement, and Agent 13 vanished into the night.

MAGGIE'S SCOOP

Maggie Darr entered room 417 of the Georgetown University Hospital. A nurse, following her, switched on a soft light. Maggie's eyes fell upon the contours of a body swathed in bandages like a mummy. A moaning sound from down the hall made her shiver, while the ubiquitous smell of hospital disinfectant, which seemed to also carry the mixed emotions of fear, desperation, joy, stung her nose.

Maggie sat down opposite the mummy in a tubular hospital chair. Much to her surprise, the mummy's eyes were wide open. Maggie leaned forward in the chair.

"Mr. Hendricks," said the nurse, "this is Kimberly Wirth, the reporter from the *New England Journal*. The doctor said she could stay five minutes. Do you feel up to talking to her?"

"It's extremely urgent," Maggie said, her voice soft with pity she did not have to feign. "I must talk to you about one aspect of the *Hindenburg* crash...."

The mummy nodded and the nurse left the room, softly shutting the door behind her.

"Now," Maggie began, "I need to know if you remember anything about a scientist named—"

"The cause can be summed up in one word," came a weak voice through a hole in the thick gauze wrapping. "Hydrogen."

"I beg your pardon?" Maggie said, blinking.

"Hydrogen!" snapped the mummy irritably. "If they had used helium, there wouldn't have been any explosion, and I wouldn't be a burned sausage. The blasted ship was designed to run on helium, but the U.S. banned all helium sales to Germany and so they used hydrogen."

"Yes," Maggie murmured, "but

about the scientist— His name was Wulfgang Heidelberg. He was an important airship designer, traveling on the Zeppelin. His body wasn't located, and I was wondering—"

"I'm considering suing, you know." The mummy's voice overrode hers. "Over the helium. You can print that...." His bandaged fingers fumbled for a buzzer by his side.

"Here, let me," Maggie said, leaning over to help.

"Thank you," the mummy said. Maggie pressed the button. A soft buzzing sound echoed down the corridor.

"Is there something I can do for you?" Maggie asked.

"The nurse will take care of it," the mummy answered.

The door to the room swung open. Maggie turned slightly—and froze in her seat. Entering the room was the German nurse! The one she had seen with Kent Walters at Bethesda! Instantly, Maggie's hand went for her purse.

"No, no, Miss Darr. I know you are not going for your lipstick."

Turning, Maggie saw the "mummy" holding a Luger with a silencer attached. The bandaged figure motioned. "Put your purse on the floor, slowly. Now, Miss Darr, have no illusions. Bodies come and go out of this hospital every day. Yours would be just one more."

"I don't understand," Maggie said, forcing herself to maintain her cover. "I'm not this Miss Darr! You've made a mistake! I'm Kimberly Wirth! This—this nurse can identify me!"

"I most certainly can, Miss Maggie Darr," said Nurse Stahlberg, stepping toward her, one hand held behind her back. Slowly, that hand emerged. Light flashed off the long, thin needle of a syringe as she grabbed hold of Maggie's arm....

Slowly, Maggie Darr became aware of the low whine of engines, the rumble of propeller blades, and the bumping of minor air turbulence. It took her a few moments to collect her senses. Then she remembered! The nurse! The mummy! A stinging sensation in her arm....

Opening her eyes, Maggie stared up into the face of the most terrible creature she had ever seen! It was a giant! In the semidarkness of the interior of what Maggie realized was a transport plane, the giant's features seemed horribly distorted and unreal.

For a moment Maggie wondered if she were going mad. Could this being really exist? Was it something she dreamed? Was she still dreaming?

Then she saw the giant turn around and heard him shout something into the rear of the aircraft.

Maggie struggled to sit up, but she discovered that she was strapped to a stretcher.

A cigarette seemed to dance in the air like a firefly. Then the cigarette's owner emerged from the darkness of the plane. Even in the poor light, there was no mistaking that stunning beauty....

"Who are you, darling?" the voice asked.

"I'm sure you rifled my purse and know exactly who I am!"

"Ah yes, Kimberly Wirth, ace reporter for the *New England Journal*,' China White replied.

Filled with hope, Maggie drew a deep breath. Had China White ever seen her? Hurriedly, she thought back. She and China White had seen each other on the *Normandie,* but there had been the smoke, the shooting—and Maggie had been disguised as Mrs. Plotkin... Maybe China didn't know her!

"Look, I don't know who you are or who you work for, but you're not going to be able to keep the *Hindenburg* sabotage secret for long," Maggie said, trying to keep up her cover. "If I don't crack this case, another reporter will. Or maybe the police. My editor knows what I was digging for. If I vanish, he's going to go to the FBI. Hoover himself will start looking around in this *Hindenburg* thing."

"Oh? Suppose your editor doesn't live to tell Hoover what story Kimberly Wirth was working on?" China White asked in an amused voice. "Suppose, like you, he has an unfortunate accident?"

Maggie swallowed. She had a feeling they weren't discussing newspaper editors anymore. But she had no choice but to keep on. "There are others who know," she said loudly.

China White laughed. It was a strange laugh, at once operatic, piercing, ecstatic, and joyless. "He trained you well, my dear."

Maggie's soaring hopes crashed. China White was playing with her as a cat plays with a mouse before killing it.

"You love him, don't you?" China White said, sitting down next to Maggie and regarding her with a look that was cool, condescending.

Maggie said nothing.

"Do you think he loves you? Because he doesn't, you know. I think you should resign yourself to exile from his heart forever."

Maggie could not let this woman see her weakness. Tossing her head on the pillow, she put on her best Scarlett O'Hara act. "Ah really don't know what y'all are talkin' about, ma'am. I don't share intimacies with folks I've just met. Why, we've never even been formally introdu—"

China's beautiful face hardened. "The tougher you act, the weaker you will become. We need no introduction. You know me. You've seen me countless times. And each time you have wondered if the Agent loves me still. And, in your heart, you knew the answer. Each time you have felt the absence of 13's love for you, you have felt the presence of his love for me!"

Maggie looked at her coldly. "I don't

know what you are talking about—"

China ignored her. "I am taking you to a place where they have elaborate tortures. They will ask you where his lair is and you will tell them. Oh, yes, my dear—you'll tell them, anything they want to know. But, right now, I'm going to indulge in a little torture of my own. It will, perhaps, be much more painful than even the Helmet of Truth. I will tell you of my affair with Agent 13."

"Keep your dirty little secrets to yourself!" Maggie said, but she couldn't keep her hands from clenching.

"It was at the Shrine." China's eyes stared out through the aircraft windows. The sky was gradually getting lighter. It was near dawn. "Has he ever told you of the Shrine?"

"It has been mentioned in passing," Maggie responded sarcastically.

Still staring into the distance, China went on, as if in a trance. "It was a wondrous place. Truly ancient. Hallowed. I have no idea where it is. It has been hidden for millennia and will probably remain so forever. Its physical beauty is as over whelming as the mystical energy that surrounds it. It is a place of dreams... but it is also a place of nightmares."

China was silent for a moment. Curious despite herself, Maggie listened in pain.

"All societies train women in the arts of seduction, just as all societies train men in the arts of warfare. Some accomplish their tasks better than others. The Brotherhood—the most ancient society on earth—does both jobs superbly. Rare is the man who could resist me—"

"They must have skipped the courses in modesty," Maggie muttered, to keep up her own spirits. Inside—as China had predicted—she was writhing in agony.

China went on. "As a final test of our skills, each of the female acolytes in the Shrine was given a male to attempt to seduce. It was a deadly game, for if the male were seduced, he would be forced to undergo an ordeal of courage in the desert—an ordeal most did not survive. If the female failed, she was disfigured, becoming a grotesque, hidden operative of the Brotherhood. You met one who failed, in fact. Once Nurse Stahlberg was one of the loveliest women in the world. You noticed she was disguised. Little did you guess why...."

China shrugged and snuffed out her cigarette. Then she went on more briskly. "Be that as it may. I was given the most difficult target—Agent 13. For weeks, months, I lured him with every charm I had been taught, plus those natural charms I have developed on my own. He resisted me. Then the unforeseen happened. I fell in love with him. I was about to concede failure when, one day, I looked into his eyes in an unguarded moment and realized that he loved me, too!"

Maggie gritted her teeth, forcing herself to lie perfectly still. This woman must not see her pain!

In China's luminous eyes, Maggie could see that first, innocent love reflected there still, undimmed by time.

China sighed softly. "One night, we met in the garden. We could resist our urges no longer. He held me. We kissed. And then, we started to part. But the priests, who had been watching us, leaped out and caught hold of me, accusing me of failure. 13 lied for me then. He told them I had been successful, that he had fallen victim to my lures long before that night." China smiled.

"He lied to spare my beauty. They took him away and sent him into the desert for his ordeal. Do you see what he did, Maggie Darr? He willingly gave up his life for me. But the gods favor those with reckless courage. One by one, he eluded all the men who hunted him. When he returned to the Brotherhood, he was hailed one of the greatest agents ever. But he knew them, then, for what they really were.

"When he had the chance, he came to me, asking me to escape with him. I agreed, of course. When I went back to my chambers, however, the priests were waiting for me. They offered me a choice—love or power. Agent 13 or the world. I need not tell you which I chose."

"Slut!" Maggie shouted. "He may have loved you when he was a boy, but now he is a man! He may have protected you then, but now you've been disfigured by the ugliness around you! He sees you for—"

The palm of China's hand caught Maggie across the jaw. The pain from the blow brought tears to Maggie's eyes, but she had the satisfaction of seeing the beautiful, dark, luminous eyes of the opera singer glisten with tears as well.

INTRUDERS IN THE SANCTUM

Late that night, the cab left Agent 13, no longer disguised as Tom Hanover, several blocks from his Washington lair.

"Thanks," he said, stepping out and handing the driver a tip.

"Thank you, boss!" the young Chinese driver said, grinning.

By the light of a street lamp, 13 looked at him closely. There was something vaguely familiar about that grin— But before he could say a word, the cab shot off into the night.

"Son of wife number seven, no doubt," Agent 13 said to himself with a smile. By turning up his collar, crumpling his hat, and picking up an abandoned whiskey bottle, 13 turned himself into a drunken derelict. Then, weaving and singing a ribald song, he stumbled down the street toward his refuge.

Coming within sight of the lair, 13's song died on his lips. The American flag was flying over the warehouse!

The signal! Intruders! Someone had broken into the sanctum!

His mind raced. They could have found out the location of his lair from only two sources—Ray and Maggie! He immediately discounted Ray. Mystery man though he was, Furnow had proven his loyalty time and again. 13 trusted Ray now, as he trusted only one other person— Maggie.

Somehow, the Brotherhood must have captured Maggie! And they had made her talk. Bitterly, he cursed them. Maggie was strong. But no one was strong enough to hold out against the Brotherhood's hideous tortures. Even he had succumbed.

At least they had not caught him unprepared. Knowing that someday the secret of his lair might be revealed, Agent 13 had devised a safety measure in the elevator known only to himself. Unless the elevator remained on the fourteenth floor at least thirty seconds before descending to the thirteenth, a small lever would be activitated that triggered a network of defenses. One of these was the automatic hoisting of the American flag on the roof to warn him that the security of his lair had been violated.

Knowing that guards would most probably be positioned around the building, Agent 13 slipped into a tenement house across the street and climbed to the roof.

From that vantage point, 13 could see a black Chrysler stationed behind the warehouse with two triggermen holding grease guns. They watched over the back entrance, where yet another guard hid in the shadows by the frieght elevator door.

Despite the fact that they looked like typical thugs, they were probably the lowly but deadly members of the Jinda-Hai.

Agent 13's mission was delicate. He had to destroy the Jindas without killing the pointer. The one member in the group responsible for "pointing" the drugged Jindas on their mission, the pointer was normally not a member of the Brotherhood, but some recruit from the underworld who was paid well to perform a single mission. The pointer must be inside the warehouse, and 13 wanted the man alive!

Agent 13 was, of course, completely familiar with the area surrounding his lair, including the sewer system beneath the streets. Sneaking though a street grate like a rat, he was able to creep up on the two Jindas guarding the Chrysler from beneath.

Staring up through a storm drain, he targeted one of the Jindas with the barrel on his lighter pistol and squeezed the trigger. The Jinda's head exploded first with blood, then with flame.

As the body collapsed, the other Jinda whipped around. Too late. There was a crack. A second later, the Jinda's flesh turned to flame.

The Agent couldn't see what the guard at the door was doing, but he must have heard the shots. 13 ran through fifty yards of sewer system and emerged on the side of the warehouse. From this vantage point, he could safely observe the third Jinda by the freight elevator door.

Apparently the Jinda had heard the shots, but had chosen to remain in the shelter of the building. This was neither through cowardice nor tactical insight. This was the assignment he had been given. A drugged Jinda-Hai never deviated from his orders.

Knowing this made it easy for the Agent to dispatch his foe. Though the elevator had only one entrance, the building had many. Creeping through a window he purposefully left unlocked, 13 sneaked through the lower floor of the warehouse and caught the Jinda from behind while the man was staring out into the night.

A single shot turned him to ash.

Prying open the elevator doors, the

Agent discovered that, as he feared, the elevator was stuck on the thirteenth floor. Grasping the elevator's steel cables, he began to climb up them.

Foot by foot he pulled himself up. Even to a man of his great strength, this was a remarkable feat of prowess. One floor. Two floors. His arms were growing weak. Three floors. Four... He suddenly heard footsteps enter the elevator car above him!

Then, he heard the loud whine of the engine. The cable he was climbing began to move, pulling him up on a collision course with the dropping car!

Faced with certain death, 13 formulated a desperate plan. With precise timing, he leaped from the cable to a small ledge just below the fifth-floor elevator door.

Seconds seemed minutes as he sailed through the air of the dark shaft. Then, slamming into the wall, his hands grasped frantically for anything! He missed the handle that would have opened the door, but his fingers gained a tentative purchase on the narrow ledge. Looking up, he saw the car descending toward him. Within moments, he would be knocked down the shaft!

With the last strength in his arms, 13 pulled himself up to the door and grabbed the outside lever. But the door, designed to be opened by the mechanical strength of the elevator and not by a mere human arm, moved only slightly.

Desperately, using the adrenaline surge that was flooding his body, 13 pried the doors apart as far as he could. Already he could feel the blast of air pushed ahead of the elevator as it bore down on him.

With a powerful lunge, 13 drove his body between the heavy doors an instant before the plummeting elevator would have sliced him in two.

His heart pounding, the Agent looked down the shaft at the moving freight elevator. Since it didn't have a ceiling, he could clearly see its deadly cargo. There were three men—two Jindas and the pointer. Apparently, they had found what they were looking for. Not losing an instant, 13 drew his pistol and leaped down the shaft into the descending car.

He had one instant to figure out who was who in the dimly lit elevator. The Jindas were probably the two with the Thompsons. The other man was armed only with a pistol.

The occupants of the slowly moving platform neither saw nor heard 13 as he dropped silently through the darkness. The first clue the Jindas had was the sensation of the Agent's slugs tearing through the roof of their skulls.

13 knew he had guessed correctly as he watched flames fill the elevator.

The pointer—a fat, disheveled thug—stared at the burning corpses in horror as the Agent landed lightly beside him.

"Who hired you?" the Agent demanded, shoving his pistol into the man's eye.

"I don't know, I swear!" the man whimpered, trying to squirm away from the flames and the gun at the same time.

"What was your assignment?"

"To find some kinda jewel and then rub out the guy that lived here. Tha-that's all I know!"

The pointer flailed about as 13 grabbed him by the throat.

The scum was probably telling the truth, 13 knew. He probably really had no idea who hired him. Pointers never did. Messages came by phone or through third parties. But 13 had to send a message, and the pointer was his best telegram. When the pointer went to get paid at his drop-off, someone would most assuredly be watching him.

"Where's the jewel?"

"He— One of those guys had it!" The pointer gestured to a pile of ash on the floor.

"Tell your bosses I'll trade the stone for Maggie Darr."

"I don't know who the bosses are! I swear to God!"

"Don't worry. They'll find you. Tell them to meet me at the Palace of Illusion, four o'clock today with Maggie. Understand?"

"Sure! Sure!" the pointer groaned. Anything to get rid of the guy!

Then 13 struck a ring on his right hand hard against the brick of the ele-vator shaft. There was a loud sizzling sound as the magnesium in the special ring ignited. The inside of the elevator, thick with smoke and the stench of the burning Jindas, turned a blinding white as the ring began to glow. Wide-eyed, the pointer let out a terrified shriek.

Gripping the pointer by the neck, 13 brought his burning ring closer and closer....

A moment later, the elevator shaft echoed with a terrible, blood-curdling scream.

When the elevator reached the ground, the pointer dashed to the waiting getaway car, holding his hand over his forehead and sobbing with pain. As he fumbled with the gears, the pointer peered into the mirror. The number 13 was branded forever on his forehead.

The Agent watched as the car sped away. Confident that his message would be sent, he spread around the smoldering ashes in the elevator. His foot hit a large object. Reaching down, he pulled it out. The Seer Stone.

Knowing that he would have neither the time nor the opportunity to move the contents of his lair and that he would never be able to return, Agent 13 began the grim task of burning the entire structure to the ground.

SLEIGHT OF HAND

When Harry Houdini died on Halloween in 1926, an era of American life came to an end. Attacked by the clergy, wounded by the Depression, magic began to die a lingering death. Sleight of hand became an almost forgotten art. The days of the grand illusion were past, and escape artists vanished from the scene, replaced by the more foolhardy but less artful daredevil.

If magic were truly dead, as many believed, then the Palace of Illusion was its tomb. Here, Blackstone had pulled rabbits from hats, the great Marmaluke had pulled fire from air, and numerous less famous illusionists had mystified, thrilled, and amazed. But the Depression, which had dimmed everything that glittered in America, had forced the closing of the Palace of Illusion.

Nobody was enthusiastic about entering the structure where were housed "The Cauldron of Horror," "the Casket of No Escape," the "Box with a Thousand Locks." Thus it was that the great structure stood, with seats and props intact, as it had on the night of the last show . . . except for some writing over the door, thought to be a curse.

China White gave the scrawl over the entry way an amused look as her agents broke into the building. Magicians? Amateurs, all of them. She herself had not only learned all the secrets in the Shrine, but many that would have astounded even Houdini himself.

"Hurry up," China said irritably, though she knew perfectly well that such things as picking locks put on by banks could not be hurried. She was looking forward to this night with as much anticipation—no, more—than she had looked forward to her debut at La Scala.

Tonight, China White would have everything she wanted—Maggie Darr in her control, Agent 13 at her mercy, and the Seer Stone. Tonight would be glorious....

China brought along all that she needed for success. The six men opening the door were elite members of the Jinda-Gol. She had Maggie Darr—drugged and completely oblivious to what was going on—slumped in the back seat of the sedan.

China had no doubt that Agent 13 knew what he'd be up against. That left her with one question—What did he hope to gain? Standing on the steps of the Palace, she glanced back at the semiconscious woman in the back seat. Had 13 fallen for this woman? Anger creased her beautiful forehead as she remembered the bullet scar in her shoulder.

She had wanted to kill the woman when they brought her in last night, but the Masque had forbidden it.

"She will be of more use to us alive than dead," he said coldly.

"More use to you, perhaps!" China said, but she said it under her breath. She had seen the look in the man's eyes as he stared at the bound and gagged blonde young woman. China sneered. Two members of the Brotherhood smitten by this little tramp. Whatever she has, maybe we should bottle it, China thought with scorn. Because she wasn't going to have it much longer!

China looked at her watch just as the Jinda-Gol succeeded in forcing the locks. It was three o'clock.

"Get the woman," she ordered one of the men. Bowing, he did as he was told. Dragging Maggie out of the car, he hauled her – stumbling and nearly falling—up the stairs and into the palace behnd China and her assassins.

"13," she called out into the darkness. It was early, but she kenw he was here.... Waiting, hidden in the shadows of the mystical props.

She caught hold of Maggie and pulled her forward.

"I have an associate of your, 13. She's unharmed—so far. I'm here to make a trade."

Still no resoponse. She would have been surprised if there had been one. China turned to the Jindas. "Find him."

The fire in the abandoned warehouse had been a five-alarm blaze, and by the time the firemen reached it it was too late. 13, watching from a distance, saw that it was completely, totally destroyed. Everything in the lair, except for the small weapons and disguise kits that he carried with him, was incinerated—years of research, a large cache of weapons he had used to fight the Brohterhood, an autogryo, and more. Turning away, he went to keep his appointment.

Sitting now in the darkness of the Palace of Illusion, waiting, the Agent sensed an aura of finality about the coming events. All the cards were in his enemy's hands. The Masque had Dr. Fischer's Lightning Gun, capable of reducing its target to ashes. The Masque had Maggie. But if, once again, he could throw a wrenchn into their works, keep htem off balance, present them with the unexpected so they didn't have time to compensate... That was his hope.

Soon President Roosevelt would deliver his State of the Union Address to the nation. Hanover and his other contacts in the White House were endeavoring to find out how Roosevelt would react, but—so far—the President had remained in seclusion. The Agent had strong misgivings. It would be political suicide to allow the Masque's threats and acts of terrorism to be made public. To go along with the Masque would cast the President in the role of a capitulator. But what havoc would be wrought by the Masque if the president failed to respond at all?

As 13 watched the six Jinda-Gol slip into the old building, flanking China White and Maggie, he realized how truly desperate his situation was. He hadn't had time to prepare the elaborate traps that would have been necessary to deal with these overwhelming odds. All he had was a plan.

Two Jinda–Gol guarded China White and Maggie Darr. He knew exactly what their orders would be— shoot the hostage first, himself second. The four other assassins were slowly and methodically working their way through the abandoned theater, checking each row of seats, each doorway. It was clear that they had no intention of trading the woman for the Seer Stone. But then again, neither did 13.

China heard the first gunshot at 3:55 p.m. In moments, her expertly trained agents had isolated the source. It came from the massive storage area in the basement of the theater. China could hear her men whistling instructions to each other in code as they disappeared down the stairs.

The Jinda-Gol slowly worked his way through the storeroom where props from the great magicians of past eras were stacked high on either side. He had determined that Agent 13's hiding place must be in one of two areas. The first area was sealed off by the other two Jindas. The second area was his.

The Jinda-Gol felt no sorrow when he found a pile of ashes—all that appeared to remain of his partner, who had obviously perished by the bullet they had heard fired. Sorrow was not a useful emotion to the Jinda-Gol. He was more concerned with trying to flush out the Agent.

Suddenly, the Jinda-Gol heard a scrabbling sound, the kind animals make when cornered and trying desperately to escape.

That wasn't like 13. The Jinda-Gol smelled a trap. Looking up, he saw a twenty-foot shaft leading to the stage above. At the top of the shaft there was a square of light which blinked suddenly, as if a figure had passed in front of it.

A trapdoor in the stage floor, thought the Jinda-Gol. The kind used by magicians for their disappearing acts.

Someone was up there. The Jinda aimed at the light and fired. There was a gasp of pain, then a scraping sound—like someone opening a door. Hurrying up the ladder leading to the trapdoor, he saw a shadow move above him and guessed what was happening.

He had wounded the Agent and now 13 was escaping through the trapdoor! The Jinda heard it scrape shut.

Whistling the code that meant success, the Jinda arrived at the top of the ladder, directly beneath the closed trapdoor. He reached up, into the darkness, to open it....

Sitting in the dust-covered seats facing the stage and flanked by her two guardians, China White looked over at the groggy Maggie. The woman was barely conscious. Maybe an "accident" would occur. Surely the Masque couldn't hold her responsible if poor Miss Darr tripped and fell, breaking that pretty neck.

One of the Jindas stiffened suddenly. China heard what he had—movement on stage.

"Lights!" she cried out.

A spotlight glared, switched on by one of the Jindas guarding the back stage. China watched curiously as a wounded man staggered out of the wings. Blinded by the lights, he flung his arm up over his face. Then she saw blood on his chest. She saw, too, that he was not one of her Jindas! His clothes, his face. . . .

Leaping out of her seat, she ran down the aisle as fear built inside of her.

Suddenly a Jinda threw open the trapdoor on the stage. Climbing through it, he leveled the cold steel of his Thompson at the wounded man.

"Don't shoot!" China shouted frantically.

But the order came too late. The Jinda's Thompson began to sing, spitting out rounds. Agent 13's body danced for an instant like a marionette, as slug after slug tore through his body in an unending fury. But the body did not burn! So it was true—somehow 13 had managed to get hold of an antitode to the mantha. A lot of good it had done him.

"You fiend!" China screamed at the Jinda-Gol, who merely looked at her with that blank stare they all had. For an instant, she considered killing the assassin for failing to obey her command. Then she forced herself to calm down. It took years and enormous amounts of time and money to train a Jinda-Gol. One did not sacrifice them lightly. Besides, he had probably been following the Masque's orders.

They had no intention of letting 13 remain alive.

Two other Jinda-Gol padded out

from the shadows. They stood motionless on the stage, holding their machine guns cradled in their arms.

Kneeling by the body, China White reached gingerly into the blood-soaked pocket. Her hand emerged. The Seer Stone was in it, covered with the still-warm blood of Agent 13, the final confirmation of all she had feared.

Even though her mission was a complete success, the man she loved was dead. . . . But she couldn't think about that now. Time was crucial.

"Pick up his body and place it in the trunk of the car," she said coldly. Like the Jinda-Gol, she had been trained to keep her remorse and her sorrow bottled up inside of her—at least until she was alone in her room.

Several hours later, at the White House, the President of the United Sates was laboring over a crucial paragraph for his State of the Union Address. Short miles away, at one of the Masque's hide-outs, a dead body lay upon a cold slab.

Peering down at Agent 13's body, the cowled figure of the Masque nodded. One of his men reached down and lifted up the Agent's cold hand. Holding the Seer Stone, the Masque looked at the Agent's palm.

"I see nothing," he growled.

"He's probably using some kind of fake skin," China suggested, trying to keep from trembling.

"I've never seen one so lifelike be-fore. Get me a knife."

Minutes later, the Masque peeled off what looked like a layer of skin from the hand. He held the Seer Stone to his eye once again.

"Ah," he purred in satisfaction. "There is the number 1..." Continued scraping removed a second layer. He held the stone to his eye again.

"A 1 and a—" His voice caught in his throat, then turned into an inarticulate shriek of rage. "A 9! You imbeciles! 19! You have killed a Jinda-Gol!"

Reaching up to the corpse's face, the Masque's hand found the thin, nearly invisible line of the rubber fleshlike mask. Furiously, he ripped it off.

The Masque's grim gaze turned on China White.

"I-I don't understand," China faltered. "Why didn't the Jinda burn up? The body should have turned to ash! And what about the Seer Stone I found?"

"Fake, probably. Another one of *your* tricks, no doubt!" the Masque snarled. "Still trying to protect the man you love?"

"That's not true!" she cried, staring wildly at the body of the Jinda-Gol.

Though the Masque, like all Brotherhood agents, was expert at containing his emotions, his rage was apparent, even through the hood.

"You have failed me for the last time!" he hissed, motioning to two of his Jindas. "Take her away! You know what to do with her!"

He turned back to China, who was deathly white. "What a pity it had to end like this," he said without a trace of feeling in his voice. He watched the beautiful woman being led, struggling, away.

Whirling, he glared at the remaining Jindas. "Where did the others go?"

"To our rendevouz—the cannery—as you told them."

The Masque seethed in fury. "That means Agent 13 is there! With *it*!" His hands clenched. "Find him! Or I'll have your lives as well!"

THE HORROR UNVEILED

Agent 13's eyes slowly adjusted to the tunnel's dim light. The passageways seemed to go on forever, with no apparent direction or purpose. He felt like a rat in a maze.

The lair was far bigger than he had expected, and it smelled strongly of fish—not surprising, since the building fronted as the Sea Breeze Fish Cannery. It covered several acres and employed vast numbers of workers who had no idea what terrible secrets lived beneath their workplace.

Disguised as China's henchman arriving with a group of her thugs, 13 was instantly waved on through by the guards at the outer doors.

Without hesitation, the thugs headed for a door at the rear of the building. They entered one by one, as 13 waited his turn. When it came, he found himself in a small, dirty latrine. There was no sign of the other thugs. His sixth sense told him he was being watched, most probably through the mirror that hung over the filthy sink.

The Agent feigned boredom. Looking at his reflection in the mirror, he pulled a toothpick from his pocket and began to pick his teeth. Immediately the entire room began to vibrate and hum. 13's inner ear told him that the latrine was actually an elevator, moving downward. After several seconds, it stopped abruptly. He opened the door and found himself in the main reception area for a large facility. Several uniformed guards were giving him the eye.

A guard caught his attention. "Where ya been? They're waiting for you in 4B." The disguised Agent disappeared around the corner. He had no intention of going to 4B. Instead, he took the first detour he came to, a roughly hewn stone staircase.

As 13 descended the stairs, he discovered a vast network of tunnels and rooms branching off from them. He kept going down, far into the bowels of the earth, until the staircase finally came to an end in a tunnel much larger than the others. 13 estimated that he was about three hundred feet beneath the surface of the earth.

The sheer size and complexity of the structure told 13 that he had found a headquarters of some kind, possibly the lair of the Masque himself. It must have taken years to carve the tunnels from the bedrock. 13 followed the tunnel downward, until suddenly it came to a dead end.

The Agent faced a pair of huge metal doors— obviously a new addition. It was also the only way out of the tunnel. 13 pressed his ear against the door's plate metal. Even through the thick fire door, the Agent's acute hearing was able to pick up a constant, rhythmic vibration.

13 recognized the throbbing rhythm as a Pratt and Whitney R-2800 Double Wasp airplane engine, an engine so advanced that it was available to the military on an experimental basis only. What would an experimental aircraft engine be doing far beneath the earth's surface?

The lock on the double door was no match for 13's talents. He had already bridged the major security barrier with his disguise. 13 silently slid the door open a crack.

Before him stood a hangar, similar to those to house the gigantic dirigibles at Lakehurst, New Jersey. But the hangar before him was entirely underground, carved from the granite bedrock! Its vast vaulted ceiling rose hundreds of feet above him. But even more amazing than the hangar was the airship contained in it. It was unlike anything 13 had seen before.

The saucer-shaped airship, the length of two football fields, was supported by massive, retractable legs. The Agent counted over twenty of the special Pratt and Whitney engines attached to the craft's sides. Considering the ship's sleek design, he surmised that the engines were enough to give it a considerable forward speed.

The airship's purpose was obvious. Plated with shiny black metal, it bristled with armaments and antiaircraft guns. 13 counted nine experimental-type fighter planes undergoing their final engine checks. How many had already been pulled into the waiting hangar doors beneath the ship?

Through an open, massive door set into the bottom of the craft, he saw a huge version of Dr. Fischer's Lightning Gun, the weapon that could deal instantaneous death to a tank ... and more.

With all of its defenses, the airship would be impervious to attack. Once aloft, it would be invincible—a device of terror.

Suddenly it all made sense—the kidnappings of the scientists, the disasters to cover their disappearances....

13 knew they were all here—Dr.

Meinzner, the helium scientist who disappeared in the chemical factory explosion; Dr. Taylor, the physicist who disappeared in the train wreck; Dr. Fischer, the developer of the Lightning Gun; Dr. Hei-delberg.the airship designer; Manny O'Brian, the test pilot; and Dr. Neilsen, the Nobel Prize winner for chemistry. All had been forced by the Brotherhood to help build this death-dealing airborne monster.

13 shook his head. It was a terrible weapon, but one of these ships alone couldn't be of much use against a nation as large and powerful as the United States. The Masque's plan must be deeper, more subtle. 13 had to find out what it was.

There was one person who might know-Maggie. He had to find her! Deep inside, he was beginning to realize that Maggie's loss meant something more to him than losing a trusted and valued employee.

Even as 13's mind weighed his options, his eyes and ears were absorbing the activities and shouted commands echoing through the vast chamber. It was obvious that the airship was in the final stages of preparation. The Brotherhood was preparing to make its move. He had to have his information quickly....

Charlie Vickers was a petty criminal on the lam. Busted in Philly for a petty rackets operation, he was looking at five to ten in the big house. Charlie was already pushing fifty, so he skipped bail and took off.

Charlie tried to lie low, but word spread quickly—he was hot. Out of money, with no place to stay, Charlie was desperate. So when a Mr. Simons approached him with an offer of work and a place to stay, Charlie didn't bother to ask any questions.

The job seemed simple at first—installing steam pipes through a network of old tunnels beneath the Sea Breeze Fish Cannery on the shore somewhere in southern Virginia.

He noted a lot of people in suits and white lab coats, who looked out of place in a fish cannery, but they didn't ask questions about him, so he didn't ask questions about them.

But Charlie felt increasingly uneasy. He'd I always figured he'd lived as long as he had by steering clear of the big boys. But now he had the feeling something really big was going on here, Charlie didn't know what it was, but he had the impression that these guys weren't to be messed with.

When the tunnels were completed, the next phase began—the construction of a giant cavern, which he later learned was to house a great airship. Charlie received a promotion. He was taken off the sweat detail and given a job in security.

The security job was easy at first. Charlie knew most of the crew in the building. But when work started on the airship, strange people began arriving—military types, Japanese, Germans, Italians. . ..

The job grew confusing. Charlie became flustered. The newcomers cursed him in foreign languages and looked at him as if he were a bug. This didn't sit well with Charlie. No one treated him as second class! But his uneasiness was changing into fear.

Then the prisoners were brought in. That's what Charlie called them at least. They seemed to have brains, but they looked either unhappy or angry most of the time. They were kept under constant guard, and it was obvious that they were being forced to work. Those who wouldn't cooperate were taken to the "special" rooms far below. Charlie was never allowed down there himself, but he had heard the horror stories.

Charlie would have been the first to tell you that he was no angel, but, for all his faults, there was a human side to him. He didn't like what he saw and heard. Even criminals had a code of honor. He was a patriot , and he didn't like all these talking about "Der Fuhrer" when they thought people couldn't hear them. He didn't like the rumors of torture chambers. He didn't like the way some of his coworkders began to disappear, particularly those who complained. Charlie felt trapped.

Maybe somehone higher up sensed a change in Charlie's attitude, or perhaps it really was a tranfer like they said, but Charlie was shifted back to the now-empty utnnels. Here he was told to patrol and watch for anything suspicious. He spent a lot of time alone, watching eh airship take shpae. And as it grew, more of his fellow workers vanished.

How much longer have I got? Charlie wondered as he patrolled the almost deserted tunnels.

Agent 13 stared at the motionless body, sursing. He hadn't intended to kill the young guard. Catching him unasare, 13 had quickly subdued him. Then, using *Shin Gesere* – an ancient form of mind probing – 13 had attempted to search the man's mind for information. The probe was too much for the guard, however. He died quickly of a sudden, massive hemorrhage.

Well, there was no help for that now. Quickly 13 exchanged clothes with the dead guard, then set about ransforming his features to those of the lifeless face on the tunnel floor. Undoubtably the dead henchman whom 13 had replaced earlier had been discovered by now. He would be safer in a new disguise.

As 13 was finishing turning himself into Scotty Cunningham, as the dead guard's name badge said, the Agent heard footsteps approaching. Their deliberate sounds told him that the man coming was older, possibly with a leg injury. Maybe this man could supply the answers 13 needed. The Agent withdrew into a rocky alcove to await the man's arrival.

The approaching winter had made the tunnels cold and damp. Even the hot steam from the pipes couldn't help ease Charlie's bouts with arthritis in his left leg, the result of being "kneecapped" when he came up short on a gambling debt years ago.

Lost in gloomy thoughts, Charlie was just wondering when his "transfer" would occur—the one to the big pine box. . . .

Charlie felt a sudden, piercing pain behind his left shoulder. Reaching back in panic, he felt a man's hand. The strength ebbed from his body as he drifted into unconsciousness.

13 lost no time in probing Charlie's mind. *Shin Geseare* was a powerful force. With it, the Agent unlocked Charlie's subconscious, discovering a lot about the human side of Charlie Vickers. Immediately 13 realized that Charlie was a possible ally. Planting certain post-hypnotic suggestions, he short-circuited Charlie's criminal tendencies. Normally 13 would have spent more time with Charlie, but there was no time to spare. He would have to take his chances.

When Charlie came to, he was confronted by a man who seemed strangely familiar. The face resembled Charlie's arrogant assistant, Scotty Cunningham. He was wearing Scotty's uniform, with Scotty's name badge. But it wasn't Scotty!

Charlie tried to remember how he came to be lying here in the tunnel. The last memory he had was of the sharp pain in his shoulder.

"Who're you?" Charlie demanded.

"A friend," answered 13.

"Oh, yeah? Well, we'll just see about that!"

Charlie reached for his pistol. It wasn't there.

"Where's my gat?" he demanded.

13 held up Charlie's gun. "We can be of use to each other, Charlie."

"How'dya know my name? Where's Scotty?"

As 13 helped the confused man to his feet, Charlie said, "I'm dizzy. What happened?"

"You had an accident, but you'll be fine. Your life's in danger, Charlie. You know that don't you?"

Charlie stared at the Agent in growing fear.

"They plan to kill you within the next twenty- four hours, to toss you away like a used dishrag, just like the others."

"N-no!" Charlie stammered.

"I can help you escape, Charlie, but I need your help."

"What do you know?" Charlie pulled away.

"I know I'm the only prayer you've got, Charlie. Look around you. Jack Yates, Tommy Meyers, Lou Tazaoli—they've all vanished. And you're next. You know too much, my friend. When that airship goes up, you're going down... if you follow my drift."

13 grabbed Charlie by the shoulders. "Take me to the room where they're holding the girl!"

"I can't," Charlie mumbled, trying

to break free of the Agent's gaze, but he seemed to be fighting himself as much as the Agent.

"You can, Charlie."

The voice seemed to come from his own head! It was as if Charlie's mind was nothing but a radio speaker for the stranger's voice!

"No one's allowed down there," Charlie whined, "Those rooms are off limits—"

But the voice in his head said, "Come on, Charlie! You can get down there. And you're going to take this stranger with you. He's a friend..."

The large iron chair was bolted to the the chiseled stone floor. A woman sat upright in the chair, held by tight leather straps around her wrists, waist, and ankles. Securing her head to the chair was a masklike device with a tangle of electrical wires running from its back to a nearby generator. 13 recognized the device—the Helmet of Truth.

Devised by the Brotherhood, the helmet could, through a process of electrical shock and thought inducement, bring to excruciating reality its victim's worst fears. Too much of the "treatment" could lead to permanent brain damage or death. But in skilled hands, it could reduce the toughest hood to a whimpering child.

The woman had passed out. Her motionless body slumped forward, indicating that her "treatment" had al-

ready started. Around her stood three uniform-clad men who, quite clearly, enjoyed their work.

The fat one was called Axel. Sweat poured from his double chin, indicating his displeasure that the woman had passed out. "Revive her!" he commanded a skinny man with glasses. "The Masque said no rest. Bring me the Praxus!"

The skinny man repeated, "No rest! No rest!" as he shuffled off toward a box of tools.

The skinny man was Dr. Natchez, the renowned scientist in the field of missile warfare. He had been one of the top designers of projectile weapons for the army until his disappearance several years ago. He had been kidnapped to design a hellish weapon for the airship. But he refused to cooperate.

Being a man of high conviction, Natchez realized that turning his secrets over to his captors could mean horrible death for millions of innocent people. Try as they might, the Brotherhood couldn't break him. Finally, they decided to make an example of him. The higher-ups recommended the Helmet of Truth. So the rebellious man was placed in Axel's "care," and he was given free reign to "experiment."

It was during his fifth session with Axel that the change in Natchez occurred. In the middle of the most horrible of tortures, the essence that was Dr. Natchez departed. When Axel finally removed the helmet, he was confronted by a blithering idiot of the most vile nature.

Natchez's new disposition amused Axel, who felt that, in a way, he had "created" Natchez. Lexner, the hunchbacked dwarf who was Axel's assistant, welcomed Natchez as someone he could lord it over.

The woman's body jerked spasmodically from a sudden electrical shock. Axel spun to see Lexner turning various knobs on the generator.

"I said the Praxus, not more voltage, you idiot!" he screamed. "Praxus, not voltage!" mimicked Natchez. Shutting down the power, the dwarf fired an angry look at Natchez, but the deranged doctor was absorbed in his assignment. A large smile filled his face as he held up a devilish-looking tool.

"Praxus?" Axel looked at the device. It was a medieval-looking contraption, consisting of a long metal bar with several hooks, a belt, and balance weights. "Good. Bring it here.... Lexner! Prepare her!"

This was clearly a job Lexner enjoyed. He ripped open the waist of the woman's blouse. Her soft white stomach would be the target of the barbaric tool. Enthralled by the woman's soft skin, the dwarf continued to rip her blouse, touching her as he did so. Axel slapped him away.

"Enough!"

Axel grabbed the Praxus and fastened it to the woman's waist. The tips of the hooks pointed inward, the

pressure against her skin regulated by the weights and balances protruding from the front.

Slowly Axel began to increase the weight. The woman started to moan as the pain increased.

"It's working!" yelled Lexner.

"Of course," replied Axel confidently as he continued to increase the pressure.

Suddenly the woman was awake, her piercing scream echoing weirdly from beneath the helmet.

"Shall we start again?" Axel said.

Disguised as a guard, with Charlie in the lead, 13 had no trouble getting past other guards and opening locked doors. The feverish activity everywhere, plus several overheard remarks about the transportation of carts filled with tanked gases, confirmed Agent 13's hunch. The airship would be launched within the next twelve hours.

Suddenly Charlie stopped. "Uh, it's through there," he said, pointing at an unlocked steel door. "But I'm not allowed in this area—"

Reaching out, 13 opened the door. Peering inside, he could see why no one had bothered to lock it—two hulking guards stood just inside.

"Let me do the talking," 13 whispered crisply.

With Charlie trailing along behind, 13 entered the door. The two guards eyed the newcomers suspiciously. The larger guard, who was built like a gorilla, immediately went for his gun.

"Turn around! Neither of you have clearance for this area!"

As he spoke, 13 heard the screams of a woman from a closed chamber off to his left.

Startled, the guard glanced around. Catching a quick glimpse of movement in front of him, he whirled, but it was already too late. Agent 13's fist slammed into the gorilla's throat. The man collapsed to the ground with a gurgle.

The second guard swung his .38, taking a bead on the Agent's heart, but the bridge of his nose was suddenly caved in. Reaching down, 13 ripped the pistol from the guard's hand.

It had occurred so quickly that Charlie was still trying to figure out exactly what had happened when he realized that 13 was gone. Leaping over the bodies of the guards, he caught a fleeting glimpse of the Agent running into the chamber.

Inside the room, the crackling sound of electric ity filled the air as the dwarf manned the controls of the generator.

"More voltage!" yelled Axel as Dr. Natchez s screams mimicked those of the tortured woman.

"Kill her!" screamed Lexner excitedly, reaching for the dial.   . .

Hearing a noise at the door, Axel turned in irritation just as a .38 slug hit him right between the eyes.

13 turned his gun on the dwarf, but Lexner managed to hit the alarm button, then flee the room. Screaming in panic, Dr. Natchez crouched in a corner.

"Maggie!" 13 gasped, recognizing her dress.

There was no reply. The woman had once more fallen unconscious. 13 tried to remove the helmet, but it was bolted in place. He turned to Dr. Natchez.

"Where's the wrench?" he demanded.

Natchez grinned idiotically. "Where's the wrench? Where's the wrench?"

Standing in the doorway, peering cautiously inside, Charlie's eyes grew wide.

"We've got to hurry!" snapped Agent 13. "Keep an eye on the door!"

Hurriedly 13 studied the Helmet of Truth. The machine was building power, and he knew that the next surge might be the last Maggie could stand. He studied the connections. The mass of wires were tightly bundled together. The slightest mistake could cause an electrical arc. Grabbing Natchez, 13 dragged him over to the chair.

"Shut it off!" 13 commanded.

The doctor rolled his eyes. 13 released him, realizing that the idiot could be of no use. He had to do it on his own.

With skilled hands, he started to disconnect the live wires. Suddenly he felt a sharp pain shooting up his leg. It was Natchez. Like a rabid dog, he had sunk his teeth into the Agent's leg. 13 froze, unable to move for fear of arc-ing the wires.

Charlie grabbed the nearest object he could find. Axel called it a Ripper, a razor-sharp instrument that could strip the flesh off living victims. Charlie wasn't versed in its use, but he had no doubt that it could be useful.

Natchez never saw it coming as Charlie brought the Ripper down hard on the deranged scientist's neck.

Charlie wasn't prepared for it when the facial muscles on the severed head continued to twitch. Horrified, he dropped the weapon and retreated to the corner of the room.

13 continued to work quickly. He knew the alarm would soon bring armed guards. His hands were steady, his steely eyes locked in concentration as he channeled his every thought to the cables in his hands. Every wire had a relationship, an interlocking code. Quickly he worked, making the needed connections to reroute the current.

"I hear 'em coming!" Charlie yelled.

Fortunately 13 was done. Gingerly pulling the plug from the rear of the helmet, he freed Maggie from the fiendish machine.

"C'mon!" implored Charlie.

13 quickly unfastened the straps holding the Praxus in place, along with the ones binding the woman to the chair.

"Maggie?"

Still unconscious, she made no reply. Again he tried to remove the helmet. Though free of the generator, it still enclosed her head in its grip. The bolts held it firm. 13 could hear shouts in the distance. Charlie was dancing up and down with fear.

Running to the power box, 13 ripped off the metal panel, revealing a tangle of wires. Quickly he began sorting through the multicolored strands.

"Do you know the way out?" he asked Charlie.

"I helped build this place! I could find my way out with my eyes closed. But if we don't beat it now, every mug in this joint will be after us."

13 touched two wires together. The lights flickered, then suddenly went out, plunging the room and the corridor into an inky blackness.

Lifting the limp Maggie from the chair, he threw her over his shoulder. With Charlie in the lead, they raced from the chamber of horror, leaving only the grim remains of Axel and poor Dr. Natchez as testimony to their visit.

A GRIM SURPRISE

Through the blackness Agent 13 and Charlie fled, the sound of their pursuers' boots close behind.

Charlie had learned the tunnels' patterns through his years of service. While the guards stumbled through the tomblike passageways, Charlie led 13 - still carrying Maggie - twisting upward until the sounds of the Klaxons and shouting guards were merely echoes in the distance.

Finally they emerged onto a level where the lights were still on. 13 brought Charlie to a halt. They would have to slow down now, to move more sedately , as if nothing were wrong. The Agent's disguise and Charlie's presence might enable them to avoid a conflict.

Near the hangar level, most of the workers were busily preparing the aircraft for departure. Anyone who gave them a second look was reassured by Charlie, whom they all recognized.

They walked through the hangar area as quickly as they dared, then were back in the tunnels again. They were nearing the surface. Only the problem of getting out of the structure itself remained.

It was a question that had tormented Charlie. Suspecting that his own days were numbered, he had been searching for an escape route, only to find heavy security at all the exit points.

Higher and higher they climbed. Charlie soon fell behind, the increasing pain in his leg slowing him. Finally he had to call a halt.

"Hey, wait up!" he implored, collapsing against the side of the tunnel. The stranger stopped. Even with the woman slung over his shoulder, he had been pushing on at an untiring pace.

"How're we gonna get out of here?" Charlie asked. "Every guard and his brother will be looking for us at those exits."

"They won't be looking for me - only you and her," 13 replied from the shadows.

"Whaddaya mean?" cried Charlie suspiciously. In answer, Agent 13 simply turned around.

"Jeez!" Charlie blurted, staring.

The face he saw was no longer that of Scotty Cunningham. It was thinner and better-looking.

"What in hell is going on?" Charlie demanded.

"It's unimportant. Where is the nearest exit?"

"Then what?"

"Let me worry about that."

But Charlie worried with good reason. The ascent from the depths had exhausted him. He could have packed it in , here and now, but something about the stranger kept him going. With him we've got a chance, Charlie thought. And any chance was better than what faced him if he stayed in the tunnels.

"The exit?" the Agent pursued, shaking Charlie from his thoughts.

"At the next intersection, turn right. Then up the stairs and jog to the left."

"Where does it go?"

"I think it leads to a secret door in the back of a storage room. The storage room opens into the main area of the cannery. But they'll have guards at every exit - " Charlie stopped in midsentence. The stranger's .38 was pointed at his chest.

"What's this?"

"You're my prisoner, Charlie. The dwarf will recognize you. Put your hands in the air."

"Why, you! I shoulda killed ya when I had the chance." Charlie scowled. "Ya think you'll skate outta here by layin' the smear on me?"

13 pulled the hammer back. "Start walking."

Looking into those intense eyes, Charlie knew the stranger was serious. Charlie's first thought was to make a break for it back into the tunnels, but that would be inviting a bullet in the back. Charlie had a vivid picture of himself lying dead on the cold stone floor.

He started to walk. "Ya think you're a slick operator, don't ya? Ya don't think they'll recognize ya, eh? Well, I got news for ya. If I go down, you and the skirt are going with me!"

13 shoved the .38 into Charlie's back. "Enough talk. Just keep walking."

Charlie did as he was told. As he walked up the stairs, he tried to figure out who the stranger was. Was he a field agent for the feds, a trigger for the mob, or just a hired muscle sent to rescue the moll? Charlie couldn't figure it. All he knew was that the man was a professional, and a good one. But even the best make mistakes, and when he did, Charlie would be ready.

When they reached the top, Charlie could hear sounds from the guard station ahead. There were no lights on here, either. Apparently it was on the same circuit as the lower tunnels. Charlie realized that the moment of truth lay just around the bend.

As they turned the corner, the beams of two flashlights suddenly hit them. There was the sound of clicking pistol hammers. Then a no-nonsense voice spoke from the darkness. "Hold it right there. What are you doing here creeping around in the dark? Let's see your clearances."

The Agent shoved Charlie forward with his pistol. "Call security," he said. "Tell 'em we caught one of the killers and the girl."

"Don't listen to him!" Charlie implored, stumbling forward. "It's me, Charlie Vickers!"

The guards sought his face with their lights.

"It's Charlie, all right," muttered one. His light played on the unconscious girl. "What are you doin' with a broad with her head in a bucket?"

"Yeah, Charlie, what's going on here?" demanded the one with the gruff voice.

Charlie was feeling a little more confident. He knew these guys. He might be able to get out of this after all. "Look," he said, moving forward a couple more steps, "I was workin' below when—"

A phone rang somewhere in the darkness. The gruff-voiced guard answered it. "Yeah?" he said. "Thanks for the tip." He hung up, then turned back toward Charlie. "That's close enough!"

The nervous guard's pistol took a bead on Charlie's forehead. Charlie stopped dead.

"That was a call from down below. Someone's rubbed out the fat man and that crazy old doctor. Now, you just back up nice and easy against that wall until we can figure this thing out."

"Put me through to security," the younger voice said into the phone.

Something hit Charlie from behind, knocking him sideways. Two pistol shots rang out in the darkness. There were two cries, two thuds, and then two flashlights were lying on the floor, their beams staring aimlessly into the darkness.

The stranger laid the woman down on the floor. Grabbing one of the flashlights, he began working on the lock to the door of the storage room. Within moments, it opened. Picking up the girl, he hurried inside.

Using one of the flashlights, Charlie managed to locate a guard's gun. Picking it up, he felt better. So, the stranger hadn't pulled a double-cross after all. Maybe the guy was all right. Charlie followed him into the storage room, slamming the iron door behind him.

A dim overhead light revealed rows of shelves containing canned sardines. "This way." Charlie motioned, hurrying to the end of the room. Here, the stranger paused and pressed his ear against a door. All that could be heard were the sounds of the cannery.

Opening the door a crack, 13 looked through. The smell of fish was overwhelming. Outside, workers were cleaning, sorting, and packing fish in the immense work area.

"No guards," Charlie said behind the Agent.

"Not that we can see," 13 retorted grimly, looking around. "Bring me those smocks," he said to Charlie as he pointed to several fish-stained garments hanging in a corner. Then he laid Maggie on the floor while Charlie went to get the garments.

"Keep one for yourself and give me the rest."

Charlie quickly did what he was told. It was clear to him now that the guy really was trying to help save his life. He would obey orders.

The Agent rolled Maggie up in the smocks until she was nothing more than a pile of rags. Then he slipped his own arms into the remaining garment.

"Now listen carefully," he said to Charlie, staring hypnotically into his eyes. "We're going to pick her up and walk straight out that door. We're not going to stop till we're outside. Understand?"

"Just like we own the place?"

"Just like we own the place. If anyone says anything, you keep quiet. I'll do the talking."

"You're the boss."

Bending down, Charlie helped the stranger lift the bundled form. Then they casually walked out the door. In the distance, a large open freight door allowed sunlight in and fish fumes out. Their footsteps rang hollowly on the iron surface beneath their feet. Seeing the stranger pause and look at the floor with a puzzled expression, Charlie nodded.

"Queer floor, ain't it?" he said. "Always wondered why it makes that hollow sound...."

The stranger's face cleared. "That's because it's really the ceiling of that huge cavern down below," he said. "See those gears and pulleys? When they're ready to launch the airship, they'll just lift up the floor and the ceiling above us."

Charlie gaped. "Jeez!" he whispered. "But why—"

"Shhh!" the stranger warned. Looking around, Charlie saw that they had become the object of curious stares from several workers.

Seeing the exit ahead and feeling the weight of the pistol beneath his jacket, Charlie felt a little better about their situation. He was good with a gat, though not nearly as good as the stranger. Still, he figured he could take down at least six of the workers if they got too curious. But that would bring the whole place down on them!

Charlie began to get nervous. Everyone in the place seemed to be looking at him suspiciously. He saw hands sneaking into pockets, and he knew they were going after guns! In a moment, he knew, he would have to drop the girl and pull out his gun and begin firing....

A strange sensation swept over Charlie. He felt giddy, lightheaded. Suddenly he knew he had become invisible! He saw himself floating through the crowded factory, but he knew somehow that no one else could see him! And then he was strolling down New York's crowded Fifth Avenue on a warm, sunlit day. No one was paying the least bit of attention to him. He even stopped and bought a daily paper at the corner rag stand. He kept walking, past hotdog stands, pretty women with long legs, kids with balloons and flowers.

Suddenly Charlie felt overwhelmed with sadness. His life had been a waste. And now maybe he was going to die. Charlie did something in those moments he hadn't done in some twenty-odd years. He prayed.

He asked God for forgiveness and promised that if he ever made it out of that cannery alive, he would lead a good life. No more scams and ripoffs. All he wanted was one more chance to prove himself. He promised . . .

"Set her down here."

The command snapped Charlie out of his dream. He felt the heat of the sun's rays and cold, fresh air blowing into his eyes. He was in a forest. Dry pine needles crunched beneath his feet, filling the air with a sweet scent.

"We're safe, for the moment," the stranger said, smiling.

Charlie gasped. In his dreamlike state, he had apparently carried the woman through the crowded factory, past the guards at the door, and into the safety of the dense forest.

He gently laid the woman down. He could hear the sounds of the sea and the factory noises through the trees. He didn't understand what had happened, but he realized that there was a lot about this stranger that didn't make any sense.

"Thanks for your help, Charlie," the stranger said as he quickly unwrapped the unconscious Maggie. "I suspect they're aware of our departure by now. There's a train station a mile up the coast. In your pocket, you'll find a hundred-dollar bill. Use it to buy a ticket and whatever else you may need."

Charlie reached into his pocket and pulled out the C-note. "I—I don't know when I can repay—"

"Consider us even. I suggest you leave while you can." With his head, the Agent gestured back toward the factory.

Charlie looked. Several guards with drawn guns were hurrying out of the distant structure.

"Say no more. Just remember that Charlie Vickers owes ya one. I'm good for it. Anytime." With that, he turned and fled through the trees, toward freedom and a new life.

BREAKING THE BONDS

The Agent watched Charlie disappear into the forest greenery. Satisfied, he shouldered Maggie and walked in a different direction to a muddy road hidden by large hedges. Laying Maggie down again, 13 removed loose brush from the largest hedge. Soon the sleek green hood of a Daimler Double-Six came into view.

During his drive to the lair, the disguised Agent 13 had thoroughly familiarized himself with the area, making notes of the towns, dirt roads, bridges, and even old Tuttle Field—now being used as a training base for pilots.

Slipping away from the thugs, 13 had made his way to the executive parking lot, had hot-wired the high-speed Daimler, and then driven it to one of the many firebreak roads he'd discovered. He had then concealed the auto with the thick brush before returning to his unsuspecting cronies.

The Daimler Double-Six clear of the shrubs, 13 placed Maggie Darr in the passenger seat, then climbed into the car and started the engine. He eased into gear, and moments later, the car stood poised at the end of a fire road, ready to spring out onto the asphalt highway.

13 waited several minutes, but there was no sign of pursuit. They were probably still searching for him in the lair. He smiled grimly, then slowly pulled out onto the road.

Next to him, Maggie began to stir. Moaning, her hands went to the mask on her head.

"You're safe now," 13 said, squeezing her hand reassuringly. "When there's a chance, we'll stop and get that thing off you."

Maggie nodded and slumped back into the seat, sighing in relief.

After several miles, the Agent pulled off onto a small, deserted side road.

He went to the trunk of the car and found a wrench in the tool kit. Quickly he loosened the bolts securing the heavy metal helmet around Maggie's head. Then the Agent's powerful hands parted the hinged device.

"Maggie—" he began softly, but his features suddenly registered intense shock as a mass of black hair tumbled down over the woman's face. Beautiful, deep-blue eyes blinked open and looked up into his.

"China!" 13 gasped.

Shaking out her long, dark hair, China coolly pulled down the visor mirror to examine her make-up. "What a fright I must look!" she remarked glancing down at her torn dress. "I was wondering when you were going to get around to getting that thing off me."

Hearing a click, China looked over and saw a .38 pointed at her head.

"Where's Maggie?" 13 asked evenly.

"I don't think that's necessary," China said calmly, her eyes on the pistol.

"That's for me to decide. Now, where is she?"

Stretching sensually, China leaned back in the soft leather seat. "With the Masque," she said. Staring into 13's eyes, China tried to look into his heart, tried to read the thoughts of the man who once belonged to her. It was impossible. Shrugging, she continued. "Don't expect to see her again. It seems the Masque has developed a fondness for your blonde friend."

"Where's the Masque now?" Agent 13 demanded, still aiming the gun.

"At the cannery, with the airship."

"You know his plan?"

"Of course." She smiled lazily.

13 pocketed his weapon. "Well," he said nonchalantly, "perhaps things aren't so bad after all."

China watched him carefully. His act might have fooled others, but not her. He really cared for this Maggie Darr, but it was obvious that he still felt something for her as well, just as she felt something for him. How could they not?

He was the only one Carmarron had truly loved. It was against him, Tredekka, that all the others had been compared and been found lacking. After his escape from the Shrine, the Brotherhood had tried to erase all memory of Agent 13 from Carmarron's mind. But even with their most sophisticated techniques, they had been unsuccessful—the very fibers and essences of the two young people had become one.

"What's the Masque's plan?" 13 asked China, pulling her back to the present.

China looked away.

"You owe them nothing," 13 persisted, moving closer to her. "They tortured you, then threw you away, like a Jinda. There's no longer a place for you with them, China. They'll hunt you down and destroy you, just as they tried to destroy me."

China hesitated as she considered

how to turn this to her advantage. Finally she answered, "He's going to bomb the Capitol building."

13's eyes narrowed. "Of course!" he muttered. "It all makes sense! Tonight, the State of the Union Address, all the top government officials present in one place—" The Agent fell silent, pondering, planning. ...

China interrupted his thoughts. "They tortured me because I failed to kill you. They thought I was protecting you."

"And were you?" he asked.

"Yes!" she cried. But she could tell his mind was somewhere else, fighting an airship she knew couldn't be defeated, not even by him. She needed to command his complete attention.

"Believe me, there's nothing you can do! The ship is indestructible." Leaning forward, she gripped 13's hands. "This is the chance that was stolen from us years ago! Fate has brought us back together again. Together we might survive. But alone, we'll perish. Let's leave this madness and the Brotherhood behind forever!"

He looked at her.

"Yes, I love you!" She answered his unasked question. "I've always loved you!"

She could see him start to yield. He drew nearer, the passion in his eyes impossible to conceal. And then she was in his arms, kissing him with unleashed passion.

Suddenly he pulled away. Drawing a deep breath, he shook his head. "No," he whispered, "we can't go back! I have a new mission. I can't run from the Brotherhood—I must stop them! Can't you understand?"

Hearing the pain in his voice, China put her hands together and looked up at him pleadingly. Never before had any man resisted her. Never before had she been forced to beg. But now—

The low rumblings of an engine sounded in the distance. China looked around. Only the pines could be seen, lining the empty road. "What's that noise?" she asked, startled. "A car—"

"No. The airship," 13 said quietly.

STORM OF DARKNESS

Captain Kiffen McSpadden had been flying since the days of the Red Baron and the Lafayette Escadrille. A hero in France in World War I, the young pilot had returned home eager to be a part of the new United States Air Force.

McSpadden, and many more like him, was doomed to disappointment. Eager to return to peace, America dismantled the airplane factories and went back to building sewing machines. The training fields and airstrips fell into disrepair. More than one fighter pilot like McSpadden shook his head in dismay, knowing that the next war, if there was one, would be fought in the air.

By 1937, Kiffen McSpadden had been promoted to captain, but his outspokenness earned him only little-regarded Tuttle Field. He was rapidly coming to accept that his days and the field's were numbered. The money coming to the almost-forgotten airstrip was barely enough to keep the potholes repaired and seven trainers in the air.

Like all ex-fighter pilots, McSpadden followed the development of aircraft in other parts of the world. He cursed loudly over Hitler's announcement of the development of the Luftwaffe and wondered why no one else in this country could see what was going to happen.

McSpadden knew that a call for rearmament in the U.S. would eventually come. He only hoped it wouldn't be too late.

McSpadden did what he could with the tools he had to work with. His twelve bush-league pilots, even though they weren't the brightest, were of sound character and spirit. They practiced weekly in their P-12s, an outdated biplane that was scarcely a match for the deadly Messerschmidts and Stukas being tested in Spain. Even so, McSpadden's cadets took pride in their machines and mastered the basics of flight.

Now McSpadden stared gloomily at the ominous bank of clouds that had been building since noon. The P-12s sitting on the strip weren't about to go anywhere for a while. In disgust, Mc-Spadden walked back into the pilot's lounge.

Twenty years ago, he thought, remembering the Great War, this room would have been packed with over fifty cadets, trying to earn their wings and get to the front. Now he looked at the four youngsters on call that day. There was Buck Dawes, a displaced cowboy who had fallen into the service because "it was the only job he could find."

Sitting next to Buck was Clay Lewis, busily replacing a tube in a radio. Lewis had joined up to escape a pregnant girlfriend in Pittsburgh.

A quick slapping sound came from the corner of the room. McSpadden didn't even have to look to know it was Juice Tanner, packing down his ever-present Luckies. Juice was a natural, as if he had been born with a pair of wings on his back. His only problem was his taste for whiskey. Juice said that if he could walk, he could fly. The problem was, McSpadden thought grumpily, Juice tended to have to crawl most of the time.

Finally there was Blake Carter, a happy-go-lucky kid who read nothing but trashy science fiction. Blake longed to be the first man on the moon, but since that wasn't possible, he had settled for the cockpit of a P-12.

"What was the last weather report?" McSpad-den asked Juice.

"Scattered clouds, no precip expected."

"Bingo!" said Lewis suddenly from behind the radio as the device hummed to life.

"Ya get it fixed?" drawled Dawes.

"You bet!"

"Well," McSpadden said, glancing at the sky, "I don't give a damn what those weather boys say. It looks like we're going to be having a storm. Lewis, Carter—I want those planes tied down."

"Yes, sir!" Rising, the two grabbed their jackets and headed for the door. If the captain said there was going to be a storm, then they were going to have a storm. It was that simple.

McSpadden felt uneasy, but he didn't know why. Perhaps it was the approaching storm, or the chill in the wind, or the President's speech. He didn't know.

"Lewis?"

"Sir?"

"What time's the State of the Union Address?"

"Nineteen hundred hours. That's in three hours, sir."

Pacing, McSpadden hoped against hope that President Roosevelt would finally call *Der Fuhrer's* bluff and start rearming. But McSpadden was doubtful. The more Captain McSpadden thought about the developing war in Europe, the more he paced and angrier he became.

Dawes found some swing music on the radio in an attempt to lighten the captain's mood. There was a sudden crack of thunder.

"Hah!" snorted McSpadden. "I told you so."

The wind was picking up, firing droplets of rain like missiles onto the heads of the two young pilots as they ran across the airstrip. A drumroll of thunder pounded. Lewis and Carter grinned at each other. The captain was right again.

By the time they reached the planes, the rain was sheeting down, and they flung themselves under the wings for protection.

Lewis looked at Carter. "Damn!" he muttered. "So much for staying dry." Carter was drenched to the bone and shivering. "Two degrees colder and this stuff'd be snow."

The thunder sounded again, this time closer.

"Almost is," replied Lewis, studying the sleetlike precipitation on his palm.

"Who ever heard of lightning in a snowstorm?" Carter muttered.

The plane rocked in the wind. "We'd better get these babies tied down, or they'll take off without us," Lewis shouted above the roar of the wind.

The two climbed out from under the wing into the rain's fury. Lewis walked to the wing tip, waiting for Carter to retrieve the tie-down straps that were stored beneath the fuselage.

"Hey, what's that?" Carter yelled suddenly.

They could see the headlights of an automobile driving down the airstrip in their direction. As it neared, Lewis and Carter could see that it was a sports car, an expensive rag-top model.

The Daimler skidded to a stop. A woman and a man were inside, the man driving. Opening the window, oblivious to the rain pouring inside, the driver motioned to Carter to come close.

"Who's your commanding officer?" the driver yelled over the sound of the pelting rain.

"Captain McSpadden, sir," answered Carter without thinking to ask why this commanding-looking stranger wanted to know.

"Where can I find him?"

"Pilots' lounge beneath the tower."

"Hey! Just a gol-darned minute!" exclaimed Lewis, just arriving at the scene. He eyed the pair inside the Daimler suspiciously. "Not so fast, buddy! What can I do for you?"

The driver didn't reply. He simply jammed the car into gear and roared off toward the tower.

Carter looked at Lewis shamefacedly and said hopefully, "Maybe it's brass from Washington."

"I don't like it—I'm going back,"

Lewis said, undoing the flap on his holster.

Captain McSpadden was still pacing when he saw the Daimler approaching through the rain.

"Looks like company," commented Juice, pulling himself up from the leather easy chair. The car stopped at the door, and a man and a woman leaped out. Running through the rain, they dashed inside.

"Captain McSpadden?" the drenched stranger asked with an air of authority.

"Yes?"

The man pulled out a badge and flashed it. "Richard Carol, Secret Service."

McSpadden took a good look at the badge. It was Secret Service, all right, but the guy had all the makings of a mobster—a stunning woman wearing a man's suit coat over her dress, a car that would've cost McSpadden two years' salary. Maybe the guy's a spy, he thought. One of ours.

"What can I do for you?" he said finally.

"I need to place an important phone call."

"The phone's over there." McSpadden replied, pointing to the table. He noted that the woman was shivering. "Dawes? Fetch some blankets and strong coffee."

"Yes, sir."

"Why don't you have a seat, ma'am?"

The shivering woman ignored the offer. She just stared out the window into the dark sky. The Secret Service man picked up the phone, frowned, then turned to McSpadden.

"The line's dead."

"The storm must've knocked down the lines."

"What about a radio?"

Lewis burst into the room, his hand poised over his pistol. "Everything all right here, sir?"

"It's all right, Lewis. Thank you." The captain turned back to stranger. "But why don't you tell me what this is all about?"

"No time. I need the radio!" the man said coolly.

McSpadden frowned. Secret Service agent or not, he wasn't about to let this guy push him around.

"I'm afraid there's nothing I can do, sir. That radio is for offical air traffic broadcasts only. Unless it's a dire emergency, I'm afraid—"

"The nation's Capitol is about to be bombed, Captain," the Secret Service man said, cutting him off. "Is that emergency enough?"

"Bombed?" repeated McSpadden in disbelief. "And just who and how?"

"An airship."

"In this storm?" McSpadden relaxed. This guy must be a nut. "I've got news for you, mister. The only things flying in this weather are sea gulls looking for caves. Now, why don't you and the lady have some coffee, and—"

There was a sudden flare of light, and they saw a large lightning bolt hurtle from the distant clouds and strike the power generator at the far end of the field. The explosion shook the room as the lights flickered, then went out.

"Jesus!" Dawes gasped and backed away from the windows. "That was some lightning!"

"It wasn't lightning," the man said grimly.

"Huh?" McSpadden started to turn away from the window to question the stranger when he stopped suddenly. "What the hell is that?"

A massive, saucer-shaped object floated into view. As McSpadden watched in disbelief, bright beams of light streaked through the air, striking the generator. Within seconds, it was nothing but a lump of twisted, blackened steel.

"What—what is that thing?" stammered Juice.

"The airship," replied the woman.

"I've been twenty years in the air," McSpadden said, "and I've never seen anything like—"

"The radio!" the man demanded.

"No good. It ran off the generator." The generator destroyed, the airship began to move again.

"Are your planes in flying condition?" the stranger asked.

McSpadden stared at him. "Yes, but—"

"Then get them in the air—now!"

"It'd be suicide in this weather!"

"Captain, you and your men are all that stand between that device and the President of the United States!"

McSpadden looked at his fliers. They were young and inexperienced. Even if they managed to get their craft in the air, their chances of being able to do anything to stop that massive machine were next to zero. He could tell that they, too, knew the odds, but one look at their faces told McSpadden that they were behind him.

"All right!" McSpadden sprang into action. "Juice, Buck, you two are with me. We'll take the three P-12s with the Lewis guns. We're going to keep a tight formation and then come down on her from above, concentrating our firepower. Stay close and follow my example. Lewis?"

"Sir?"

"You and Carter fly to Fort Myers and let them know what's going on here. The moment you're in the air, try reaching someone on the radio."

"Yes, sir!"

"Now, let's get those birds off the ground!"

A static electrical charge suddenly filled the room, making their hair stand on end.

"Get out of here!" yelled the Secret Service man. Running forward, he grabbed the woman and pulled her out the door and to the ground as a bolt of energy burst into the tower above them. A flying board slammed into McSpadden, knocking him to the airstrip, unconscious. The captain wasn't going to be flying anywhere.

"Keep going!" 13 yelled. "Get those planes up!"

"But—the captain! Who'll lead—"

"He'll be fine!" 13 was already taking off the captain's goggles and flight jacket. Another beam struck the Daimler, sending it flying into the rubble of the burning lounge. "Come on!" 13 shouted. "Those planes'll be next!"

The pilots ran off down the concrete as the airship hovered above. Agent 13 quickly slipped into the captain's flight jacket, cap, and goggles.

"What are you doing?" China cried.

"I'm going up to lead those boys."

The deadly chatter of machine-gun fire began to rain down from above.

"Let's get out of here! You've done what you can!" China implored.

"There's still a chance...."

"Don't I mean anything to you?"

13 looked at her. "I didn't kill you, did I?"

She shrank away. One look in his cold eyes told her it was over.

"You have your freedom, China. Take it." The Agent turned and sprinted away.

SCRAMBLE!

Agent 13 was no stranger to airplanes. Under an alias, he had flown for the French in the Great War, racking up enough kills to qualify his fictitious alter-ego as an ace. Then before the publicity hounds could expose his true identity (or the fact that he was too young), he had disappeared as mysteriously as he had arrived.

By the time Agent 13 reached the captain's P-12, the other pilots were already grinding their engines up to full throttle. Through the dim light and the wind and the rain, they could see the stranger climbing into the cockpit.

13 glanced behind him. The control tower lay in ruins, and the airship was heading for the planes on the apron. Fortunately, the gigantic ship was slowed by the strong headwind. Even so, the direction of the runway would take the planes almost directly under the monstrous death machine.

His voice crackled crisply over the radio. "It's no good trying to use the runway! Sit tight, then follow me!"

"Like hell I will!" Blake Carter snarled.

13 watched as Blake's P-12 raced down the runway trying to become airborne. The airship hovered above, waiting for its victim.

As Carter's P-12 passed beneath the ship, he felt his wheels leave the concrete. A lightning bolt suddenly crackled from an open port beneath the airship, striking the fragile biplane's engine cowling. Instantly the airplane vanished, leaving in its place a searing ball of flame.

Buck Dawes was right behind Carter. Seeing what had happened to his buddy, fear and nausea welled suddenly in his throat. He quickly jammed the throttle forward and slammed the rudder pedal, attempting to stop. Unfortunately, he was too late. Gunners from the turrets ringing the airship opened up, and lead cut through Buck's P-12 like knives through melted butter. The plane nose-dived in a flaming ball of death.

"Follow me!" 13 repeated coolly over the radio, his plane finally ready for takeoff. The two remaining young pilots glanced over at the Agent, then shrugged and decided to follow him to what they felt was certain death. To their amazement, he motioned for them to follow as he turned his plane down a service road leading out of the base.

"He's crazy!" Juice gasped, bouncing and jolting over the rough surface, expecting his plane to shake apart any moment.

"Like a fox," muttered Lewis, suddenly understanding the Agent's plan.

After a rough quarter mile, the three aircraft reached the highway. The road was wide enough to accommodate the craft. The next concern was the possibility of crosswinds, which could force the planes into the tall pines lining either side of the road. But the Agent had no time to worry. The airship was right on their tails.

13 jammed the throttle forward, and the plane surged down the road. Lewis and Tanner immediately followed, breathing a prayer that nothing would go wrong.

Agent 13 felt his craft leave the ground. Suddenly a truck, loaded with lumber, appeared out of the fog directly ahead. 13 slammed the control stick back. The plane shuddered in response, then pitched upward, slowly gaining altitude. The driver of the truck hit the brakes as the aircraft's black rubber tires grazed the roof of his cab. Then the truck lumbered into a ditch.

The truck driver watched in disbelief as two more aircraft soared overhead. He froze for a moment, then stuck his head out the window.

"Jerks!" he screamed, shaking his fist. Reaching into the glove compartment, he pulled out a bottle of scotch, took a drink to calm his nerves, then got his truck back onto the road. Suddenly he slammed on the brakes again.

"Great jumpin'jehoshaphat!" he murmured in awe. The night was lit by flickers of lightning. Looking up, the truck driver saw a giant saucer-shaped airship. Lightning bolts streaked down from it, setting trees ablaze. He could see machine guns protruding from the great ship.

The death machine passed quickly overhead, disappearing in the direction that the planes had taken. Suddenly the night was still, except for the rumblings of the dying storm. The truck driver took another long look at the road ahead, wondering if perhaps Noah's ark would be next. But nothing came. He studied the scotch in his hand, then looked back at the sky. His wife had often told him he had a drinking problem. Maybe she was right.

"I think it's over between me an'

you," he said to the bottle, tossing it out the window.

The P-12s climbed quickly into the thick thun-derheads. Visibility fell to near zero, and the turbulence banged them around like marbles in a washing machine. But 13 knew that the clouds afforded them protection from their deadly pursuer. Higher and higher they climbed, flying on instinct and the dials of their control panels.

13 watched as his altimeter continued to spin through the numbers—one thousand . . . five thousand... ten thousand—and still they were in the inky clouds. The slushy rain had turned to snow, icing up their wings, sending arctic-like temperatures through their open cockpits.

Their faces grew numb, but they had no time to notice. They had a new fear—possible midair collision with each other. They were flying blind, the only light coming from the greenish streaks of lightning that ripped the murk apart, followed by earsplitting thunderclaps. But the sporadic flashes permitted them to see the dim outlines of their own frail craft. At eleven thousand feet, they finally broke through the cloud cover.

The full moon provided a celestial peace to the gray sea of clouds beneath them. Sheets of lightning rippled in the distance. But they weren't lulled by the beauty, knowing the sinister evil that was rapidly approaching them.

"Try to raise someone on the radio," 13 ordered as Lewis and Juice came up beside him.

"No, luck, Cap—uh, sir," Lewis stammered. "All I'm getting is static. Must be the storm."

"Not likely," 13 muttered. "More likely a jamming device. Make certain your guns work."

Both young pilots checked out their weapons, glad to have something to do to keep their minds off their fears and the intense cold.

They circled, waiting for the ship to appear. 13's mind drifted to Maggie. There was every possibil ity she was aboard the fortress he was about to attack! 13 drove the thought from his head. He couldn't let it interfere with his mission! The air ship was somewhere in the storm beneath him. It had to be stopped—no matter what the price. Maggie would understand....

Then, through the clouds beneath him, 13 saw lights, and a saucer-shaped airship appeared, rising up out of the clouds, coming into focus. He was Ahab, watching as the Great White Whale— his destiny—rose from the murky sea of clouds.

It was the first time Agent 13 had seen the airship from above. The bottom and sides tapered into a saucer configuration, but the top was flat. Along its center, like the spine of a serpent, was a lighted airstrip. Two elevators operated on either side of the strip, ferrying planes to the surface. Behind them were four autogyros, tied down behind small aerodynami-cally tapered enclosures. The entire runway was ringed with tur-reted ma-chine-gun emplacements.

13 marveled at the evil genuis of the Brotherhood, but he had no time to waste in grudging praise. Below, he could see pilots scrambling in an attempt to get their planes in the air.

"Commence attack!" 13 signaled to Lewis and Juice as his own plane peeled out of formation.

Jamming the stick forward while tramping down on the rudder, 13 banked, then dove at the target. Slow-ly his thumb fingered the trigger but-ton, holding his fire until the last pos-sible second. Then the Lewis guns spat forth a short burst.

He watched as several tracers slant-ed off to the right, made the proper adjustment, then fired again. His guns began to shake and shudder, spitting forth spears of flame into the night.

Suddenly he scored a hit! Down on the airship, he could see a plane that had started to take off burst into flame. A dark figure leaped out of the burning plane, running for cover with 13's bullets following him. Two other pilots raced for the walls protecting the autogyros. The Agent fingered the trigger once more, and again the trac-ers found their mark. The dark figures spun and crumpled.

13's bullets merely ricocheted off the ship's armored surface. By this time, the turret gunners had gotten their bearings and were zeroing in on the Agent's craft. Their bullets tore through the wings as he pulled back on the stick, to end his dive.

The G-forces of the maneuver forced the blood from his head. The Agent struggled to maintain consciousness. Once out of range, he leveled off and glanced back. The plane he had hit was still burning. Live rounds from the plane's guns were exploding and firing in all directions.

Lewis was next into the foray, his guns ratatat-ing like cracking whips as he descended. His bursts struck the autogyros, causing them to explode in balls of flame. His guns continued their deadly chatter until suddenly 13 saw him slump forward.

Lewis's plane began to tail off to the right. The airship's gunners kept him in their sights, the staccato impact of their 50-caliber slugs ripping through the fuselage of the P-12.

The wing of Lewis's plane sudden-ly broke away, sending the craft into a spinning nose dive. Blazing like a rocket, the craft disappeared in the sea of clouds while the remains of the broken wing drifted down lazily after it.

13 could hear Juice swearing in rage and grief.

"Keep calm, son," 13 commanded, though he knew it wouldn't do much good.

Furious, Juice dove at the airship with a vengeance. At five hundred feet, he opened up, aiming for the gun ports. The glowing barrels of his dual machine guns explored the surface of the ship with fingers of destruction. A machine-gun turret shattered in a hail of ruin as the gunner was sent twirling sideways. The flaming figure of another gunner suddenly leaped from the destroyed port.

Juice fired another burst as his P-12 dove past the airship's port side, obviously taking hits from the deadly fusillade. Somehow he managed to survive and fly out of range.

But he was in trouble. He was diving too fast. Summoning all his strength, he hauled back on the stick, attempting to bring the nose of the craft up from its sickening descent, but nothing happened. Juice glanced at his wings as he struggled to pull up. Half his fuselage had been opened like an eggshell, the control cables destroyed. He was still struggling for his chute as the shattered hulk hurtled to its fiery doom.

13 was alone. The airship was still practically unharmed. 13 knew what had to be done. Down he plummeted. Pushing the throttle full forward, he gave the craft everything he could. Blood rushed to his head and his temples throbbed with pain as he pushed his craft past its limit.

The wings vibrated in defiance, threatening to rip from their supports. Still 13 didn't let up. With every passing second, the P-12 picked up speed. The gunners had him in their sights, but they couldn't stop him. 13 aimed his plane at the center of the runway as the flames of lead licked at his wings. At twelve hundred feet above the airship, he undid his harness. Tracers suddenly ripped into the prop blades, splintering them into thousands of deadly fragments. Sparks and oil showered from the cowling, but the plane's momentum couldn't be stopped.

For 13, the world began to spin as up became down and time slowed to a stop. Images flashed before his eyes—the parents he barely remembered. A little girl playing with a broken tin soldier. The glowing temple of the Shrine. Carmarron, her body naked in the moonlight. The skull of the Brotherhood, the Masque of death, dealer of destruction. Maggie in a delivery room. Cries of a newborn infant. Someone slaps it. The infant's head turns—it's him!

13 was suddenly jolted back to reality. He was inside a flaming cockpit, his head ringing with the explosions of the faltering craft. He felt pain, but it was a dull, unreal sensation. The wind screamed in his ears as his reflexes took over. Fighting the rushing wind, 13 grabbed his chute's D-ring and rolled out of the cockpit, disappearing into the black void of infinity.

The gunners heard the feverish whine of the approaching engine even as they saw the plane plummet from the moonlit sky. They had endured three previous attacks, but they weren't prepared for the speed at which the aircraft was descending. They opened fire in unison, their tracers arching into the blackness like crimson fireballs. Their murderous slugs tore into the craft, eating it away in jagged chunks of metal. But the pilot didn't veer. He seemed determined to crash his plane into their ship.

Nine hundred feet above them, the plane burst into flames, and the craft became a deadly fireball as it continued its path. But the gunners didn't give up. Their concentrated fire continued to find its mark until, less than two hundred feet above their heads, the remains of the marauder exploded in a blinding flash. The sudden concussion knocked the gunners to the ground, showering them with flaming debris. Moments later, they pulled themselves from the wreckage, half deafened and blind from the blazing light.

Thus they never noticed the parachute silk as it drifted silently off the port side of the ship like a ghost.

BELLY OF THE BEAST

When 13 landed on the airship, the runway was empty. Everyone had taken cover when the attack began. He knew, however, that they would soon return to deal with the damage. One look around told him that the P-12s' attack had been largely ineffective. The ship was still proceeding on course. The fires he saw were fueled by the debris of the destroyed planes and autogyros, not the airship itself. As 13 had foreseen, the ship was impervious to air assault. Even if 13 and the other pilots had managed to knock out the airstrip, the airship had other weapons just as deadly.

Slipping out of his chute, 13's first order of business was to gain entrance into the airship. On the port side, he found the gun turret that Juice had destroyed. Nearby were the bloody corpses of the two gunners. 13 quickly set to work removing the blood-soaked uniform from one of the dead men. Once done, he slid the naked corpse off the side of the ship.

Disguised as the gunner, he entered the smoldering gun emplacement. Here he found an iron ladder that led to the ship's interior. Grabbing the steel rungs, he grimly descended hand over hand, into the darkness.

The ladder led 13 to an iron catwalk, which in turn led him to a central gangway running directly beneath the airstrip. All around him was the austere coldness of the metal interior. The ship's basic design appeared to be similar to that of the *USS Akron*, an airship that had crashed in 1933 while at sea off Barnegat. The Akron was a ship of rigid frame construction. Its aluminum girders and bulkheads provided the structural support for the immense helium gas cells that filled ninety percent of the craft's interior. Lift and descent were achieved by changing the balance of gas against the water ballast located in the lower part of the ship.

Once airborne, *Akron's* eight Maybach VL-II engines' 4480 horsepower could give it an airspeed of 79 miles per hour.

But 13 knew that the craft he was in now was vastly superior to the *Akron*. While *Akron* used aluminum for structural purposes, this new airship used a lighter weight metallic alloy whose superior strength was capable of supporting the armor-plated skin and the added weight of the airstrip above. The craft's saucerlike shape offered an aerodynamic advantage over the standard cigar-shape configuration of other airships. This, combined with the latest Pratt and Whitney engines, gave the airship greater maneuverability and an airspeed of at least one hundred and fifty miles an hour—nearly twice what the ill-fated *Akron* could achieve.

At that speed, the airship would be over Washington in less than two hours.

13 saw two chances to stop the flying leviathan. If he could locate the armory, he might be able to find a device capable of blowing the ship's bulkheads. Or, if he could gain entrance to the control room, he could empty the ballast, sending the ship rising into the air, out of control.

Logic told him that the service decks and flight centers would be located beneath the pressure of the gas cells, somewhere in the lower por-

tion of the ship. Proceeding along the gangway, he was amazed that there seemed to be no response to their attack. Only the muffled hum of the Pratt and Whitneys reminded him that he was in an airship two thousand feet above earth.

The Agent came upon a large freight elevator, but ignored it—too many people. He preferred to take the less obvious approach, a ladder that descended into the bowels of the craft. Reaching the bottom of the ladder, he was confronted by a hatchlike door. He pressed his ear against its metallic surface. The lack of activity above contrasted sharply to the buzz of activity on the other side.

13 cracked the door slightly. Technicians and mechanics hurried to and fro in preparation for their attack on the Capitol. Feigning the injuries that his blood-drenched uniform suggested, 13 stumbled out of the hatchway and into the lower gangway. His legs buckled beneath him as he collapsed to the steel-plated floor in apparent shock.

"Get him to the infirmary!" commanded a voice with a German accent. 13 was immediately lifted by two uniformed men and helped down the hallway. Though he appeared to be unconscious, he was in reality peering out from beneath his lashes, memorizing his surroundings.

One doorway especially caught his interest. In the glance he was afforded, he saw a large number of technical people working with many banks of electrical machines and generator-type equipment. As he was hauled past the next door, he saw what they were working on—a large towerlike apparatus bristling with capacitors, transformers, insulators, and other electrical equipment. It was a gigantic version of Dr. Fischer's Lightning Gun!

The same device had been responsible for the vaporization of Carter during takeoff, as well as the destruction of the airfield's generator and control tower. And it was the same diabolical device that would soon be turned on unsuspecting Washington unless he was able to stop it.

But even as he tried to concentrate on his prime objective, another thought intruded in his mind. What about Maggie? Was she somewhere on board? He tried to forget about her, but he caught himself trying to guess what they might have done to her and where she might be as the men carried him through a hatchway into the sick bay.

"Another one?" growled an old doctor, pulling a white cotton sheet over the charred remains of what was once a man's face.

"This one's still alive," responded one of the men as they placed the Agent on a steel table.

"Take this one away," said the doctor, gesturing to the corpse as he moved to Agent 13's side.

The doctor immediately went to work. First he checked 13's vital signs. Then he pulled back the unconscious man's eyelids. Nothing but whites. He felt the carotid artery. There was barely a pulse. Death couldn't be far away. He carefully opened the man's shirt, prepared to see his intestines spill out on the table. The doctor blinked in astonishment. No apparent injuries! Plenty of blood, but unscathed flesh. He opened the shirt wider. Still nothing.

"What the—"

The Agent's powerful, viselike hands grabbed the doctor by the throat. Leaping off the table, 13 slammed the baffled man against the wall, well out of sight of the open hatchway.

"Let's talk," Agent 13 said grimly.

A CHANGE OF MIND

When Dr. David Fischer was captured by the Brotherhood, the reason was easy to understand—they wanted the Lightning Gun. They believed in him, having followed his lectures and attended his demonstrations. They had seen his proposals for a full-sized version of the weapon, and they knew it would work. So they had plotted to kidnap him.

It was because of the Brotherhood's influence that the United States Army refused to take Fischer seriously. Acting behind the scenes, the Brotherhood had destroyed his dreams and his career until finally he was a shattered wreck.

They enticed him aboard the *Normandie*, then kidnapped him as they had so many other crack scientists. But they didn't bother to torture Fischer. They figured they had already reduced him to emotional rubble. They came to him as friends.

"We can help you fulfill your dream!"
the Masque said. "We have money, resources, manpower. We'll help you create this revolutionary device. You're a visionary, professor—a man ahead of your time. The ignorant masses cannot possibly see this. But *I* can! Together we will show the world!"

Fischer proved stronger than they'd anticipated. He knew what horrible power might be unleashed if his Lightning Gun fell into the wrong hands. He didn't trust this masked figure. He didn't trust any organization that had to resort to kidnapping, and he bluntly said so to the Masque. He then demanded to be sent back home.

As a result, Dr. Fischer ended up beneath the Helmet of Truth. After several sessions, the wretched man was more than willing to cooperate. To ensure his "enthusiasm" for the project, his sister and her husband were kidnapped and held at an undisclosed location.

Fischer began work. Whatever he needed, he received—including other scientists. After several months of forced labor, the device was finally finished, and a test was arranged. The cannon was fired at the USS *Trent*. After two direct hits, the ship simply ceased to exist.

The results exceeded even the Masque's expectations. He sent Fischer a congratulatory bottle of champagne, which the scientist promptly smashed. Even as the completion of the Lightning Gun was Dr. Fischer's dream, the hands that now controlled it were his nightmare. He wanted to destroy his demonic child. But how? He was guarded day and night.

When the airship was complete, the Masque's men loaded the cannon into a special chamber designed to house the gun. Large bomb-bay doors could be opened, permitting the cannon to discharge its tremendous power.

The Masque personally led Fischer and four other scientists on a tour of the awesome ship. As they stared at it in helpless horror, armed guards began prodding them up the entry ramp, forcing them inside.

"Surely you want to witness the tremendous capabilities of your wonderful weapon, Dr. Fischer," the Masque said.

"I'm a scientist, not a murderer!" Fischer protested helplessly.

"Precisely. And as a scientist, you will appreciate why I need you. Nothing must go wrong! If it does, I want you there to fix it."

There was nothing Fischer and the other scientists could do. Heavily armed guards watched them every second.

The airship had been in the air only thirty minutes when the command was given to open the doors beneath the Lightning Gun. Generators hummed, channeling power into the cannon's massive capacitors.

"What are you doing?" Fischer demanded.

"We've got orders to commence firing, Doc," said one of the workers.

"No!" Fischer began, but he heard the click of a rifle bolt behind him and could do nothing. He watched helplessly as a gunner donned goggles and began to operate the hydraulics that controlled the movements of the Lightning Gun.

Fischer watched in anguish as the gentle countryside rolled beneath them, wondering what their target was going to be. Breathing in the sea-scented air, watching the peaceful countryside drift by below, he thought of his past, remembering walks on the beach. Suddenly the picture stopped. Frozen below them, like a picture suspended in time, was a telephone relay terminal.

Suddenly the gun surged with electricity. A green light flashed, signaling that the power was sufficient to launch the deadly bolt.

"Fire!" a voice commanded. All heads turned aside as two hundred million volts filled the room and a plasmic bolt of electricity left the gun. A split second later, a thunderclap jolted their ears as the shock wave blew hot wind into their faces. It was an awesome display of power—except this time it wasn't a test.

Below the ship, the relay terminal lay in ruins. Fragments of twisted metal and wires were everywhere. All eyes in the room stared at the destruction they had wrought. No one spoke. It was as if the power of God had been harnessed.

A second order to fire snapped them back to their senses. They quickly turned their heads once more as the green light went on for the second time. Again the flash filled the room. As they looked below, they saw charred earth and a gaping hole where the station had once been.

The airship started to move as the Lightning Gun recharged for a third time. Storm clouds closed in, and rain blew through the open bomb-bay doors. Soon the gunner found a new target— the power generator of a distant airfield. The gun's tongue spat once more, and again came destruction. Next—a control tower. Next—a fighter plane. There was no end to the nightmare.

Dr. Fischer buried his head in his hands. What had he done? How many more deaths must he be responsible for? If he had only been stronger, if he hadn't submitted to their will. ..

Finally the bomb-bay doors closed,

and the airship ascended into the clouds. The sound of an air battle above told Fischer that something was trying to stop the menace. Fischer prayed for the giant airship's destruction. He didn't care if he went down, too. All he asked was that his tormentors and the Lightning Gun go with him.

One by one, the sounds of the attacking engines swept past the ship, and one by one they were silenced. The men in the room began to cheer. Dr. Fischer started to weep. He knew that the attack had failed. The airship truly was invincible.

The guards shoved the shattered man into a corner. Alone, frightened, Fischer was considering hurling himself out the bomb-bay doors when suddenly he felt a hand upon his arm.

Startled, he spun around. A man wearing a gray technician's jacket stood beside him. He held a clipboard in his hand and appeared to be checking the settings on a bank of dials on a nearby generator. Fischer couldn't recall having ever seen this man before. The eyes, especially, were arresting— piercing, intense, intelligent.

"I'm a friend," the technician whispered. "I have no friends here!" the scientist cried out.

At the sound of Fischer's voice, his guards turned. Who was he talking to? The only person near him was a technician, who looked at the professor blankly and moved away. The guards shook their heads and resumed talking.

"Dr. Fischer, listen to me!" The distraught scientist heard the whispered voice again.

He looked dazedly around. No one was even near him! Was he finally going mad?

"Who—" Fischer started to ask.

The voice cut him off. "Don't speak out again, Doctor. Just listen. I repeat—I am a friend."

Fischer spun around and looked. The technician wasn't even facing him!

"Don't be alarmed. I am able to ventriloquize my words so that only you can hear them. I have come to destroy the Lightning Gun and this airship, but I can succeed only with your help.

"If those who forced you to build this weapon are allowed to continue with their plans, thousands, perhaps millions, will die. The planet will be plunged into darkness such as it has never known. You and I are all that stand in the way, but I can't do it without you. If you will help me, cough softly. I will hear you."

Fischer's head whirled. Could this man be telling the truth? Or was this another trick of the Masque's? If it was a trick, it was a clever one. But why now? The ship was already in the air. If he had been going to sabotage it, Fischer surely would have done it before the gun was completed.

It only made sense if the technician was who he claimed to be. But how could he have gotten aboard? Questions spun through the professor's mind. He had to admit he didn't know the answers. Through his months of captivity, Fjs. cher had learned to trust no one.

Fischer was about to decide to ignore the man when several guards suddenly burst through the door. A burly guard pulled out a pistol a.nd, approaching the technician, shoved the cold steel of the barrel into the man's temple.

Another guard, tall and muscular, grabbed the technician by the hair and jerked his head around, holding his face up. Behind the guard, someone whispered, "That's him!" The ship's doctor was being held up by two guards, but tifter speaking, he slumped into unconsciousness.

"Hey, what's going on?" the technician cried, his clipboard clattering to the floor. "I—"

Without a word, the guard struck the technician on the temple with the barrel of his gun. Quickly they caught the unconscious technician and dragged him to the door.

"Back to work, everyone!" commanded a Voice over the radio intercom.

So it wasn't a trick! Fischer thought disappointedly as he watched the guards haul the man away.

"Hey!" One of the guards loomed up before Fischer. "What did that guy say to you?"

Dr. Fischer blinked and said, "Nothing... nothing at all."

A SINISTER SCHEME

Darkness. Nothing but darkness. His brain told him he was alive, as did the pain throbbing through his head. 13 automatically recited the ancient words that banished pain.

The vibrations set up by the repeated words enveloped his body in soothing waves of energy. Agent 13 could think again.

He recalled the events that led up to the moment he'd been struck. What had gone wrong? The ship's doctor should have died from the poison. Somehow, someone had gotten to him in time, someone who knew the antidote....

The Agent remained motionless, his senses exploring his environment, assembling the facts.

A redness through his closed eyelids indicated there was light in the room. He was lying flat on a table apparently cushioned with leather. He was barefoot. His clothes appeared to be some sort of hospital gown. His watch and rings had been removed.

Elastic bindings held down his arms and legs. He could hear the din of the Pratt and Whitneys, so he was still in the airship. But his acute hearing picked up something else—someone breathing. And there was a scratching noise. 13 was not alone.

He opened his eyes slowly. The gray, slanted wall he faced contained large rectangular windows that afforded a sweeping view. He could see armor-plated shutters that could be shut quickly. It was dark outside the windows.

The Agent turned his head. He saw more blank gray walls, then a metal desk, cold and austere. Then he saw him.

The man was masked, as he had appeared in the filmed threats 13 had viewed in Washington. The Omega and Star symbol of the Brotherhood was affixed to his hood, and a Seer Stone hung from around his neck. The Masque!

He sat at the desk, fountain pen in hand, writing on paper before him. Except for the movements of his hand, he was motionless, deathlike.

His raspy breathing echoed through the chill room like the hiss of a reptile. He paused for a moment, as if in thought, then set the pen down.

All was still. Then 13 heard a low, dry chuckle.

The Masque rose from the desk, his face obscured in his hooded garment. "Welcome, Agent 13. At long last we meet. I congratulate you. It took an extraordinary man to spirit China White from my fortress, attack my airship, then manage to sneak on to it as well. You have been a worthy opponent—but the game is over!"

13 saw the Masque reach beneath the desk. There was a click, and the Agent heard the soft horns from Wagner's *Tannhauser*. The Masque rose and walked over to the bound Agent.

"Did you really believe you could stop me?"

13 did not answer but merely smiled.

The Masque stared out the windows. Flipping a switch, he turned on large spotlights outside the ship. The lights illuminated the cottony tops of the gray, puffy clouds below them. He seemed lost for a moment in his thoughts and the music.

"Beautiful, isn't it? The sea of clouds, so peaceful and serene.

Yet capable of so much destruction—hailstorms, blizzards, tornadoes, thunderbolts ..." He turned back to face 13.

"You are a fool. Our forces stand poised to strike. Soon we will be the earth's supreme masters, an opportunity we should have seized long ago. It was a destiny you might have shared—but you heard a different calling." He sneered. "All your efforts have been wasted, smashed like a grain of sand beneath my heel!"

13 stared hard at the hooded presence before him. "Why Washington?" he asked curiously.

"Because the United States stands in our way. We tried to achieve our ends by more subtle means, but your leaders refused. They've resisted long enough. Now they shall pay!"

"Your terrorism will unify the country against you."

"That's precisely what we plan. Tonight the governing body of this nation will cease to exist. It will be an animal without a head...."

"For every one you kill, another will step forward with even greater resolve to oppose you."

"Exactly right, 13." He chuckled again. "And who do you suppose that other person will be? Who more qualified than—" The Masque removed his hood.

It was Kent Walters, the National Security Advisor! The entire plot was suddenly clear to 13. Kent Walters, supposedly still recovering from his wounds, would be the only major political figure who wouldn 'the present at the State of the Union Address—and thus, the only survivor.

"With everyone else killed, you'll be able to take over the Presidency!" said the Agent.

Walters smiled. "Precisely. I've already laid the groundwork. I'm a hero to the public since the assassination attempt. With most of the members of Congress dead, I will step in and console a grieving nation. My first task as the new President will be to crack down on the terrorists responsible for the tragic deaths of the goverment leaders.

"The Masque will deliver yet another threat. This time it will be directed at a dam. The lives of thousands will be endangered. Would you like me to read it to you?" Grinning, Walters produced the sheet of paper that he was working on earlier.

"Not particularly," 13 responded dryly.

Walters returned the sheet to his pocket. "It doesn't matter. What's important is the result.

"At the last moment, the Armed Forces, under my direct command, will discover, then destroy, the airship and the Masque. It will be *I* who delivers the nation from the evil that threatens it. Once again, I will be the hero.

"And when war finally breaks out, the people will follow me blindly as I bring the United States to the aid of the misunderstood Axis powers. With the vast wealth of this nation, nothing can stop us from taking over the world! Then the Brotherhood will rise from the shadows and take possession for all eternity!"

13 said nothing. His mind raced through the scenario Walters had described. Once again, he marveled at the Brotherhood's genius. Their plan could work! Had he fought and struggled all these years only to fail now?

"It's a pity you won't be here to see it, 13. You are to be returned to the Shrine. There the brainwashing techniques will be continued. The Jindadii awaits. ..."

13 went cold. He feared only one thing—and that was it! He would become the Serpentine Assassin once again! Who would he be instructed to kill this time?

Seeing 13 pale, Walters began to laugh maniacally. A red light began to flash on the wall above his desk. Turning, Walters pressed the intercom switch.

"Yes?"

"We'll be over Washington in thirty-five minutes," a voice crackled over the intercom.

"Good. Any sign of resistance?"

"None whatsoever."

"Good. Send four guards to my office immediately."

"Yes, sir."

Walters turned back to Agent 13, smiling grimly. "You will be given the same drug that was administered to you previously. The next face you see will be the face of the Jinda-dii."

"What about Maggie Darr?" 13 asked.

"Ah, yes, the sweet Maggie. What a treasure you found there. She's quite safe, I assure you."

"Is she aboard?"

"Oh, yes," he said, leering.

"I want to see her," 13 said.

Walters sighed. "I'm afraid that's impossible."

"I still have the Seer Stone. Let me see her and I'll tell you where it is."

Walters chuckled. "With your return to the Shrine, the stone is nothing but a worthless rock."

"If I fail to come back, I've left instructions with my agents explaining its use. They'll carry on the fight without me."

"And therefore I don't believe you, 13. You are too strong to compromise your agents for the sake of seeing a woman, no matter how sweet her flesh might be. No, you would give me a location, but I have no doubt that the Seer Stone would not be there."

"Can you afford the risk?"

"Indeed. You see, one of your first assignments, my fledgling Serpentine Assassin, will be to track down and destroy all of your own agents...."

Four guards filed into the room and stood at attention in the doorway.

Walters looked at the Agent one last time. "I am disappointed in you, 13," he said coldly. "Look at you, carrying on like a lovesick schoolboy. Perhaps the Brotherhood was mistaken about you." Walters turned to the guards. "Take him away! Make sure he is given a full view of the coming event, then administer the drug."

The guards picked up the top of table that the Agent was strapped to. It turned out to be some type of stretcher.

"Good-bye, 13. I hope your journey to the Shrine is a pleasant one." Walters smiled.

The last thing 13 heard as he was carried off was laughter echoing from the cold, gray walls.

COOPERATIVE DEATH

Dr. Fischer didn't know who the man was that the guards had dragged away. It didn't matter. What counted was that someone finally had the courage to stand up against them!

The incident snapped Fischer out of his own shock. Perhaps something could still be done! Any doubts he might have had as to how they intended to use his gun had been quickly dispelled at the airfield.

The stranger was right. It was only going to get worse. He would be responsible for the deaths of thousands! He had to act quickly to stop it, before the next fiendish event occurred!

He was being watched constantly by three guards. Besides them, there were two technicians and two other scientists who, like himself, had been kidnapped.

So they outnumbered the guards. But what could they do? The answer was simple. They could destroy the gun. It would take some doing, but it was possible. He would need the help of the others, however, to deal with the guards.

"Uh, I don't think that dial is reading correctly," Fischer said, hurrying over to make an adjustment. Standing next to the dial was Dr. Floyd Stockwell, the designer of the massive capacitors that stored the charge for the cannon. Stockwell and Fischer had worked closely together for the last several months. Though Stockwell wasn't any more of a fighter than Fischer, he was resourceful. If there was one man that Fischer thought he could trust, it was Stockwell.

When Fischer approached Stockwell, the guards didn't give a second look. They were used to seeing the two involved in long technical discussions.

"We've got to stop this!" Fischer whispered.

"You're right," Stockwell replied in a low tone. "I don't care what happens to me anymore, but we mustn't let more innocent people die!"

"Can we take the guards?" Fischer asked.

"Get O'Brien," Stockwell suggested. "He's been in enough barroom brawls in his time."

Fischer looked dubious. Curly O'Brien was a large Irishman with a taste for whiskey. He was also the designer of the generators that created the power for Fischer's gun. But O'Brien believed that it was Fischer who had been responsible for his kidnapping and didn't trust him.

"Let me talk to him," Stockwell said, noticing Fischer's hesitation. "We've discussed escape before. We can trust him."

The technicians were another story. Two of them were small-time hoodlums with technical skills, who had become indebted to the Brotherhood.

"Don't worry," Stockwell said. "They'll follow whoever's got the guns.

"Dr. O'Brien," Stockwell called. "We have a minor problem here, but it could turn into something major. Could you come and have a look?"

O'Brien approached, scowling at Fischer as usual. In a low voice, Stockwell explained the situation. O'Brien smiled grimly.

"I've been waiting a long time for this!" he growled. "I never thought you lily-livered cowards would make up your minds. But, if you have-"

"We have, I assure you," Dr. Fischer said.

O'Brien thought a moment, then proposed a plan. Pretending that there was an emergency with the gun, O'Brien, Fischer, and Stockwell would assign the technicians jobs "of the utmost urgency." Once they were busy, a minor disaster would occur with one of the power cables. This would require the assistance of the three guards. When the guards were holding onto the cable, a switch would be thrown, sending two thousand pulsating volts through the cable.

The "accident" would take care of the three guards permanently. The scientists would then grab their weapons and seal the hatch leading into the room. Then they would destroy the gun itself.

Precisely on cue, the "emergency" occurred.

"Hey, you!" O'Brien bellowed at the technicians. "Check those readings!"

The technicians scurried off. O'Brien was about to create the cable "disaster" when he saw movement in the hatchway. The scientists turned nervously, staring as four more guards entered the room carrying a man strapped to a wooden slab, like a tabletop.

"That's him!" Fischer whispered to Stockwell. "That's the technician they hit over the head. He's the one who suggested this to me."

The guards carried the bound stranger into the room and were starting to set him down on the floor when a hunchbacked dwarf appeared in the doorway.

"Put 'im in the bomb-bay door!"

urged the dwarf.

The guards gave a start as Lexner produced a submachine gun and leveled it at their chests.

"Do as I say!" the dwarf commanded.

"What's this?" a guard asked as the other three carried the man out onto the closed bomb-bay doors. "The Masque said we were supposed to give this guy a good seat, but this is ridiculous! When the gun goes off, the guy'll fry!"

"That's the idea!" cried the dwarf. "He killed Axel and Dr. Natchez! Now he's gonna pay!"

"But orders are—" the guard began.

"It'll be an 'accident,' " the dwarf interrupted. "And if there's any more arguing, the accident won't stop with him! Now, move!"

The scientists watched helplessly as the guards carried the man out onto the bomb-bay doors.

"Tie him to those hinges!" ordered the dwarf.

Stockwell glanced at Fischer, standing near the lever that controlled the doors. He made a subtle motion, as if pulling the lever. Fischer shuddered. He couldn't send those men to their deaths!

The guards set down the table, then went to work. Lexner stood over them, grinning widely. Fischer wondered about the stranger, who seemed resigned to his fate.

The guards lashed the stranger's wrists and ankles with heavy rope,

then began to tie the ends to the door hinges. When the doors opened, he would be suspended directly in front of the gun. When the Lightning Gun fired, he would be vaporized instantly.

Fischer began to sweat. The four guards and the dwarf obviously weren't going to leave until they had achieved their sinister objective. The tension in the room was building. They couldn't take much more of this!

The stranger turned his eyes toward Dr. Fischer. "Go ahead," he told the professor silently. "Do it!"

The first guard finished his knots, and his glance followed the stranger's gaze. The guard saw Fischer standing next to the lever and sensed what Fischer was planning to do. But it was too late!

"Hey! Get away fr—" The guard's words trailed into a scream as the bomb-bay doors suddenly swung open. Everyone standing on the doors, including the dwarf and the stranger, dropped from sight.

Fischer froze, horror-struck. But he had no time for remorse. One of the remaining three guards whipped out a pistol and fired. The slug slammed into Fischer's shoulder, spinning him back against the wall. The guard took aim again, intending to finish the job, when suddenly he was hit from behind with an iron wrench. The guard collapsed to his knees, clutching his head in agony as Dr. Stockwell stood over him, staring at him grimly.

The second guard reached for his

gun just as an uninsulated electrical cable, thrown by O'Brien's powerful arms, wrapped around his neck. O'Brien threw the switch and it was over instantly. The man's hair stood on end as thousands of volts fried him to a crisp.

The third guard was still fumbling for his gun when the two technicians, seeing who was coming out on top, knocked him down and pummeled him into unconsciousness.

Grabbing the guns of the guards, the scientists suddenly found themselves in charge.

"Someone get the door!" barked Stockwell, hurrying to the injured Fischer.

"You—" O'Brien growled to the two technicians, "are you with us or not?"

Glancing nervously at each other, both technicians took this opportunity to beat a hasty retreat.

O'Brien slammed the door shut and closed the locks. They were safe for the moment.

"You all right?" Stockwell asked, helping Fischer to his feet.

"I—I think so," Fischer breathed, looking at his blood-splattered smock. "It seems to have missed the bone."

"What about the bleeding?"

"It'll be okay."

Fischer felt pain, not so much from the wound, but from the knowledge that he had dropped the stranger and all the other men to their deaths. Unlike his Lightning Gun, when some-

one else pulled the trigger, this time it was his direct action that led to people's deaths. He had committed murder.

"I need help here!" yelled O'Brien urgently from the bomb-bay doors. Fischer and Stockwell ran to his side. Looking down, Fischer gasped. The stranger, still strapped to the table, was dangling upside down beneath the ship by a single strand of rope secured to his ankle. Clinging to another rope, attached to the stranger's wrist, was one of the guards!

The stranger was unconscious. The strain on his leg must be tremendous, Fischer thought. The guard was screaming and kicking at the empty air in a desperate struggle to hold on to life.

"Someone give me a hand here!" yelled Stock-well as he dropped to his knees and began pulling.

O'Brien and Fischer reeled in the stranger, but as they did, the table caught on the door. They couldn't pull it up any farther. The guard began losing his grip on the rope as the rough hemp slipped and tore into the flesh of his palms.

"Hold on!" yelled Stockwell in a moment of compassion as he extended his arm down to the guard.

The panic-stricken man reached out with his hand, his fingertips only an inch from Stock-well's. Beads of sweat ran down the guard's forehead as he struggled to reach him.

"I—I can't..." he gasped.

"Reach!" yelled Stockwell, his fingers stretching for the extra distance.

The man slipped.

There was no scream, no yell, only silence as he plunged into the darkness, disappearing into the void of the passing cloud cover below.

"It's probably just as well," O'Brien muttered.

With the guard's weight gone, the scientists were able to pull the table and the stranger in the rest of the way. Resting the table on the deck, they removed the straps from the stranger's wrists and ankles.

"Listen to the way he's breathing," said O'Brien. "Look at his face! He's not unconscious. He's in some kind of trance!"

Soon the strange, hoarse breathing subsided. The stranger opened his eyes. He was instantly alert. Instead of being contorted by fear or confusion, his face was calm and clear, his mind lucid.

Quickly he rose from the table, fully awake. It was almost as if he had just returned from a relaxing vacation, thought Fischer in amazement.

13 looked around him, quickly assessing the situation. The guards had been taken care of. The room had been sealed off, the scientists inside apparently united in cause and purpose,

"Tie up those guards. They'll be coming around shortly," 13 commanded.

Stockwell hurried to obey, but O'Brien remained behind, staring at the stranger suspiciously.

"Who is this guy?" O'Brien demanded.

"I don't know! He said that he—" Fischer's voice faded as loud pounding and hammering began on the hatchways.

"Open up in there!" shouted a voice.

"Now what?" Stockwell looked alarmed.

"How do I destroy this gun?" asked 13.

Fischer stammered. "Well, there—there are several possible ways. The first would be—uh—"

13 impatiently cut him off. He didn't have time for long-winded explanations. He had but one purpose now—to destroy the gun.

As Fischer rambled on, O'Brien and Stockwell began shoving tables against the door. 13 quickly sized up the device, its massive capacitors towering upward in rings of iron and steel, the monstrous, snoutlike barrel pointing downward, waiting to be fired again. With several large coils of wire, he saw a way to create a back-surge that would destroy the gun. Unfortunately, it would also destroy everything else in the room, themselves included. Suddenly he had another idea.

"What kind of gases are in the cells?" the Agent interrupted Fischer.

The doctor blinked, thinking a moment. "It's a helium and oxygen mix."

The gas wasn't flammable.

"They're coming through!" Stockwell shouted.

The metal door was beginning to creak and bend under the repeated blows from what sounded like sledge-hammers. "Put down your weapons and surrender!" a voice crackled over the intercom. "You are surround—"

The retorts of O'Brien's pistol, firing into the speaker, shut the voice up for good.

"God, that felt great!" O'Brien grinned.

Ignoring the commotion, 13 leaped into the gunner's seat and began spinning the cranks that controlled the Lightning Gun's movement. The snout began to tilt upward. The moment it started to swing above the bomb-bay door, however, it stopped. 13 looked down at the gears. There was a safety catch that prevented further movement. It could not, therefore, be turned inward.

Leaping away from the gun, 13 grabbed a pistol from Stockwell's hand.

"What are you going to do?" Stockwell cried.

"Stand back!" 13 yelled as he leveled the pistol at the gears.

13 fired four times, each spinning slug ripping away a pin that prevented the gears from swinging upward. The grim-faced Agent quickly leaped back into the gunner's seat and began to crank the gears once more. The cold black snout of the gun slowly rose toward the ceiling of the airship.

"What's he doing, for God's sake?"

shouted O'Brien, backing up as the hatch door slowly caved in.

"Get ready to fire this thing!" 13 commanded.

The men in the room looked at each other, suddenly realizing that he was going to fire the gun into the airship itself.

"Let's do it!" yelled O'Brien to the others.

"We could all die!" Stockwell said, putting into words what they all knew. Without hesitation, all three men ran for their posts.

Slowly they brought the generator up to full power. Grabbing the protective goggles dangling from the gunner's chair, 13 watched the dials, waiting for the green light that would tell him it was ready to fire.

Suddenly bullets filled the air. 13 looked over at the hatch. The crew of the airship had managed to bend open one corner of it. One of the guards was taking potshots at anyone he could see.

Lifting his pistol, 13 fixed his eyes on the target, then fired.

The bullet's impact knocked the pistol from the guard's hand and splintered his wrist into thousands of fragments. As the man withdrew the remains of his hand, 13 knew it would be a while before they tried that again.

The scientists, meanwhile, had never left their posts. They, too, affixed their goggles. The generators hummed, filling the capacitors with millions of volts. Suddenly the green light came on.

"Take cover!" yelled the Agent.

He waited seconds more while everyone else scrambled for safety. Unfortunately there wasn't much to hide behind.

The Agent squeezed the trigger. The blinding white light was instantaneous with the explosive concussion. Fragments and shards of twisted iron tore through the room in a fiery maelstrom of destruction.

13 was slammed back against his seat, his face blasted by the searing hot winds of the flames. The glass of the instrument dials cracked and sparked. The din of the explosion filled their ears.

Agent 13, who had been protected by the huge apparatus of the gun, took off his goggles and looked at the remains of the room around him. The blackened steel walls looked as if they had been peppered by shotgun blasts. A massive whirlwind of escaping gases spun through the room, creating a storm of debris. Shielding his eyes from the damaging splinters, he scanned the room.

Stockwell, his shirt torn to shreds, stood in a daze, his face covered with blood that gushed from a deep gash in his forehead. O'Brien rolled on the steel floor, groaning in agony, pulling at a five-inch shard of steel protruding from his knee. Fischer, apparently unharmed, knelt beside O'Brien, trying to help.

The efforts of the crew to get into the room had stopped. There was no sound outside.

13 pulled himself from the wreckage of the gun. The entire device had been blown off its support stand and thrown backward by the force of the explosion. Freeing himself from the gunner's seat, he inspected the damage to the airship.

A fifteen-foot hole had been blasted through the ceiling. Girders and cables dangled like dead vines as the helium winds from the torn gas cells rushed past his face.

Staring upward, 13 could see no end to the hole. It disappeared into darkness. He wondered how many gas cells the blast had ruptured. He could see two. There might be more. Was that enough?

Then 13 felt something. His acute sense of balance told him the floor was beginning to list. Was it the ship itself or just a buckled floor plate, damaged by the explosion?

Suddenly, outside the door, he could hear pounding footsteps, voices shrill with panic shouting confused orders. Falling flat, 13 peered out the open bomb-bay doors. The ship seemed to be losing altitude, but it was hard to tell for certain. A loud, painful moan seemed to come from the airship itself. Was it collapsing?

"She's going to break up! Are there any chutes?" 13 asked.

"Yeah, I'll get 'em!" answered Stockwell, wiping blood from his face.

Hurrying to a supply compartment, he yanked it open and began pulling out belly chutes. Suddenly they heard what sounded like a rushing stream beneath their feet.

13 saw hundreds of gallons of water plummeting toward the ground. The crew was dumping the ballast of water in an effort to keep the airship aloft.

The craft shuddered. Everyone in the room looked at each other. Even the injured O'Brien quit moaning. Fischer had managed to remove the sliver of steel and was wrapping a crude bandage around O'Brien's bleeding knee. He sat back. The slant of the floor was now plain to everyone in the room. The airship was beginning to list!

"Put on the chutes!" commanded 13.

Then, from deep in the hull's interior, came an ominous cracking noise like the breaking of matchsticks. The aluminum girders were snapping! Klaxon horns of alarm began to resound throughout the stricken ship.

Stockwell and Fischer helped O'Brien into a parachute. They were getting into theirs when a nearby beam supporting the bomb-bay doors suddenly snapped with a sickening crack. The beam dangled for a moment beneath the ship's hull, then wrenched itself free, tumbling end over end to the earth, thousands of feet below. The entire structure was breaking up!

Like a speared whale, the enormous craft began to screech and moan its death song to the heavens. The mighty airship was finished.

"Get out of here while you still can!" barked the Agent.

"What about you?" asked Fischer, noticing that 13 wasn't putting on a chute.

"I still have something to take care of! Now, get out of here!"

Fischer stared down into the inky blackness. "I—I can't!" he moaned.

The Agent looked at Fischer's chute. It was fastened on properly. Grabbing the professor, 13 hauled him over to the bomb-bay doors.

"Count to three, then pull the ring!" 13 instructed, then he shoved Fischer out. The scientist shrieked, but 13 thought he could hear a faint voice counting. He turned around.

"Who's next?"

Stockwell jumped forward. When O'Brien limped, grimacing, to the door, the Agent stopped him.

"Give me your pistol."

"You got it," O'Brien said, happy to be rid of the thing. The next moment, he was gone, falling through the black void on his way to freedom.

13 was alone. He had two priorities—the first, to make certain the Masque did not escape alive; the second, to find Maggie.

Taking two of the parachutes, he hid them beneath some debris. Then, pistol in hand, he spun open the undamaged hatch door and ran out into the corridor.

FOR WHOM THE BELL TOLLS

No one gave 13 a second glance as he hurried to the command room. He was only one of many who were rushing frantically through the stricken craft.

Passing the hangar, 13 noticed that the floor was listing so badly that the elevators wouldn't function. Planes were stuck down below, with no way to get them to the airstrip on top. Men scrambled for chutes as officers barked final commands.

13 noticed the planes beginning to slide along the floor, unbalancing the weight of the ship toward the bow. Everyone ignored them, too busy trying to save their own lives.

The stern of the ship began to rise upward. Oil drums broke free, rolling along the floor and knocking men down like tenpins. Flames erupted as the contents spilled over the hangar floor.

13 ran on, until he reached Walters's door. He kicked it open. It was dark inside, apparently empty. He dashed inside. Light from the corridor outside gleamed on something bright and shiny on Walters's desk—13's rings!

The Agent grabbed them. He would have a use for at least one of them, he hoped.

Racing out into the corridor, he grabbed the first body he saw. He shoved the pistol barrel into the crewman's chin with such force that it slammed the man's head back against the wall.

"Where are Walters and the girl?" 13 demanded.

"Wal—Wal—Walters?" the man stammered in panic.

13 pulled the hammer back. "The Masque!"

The man shook his head from side to side.

13 fired the pistol, missing the man's face by a quarter of an inch. Blood

dripped down the side of the crewman's head, his eardrum shattered.

13 moved nearer, shoving the pistol into the man's throat. "Where?"

"The airstrip! He took her up on the roof!"

Tossing the man to the floor like a used dishrag, 13 ran down the slanting corridor, heading for the iron stepladder he had used when he first entered the ship. As he ran, he wondered why Walters would go to the roof. The autogyros were destroyed. Did he have a plane up there?

Slamming open the hatchway, 13 grabbed the cold steel of the ladder. The ladder was tilting with the ship. It would be a difficult climb, but he had no choice.

Something caught his eye—movement! In the darkness above, he could see shadows moving upward. Was it them?

Seconds seemed like minutes, minutes like hours as 13 climbed hand over hand. The air was rapidly filling with smoke, becoming heavy with heat from the fires somewhere far below.

The weight of his body seemed to increase the higher he went. He tried to block out the fatigue, but his mind found it difficult to concentate. Finally he gave vent to his pent-up anger, letting it pump needed adrenaline into his system.

He was filled with a kind of madness, akin to battle-rage. The tilting of the ladder no longer affected him. He was a ravenous predator, stalking the game he must kill.

Consumed with fury, he climbed the ladder at an almost superhuman rate.

Suddenly he came to the top of the ladder and jumped off it, landing on the steeply pitched gangway. There was nothing in sight but an open hatchway in the distance. 13 sprinted down the pitched steel deck to the open hatch. Crawling through, he saw that it led to the airstrip above.

Sweat streamed down his face as he raced up the tilting stairs three at a time. Then, kicking open the final hatch that led to the airstrip, he was out in the open.

Chilled winds blasted at his face as he stared into the blackness of night. The airship's bow was pitched in a steep dive. The airstrip and surrounding surface were still littered from the debris of their earlier attack. Beyond that, the area appeared abandoned, the gunners who survived the attack having left their posts long ago.

Suddenly 13 heard the click of a bolt, then another. Whirling, he examined the pitching deck closely. 13 saw a huge steel device, strong enough to be pressurized, apparently buried in the deck. Explosive bolts were snapping back along its side, releasing it from the ship, raising it up. The device was ringed by thick glass portholes. What was this thing?

Then, through the portholes, he saw Walters, moving around in the greenish light within the capsule.

13 began to claw his way toward the device. The pitching deck made his journey difficult; one misstep and he'd slide to his doom. But he was like a fly. Every hairline fracture and rivet in the deck supplied him with the purchase he needed.

Then he heard the hissing of rushing gases. A large port cover exploded off the roof of the bell, and a canvas bag began to inflate and rise upward. It was a hot-air balloon! Walters was using a balloon with a pressurized gondola to escape!

The massive balloon inflated rapidly, slowly pulling the rounded escape bell from its protective cradle in the ship's deck.

13 lunged at the rising bell. For a moment, he was suspended in mid-air, the airship slanting away beneath him. If he missed, it was certain death, but it no longer mattered. 13 was consumed by one thought, one mission—to destroy Walters.

His hands closed over steel, and his body slammed into the side of the bell. Rivets bruised and tore at his flesh unnoticed. His hands, their knuckles white with anger and strength, clutched at a cable. Clinging precariously to the cable hanging from the ship's side, he hung on as the craft began its rapid ascent.

Slowly, using all of his incredible strength, 13 pulled himself up to the flattened top of the bell. Looking up, he could see the hemp ropes that held the pressurized bell rising upward to encircle the massive fabric balloon as it continued to inflate. The entire device rose rapidly into the heavens. The chill of the subzero winds tore at his flesh. 13 looked below him.

The airship was growing smaller. Flames poured from her inner ports as she began to sink, bow first, into the great sea of clouds. It was destroyed. It could hurt no one now.

Leaning over, he looked through the thick, round plate of a port window. 13 could see Walters clearly. His hands wanted to reach through the window and tear him apart, shredding him piece by piece.

There were two others inside the small bell, a pilot—and Maggie! She seemed more angry than frightened, but she appeared to be uninjured.

Abruptly, 13 was aware of a new danger-anoxia! The air was thinning rapidly with the increased altitude. His oxygen was running out!

What could he do? There was no way to force himself into the bell. The small, thick glass portholes cranked shut from the inside and were designed to resist massive pressure. The glass was undoubtedly bulletproof as well.

The blood pounding in his head told him his body was screaming for air. He struggled to maintain consciousness, but things were beginning to blur. In addition, 13 began to freeze in the severe cold. He was getting lightheaded. Feeling weak, he slipped back against the top of the bell.

13 looked up. The stars were bright and clear. He seemed to be floating, journeying across the black void to those distant worlds. He looked down and saw himself lying flat on top of the bell. He appeared very small in the scheme of the universe—small and very fragile.

He no longer felt pain and torment, only peace. There were others around him, welcoming him into this strange new world.

13 felt a power directing him. Was it the dead leaders of the old, beneficent Brotherhood? God? He didn't know. Whatever it was, it was all-consuming and filled with warmth and goodness.

But something wasn't right. It wasn't time ... not yet. . . not until his mission was complete. Then the answer was given to him in a moment of crystal clarity. He flew back to his body at a speed greater then light. A moment later, he opened his eyes.

13 pulled out his pistol, its cold grip like ice in his hand. He raised his hand, pointing the gun upward. His finger squeezed off two shots in rapid succession. The bullets passed through the fabric of the balloon. The force of their passing tore a rip in the balloon. Within seconds, their ascent began to slow as gas began to escape from the bag.

His finger tensed again, and once more the pistol belched flames. He heard another tearing sound high above him, followed by the rush of air. The balloon began to descend ...

ever so slowly.

Then he heard another sound— the lever that opened the hatch. He ducked low as the whooshing of air told him the door seal had been broken. Someone was coming out to investigate!

A weathered hand groped for the iron hold only inches from 13's face. The Agent waited until he saw the pilot's eyes widen in surprise.

"What the—"

It was all the pilot had time to say as 13's hand snaked out. Grabbing the shocked man, he dragged him up onto the roof of the bell. Then he catapulted the horrified pilot out into space.

"What's going on up there?" Walters's angry voice called from inside.

"Problems! Get out here!" called 13.

He moved back away from the hatch and waited, his face tense, his frostbitten fingers clutching the pistol, his eyes cold with hatred and anticipation. He imagined his bullets turning Walters's face into crimson mush. It was almost too easy! Suddenly he heard a click.

Another hatch!

He turned quickly, but it was too late! Walters's arms grabbed him from behind. Encircling 13's neck, Walters pulled the Agent down to the roof. 13 struggled for a grip as his pistol clattered off the bell, disappearing into the dark sky.

Flinging 13 onto his back, Walters was on top of him in an instant. His clawlike fingers dug into 13's neck, trying to squeeze the life from him.

13 twisted and turned, struggling to hang on. But his opponent had also been trained by the Brotherhood.

"Say hello to your maker!" the Masque snarled.

A power suddenly welled up from somewhere inside 13. His ankle touched a tether line on the bell's roof, and he forced his foot beneath it. Then, with every last ounce of strength he had, he shot his knee upward with sledgehammer force.

The Agent's knee found home, ramming hard into Walters's gut. There was a cracking sound. 13 had hit the man's spine. Walters gurgled with infant-like sounds. His once-steely fingers relaxed and turned to Jell-o around the Agent's throat. His spine broken, he slid to the roof, a helpless— but still conscious—doll.

13 pulled himself to his feet. Leaning over Walters, he removed the man's belly chute. Walters's lips mumbled inarticulate words as his eyes pleaded for the mercy of a bullet.

13 looked down at the man. The battle-rage had subsided. 13 could easily have tossed the pathetic creature off the roof, but he didn't. Walters would pay for the untold misery and suffering he had caused with his own. He would leave him atop the falling balloon, let him linger to wonder just when the ground would slam into it, ending his misery forever.

Reaching down with his hand, the Agent struck the ring he wore against the metal surface of the bell. It began to glow white-hot. Then, leaning over Walters, the Agent pressed the burning ring against the man's forehead.

Walters's eyes registered shock as the rnark of the Agent's continuing battle against the Brotherhood was branded onto his head—the number 13.

Turning away, 13 quickly slipped into the parachute. Then he leaned into the hatch. "Maggie!" he shouted.

Her face looked up at his. He saw amazement, then swift, sudden joy.

"Thank God you're alive!" she cried. Tears streaming down her cheeks, she grasped his strong arm. He tried to pull her out of the bell, but the tremendous wind pressure caught her, holding her half in and half out. The whipping wind tore and shredded her shirt, exposing her legs and thighs to its biting chill.

"I—I can't!" she cried, struggling to free herself.

Faster and faster the balloon fell.

Holding onto the iron ring on top of the metal roof of the bell, 13 fought the winds as he climbed down inside the bell.

Grabbing Maggie about the waist, he added his strength to hers and they both struggled up the ladder.

"Hang on to my back!" he shouted. Maggie flung her arms around him, and he leaped outward from the falling balloon.

Down they tumbled, through the

blackness, freefalling toward the clouds below. Then suddenly the sensation of falling vanished. They had reached terminal velocity. It was as if they were floating.

"Hold on tight!" 13 yelled.

He jerked the D-ring with all his might. The parachute snaked out, jerking them sharply upward.

Maggie shrieked but managed to hold on as the chute jerked full against the rushing wind.

Then they were drifting slowly. Hearing a rushing, flapping noise above, they looked up to see the balloon hurtling past, the mouth of the paralyzed Walters open wide in a silent scream.

Maggie held 13 tightly. Tears froze on her cheeks as they floated lazily downward.

"I thought I'd never see you again!" she cried into his ear.

"I'm sorry it took so long," he shouted.

"Better late then never."

"I love you!" Maggie murmured, pressing her cheek against his strong back. He couldn't hear her, but it didn't matter to Maggie. She would never leave him. She would follow him to the bitter end, wherever that might lead.

They floated from the cloud cover toward the waiting ground below. For this brief moment, they were at peace.

The Hand Sinister sat on his huge throne. He was alone. Those minions who were fortunate I had been able to flee his anger. Corpses of the unfortunate littered his stairs.

Itsu felt the emptiness of the aura that had been the Masque. He felt the triumph of Agent 13.

The Hand Sinister's elaborate plans were crashing down about him. And, what was worse, it was time—time for him to undertake the journey for the *Juvita-ta*, the ceremony of rejuvenation, the I only time he ever left the safe, sacred grounds of I the Shrine.

It was also the only time Itsu was vulnerable, and he could sense the aura of Agent 13 reaching out to destroy him.

"Jinda-dii," Itsu whispered into the darkness. "You must go. Find your pupil. Bring him back...."

* * *

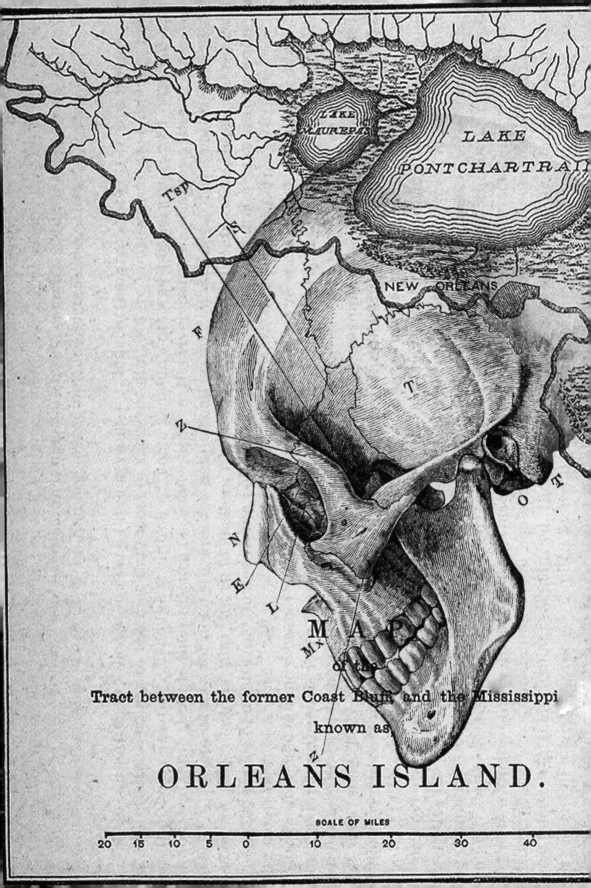

MAP

of the

Tract between the former Coast Bluff and the Mississippi

known as

ORLEANS ISLAND.

SCALE OF MILES

20 15 10 5 0   10   20   30   40

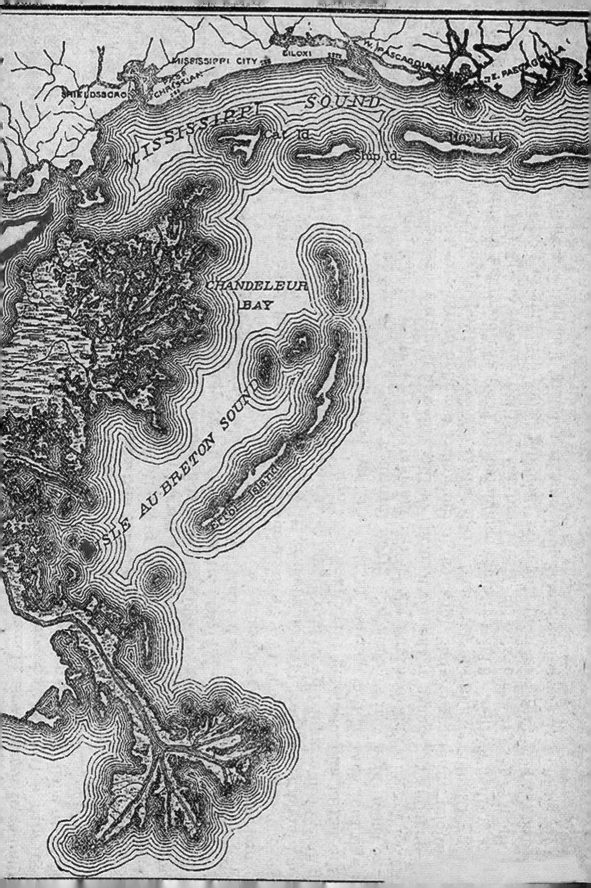

MISSISSIPPI CITY   BILOXI   W. PASCAGOULA
SHIELDSBORO   PASS CHRISTIAN   E. PASTGOU

M I S S I S S I P P I   S O U N D

Cat Id   Horn Id

Ship Id.

CHANDELEUR
BAY

ISLE AU BRETON SOUND

Errol Island

A WORLD ON THE BRINK OF WAR!

From the dawn of recorded history, the Brotherhood had worked secretly, behind the scenes, guiding the course of human history, using secret knowledge far beyond that of humanity. At first, its purposes were beneficent. However, the Hand Sinister seized power and those purposes became corrupt, perverse, evil. Now the Brotherhood sowed death and destruction through the pages of history, and it was about to write a new chapter more bloody than any that had gone before.

Hitler, Mussolini, Tojo—none of these dictators suspected that they were but pawns in a much greater plot. And neither Roosevelt nor Churchill, the two truly great leaders in the powerful democracies, suspected that they were about to engage in a struggle with a power far beyond that of any fascist state. Nor did Joseph Stalin imagine in his wildest paranoia the true depth and nature of the plot that existed against him.

But there was one man who knew, a man raised by the Brotherhood, trained in many of its secret ways. This man had discerned the true nature of the Brotherhood. Instead of rising to become one of its most trusted operatives, this man chose instead to oppose it with all his knowledge, will and might.

This man was Agent 13.

AGENT 13

CHAPTER III

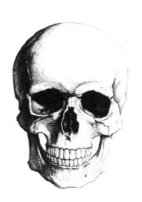

ACOLYTES
OF DARKNESS

A COLD CORPSE IN MOSCOW

For just a moment, Lavrenty Pavlovich Beria was seized by a sickness of spirit. As he crossed the vast, empty whiteness of Red Square, he had a disheartening awareness of his own inadequacies and a profound sense of impending doom. He quickened his step.

Five men, men with the stolid, heavy-browed, sunken-eyed faces of Soviet bureaucrats, huddled against the high red-marble wall of the mausoleum, watching Beria's approach. None spoke. Occasionally, one coughed hoarsely. Another stomped his feet trying to drive the freezing cold from his burning toes.

Beria, an irredeemably ugly man with deep-set eyes, thin, cold lips, and disproportionately large hands, walked directly up to the small group. Without a word, he lifted one eye to glance up the staircase and walked quickly forward, leading the way up the stone stairs. Around the

outside of the memorial, he went, and up to the top of the mausoleum where Lenin's body was on display. The five silent men fell in behind Beria, forming a single file procession that snaked up the staircase.

The only observers of this strange, silent parade were the handful of Kremlin guards who maintained a constant, solemn vigil over the great square from the high walls at the heart of the Soviet empire. For most of the soldiers, the sight of Beria and a handful of bureaucrats provoked only mild amusement. Even top officials, they thought, must suffer from the cold. But for a few special soldiers, the scene was of intense interest. They all watched carefully, and were ready for action.

Although no trace of anxiety showed in his face, Beria was very tense. His heartbeat quickened and his large, gloved hands clenched into tight fists as he thought of the order insisting that he hold visible meetings in public places.

Beria worked best in the covert battles of the state. As head of Joseph Stalin's secret police, and the chief instrument of the dictator's endless bloody purges, his cold fingers had silently roamed at will across two continents and their icy touch brought promised death.

But Beria was also a man who obeyed orders. And these orders had come from a power far greater than that reflected in the high, red walls of the mausoleum. They had come from the Hand Sinister, Itsu, Head of the Brotherhood.

A cold, white moonlight flooded through the windows of the mausoleum, casting eerie shadows. Beria took his place near the head of the great glass case. He looked down into the dead eyes of Lenin for a brief moment before beginning the meeting. Then he raised his ugly face to his five followers and smiled a thin, weasel-faced smile.

"Brothers, we may speak freely. As head of Soviet internal security, I can assure you that this place is not subject to scrutiny by hidden listening devices."

The five men arranged around the glass case chuckled and snickered. Beria's smile vanished. "We must decide what to do about Stalin." His voice was calm, incisive, and betrayed none of the anxiety that was bottled up inside him.

"Hitler and Mussolini are mere pawns of our agents in their countries, and the entire Japanese military establishment marches to music composed by the Hand Sinister. Stalin, however ..." His voice faded and he shook his head slowly. With a soft, coaxing, penetrating gaze, he eyed his men for suggestions.

"But why cannot Stalin be persuaded differently? We all know there are techniques," began a baby-faced man with a delight of the grotesque, of the obscene.

"That will not work on some men," Beria snapped. "We have not been able to control Stalin as we have many others, because the man is both a genius and a psychotic paranoid. His very insanity makes him a match for the best of our infiltrating agents. He trusts no one—not even me. And he weaves plots within plots, sometimes plots so complex that the Hand Sinister himself is unable to follow all the threads."

"Then we assassinate him," persisted the man, a strange glint in his eyes.

"No! Killing Stalin would initiate another power struggle for which we are not prepared," said a distinctly unremarkable figure bundled up in layers of fur and wool.

"I have reflected on this situation for some time," he continued. "And I believe I have a solution to our problem."

"Proceed," Beria encouraged.

"A temporary truce with Hitler. A temporary non-aggression pact between the Germans and ourselves would give Stalin a false sense of security, and it would buy Hitler time to deal with France and Britain before he invades our country. Stalin has hoped for some time that he and Hitler would reach an agreement."

The circle of men again fell silent. Gradually, a smile played at the corners of Beria's mouth and a fire came to his dark eyes as he envisioned the plan.

"The matter is decided," Beria stated curtly. "Goodnight, comrades." As an afterthought, he added, "Before we go, let us, as good Communists," Beria grinned at the irony, "pay our respects to Lenin."

He glanced again at his five subordinates as they lowered their heads for respectful viewing of Lenin's body. Then he looked down himself and recoiled in terror.

A BLAST FROM THE PAST

Vladimir Lenin's blue eyes sparkled brightly as they saw the look of utter terror on Beria's face. But Lenin's corpse couldn't waste time admiring the view. Before Beria and the five other Brotherhood agents could react, the right arm of the fallen Soviet leader raised a sawed-off pump action shotgun, and the finger fired the first shell straight through the foot end of the glass case.

The blast shattered the entire glass structure in an instant.

The red-hot lead pellets and countless glass shards ripped through the abdomen of the baby-faced man. The man flew back and upward a full five feet, crashed against one of the enormous columns supporting the mausoleum roof, slid to the floor sitting upright, then collapsed forward like a broken rag doll, his forehead smacking the concrete between his snow-covered boots.

The remaining Brotherhood agents stepped backward in shock and horror. Lenin sat upright, swinging his legs over the side of the bier as he pumped the next shell into the shotgun's chamber. Chunks of broken glass tumbled from his head. He raised the weapon to his shoulder and fired, downing another man.

As his comrades fell around him, Beria managed to slip quietly down the stone staircase.

Lenin jumped to his feet, and kept the trigger pulled as he worked the shotgun's pump. Three more explosions echoed through Red Square. The remaining three Brotherhood agents toppled forward down the stairs, collapsing in heaps of freezing flesh, steaming blood, and shredded cloth.

Quickly, Lenin glided across the marble floor to the first sprawled body. It's glassy eyes stared up at the vaulted ceiling in disbelief of their final vision. Lenin lifted the dead KGB officer's hand and held it open. Holding a strange amulet, he viewed the officer's palm through a crystal of a color and shape not found in nature.

He felt no surprise when he saw the tattooed number "6" appear on the palm. Invisible to all, save the user of the crystal, the numbers served to identify Brotherhood agents.

Then, in a series of actions that would have been most mysterious to the outside observer, Lenin struck a large ring he wore against the cold stone floor. The white-hot ring sizzled and smoked as he pressed it into the forehead of the dead Brotherhood agent. When the killer removed the ring, the branded message was clear . . . the number "13."

Before branding the next corpse, Agent 13 moved to the window and cautiously surveyed the situation. Guards were scrambling down the Kremlin wall, fanning out around both sides of the huge mausoleum.

13 had eliminated five Brotherhood agents, but the sixth and most important, Beria, had escaped. And now, it was obvious to 13 that this meeting was a cleverly laid trap for him. Those "Soviet guards" who so skillfully descended the Kremlin walls were not ordinary soldiers, 13 knew. They were Jindas— specially trained and drugged assassins whose sole purpose was to kill on command of their Brotherhood superiors.

13 exited down the stairs taken by Beria, pausing when he reached a small landing from which he could not be seen by any of the approaching guards. Quickly, he stripped away his outer garments, exact duplicates of those in which Lenin lay in state. Beneath those clothes he wore the uniform of a Soviet private attached to the Kremlin guard.

Seconds later, his face was devoid of the characteristic mustache and eyebrows of the dead Soviet leader. Without them, his face looked like that of countless other anonymous Soviet soldiers. Finally, 13, indifferent to the pain, smashed the side of his face hard against the cold, red-marble wall. Blood trickled down his cheek, and the side of his face began to swell.

His transformation thus complete, Agent 13 trampled his discarded Lenin disguise beneath the deep crusty snow, dropping the shotgun there as well.

As he continued down the outer stairs of the monument toward Red Square, 13 saw the enormity of the trap prepared for him by Beria. The jeeps had arrived, one at the foot of the main set of stairs.

13 stepped onto Red Square. The machine gunner on the jeep eyed him coldly.

The troops following the jeeps were shoulder to shoulder, starting to form an impenetrable barrier surrounding the mausoleum. The more thinly spread Jindas advanced ahead of the main line of troops, sensing that their prey was very near.

"Comrade!" Agent 13 shouted to the machine gunner. "Up there! Quickly! The assassin is escaping. Send your men to cover every inch of the mausoleum!" Agent 13 ran as he shouted, nearing one of the Jindas.

"Halt, comrade," the machine gunner shouted in reply. Agent 13 heard the distinctive "click" signaling that the man had prepared the weapon for firing. "You have forgotten something."

Agent 13 looked at the nearest Jinda, saw the crazed, glassy eyes of the drugged man, and knew that somehow his identity was known. He stopped and turned. Behind him, the line of regular Soviet troops raised their guns and tensed, ready to fire.

"What have I forgotten, comrade?" Agent 13 asked, running the bluff to the end. "I have urgent business concerning the protection of comrade Beria, who even now ..."

"Comrade assassin," the machine gunner replied, "you have forgotten your boots." The man grinned broadly. "A clever disguise, but you forgot about the boots!" The man laughed uproariously as he ordered the troops to seize Agent 13.

"Well done, Lieutenant Sokolov," roared a voice from high on the Kremlin wall. "This man is the prisoner of the KGB. Escort him at once to the Lubyanka for interrogation."

Agent 13 looked up. Peering down on the scene in Red Square was the cold face of Beria, his thin lips smiling in victory. Beside him towered a dark-haired handsome man. Although years had passed since he had last seen this man, Agent 13 immediately recognized him. He was the Jinda-Gaa, prize pupil of the Jinda-Dii and the most lethal assassin in the world.

Agent 13's and the Jinda-Gaa's eyes met momentarily in an expressionless stare. Then each man smiled. There was a deep understanding between these two men who had both been trained in the knowledge and arts of the Brotherhood. At one time, they had been both friends and rivals.

Beria and the Jinda-Gaa turned and walked away, disappearing into the Savior Tower, the huge gothic structure that is the major public entrance to the Kremlin fortress.

Agent 13 shifted his gaze to the ground and stomped his feet. They were nearly frozen in the thin leather shoes that were exact duplicates of those on the corpse of Lenin.

RED STREETS IN MOSCOW

The sky over Red Square held only the barest hint of dawn, a subtle gray in the overcast blackness above, as Agent 13 was handcuffed and shoved roughly into the back seat of the Soviet military jeep. One armed guard sat next to him. Lieutenant Soko-lov, the grinning officer who had trapped Agent 13, stomped the snow from his boots and took his place in the driver's seat.

13 studied the scene around him and considered his best chance for escape. The eyes of the guard next to him in the back seat had the dull glaze of a Jinda assassin. 13 knew that this man would be extremely dangerous if he were to make a move.

The Jinda's goal, his entire life's training, and his drugged compulsion would drive him to kill. If the assassin himself were to die, his body would burst into flames. Low-ranking Jindas were forced to drink mantha, the oil of fire, an Eastern serum that interacts with strong natural chemicals released during death and causes a combustible reaction. Should the Jinda die while trying to carry out his mission, no trace of his body would remain.

The driver turned the jeep off of Red Square and headed northeast onto Chernyskevsky Street. Soon the snow-covered thoroughfare would be thronged with early-morning pedestrians, and a stream of small, cheap Soviet cars as they made their way southeast, bearing minor Party officials to their day's work in the Kremlin. But now, the road was deserted.

Lieutenant Sokolov abruptly pulled the jeep to the side of the road and in a deep, throaty voice directed the Jinda guard to step out.

"You have failed me," Lieutenant Sokolov commanded. "Pay the price for your failure."

13 watched with increasing interest.

Who, he wondered, was Lieutenant Sokolov? He knew that the lieutenant must be a high-ranking Brotherhood agent, because the Jinda would only respond to a Brotherhood superior. Yet he was bewildered by the command. The price for failure for a Jinda was seppu-ku, death. The Jinda guard's death would leave the lieutenant sufficiently vulnerable to an attack by 13. The command, therefore, made no sense. 13 suspected a trap.

Yet, without a sound, the Jinda removed his sword and fell forward onto the blade, wrenching the cold steel from left to right.

Disemboweled in the snow, he waited patiently in a puddle of blood for his life to run out. Seconds after his last breath, a wisp of blue-green flame emerged from the man's back.

The tiny flame grew rapidly; the man's flesh crackled and popped. The flame continued to grow until it became a consuming white-hot fire. The stench of burning flesh lasted for only a moment, and then there was nothing except fine ash on the snow next to the jeep.

"Who are you?" 13 demanded, turning to the lieutenant.

Lieutenant Sokolov pulled the latex mask from his face and turned to look straight at 13. . . . She didn't say anything. She just looked at him with her large, bewitching china blue eyes.

It was always this way when he saw her. And he knew it was happening again. Yet he felt incapable of changing his reactions. He no longer felt like himself. He felt different. He felt at a distinct disadvantage.

Once, in another place and time, when his name was Tredekka and hers was Carmarron, he had loved this woman. Many years had passed, and Tredekka had become Agent 13, while Carmarron had become China White. Yet every time he had seen her since, which was surprisingly often, he felt, for that first fleeting moment, intimately bound to her as though they still shared a wonderful secret.

Agent 13 knew that at the core of China White's being there raged a constant struggle between her love for him and her love for power. When last they met, her love for him had almost won that struggle. It was she who had freed him from certain death. In saving his life, China White had risked her own. If her treachery were discovered by Itsu, there would be no place on Earth to protect her from his vengeance. 13 could only guess that the Hand Sinister was unaware of China White's betrayal.

She took off her hat—her raven black hair whirled wildly in the cold Russian wind as she started up the jeep and drove on.

"Why?" he queried, breaking the silence, his voice remarkably calm and unemotional. "What is this all about?"

She laughed the disarming, engaging laugh of an opera singer, deep and melodious. China White gave little away.

"I would tell you that I still love you tremendously and could not let you be captured, but I'm quite certain that you would not believe me."

"Even now, the Brotherhood hunts you, as well," he challenged, regaining his confidence.

"Do you really believe that Itsu has discovered that I saved you?" she questioned softly.

He made no answer. The jeep sped down Cherny-skevsky Street, past Boulevard Ring, away from central Moscow.

"Your work here is done. The Brotherhood's ring in the Soviet state is smashed. Their attempt to trap you has failed." China White spoke softly, not pleadingly.

"Beria is still alive," 13 responded.

"You're not after Beria. You know that without his agents to support him his power is limited. You will come back for him another time when he is not on guard against you."

Agent 13 said nothing. He kept his silence until the jeep pulled into an obscure garage tucked between two large factories. Across the street was one of Moscow's many large, open parks. Inside the garage, 13 saw a small catapult-launchable aircraft, an Aristotle 1-15.

China opened the door of the jeep, stepped out, and motioned for 13 to join her. He stood beside her and looked down into the deceptively soft features of her face. She was a woman of remarkable beauty with her high Slavic cheekbones, tiny nose, full sensuous lips and large, intense, smiling eyes.

"Of my motives, I will leave you to ponder." Her blue eyes glowed passionately as she stood in the enormous parka and large boots she had used to disguise herself as Lieutenant Sokolov.

"But know this, my love. Itsu's health is failing. He is making immediate preparations for the Juvita-ta."

Agent 13 listened carefully. The Hand Sinister's need for the Juvita-ta, the ceremony of rejuvenation that could bestow almost eternal life to the flesh, would force Itsu to leave the Shrine. He would be vulnerable.

"Remember," she whispered like a small child imparting a secret, "distant days at the Shrine and the rumors of a man named Brother Du Lac who lived at the Abbey of the Dead in Jaca. He will help. I promise."

"Why would you help me?" 13 finally asked coldly. "You know that we can never be together again."

"Perhaps," the softness of her answer was almost carried off into the darkness, as she turned toward the door of the jeep. "Perhaps now we are even."

A hundred questions were on 13's lips, but he asked none.

She quickly pulled her long legs into the jeep and slammed the door. The jeep sped off, glittering like a precious stone, reflecting brilliantly in the early morning light.

The Aristotle 1-15, a single-seat monoplane fighter, parked in the garage, looked almost new. 13 tried to start the engine. To his surprise, the carburetors fired with an explosion of black smoke, then hummed rhythmically. Their reputation for performing well in the cold, he thought with a smile, was well deserved.

13 jerked out the throttle for all it was worth then slammed the catapult release handle downward. The device threw the Agent back hard into the leather seat. He counted to himself as the plane skidded quickly down the makeshift runway . . . one thousand, two thousand, three thousand . . . and then he was airborne. Soon, the collective farms and dashas were but small black dots floating far beneath him in a sea of white.

He flew southward until he spotted the Minkoje Sosse, a winding, muddled waterway that led directly to freedom. If his fuel estimates were correct, he could fly six hours before running out of gas.

Barring contact with Soviet interceptors, 13 reasoned that six hours would be more than enough air time to take him somewhere over Poland. Perhaps even to Warsaw.

His escape nearly complete, Agent 13 thought about the strange events of early morning. He cursed his own stupidity for allowing himself to be set up by the Brotherhood, and he questioned the motives of China White.

Why would China help him? Was it that her love for him, borne so many years ago at the Shrine, had returned? Was it a strange kind of "repayment" for saving her life at the hands of the Masque? Or was there a deeper, more sinister reason?

13 knew that it had obviously taken considerable planning for China White to have authentically disguised herself as the lieutenant. No doubt, he thought with assurance, the real Lieutenant Soko-lov's body would be found with the abandoned jeep. Beria and the Jinda-Gaa would assume that Agent 13 had once again escaped. No one would suspect China White's involvement.

13 could not bring himself to accept the simplicity of her tale. Rather, he suspected that her motives were far more complex. But, for the moment, he had no choice but to go on the information she had given him. If her intention was to betray him, he would be walking right into her trap.

The questions of why China White had saved him and divulged Itsu's vulnerability continued to plague him and he turned them continually around in his head as the morning sun warmed his face. He began his journey to the mysterious Brother Du Lac.

FEARS OF THE DARK ONE

"Why?" The words of Itsu formed as a trickle of air was, with great effort, pushed from the paper-thin, crumbling lungs through the dying throat and fleshless lips.

"Why did you fail me?" Itsu rasped to the hacked corpses that littered the steps to the huge onyx pyramid that served as the base for his throne. The frenzy of the mass suicide, which he had ordered, was finally over.

The Hand Sinister felt no remorse. These men had mocked him with their failure to entrap Agent 13. They understood that the price for failure was death.

As Itsu had watched the knives dive deep into their abdomens and the blood stain the marble steps, he had felt inextricably linked to these men. Watching the cascade of blood had cleansed him momentarily, had purifid the dark thoughts that had increasingly invaded his mind.

The Hand Sinister uttered a harsh whisper that grew to the force of a very deep shout, punctuated with bubbly tremeors as if his breath were forced through water on its passage to his mouth. "Jinda-Dii!" he shouted. His words echoed for some time in the cavernous throne room.

The old man who stood before the entrance to the hollowed-out fortress of stone, deep in the Andes mountains, heard his name reverberating through the Shrine. For a brief moment he failed to acknowledge the call and continued to look out over the dark horizon of other snow-capped mountains. Standing there, oblivious to the pentrating cold, he might have been mistaken for a medieval monk or abbot. His austere, commanding figure was humbled by the simple red robe that he wore, and the cowl that covered his face.

Like a monk, the man had inherited a tradition of knowledge and ritual, of great effort and discipline, of the mysteries of the mind, the body and the spirit. But there the resemblance ceased. For whereas the tradition of the monk was founded on the knowledge and discipline of love, the tradition of this man was founded on all things unholy, base and bestial, on all things that corrupt and destroy, all things that decay the human soul.

This man was the legendary Jinda-Dii, head of the Order of Serpentine Assassins, chief of those privy to the wills and acts of Itsu, the Hand Sinister. The Jinda-Dii had chosen evil with open eyes, embraced it with open arms. His lips had kissed the worm of death freely, and its white, cold lifeless lusts he had made his own.

The jinda-Dii was troubled by his strange thoughts, however. Once again his men had failed to capture Agent 13. Yet, he had a strange sense of relief. For Agent 13 had been the pupil of the Jinda-Dii, his greatest pupil, who would have become the Brotherhood's greatest agent. It was the thought of Agent 13 that made the Jinda-Dii hesitate now, that made whatever still lived in his own soul yearn for that other path so long ago forsaken.

He turned and entered the great fortress, hewn from rock before the memory of humans began. As he entered he felt himself spiritually contracting and a wave of peace set over him as he walked through the high arches and pillars. His own shadow merged with ghastly purplish images that were lit by black flame.

The stifling, repressive atmosphere of the Shrine pleased him and secretly affirmed his very being. Within the Shrine, his malignant soul was allowed to deny any other choice. Within the Shrine, Agent 13 became merely a menace to him, one who must be destroyed.

As he entered the throne room, an unmistakable and repellent stench of death caressed him. The Jinda-Dii briefly studied the agonized faces of his dead men horribly highlighted in the dark flame's lurid light and stepped over their bodies. At length, the Jinda-Dii halted twenty steps below the chair in which the body of Itsu reposed. Those final twenty steps, made of gleaming gold, could be trod upon only by the Hand Sinister.

The Jinda-Dii stared directly at the living death who was his master, his own hard, shining dark eyes boring into the sockets through which Itsu saw the world.

"My death shall be yours...." the Jinda-Dii said simply, his voice betraying no emotion, his blade held to his stomach.

The Hand Sinister smiled a ghastly smile. A robed, deathly thin arm rose from one of the armrests on the throne, and a skeletal hand made small circling gestures in the air. "Death shall not come to you so easily."

The Jinda-Dii saw the glint of rage in the lifeless eyes, shrunken to an almost nonexistent rot in the blackened skull.

"Summon the Mondra Lava and the Bludda Dak for the Juvita-ta," the Hand Sinister commanded. Then anger seemed to well up in the mummified figure like an earthquake from within.

"Do not fail me or I shall inflict things upon you that are far more searing than the knife you hold to yourself!" he shrieked. "Now go. Time is short."

Without words, the Jinda-Dii bowed to his master and quickly departed, grateful that instead of death, he could be of help in the ancient rituals of the Juvita-ta.

I am perishing, the Hand Sinister thought with terror as he took a painful inventory of his decaying body. The flesh was nearly gone. He had lost all of his strength. Only the use of the most advanced mental and spiritual disciplines had imparted enough power to the shreds of muscle tissue remaining to enable the body to slowly move.

To escape from his agitation and torment, Itsu closed his eyes and his soul departed into the dark region of the Shadow Zone.

There, Itsu's soul swirled in the refreshing blackness of its own evil, giving off a light that was not a light—a radiant darkness. The Hand Sinister soared in this zone, which was a realm of pure spirit, beyond space and time.

From that timeless realm, the Hand Sinister willed himself to see the Earth as if he were soaring high over it. Through thick white haze, Itsu saw the forests, mountains, plains, rivers and seas of the Earth flying by below him. Soon, he thought, there would come a day when the earth, the air, and the sea would reverberate with the screams of human pain and death, when the water and the soil would drink human blood on an unprecedented scale. From the ashes of this worldwide conflagration would arise the new world, a world ruled by Itsu, the Hand Sinister himself.

As Itsu serenely meditated on these events and sadistically anticipated world domination, he felt the dreadful presence of a lesser darkness in the Shadow Zone. This lesser darkness attempted to engulf him and smother his soul. A traitor, he thought in despair. Yes, the Hand Sinister knew this presence was the soul of a traitor, a traitor within his inner circle of Bishops and high-ranked Jindas. He could not, however, identify to whom of his trusted confidants this soul belonged.

The Hand Sinister hastily returned to his body. In the murky twilight of the dark flame, Itsu once again felt a prisoner of his body. He had a devouring restlessness to hasten the Juvita-ta even though Agent 13 was still at large and a deadly traitor was very close at hand.

For the first time since his youth, the Hand Sinister was consumed with fear. He sank deep into his cowled robes.

MIDNIGHT JOURNEY

Agent 13 was hidden deep in the cowl of his British monk disguise, as the Sud-Express left the Gare d'Orsay in Paris in darkness. Even though the train had several luxurious first-class Pullman cars, 13 preferred the Spartan comfort of second class.

Three girls amused themselves by attempting to see the face hidden behind the holy cowl. One girl could make out the pale, beaklike features of a man who had apparently spent his adult life in a closed, dark room poring over old musty books. She could also make out his eyes. They were deep blue and frightening, watchful and cold. The girl never suspected that only days earlier this monk had masqueraded as the "father" of the Russian Revolution.

After an otherwise uneventful night of travel, the Sud steamed into the Spanish frontier station of Irun. The morning sun slowly rose in the Basque sky while the air brought moist hints of the nearby Bay of Biscay. The disguised 13 transferred to a provincial train which took him east along the southern base of the Pyrenees mountains. The train's destination was Jaca.

In the train's cramped quarters, he appeared to spend his day in seemingly "pious" meditations. In truth, he thought of his own life. As he watched the emerald green waters of the bay sparkle with rays of sunshine, something rose from the depths of his mind—a ride in a carriage many decades before. He was a child. His parents were American missionaries in South America. As their wagon rolled through the rutted jungle, they hummed a hymn. And then, suddenly, the jungle erupted in explosions and flames.

Agent 13 abandoned himself to reverie and took possession of these vague memories and lost times. His parents were dead, and he was carried by brutal hands to a secret camp deep in the jungle. He looked for the first time into the diabolical eyes of the man who would be his master and tutor. This man was the Jinda-Dii.

From there, he was taken to the Shrine—a realm of darkness, a place whose location was so secret that only the Jinda-Dii and Itsu knew the route.

13 recalled his childhood. He was raised to be a Brotherhood agent and taught science, politics, art and the true history of the world as it came from the Brotherhood's sacred texts. He very quickly learned to embrace this malignant world. He became the favorite pupil of the Jinda-Dii.

Then it happened. At.seventeen, he was seized by a sickness of spirit. He found it difficult to concentrate on his studies. All he could think of was Carmarron. Her china blue eyes. Her raven black hair. Her warm touch. When he was near her, he felt that he had been waiting for this for all his life. He desperately wanted to be with her. To make her laugh. To escape what he now viewed as the imprisoning, stifling cloisters of the Shrine.

When Agent 13 discovered in his research one night that what he had thought was the truth about Itsu and the Brotherhood, was in fact a lie, he knew that he must escape. He planned the night when both he and Carmarron would depart. However, when he sneaked out to the garden where she was to meet him, she was not there.

Instead, he was nearly caught by Brotherhood agents who had learned of his intended defection. He fled. And was hunted.

A strange, wonderful, magical little man named Ray Furnow befriended him, protected him. Ray gave him a place to rest and the time he needed, quite literally, to collect his thoughts. Ray helped 13 re-evaluate his own preconceptions of the world and gave him access to his former self.

It was Ray Furnow who one night, while peering into a beautiful crystal, awakened in 13's mind the mystery of his kidnapping in South America. It was Ray Furnow who led him to the cemetery where 13 saw a tomb with his own name on it: "Tedd Phillips." It was Ray who convinced him to fight the ugly, senseless evil of the Brotherhood. But Ray Furnow was dead now, a victim of the Brotherhood.

Agent 13 wished he could have the memories without the bitterness, without the all-consuming desire for revenge. As he watched the dazzling sunrise from the train, he felt a sad estrangement from humanity. His insular life was full, he concluded, of many private experiences that could be shared with no one.

His self-imposed mission to destroy the Brotherhood was at times barren. Sometimes, in a disheartened mood, it seemed to him that his identity had become so inextricably linked to the Brotherhood's demise that he had no sense of normalcy. Without his fanatical quest to destroy the Brotherhood, he decided, he would have nothing.

Although he briskly put a period to these thoughts and felt the movement of the train underneath him, it seemed as if he were not moving at all.

A STRANGE MEETING

Arriving in Jaca, the hook-nosed monk begged passage on a horse-drawn carriage with an elderly man and woman who were heading to their home in the Pyrenees.

The husband, who 13 estimated to be nearly seventy, smiled reverently as he helped the monk gain access to the wagon. Secretly, 13 suspected, the man counted the blessings this act would give him in heaven, as some men might count money. His wife, whose face had the cheerful yet distorted look of a rotted jack-o'-lantern, bowed her head to him and made the sign of the cross.

The carriage departed, and 13 nodded his head several times as though in prayer. Imperceptibly, though, 13 painstakingly surveyed the surrounding area. He could not trust China White. Any one of the dozen beggars they passed could well be a Brotherhood agent. Well did 13 know that the knotted fingers of a widow could conceal the trained barrel of a pistol, the drunk's bottle could be an incendiary bomb, and the farmer's scythe could,

in trained hands, as easily behead the Agent as a stand of wheat.

13 had chosen not to wear a weapon. Civil war raged in this country and although he was in the most rural part of Spain, the mountains did not escape the ramifications of war. Afraid that he would be checked by local authorities on his departure from the train, 13 had chosen instead to rely on his lightning reflexes and sharp perception.

For hours, as the carriage travelled up and down the hilly terrain, the peasants spoke only to themselves. 13 remained silent. His cowl masked a mind that had abandoned his earlier disquieting thoughts and was now racing ahead to his encounter with Brother Du Lac.

So often this man's name had been whispered in the shadows of the Shrine. 13 had heard the rumors-Brother Du Lac, Itsu and a third man named Sharu had started the Brotherhood. 13 wondered if Brother Du Lac was a spirit or if he, too, partook in the mysterious ceremonies of the Ju-vita-ta.

The mountains were startlingly silhouetted against an icy gray sky and the moist dusk air was perfumed with blossoms. As the sky was turning from gray to black, 13 eyed the ruined monastery. Its broken walls and towers rested like jewels in the crown of the craggy heights. Agent 13 noisily cleared his throat. "Leave me here...." he said to the peasants in broken Spanish.

"But, Father, the building is but a ruin. There is nobody up there. . . ." the husband responded.

13 smiled in the shadows of his cowl. "Please, good people, stop the wagon," he insisted.

The wife turned to him, her face wrinkling like a handkerchief. "There are ghosts in there. It is called the Abbey of the Dead."

The Agent bowed in his seat. "Yes, and these ghosts must be sent to heaven. . . . Thank you for the passage. Go with God."

13 waited for them to pass out of sight before he began the steep ascent to the gray-black building which looked down on him like a mourner looking into a fresh grave.

At one time, the devoted would have climbed a narrow and winding path to the great, bleak structure. The passing centuries had, however, played havoc with the path. Rain had eroded whole sections of it. Landslides had covered other sections with rubble. And small

bridges had rotted away. Everything about the monastery was softened in the dusk. 13 crossed the obstacles on his way up with tremendous agility, a skill that would have betrayed his monk's disguise had anyone been watching.

And he did feel watched . . . watched from above. Thus, when the night mist drifted in across the Pyrenees, obscuring the peaks, and a wind hummed up the valley like a Gregorian chant, 13 felt a sense of relief. His approach to the monastery was concealed in the murky dusk.

13 walked the final passage in darkness. Though the monastery had been a place of worship, he could not help but be aware of grim reminders of what this place once was. The stone wall was stained where hot oil must have been poured on invaders. The broken tip of a battering ram stuck through the metal frame of a gate whose wooden parts had rotted away. And below him, filling a pit which was once crossed by a drawbridge, was a pile of bones.

As there was no other way across, 13 waded through the mass grave. The sodden earth gave way, and he often sank in the mud and bones. Surveying the pit of human rubble, 13's gaze fell upon a telltale Jinda knife. Though it was ancient, he could not mistake its shape. There could be no doubt but that he had come to the right place.

Suddenly, a Spanish voice cut through the gloom, jarring the Agent's thoughts.

"By what right do you desecrate this hallowed abbey?"

13 looked up to see a figure standing above him within the gates of the monastery. He held a rifle and was dressed in the uniform of a Loyalist. As 13 had anticipated, even the unpopulated mountainside was infiltrated by Franco forces attempting to overthrow the government, and Loyalists attempting to secure the regime. 13 quickly assessed the figure. He was only an adolescent, his face smooth and unlined, his posture erect and confident. Yet, he took short, gasping breaths. His nervous hands held the gun imprecisely. His tightly compressed lips excitedly twitched in a smile. And his desperate eyes— there was a wild look of madness in the young boy's eyes that 13 recognized even in the fading light.

Assuming the identity of the British monk, Agent 13 responded in English. "It is you who brought weapons into a house of God . .. and you are a Loyalist, no less." Loyalists, 13 knew, were devoted followers of Catholicism.

"Weapons are sometimes needed to fight God's wars," the boy said in fluent English. The last word was spoken with an edge of sarcasm. Then, his voice changed to a command. "Go no further."

Agent 13 froze in compliance. The boy drew a flashlight, ignited it, and vanished in the darkness behind its intense light. The light played on 13's robes, penetrating under the cowl.

Though it seemed the boy was unsure of what to do, 13 was never one to trust fate. As the boy shifted his balance, the Agent dove into the pile of bones, grasping for the Jinda knife, which glimmered in the sea of bones. Bullets crashed from the boy's gun. 13, however, took advantage of the boy's need to wield the gun and the flashlight simultaneously and used his own speed and dexterity.

In a single motion, 13 grasped the knife and advanced quickly forward into the light. He planted the point of the knife firmly against the boy's belly and thrust inward and upward as hard as he could. With his left hand, he reached out and took the boy's gun while the boy gasped in surprise and pain. The boy let out a gurgling moan as his eyes rolled back. He sank slowly, his knees buckling and his head falling forward. A strange emotion welled up from deep within 13.

He felt inexplicable remorse. He never liked to kill. Yet he did it easily, efficiently, when it was necessary. This boy had threatened his mission and 13 suspected .. . "

Reaching into his cloak, he drew out the seer stone and grasped the boy's hand. Though the day had turned to night, and there was no real illumination, 13 could read the tattoo that seemed to glow with its own light. It was the number "58" within an ancient symbol. As the Agent had suspected when no other Loyalists had scrambled the walls with guns, this dead Loyalist was not loyal to the regime at all. He was loyal only to the Brotherhood.

Yet, something was wrong with this boy. Something connected to the madness in his eyes and his presence at the Abbey of the Dead. 13 knew China White well enough to know that she would have the best-trained Jindas here to greet him if she wanted to trap him. 13 was again perplexed and suspicious.

In a grim ceremony, 13 struck his ring upon a rock. Suddenly the entire portal of the monastery was bathed in a searing white light.

Before the ring could touch flesh, a voice cut through the magnesium sizzle.

"And for what purpose was my best pupil slain?"

13 was so startled that he grabbed the boy's rifle and blasted several shots into the gloom.

The echoes of gunshot on stone finally died away and were replaced by uproarious laughter. 13 peered into the darkness waiting for death. Waiting for a dagger to strike him squarely in the eye. Or a bullet to lodge in his heart.

"You have just killed my best pupil," the voice in the darkness said grimly. "It took me months to convert the boy from Itsu's madness to my madness."

13 lifted himself off the ground. He shouted, "Are you Brother Du Lac?"

"The Brother Du Lac died in sixteen forty-seven," came the voice from the velvety fog.

A grim smile crept across 13's face. "That does not answer my question."

Laughter echoed in the air. "You are called Tre-dekka by some, Agent 13 by others. I knew this when you dispatched the boy so quickly and so heartlessly."

13 instinctively recoiled. After living half a life with a disguised identity, it came as quite a shock to have his mask of anonymity so easily torn from him. "You are the one known as Brother Du Lac," 13 stated with conviction.

"If you must know me by a name..." the old man said.

"What are you? A spirit?"

"Indeed," the deep voice said solemnly.

The answer did not surprise Agent 13. He continued, "I was sent here by one who told me you might be of help. Her name is China White. She said the Hand Sinister would soon be vulnerable."

The spectral figure nodded. "China White spoke the truth. Itsu must soon go for the Juvita-ta."

"Will you explain it to me?"

"I must begin at the beginning. This will take time," Brother Du Lac stated. "My story begins five thousand years ago. Human history had not begun to be written and yet a great, benevolent civilization flourished. It was our civilization, and it is known to you as Lemuria."

"I am aware of the ancient legends," 13 responded.

"Yes, but you only know them as Itsu would have you know them."

The old man cleared his throat. "As a young man, Itsu forsook the heavenly world of Lemuria which he was born into, and entered the world of primitive humans. So great was his knowledge, that shortly they began to worship him as a god.

"He revelled in this adoration, became their king and deity, and for a time reigned over an empire.

"But, alas, there was a limit even to his power. Eventually, his subjects saw him as flawed and turned on him. Had he consented to die then and there, Lemuria, the Golden City, might well have flourished to this day. But the greedy Itsu valued his own life above all others, and fled to his homeland of Lemuria. He was pursued. The barbarians swarmed down on the city, and Lemuria died in bellicose flames.

"However, the precious secrets of Lemurians were preserved in the Crystals of Uru. These crystals-Science, Religion, and Politics—contained all the knowledge of the universe. It is rumored that they were forged in a distant place in the heavens.

"Not knowing that it was Itsu who brought about the city's demise, the great fathers foolishly trusted him to protect one of the crystals. Sharu and myself were trusted with the other two. We were all to hide within a hol-

lowed mountain shrine near Lemuria and wait with the crystals until we felt it was safe for our great civilization to rise again."

13 interjected, "One day not long before I fled the Shrine, I came upon information that led me to believe that Itsu's version of the fall of Lemuria was a lie. Once I knew he told one lie, I suspected many more. I fled the Shrine."

"And you attempted to take Carmarron with you. Now, it is fortunate that you failed. Even now, she rots the Hand Sinister's power from within," he said musingly.

"Or at least that is what she leads you to believe," 13 responded.

Brother Du Lac smiled with conviction and then continued.

"For thousands of years, Itsu, Sharu and I remained in our mountain shrine. We partook in a much different form of the Juvita-ta. The ceremonies were benign and beautiful. Itsu, of course, now has altered them immensely.

"Together, we formed the secret, eternal Brotherhood. From our knowledge founded in the Crystals of Uru, we acted as a guiding hand over humanity's fate. Gradually, however, the differences in our individual personalities became more apparent.

"Sharu was most like a true Lemurian. He believed only in goodness, love and beauty. His happiness was found in the white, pure spiritual region of the Shadow Zone—a place where his soul could soar to new heights of perfection.

"Itsu, on the other hand, perversely denied the Lemurian doctrines. With the ambitions of a diseased mind, he became fascinated with the idea of violence, delighted by the pleasures of terrors. He found his happiness in the darkest regions of the Shadow Zone—there his malignant soul could flourish.

"I became the balance between these two, the mediator of their disputes, the ruler of the three. I lived in reality with a love for both the imperfections and the beauty of humanity. Even then, I disliked the Shadow Zone.

"Itsu, whose evil could allow for no compromises, plotted to topple me. This he did through elaborate potions that altered my thoughts. For a time, I became his pawn and embraced his ugly, senseless evil. Sharu could only watch in horror as we plotted and schemed for world domination. That period of time was known to humanity as the Dark Ages. Itsu, through his dark magic, was able to release plagues, pestilence and the jackals of war.

"Sharu, meanwhile, saw the evil that was controlling me and tried to release me from Itsu's bonds. He locked me up in this monastery." He gestured around himself. "For a time, it worked, and the veil of darkness slowly began to lift from the Earth. Mongols and Huns stopped ravaging the land. The Crusades were abated.

"Itsu, however, plotted still. He secretly kidnapped small children from the world. These children were ranked according to their intelligence and physical prowess. Slowly, Itsu developed an intricate hierarchy whose membership had multiple levels and purposes. Within the hierarchy existed separate orders each with its own levels and purposes. Itsu created the orders of Bishops, Knights and Rooks—the men within these orders were especially trained in politics. Their job was to infiltrate all of the various political institutions of the world. Another order, the order to which you, Agent 13, belonged, was the Order of Serpentine Assassins, a secret cult of ruthless killers. I'm quite certain that you realize you were one of the highest-ranked Jinda agents of the Serpentine Assassins.

"Sharu realized that Itsu, who now chose to call himself the Hand Sinister, would never rest until I was in his hands. His Serpentine Assassins infiltrated the monastery. Rather than have me recaptured, Sharu slayed me here."

"Hardly an act of goodness," 13 stated.

"Good is not always passive. But we will save philosophy for another time. I sensed Sharu's intent, and decided to save my soul by departing into the Shadow Zone. A foolish choice. I do not belong there. Both Sharu and Itsu found happiness there.

"I have found none. I belong to the

world. I desire to live. To truly live," he said passionately. "To once again breathe the air. To be free."

"And how is that done?"

"There is an elaborate ceremony, but it can only be carried out by one who has the Crystals of Uru. Sharu, although no one really knows if he still lives in the physical realm, has one crystal, the Crystal of Religion. Itsu still has the Crystal of Science and the Crystal of Politics. I want those two crystals."

"Hence your alliance with China White," Agent 13 concluded.

"Hence my alliance with you."

"Why? Why would I ally myself with you?"

"Because our interests are aligned. Time is on Itsu's side if he can complete the Juvita-ta. Already, Itsu's poison has contaminated the world. If Itsu lives, the world will be forced to embrace an all-encompassing evil. An evil that will invade every aspect of life, that will allow no freedoms. Itsu is the heart of all evil."

"You need not say any more, Brother Du Lac. How might I destroy Itsu before the Juvita-ta?"

"The Juvita-ta consists of three ceremonies—the Water Ceremony, the Powder Ceremony and the Blood Ceremony. Soon, the Bludda Dak, a vampire and high priest of the Blood Ceremony will be summoned from Egypt. The Mondra Lava, a woman gifted in voodoo and the high priestess of the Powder Ceremony, will be summoned from Africa."

The Mondra Lava, 13 thought to himself. He knew her name. Already he had one of his agents watching her. She was a suspicious woman, but he had not realized that she was so intimately involved with the most sacred of Brotherhood ceremonies.

"The Water Ceremony is performed by an ancient tribe of Mayans. The location of this ceremony is extremely important. It is the site for the entire Juvita-ta," Brother Du Lac said. "Unfortunately, all my knowledge of this ceremony was sealed before the Modern Age, so I do not know exactly where it happens.

"But I can tell you this. The location of the Juvita-ta was once seen by humans and was sought after for centuries afterward. Find out where the Fountain of Youth is believed to be, and you will find the site of the Juvita-ta.

"Once you have destroyed Itsu, take the crystals. Then, you will know how to repay me ..." The last of the monk's words drifted out of his mouth like smoke from a cigarette and floated toward 13.

For a moment, Agent 13 watched the swirling patterns. Suddenly, he realized his companion had vanished into ether. Only his echoing voice remained.

"Do you understand? I want to live. To be free ... to be free. Help me to that end and I will be an ally of great value to you."

THE LOST MANUSCRIPT

"Help me to that end and I will be an ally of great value to you." Maggie Darr repeated the words Agent 13 had just spoken to her. She struggled to suppress a laugh.

The large, airy room, bathed in the early morning light, was the color of orange sherbet. Maggie stood in the middle of the room in a tight red dress that mirrored the colors of the sun.

"Is this guy for real?" She turned impulsively toward him. Her eyes sparkled and she smiled.

He looked up at his closest confidante. He knew that his existence had become complicated by the presence of Maggie Darr. She was sensual, self-assertive and an expert with a gun. Her long, sun-streaked blonde hair cascaded in loose golden locks over the red dress. She seemed to radiate in red. And it seemed to him that for this moment she did not belong to him at all. She belonged to another world— a world of elegant parties, sophisticated people and romantic adventures. He was conscious once again of his desire for her. A desire to capture her warmth and beauty.

"Maggie," he said in a voice carefully cordial and impersonal in order to dismiss his emotions, "you have touched on the truth. Brother Du Lac is only a spirit."

She gave a mock shudder, like a child who has just heard an unearthly delight.

"That's charming," she said with an irrepressible laugh.

At one time, several years before, the idea of spirits, burning Jindas, a Shrine, a Brotherhood, a Hand Sinister would have struck her as the absurd notion of a lunatic. She had, however, abandoned familiar notions of the world and embraced a much stranger philosophy.

As 13 continued his account of his

meeting with Brother Du Lac, she studied him. His face was cold, ruthless and handsome. He had strong Aegean features, deep blue eyes, curly dark hair.

13 was sitting in front of a large map on the wall where several circles had been made in red. For years, 13 had been searching for the Shrine, the secret place that was the heart of the Brotherhood. This room, Maggie thought to herself, was 13's Shrine, his sanctum.

One wall contained a small but comprehensive library. Another was lined with weapons—from automatic weapons to swords. Opposite the map was Agent 13's disguise atelier. Tables were filled with makeup, and hundreds of wigs covered endless faceless heads. At night, Maggie would often wait in the dark for 13. She knew that in the moonlight these faceless heads became hauntingly real.

Maggie knew all of Agent 13's disguises. She had seen his many faces, his many moods. She knew 13. She believed in him. She believed in his world of enlarged dimensions.

He could feel her warm, delicate breath laughing on the back of his neck. "I need your help," he finished. "We have very little time."

"I know," she said, suddenly serious.

The warm, comforting smell of mustiness emanated from the walls of the library. After several frustrat-

ing days spent researching ancient records, both Agent 13 and Maggie were discouraged. They realized they could research for years before discovering the location of the Juvita-ta.

It was a rainy, dreary day, however, and Maggie, although disappointed by their progress, was glad to be sharing some time with 13. Maggie adored Agent 13. She truly loved him. She thought that he also loved her, but he so rarely showed her. She vaguely wondered if he had been different with China White. She could not bring herself to think long of Agent 13's past love affair.

Maggie turned the faded pages of a document that had not been read in nearly four hundred years. Its words, written by a ship's scribe whose name had been lost to history, told the tale of a fabulous quest for the Fountain of Youth. It was as though this document had been magically placed in front of her, intended to be read at that very moment by her alone.

"I have it," she said quite simply. She read the manuscript aloud through the noise of the falling rain.

"In 1591, two explorers, Alvarez de Pineda and Cabeza de Vaca, were ordered to explore the New World territories west of Florida. This is the same location where Ponce de Leon had earlier searched for the Fountain of Youth. The two men came upon a great river. They named it Rio del Espiriru Santo. At the mouth of the river, Pineda came upon a large town inhabited by a tribe of men wearing loincloths and bright masks."

Agent 13 looked at Maggie with increasing concentration.

"There, they discovered an underground labyrinth. On their first expedition, they reported the discovery of a huge red room with a large pool of water. Many of the tribesmen were in this room dancing frantically around the pool. The water began to bubble and eventually erupted like a geyser, a fountain." Maggie interrupted herself. "This next part sounds a little far-fetched," she commented and then continued.

"Suddenly from the pool of water arose a gigantic, obscene creature—half mammal, half fish. Terrified of the creature, they made their way back to the ship. They called the creature the Salamis. The next day, with renewed courage, they mounted a second expedition. No more was ever heard from them, and the underground labyrinth was never discovered by any of the rescue parties sent out by the ship."

13 took the document and held it under the reading lamp for a moment. Although 13 quickly dismissed the presence of the huge creature as pure legend, he had little doubt that these explorers had accidentally stumbled upon the location of the Juvita-ta— and had paid for their knowledge of it.

From years of history lessons at the Shrine, he knew that the river that the Spaniards had named Rio del Espiriru Santo became the Mississippi River,

and that the large village where the river met the ocean might well be the site of modern day New Orleans.

"You are brilliant," he said to Maggie emphatically.

"This means everything to you," she said, turning her luminous eyes toward him, a shadow of disappointment in her pale face, a tinge of regret in her voice.

"Yes," he said.

"Perhaps once Itsu's dead," she started, "perhaps then we shall have lives again that are simple and clear."

"Perhaps," he said softly, "perhaps."

By late afternoon, the rain had ended and 13 was standing in a dark, seedy Chicago hotel room looking around at the men he had carefully brought together. He smiled. They were all good men. Their help would be invaluable.

None of the four men knew why Agent 13 had summoned them to Chicago on this hot, summer night. They simply knew that 13 needed them, and he was a man worth risking everything to help.

Agent 13 looked across the room at FBI Agent LaMonica, in a crisp white shirt and immaculate pants, who leaned casually on the back of a pinkish, bedraggled couch. He was oblivious to the sweltering heat. His dark, hawkish eyes were surveying 13 for clues, although his stoic face betrayed no indication of his curiosity.

LaMonica unconsciously ran his finger up and down a long bullet scar on his neck. He had been a detective with the capital police in D.C. when he was called to the scene of the brutal assassination of several high-ranking National Security Advisors. He was shot in the neck by a Jinda fleeing the scene. Another inch and another minute without medical attention, and LaMonica would have been dead. Agent 13 intervened and saved his life.

13 felt comfortable with LaMonica. His matter-of-fact attitude toward life and death mirrored his own. And his quick intelligence, loyalty and honesty were indispensable.

Next to LaMonica stood Karlton Gould. Gould was a large man with an easy smile and the stature of a quarterback. Years earlier, in Nepal, Gould had been an obscure diplomatic attache who had run into some problems with the Brotherhood.

He very nearly met his end in an "unfortunate accident," but 13 pulled him out at the last minute. Now in his mid-thirties, Gould was a high-ranking member of the State Department.

Gould's eyes twinkled with anticipation. He enthusiastically embraced 13's assignments. They were great relief from the tedium of State Department work. Agent 13 caught the excitement in Gould's eyes. He respected Gould immensely and enjoyed his candid, friendly disposition.

Squatting on the floor in jeans and a faded shirt, his elbow resting on his knee, was Gunnar Holt. Gunnar was a passionate, intelligent man with a thirst for adventure and a wave of shocking white hair. For twenty years, he had lived in the Congo, making frequent trips to the United States to visit his teenage children.

Gunnar liked the predatory darkness of the jungle and the frightful, primitive urgency of the natives. Gunnar remembered his first meeting with 13 well. 13 had come into the Congo on a mission. Although Gunnar had never seen him in the Congo before, he recalled that 13 spoke the language of the natives fluently.

Gunnar had been impressed by this young man. When 13 asked for help, Gunnar willingly complied. Now Gunnar saw 13 on his trips to the States, and eagerly embraced any new assignments.

13 knew that Gunnar would be especially helpful now. Brother Du Lac had informed him of the importance of a woman named the Mondra Lava. Gunnar Holt had traded with the woman for several years. Gunnar had shared with 13 his suspicions about the Mondra Lava, and 13 had always suspected she was linked to the Brotherhood. Now he knew.

The last member of Agent 13's group was a nondescript man of forty. Benny Meyers sat awkwardly in a chair playing with the buttons on an old radio. Affectionately known as Benny the Eye, Benny had been strangely withdrawn most of his life. He had wandered New York City for years living in fear. Fear of the gutter. Fear of a knife jabbed through his throat in a dark alley. Fear of losing at the races. Agent 13 had given Benny a place to rest.

Benny, in the last several years, had learned to carry himself better. It was only at meetings like this that he was uncomfortable, and felt out of place. He did not belong with these men. He felt he was their inferior.

As Agent 13 gave Benny a warm smile, he realized that it was virtually impossible to disentangle Benny from his metal-framed glasses, his baggy pants and his badly fitted shirt. Benny, however, was intuitively streetwise and tremendously loyal.

"Gentlemen," Agent 13 began in a moment of rare humor. "I promise you high adventure in New Orleans.

"And perhaps even the Congo as well," he said to Gunnar.

HIGH PRIESTESS OF POWDER

A week after the Chicago meeting, and a continent away, a small paddleboat slowly churned its way up a steaming jungle river.

Gunnar Holt wiped the sweat and insects from his forehead with a soiled bandana. He knew that he would have to do it again in a few minutes, but that was all right. It relieved the tedium of the long, uneventful ride. So did the bottle of European whiskey that he tipped to his lips.

Finishing the bottle, Gunnar pitched it into the muddy brown water, which concealed disease and alligators with equal ease. As Gunnar watched the bottle float down the dark river, he was struck by a disturbing realization. Something had changed about the river.

For almost twenty years, he had lived in the Congo, and now he felt a part of it. The natives referred to him as the "White Warlock" in reference

to his skin color, shocking white hair, and the magic "Fire Sticks" he brought to them from the United States. These alien weapons, the natives knew, could turn the tide of wars and change the rules of hunting that had existed for thousands of years. The magical nickname "White Warlock" had kept him safe in an era when arrows shot from the dark had struck other Americans and Europeans.

At dusk, the jungle sounds grew softer and the wind started blowing gently. The sky turned a beautiful peach color. As the boat passed through a fork in the river, Gunnar became aware of the rhythmic throbbing of drums in the distance.

Despite the beauty of the setting, Gunnar could not help but notice the nervous expression on the face of the boat's black pilot. As nightfall drifted over the jungle, Gunnar lit the kerosene headlamps that guided the boat after dark.

It was then that he saw the first of the poled skulls. He had seen these ghastly warnings endless times. Yet, no matter how often he viewed the skulls, he always found the stench of their rotting flesh and the abject horror frozen on their faces very disturbing.

Lighting a pipe, he studied the twisted faces as they drifted by in the black night. In the flickering light, the black faces seemed to greet him with blood-chilling, sardonic smiles. Suddenly, Gunnar saw something that sent a shudder down his spine.

It was the freshly poled head of a white woman. Her blue eyes still screamed from their sockets, and the blood that dripped down the pole was still fresh and red. He had seen the woman at a trading post upriver. She was a Dutch missionary who told Gunnar that she had come to study the tribes. It seemed to Gunnar that they must not have appreciated her academic concern. Nevertheless, Gunnar knew that his instinct was right. The river had changed. The taboo against killing Caucasians had been lifted.

And what of the Mondra Lava? Gunnar took another puff from his pipe. The aromatic tobacco helped to conceal the stench of severed heads. She was the real power in Central Africa, despite the Spanish, Dutch, British and Belgians who had alternately tried to lay claim to the southern kingdoms. She practiced strange witchcraft that had won her tremendous respect among the natives. Of her birth and upbringing, nothing was known. The only clue was to be found in a literal translation of her name: "Daughter of Fire."

His first meeting with the Mondra Lava had been unlike any other subrosa business dealing on which he had embarked. ...

She stood before him in a tight, white dress and black heels, an unusual outfit for the jungle. Her sparkling eyes were fixed on Gunnar, greedily seeking every detail of his reaction to her loveliness. She ran her hands down her light brown body. His eyes drank in the subtle curves of her hips in the tight garment. Her legs were long and willowy. Her slender fingers were accented by long, red-lacquered nails. Around her neck, in bold contrast to the white dress, was a necklace of animal skulls.

She was at once a witch and a saint.

"I need someone among the whites who travels frequently to the States," she said provocatively and at the same time harshly. "White Warlock, will you be that one?" Her large, dark eyes bore into him.

Even though Gunnar was terrified and at the same time tantalized by her, he was determined not to show it. As every white man in Africa knew, to show fear was to sign a death warrant. He nodded and said, "If your prices are good. ..."

"I believe you are a man who can be

trusted as long as I meet your price," she stated matter-of-factly. "I do not expect loyalty from you, but I do expect you to honor the confidentiality of our dealings. . . ." Later, Gunnar would stop to contemplate the fact that her grasp of the English language was better than his own.

After their unusual first meeting, business settled into an even flow. Most of the time, she asked for foodstuffs and weapons. He knew that she was a woman who had obviously spent a great deal of time in the civilized world, and he did not find her requests unusual. Of course, there were those strange requests for birds.

Every month, Gunnar would take a caged, black featherless bird, delivered to him by a strange Chinese man, upriver to the Mondra Lava. He thought it strange that although he had delivered more than twenty of the featherless birds to her, he had never seen one of the birds again. He could only assume that the birds were for her witchcraft.

Now, as his weather-beaten paddle boat drew up to the Mondra Lava's dock, Gunnar was greeted by the woman herself. How odd, he thought.

When he stepped off the rickety dock, he bowed and greeted her. In response, she held out her hand and said, "The bird." Startled by her rudeness, Gunnar turned awkwardly, stepped into the boat and handed her the cage with the bird in it.

Without another word, she quickly retreated to her strange temple, of an architecture he had never seen on the African continent before. Gunnar stood on the dock and recalled his meeting with Agent 13 in Chicago. 13 had insisted on the urgent need for Gunnar to follow all movements of the Mondra Lava.

With this in mind, Gunnar boldly stepped off the dock and walked quickly to the temple. Only his blind determination prevented him from being struck by the horror of the temple. Human skins hung from the ceiling, drying like parchment. All around were shelves of eyes and ears and carafes of blood. In other places in the room, Gunnar could see other human parts floating in glass containers.

The Mondra Lava herself knelt before a sacred perch upon which the bird sat. Lost in her meditation, she hummed a chant, and the bird seemed to respond by echoing it. Then, to Gunnar's amazement, the bird spoke. "Juvita-ta," the bird said clearly, "Juvita-ta."

The Mondra Lava turned toward Gunnar. Her beautiful face seemed greatly changed in the obscene candlelight of the temple. She wore a hideous expression on her face. She spoke to him in harsh words, "It is fortunate that you spied upon me; otherwise, you might have viewed your death as unjust," and then she laughed a high-pitched tinkling laugh, which sounded like wind chimes in a gentle breeze on a freezing night.

She stared hard at him, focusing her trained powers on Gunnar Holt. Flames shot straight through Gunnar's body, searing every cell in every organ. His suddenly pain-numbed brain understood only one of the many inputs coming from his own burning flesh. His ears heard, but his brain did not register, not yet, the sickening sizzle of his body as it popped and boiled. For Gunnar, his brain understood only the pain, a pain more intense than any he had ever imagined, a pain accompanied by the stench of his own combustion.

As the sun rose the following morning, the charred face of Gunnar Holt, locked in a permanent screaming rictus, sat on a pole, and decorated the side of the great river.

Things *had* changed on the river.

DEATH TIDINGS

Four days later, Agent 13 received a terse telegram from Karlton Gould.

STIR CAUSED AS CHARISMATIC AFRICAN PRIESTESS MONDRA LAVA SETS OUT ON PILGRIMAGE ABOARD SHIP KNOWN AS "SACRE COEUR" STOP MONDRA LAVA KNOWN FOR EXOTIC "ZOMBIE POWDERS" STOP THOUGHT YOU WOULD BE INTERESTED STOP FIRST MATE OF SHIP AND CAPTAIN FOUND DEAD ON SHORE STOP NO REPORT FROM SHIP DESPITE FUNCTIONING RADIO STOP NO WORD FROM GUNNAR HOLT END

Agent 13 had no trouble understanding the implications of the note. The Mondra Lava, priestess of the Powder Ceremony, had been summoned from Africa to the site of the Juvita-ta.

Having no transport, she and her faithful had hijacked the French freighter and killed at least some of the crew. No doubt, he thought, she would turn up at one of the many New Orleans voodoo parlors. He would have Maggie check them out when she arrived in New Orleans.

As he picked up the phone to contact Gunnar Holt, he had a strange, sickening feeling in the pit of his stomach. Only one explanation would have prevented Gunnar from contacting him. Gunnar Holt was dead.

HIGH PRIEST OF BLOOD

As Gunnar's head decayed in the stifling jungle heat, an old man, his face etched by sand and sun, his palm carrying an invisible tattoo, moved slowly, purposefully through the Moab under a red-hot desert sun.

At noon, the old bedouin paused beside his tired mule and cloth-covered wagon to wipe the streams of sweat from his leathery brow. He cursed to himself, glancing at the relentless glare above him. Then, as if resigned to the task before him, he slowly pulled out an ancient parchment from beneath his cotton robes. His eyes stung as he tried to focus on the fragile document. Beads of perspiration dripped from his chin, dotting the document which now absorbed his concentration.

The parchment map was to a place that was lost and forgotten centuries ago. Although the starkness of the landscape made identification virtu-ally impossible, the bedouin had traveled the desert many times. He recognized through the waves of rising heat the distant peak of Machaerus, site of King Herrod's fortress where John the Baptist had been imprisoned and beheaded. He knew from the map that when he reached the fortress, his journey would end.

Although the sun's light increased in intensity, the bedouin felt as though he were moving further and further into darkness. The painful stillness of the parched air agitated him, the waves of heat blurred his world, and he felt a part of a nightmare of which he had lost the beginning and end. The old man had been a low-ranking Brotherhood agent since childhood, and he had never questioned the strange missions on which he had been sent. But today, today he felt violently swallowed up in the sun and the sand, lost in a dark, dark evil.

Soon, the mercy of the approaching night arrived. A calm serenity descended on the desert, and his agitation lessened as he reached the base of the rocky hill. He looked up to see the bleeding sun, a red fireball, melting behind the hills in front of him. The map matched exactly the rough landscape before him.

He quickly stepped to the rear of the covered wagon and threw back the canvas to reveal its mysterious contents. The Bedouin gazed upon the body of a tall young man. The man's face was deep in concentration.

The Jinda-Gaa slowly opened his eyes and sat up. His breathing sounded rough and uneven. Again the man closed his eyes in meditation. Slowly, his breathing and movements became regular and controlled. After several moments he again opened his eyes and locked his vision on the old man.

"Where is the map?" he said finally, so softly that the bedouin was convinced he had only imagined the words. The bedouin handed the document over to the young man. Quickly, the Jinda-Gaa scanned the parchment with clinical, detached eyes. He compared it to the surrounding landscape and was satisfied.

"Help me with this casket," he commanded the bedouin. Next to the Jinda-Gaa was a coffin of an exotic hardwood. With great strength and effort, the old bedouin slid the box from the wagon. He then pulled the ropes that bound the coffin. The lid came off with a soft squeak.

Inside, the bedouin was stunned to see a striking young woman. Her hair was twilight black, and her gowns were simple yet elegant—reminiscent of ancient Egyptian clothing. Around her neck was a magnificent collar inlaid with jewels.

Reaching into the back of the wagon, the Jinda-Gaa extracted a small flask. As he opened the top, the bedouin shrank from the liquid's foul-smelling fumes.

He watched the Jinda-Gaa pour the wretched liquid down the woman's satin-smooth throat.

The stunning creature slowly came to life as though after a suffocating sleep. The woman said nothing as she opened her mysterious lavender eyes. They remained glassy . . . trancelike.

The Jinda-Gaa reached into the wagon and pulled out a torch soaked in oil. He then took the woman by the hand and turned to the bedouin.

"You will stay here. I shall return before the sun rises."

"As you wish," the bedouin replied in uninterested tones as he turned his attention to feeding the mule. But the old man of the desert was tormented by a peculiar insistent need to learn the truth of the journey. Controlled by his incessant desire, he decided he would follow them. After all, he rationalized, he was one of them. It would cause no harm.

"Your mind betrays your voice." The words were somehow generated from inside the bedouin's own head. He spun around to find the Jinda-Gaa standing directly behind him, a strange, eerie glint in his eyes. With indifference, the Jinda-Gaa removed the bedouin's knife and as the bedouin stared with uncomprehending eyes, the Jinda-Gaa plunged the knife through the old man's throat.

As the Jinda-Gaa and the beautiful woman climbed the rocky hill, the Jinda-Gaa thought of his orders. The thought that he, the Jinda-Gaa, prize pupil of the Jinda-Dii, had been sent on this mission to awaken a miserable vampire, struck him as particularity degrading. Ah, he thought, the heavy price for the Moscow failure. How, he wondered, had Agent 13 escaped?

Arriving on a ridge, the Jinda-Gaa and the entranced woman were confronted by a series of cave openings. The Jinda-Gaa did not hesitate. Lighting the torch, he and the woman entered one of the smaller caves. There they began their silent descent into the darkened void.

The air was chilled and damp. After one hour, they had descended almost one thousand meters beneath the water level of the Dead sea. Passing under a three-foot archway, the Jinda-Gaa and the young woman were confronted by a large chamber whose walls were fashioned of massive cut stones that had been carefully fitted together by ancient hands long before.

In the center of the chamber was the object of the Jinda-Gaa's search. Be-fore him was a large, enclosed pool filled with a brilliant red liquid that looked horribly like blood. Floating in the center of the pool was the humanlike body of the Bludda Dak.

Stepping into the shallow pool, allowing his robes to be soaked by the liquid, the Jinda-Gaa began to recite an ancient passage while approaching the floating priest of the Blood Ceremony. He took the same vial he had used to awaken the woman and poured the liquid between the Bludda Dak's thin lips, while continuing to chant the ancient words, as if they would protect him from whatever it was he was about to awaken.

The being began to stir, opening its eyes to reveal only the whites. Its thin face was an unnatural pallor. Like a primitive animal, the being slowly rose from the aged pool. It sensed the presence of the woman. The creature knew that its centuries-long thirst would be quenched.

The Bludda Dak moved slowly toward her. She made no attempt to run or shriek in horror. Though, thought the Jinda-Gaa, if she had, she might have gotten away. She only whimpered slightly as his white arms circled her flesh.

The Bludda Dak struck without warning. Her skin broke easily under the pressure of his canines. Her jugular vein was ripe, he thought, and he ravenously depleted her body of its lifeblood.

The Jinda-Gaa watched the offering in horrified fascination. When the body was a drained husk, the Bludda Dak stepped over her remains and approached the Jinda-Gaa.

"For what purpose have I been summoned?"

The Jinda-Gaa's answer was simple. "For the purpose of the Juvita-ta."

BLOOD JOURNEY

Inspector Pierre Moulon surveyed a terrible scene. A beautiful woman lay dead on the floor of Room 238 of the Grand Dame, a first-class hotel overlooking the shore of Tangier. Her throat was horribly gashed.

Moulon knew that the woman who lay dead on the floor was a prostitute known as "Madame Night-flower." So striking was her beauty and so great her charm that neither the Church nor the authorities made any effort to punish her.

The killer, it was assumed, was the foreigner who had been registered in the room the night before. Of him, depressingly little was known. His name was Count Ghiza, and he was described by the desk clerk as a swarthy, handsome Egyptian. Moulon was certain that the man's name and title were far from legitimate.

"There is no blood," Moulon said, observing the most disturbing aspect of the case. "How does a woman have her throat ripped out and yet not bleed..." Moulon said in a heavy French accent.

Moulon's protege, Jacques LaPore, had no response.

They both turned, as a terrible hissing sound came from across the luxurious suite. What they saw was both comic and horrifying. The hotel captain, a dignified Arab, made a strange sign with his fingers and uttered ancient and terrible words. Gone were his cosmopolitan affectations, and summoned was his native upbringing.

"What is it?" LaPore asked.

The Arab, whose mutterings had risen to a frenzy, did not respond to the young investigator. However, Moulon did. "I think it should be obvious that he believes this to be the work of a vampire."

LaPore scoffed. "Superstitious natives . . ."

Moulon turned to his young assistant. "Does a better explanation present itself to you?"

LaPore could not find an answer.

As he ordered the body slipped discreetly through the back door of the hotel, Moulon began to speak to the terrified hotel captain. He told the man to come out of his panic. These things happened. He could be assured that the authorities would do everything they could. And that much was true. Moulon would make every effort, but he had a strong suspicion that the bizarre killer would vanish into the mysterious tapestry of North Africa as invisibly and as silently as he had come.

Upon returning to his office, Moulon sent wires to all the capitals in the Mediterranean area. A day later, the wires sizzled with news of similar scenes in the grand hotels of Cairo, Tripoli and Tunis. Moulon's blood ran cold. Stepping to an enormous map on the wall, he traced the mysterious man's movements from Egypt to North Africa to Tangier. He asked the respective police forces for any information they might have.

Working all day and into the night, Moulon began to put together a picture of the murderer. He was an Egyptian whose skin was white, and whose hands were unnaturally cold to the touch. Moulon shuddered and filed away his notes.

Days later, Moulon read a terrible account in an English newspaper. The body of an American heiress had been thrown from the great ship Normandie, and had washed up on the coast with a telltale gash in the neck. Moulon knew who the killer was and where he was going. The inspector, however, was too late. By the time he had notified authorities, the mysterious Egyptian, traveling under a new name, had blended into the myriad crowds in America—an ancient figure in a new land.

The Bludda Dak, high priest of the Blood Ceremony, had crossed the world.

TRAIL OF TORMENT

No living thing has ever been so hideously diseased, thought the Hand Sinister. The time has come for the journey. It is well.

As his traveling entourage surrounded Itsu—the Jinda-Dii, China White, a few notable Bishops and high-ranking Jindas—they were tormented by the acrid smell of decayed flesh.

One of them is mocking me, he thought. One of them is the Betrayer. He scanned each one of their faces.

Was it China White? Had she once again fallen in love with Agent 13 as she had when she was a young woman? Her raven black hair cascaded over her purple robes and her lavender-blue eyes twinkled innocently at him.

Next to her stood the Jinda-Dii. Could it be the Jinda-Dii? Could he be a puppet, even unknowingly, on Agent 13's strings? Itsu nearly shuddered at the thought.

He scanned the gaunt faces of his elderly Bishops. All seemed devoted.

Ah, he thought, betrayal is a cruel game indeed. He could not identify the traitor. He had no defense against this unknown enemy. He would sacrifice them all. . . yes, all. Yet, each was invaluable to the success of the journey.

"I will meet you below," he wheezed. "Leave me to prepare." Then the red-cowled living skeleton sank inside his robes, exhausted by his troubling thoughts and physical pain.

His entourage walked from the throne room into the great nightmarish three-dimensional labyrinth that was the Shrine. The maze had been designed centuries before. For the unwanted, it was a certain deathtrap.

The throne room was empty at last. Now, he thought, no eyes will see my struggle simply to walk. No tongue would ever tell the secret of the hell below the Shrine that he was about to enter. It was a place whose existence, while sometimes rumored among the agents, was known only to himself and the Jinda-Dii.

Itsu was ready, his power fully concentrated on the locomotion of his body. His ears heard the "click" of his skeletal hands on the arms of the onyx throne. They heard the scraping of dying bones in ball and socket joints as Itsu pushed his body upward, out of the throne, slowly bringing the embodiment of Living Death to his feet. Itsu inched his way toward the first of the twenty golden stairs where only his own shriveled foot was allowed to tread.

He stepped through pain, into pain, willing his body, again and again, down the twenty golden steps, the two hundred marble steps, then onto the vast floor of the empty throne room.

Gleeful, sinister laughter coughed from Itsu's throat as the effort of controlling the pain brought him to the edge of insanity. Still, the figure moved forward, now stumbling, now lurching, now standing immobile while his mind again and again gained control over the lifeless body.

Slowly, Itsu made his way to the back wall of the Shrine's vast throne room, to the flat, cold, seamless wall of rock, smoothed by hands dead before the dawn of history. At last, his skeletal fingers scraped against the unrelenting hardness of stone. Then Itsu spoke a single word of an ancient Brotherhood language. And the stone opened.

Itsu stood framed in an archway on the edge of a vast, glowing pit. Blasts of red-hot, dry air rushed up toward him, carrying with them the subtle sounds of human agony heard from afar.

Looking downward, Itsu could see no bottom to the pit. Instead, he could see only the molten agony of the Earth, the dull red glow of magma a great distance down.

Itsu stepped forward into free-fall. So light was his body and so violent was the force of the red-hot updraft that the Hand Sinister was very nearly suspended in midair. Gradually, like a leaf in a gentle breeze, his body drifted downward toward the hellish bowels of the Earth.

The fall brought release from gravity, and with it, release from pain. Itsu's sigh of pleasurable relief mingled in the turbulent hot air with the mad howling from below, which grew louder as he descended. A smile crossed the face of the Living Dead. So pleasant was his descent that Itsu saw his destination approaching with some reluctance.

Concentrating, the Hand Sinister reached out with the power of pure mind and caressed the air about him with the energy of his thought. In this way, he guided his descent so that it was no longer straight down to the magma below, but angled toward the side of the pit and an archway. Within moments, Itsu floated gently into that archway. He landed with his back to the pit, facing a vast underground room from whence the screams and howls emerged.

"Silence!" Itsu roared. And below

him there was silence.

Ahead of Itsu, in an underground room whose ceiling was lost to sight, stretched a vast plain of simmering, bubbling mud. The plain extended as far as Itsu's dead eyes could see. And this vast chamber was illuminated by a strange quality of the mud itself.

In the dim light, Itsu saw the mounds into which the barely boiling muck had been formed. Within each mound, preserved in a boiling living death, was a former successful Brotherhood agent. This bubbling hell of mud was the Hand Sinister's reward of eternal life to those who pleased him.

Once, Napoleon had commanded soldiers so loyal that they swore they would rise from the grave to follow him again onto the fields of battle. These, Itsu knew, were but idle human boasts. But here, in a sea of muck, Itsu kept soldiers more loyal and better trained, soldiers of the Brotherhood. Here they remained entombed in rotting, half-preserved flesh, waiting to serve the Hand Sinister. They awaited with eternal patience the call to march again under the banner of evil.

The Hand Sinister wheezed with pleasure as he inched his way through the mud, past the preserving mounds of men he had known when the world was young. His mind reached out to touch them in their patient suffering, to encourage, and to counsel yet more patience.

Here was a man who had instigated the condemnation of Socrates; here was an Aztec priest, skilled in cutting out the hearts of men and offering them to the sun. As Itsu passed each mound, a groan of response, of dedication, came from the undead figures preserved within.

By the side of one mound, Itsu halted. From deep within his red cowl, his living dead eyes searched the bubbling pile of muck at his feet. Itsu focused his will deep into this mound, calling with the full power of his mind to a soul gripped in the hellish limbo of living death.

Slowly, the mound of mud began to move. At first, there was nothing but a slow rocking motion. Then, as the mud began to take on a more animal form, a slithering could be seen in the steaming, slippery muck. There emerged an arm, then another, and then, at last, something recognizable as a human head was lifted, mud covered, to stare into the face of Itsu.

Itsu muttered the words, *"Mua ... ayam... natsay-nas... auvas ..."* The words were weak but the meaning strong. "Arise flame keeper... Let our journey begin."

RIVERBOAT PERIL

Agent 13 sank deep in foul-smelling Mississippi mud as he ran, or more accurately, trudged to a riverboat. Its destination was New Orleans, and its passengers included the spectrum of society, from stowaway to aristocrat. Like most of the boats of the era, it also contained a small cadre of professional gamblers who played games of chance in a secret room located behind the engine room.

Once aboard, Agent 13 cleaned the mud off his shoes and adopted the identity of a small-time grafter named Joe Barton. His name sounded phony and so did his story. His hope was that the shipboard gamblers would assume he was on the lam and therefore important. It was a complex ruse, but one that was most effective against the twisted minds of professional criminals.

Apparently, it worked. While conspicuously smoking a cigar and watching insects swarm around the light at the bow of the boat, 13 was handed a discreet invitation.

Agent 13 stood in the middle of the gambling room in a well-tailored navy suit, and surveyed the room. It abounded with the evidence of many fights. The walls revealed an occasional knife slash or enlarged hole where blades, intended for human breasts, had missed their mark. Shotgun pellets decorated the bathroom door. The slash marks and pellets, decided, gave the place character.

Tinny torch songs from a favorite radio station filled the smoky air of the room. 13 lit up his own cigar and quickly eyed the other players. First names and nicknames were exchanged.

"What I say is, this is no good," a short, fat, balding Irishman named Red O'Hara said, slamming the palm of his thick, stubby hand down on the table as 13 sat down. The thick gold rings on two of Red's fingers clicked against the table. It wasn't tough to figure out where he got his nickname. Atop his sunburned head was a small, fiery thatch of crimson hair. O'Hara's face was hard to read. Each dealt card, whether good or bad, drew the same outcries, gnashing of teeth and darting eyes.

Next to 13 sat Holiday Moran. Holiday was a man of chance. The euphemism was much kinder than those used to describe the woman with him. She would have been striking had her face not been coarsely painted with intolerable amounts of rouge and lipstick. She looked like a parrot. The difference, 13 concluded with a silent chuckle, was that a well-trained parrot would have a better-modulated voice.

Holiday was an average gambler with no capacity for guile. When his hand was good, his eyes lit up like fireworks on the Fourth of July. When his hand was bad, he took on the look of resignation of an overstuffed turkey. And if his own behavior wasn't a dead give away, the Parrot all but chirped the rank, suit and placing of the cards with a multitude of grimaces, condolences and smacking kisses in his ear.

The Agent could not help but be intrigued by the man with the top hat who sat across from him. An expert at reading faces, 13 could make neither heads nor tails of this one. He had a Southern face, haughty and handsome. His manner was cool, distant. He showed neither pleasure when he won nor displeasure when he lost. His eyes were inscrutable, like those of a man contentedly watching the waves on a beach.

All 13 had been able to learn about this mysterious fellow was that his name was DePeaux and he was a notable crime boss. He made no effort to ingratiate himself to the other players. DePeaux, 13 surmised, kept two bodyguards. However, unlike some of the showier crime bosses to whom bodyguards were a status symbol, DePeaux kept them discreetly out of sight. While the games were played, one of the bodyguards, wearing a butler suit, stood not far from his employer, procuring cocktails.

13 had come aboard in search of a man who was a trained smuggler and knew the river movements intimately. He knew that the Hand Sinister would, more than likely, take a boat to New Orleans. 13 suspected DePeaux was the man. He must, at all costs, gain the confidence and respect of this man if he is to succeed.

Only at that moment was 13's plan beginning to take form.

The game was Five-Card Draw, pure and simple. 13 acted as the dealer. He used techniques of shuffling and arranging the cards that were unknown even to the most professional cardsharps. He hoped DePeaux would be impressed by his skill, and would understand his subtle message when he allowed DePeaux to win almost every hand.

Whether shuffling, cutting or dealing, he was able to manipulate every hand. A few quick hands and, as 13 had intended, Red O'Hara became livid over his bad luck and began to mumble allegations of cheating. When he threatened to quit, 13 saw to it that he had a small victory. Holiday appeared unconcerned that his luck continued to be bad. Agent 13 made sure that nearly every victory went to DePeaux.

As the game progressed, 13 noticed DePeaux studying him with intense curiosity. No doubt, 13 thought, DePeaux is wondering who I am and what my stakes are.

The final coup de grace came when the butler was in the bathroom. 13 rigged the hand so that Red received a natural three queens. Meanwhile, he dealt DePeaux two kings. Holiday Moran and 13 were dealt a pair apiece.

Red received two deuces on the draw, and sat with a powerful full house. His crimson countenance glowed with his good fortune. His talk became more calm. Agent 13 sat quietly with a pair of tens.

DePeaux picked up a king and two fours. Thus sitting pretty with a higher full house.

Holiday folded.

Red raised high, and DePeaux matched the raise.

In the second round, 13 protested that both men were bluffing and bid high. The emotional ante went up as well. Red, as Agent 13 had suspected, went for the bait and raised again.

DePeaux quietly raised again, and 13 dropped out.

The two men faced off.

Red, convinced his opponent was bluffing, bid high, a giddy giggle arising from his throat.

DePeaux smiled and met him.

Red showed his hand and reached for the pot. DePeaux stilled the redhead's hand, then laid out his own cards.

The redhead didn't hesitate for a moment. Whipping a pistol from under his arm, he addressed DePeaux and the rest at the table. "You three have got a scheme going and I'm no schmuck. The pot's mine, and if you try to take it, you're gonna have more leaks than a sieve," Red said with an obscene, guttural laugh. His face became even pinker.

13 cursed himself silently. Although he hoped that DePeaux would realize that he was giving him the hands, 13 had not expected to see Red whip out a gun in a towering rage. He realized now the enormity of his blunder.

"My good man," DePeaux, ever the gentleman, replied. "I do not approve of your manner . . ."

Red tried to do too many things at once. He held the gun on DePeaux, he watched Agent 13 and Moran, and he tried to scoop up the chips. He shook as he spoke. "I know what you're doing, DePeaux, you're buying time for that monkey to come back in here. When he does, you better tell him not to try nothing ..."

It was silent for a moment.

Then, the bodyguard entered, zipping his fly. The Parrot squawked, and 13 dove from his seat. The flustered Red panicked and fired at the bodyguard who just stood looking dumbly at the bullet wound in his chest until it began to drip blood.

13's movement was barely any movement at all. In a heartbeat, he glided across the room, grabbed Red's left foot and yanked. Red landed hard, toppling over on his back, cracking the back of his head against the table. 13 rolled him over and planted a knee in Red's groin, then leaned forward, putting as much weight as possible on his knee. Red made pathetic gurgling noises. His eyes stared from his pain-contorted face, which eventually took on an unhealthy blue color. 13 bashed Red's head twice against the table, hard enough to knock him out.

The crime boss instinctively took control of the situation. He pushed himself up from his overstuffed leather-covered chair. He gazed around the room, taking a second to fix on the eyes of each of his listeners.

"There can be no bodies," he said simply.

13 went to the bodyguard's side and assessed the wound. The man might have lived had there been a hospital nearby. But there wouldn't be one for hours.

Holiday lifted Red and dragged him toward the door to the boiler room. Without a word, he fed the unconscious body to the flames, then Holiday Moran dusted his hands off and said, "That'll give him something to do with all his hot air."

13 vaguely wondered how many previous players had ended the game in the boiler room. He said nothing, and turned his attention to the crime boss, wondering what he would say or do.

"I do not suspect that Mr. O'Hara had long to live," DePeaux said without a trace of remorse, "and neither, unfortunately, does my bodyguard." He then motioned to the moaning man.

His bodyguard was very quickly and simply handled. Holiday lifted the body and fed it to the coals.

"Shall we?" DePeaux said and entered the boiler room himself.

The room was deathly black except for the smoldering light of the furnace flames. The Agent instinctively reached for his Luger. He heard a click as DePeaux flicked his lighter and lit his cigar. The image was striking. The Southerner's face, lit by the glowing embers of the fire, looked like that of Lucifer.

"I do not feel that any of us is in a position to want the kind of attention that these deaths might bring. Therefore, I suggest that we all depart, and take the knowledge of this evening's events to our graves," DePeaux said soberly. In the lurid light, he scanned the faces, searching for any gesture, any expression, that might reveal a hidden intention. He gestured with his arms outstretched, the palms angled upward, like a pope offering a benediction.

Holiday opened the boiler room door, and framed in it, like a cheap French postcard, was the Parrot. She was shaking with sobs. "You killed them . . . killed them in cold blood ..." Holiday stepped out of the boiler room and wrapped his arms around the woman.

"It's all right, baby ..." he muttered, trying to comfort her.

From the corner of his eyes, 13 could see DePeaux studying the situation.

That night, 13 tossed his head on his tiny pillow and lay awake watching the moonlight play against the sheets on his bed. The riverboat swayed softly. Greed, he thought, such a contemptible motive for murder. But is revenge, he wondered, even revenge for a good cause, any more justifiable. He slept very little that night.

It came as little surprise to 13 that neither Holiday nor the Parrot were in evidence at breakfast the following morning. Nor did it come as any surprise that DePeaux failed to acknowledge him.

THE VOODOO QUEEN

Hiding is something Maggie Darr had always been good at. She loved the romantic notion of hiding together with 13. But it was never like that. No, she concluded, it was always like this. Here she was alone in the most terrifying of surroundings, a knot in her stomach, playacting, while he was on some beautiful riverboat playing games. It's just not fair, she concluded. But Maggie learned early that life is often nasty, brutish, and, if not short, certainly unfair.

Maggie attempted to concentrate on her part. Her life prior to her first meeting with Agent 13 had prepared her well for this role. Her husband had been slain by vengeance-seeking gangsters, and she had been beaten, mauled and raped by one of them ... a man named Waxface. She concentrated on his hideously distorted features—purplish skin surrounded misshapen, bulging eyes and a drooping hole of a mouth that could never close all the way. Waxface was dead now, killed by Maggie. Yet, the memory of this horrible man almost caused her to be completely overcome by feelings of absolute repulsion and seething rage.

"Please, my good woman," Maggie began in a harsh voice. "An awful man has raped and tortured me. I want him dead. The high priestess must prepare a gris-gris. Please. Money is no object." Maggie was wearing a tight black dress that shook as she insistently made her request.

Across from her, a thin black woman nodded and held her hands. "I will see what I can do..." Then the black woman stood up and stepped through a draped doorway, leaving Maggie alone to contemplate her gruesome surroundings.

Maggie felt a chill from the palpable evil that seemed to surround her. She became noticeably paler. A crucifix had been bathed in what she hoped was animal blood, and defiled with strange words that she did not know. On either side of the crucifix were carved masks depicting shrieking demons, and a tall candelabra with red tapers sticking out of it like devils' nails. In ajar before her was a preserved human heart flanked by statues of two African demons, whose powers she did not wish to know. The room seemed to grow darker.

Maggie felt the other presence in the room before she saw or heard it. It was a cold, dark feeling.

"To get what you want, you must put all of your trust in me," the voice said. Then cold hands grasped Maggie on the neck. "Do not turn and look..."

Maggie had to stifle every instinct in her body to resist reaching into her purse, drawing her Luger, and spraying bullets around the room. The voice, high and singsong, tingled with an accent Maggie had never heard. "Will you grant me your trust?"

Summoning the defiant voice of an angry but frightened aristocrat, Maggie responded, "Surely I will... But quickly. Only his death will give me satisfaction."

In an instant, a thick fabric sack was dropped over her eyes. Her hands were roughly tied with rope. Strong hands carried her through the draped doorway and laid her on a table. The blindfold was removed. The room was pitch black.

"Now, what is it you came for?" asked the voice in the darkness.

Maggie held her wrists, which had been rubbed raw by the ropes that bound them. She tried not to look around the room, but instead tried to focus on her ostensible purpose at the voodoo parlor.

"I need a gris-gris to kill an evil man who has terribly violated me."

"And for this, you are willing to pay?" the voice in the darkness asked softly.

"Yes. I will pay anything. If you look in my purse... where did my purse go?" she said boldly, flailing around like a bird with trimmed wings.

"I have your things, and we have looked at them. We know you have the money for a gris-gris, and we know that you do not want one! In fact, you are attempting to deceive us."

Suddenly, the voice lit up a candle. Maggie turned. The beauty of this woman was evident. Her skin was deeply brown, but her features revealed the rich mixture of her African, Japanese, French heritage. She wore her long, thick, gleaming black hair up in a geisha style, held in place by pins that vaguely resembled bones. Her gown seemed to glow like the flames from hell.

"You were a fool to trifle with us. You and your entire haughty white civilization will be brought down through your condescension and ignorance. I am the Mondra Lava, or Mondra Love, if you please, and you are ..." She dropped a cup of tiles and meditatively began chanting and moving them around in a way that suggested years of practice.

Maggie looked for an exit. There were two doors and both were guarded by large black men in African tribal dress.

"Your name is . . ." Mondra Lava searched around some more and said, "Margaret Darr . . ." Maggie was terrified. She tried to stand but couldn't. She was held in place by a weird force that she could not master.

"Strange... strange ..." the Mondra Lava muttered. "There is another, but I cannot find a name. I find only a number. Perhaps he is known only by numbers." Suddenly a bright flash filled the room, and the number "13" glowed in midair.

As the number faded, the Mondra Lava dropped to her knees and began chanting. Maggie was released from the force that had held her, and she jumped to her feet. The Mondra Lava, her eyes piercing like daggers, glared at Maggie. She raised her hand and twisted her fingers in an unholy way and hurled terrible, guttural words at the fleeing woman.

Maggie ran to the door where the two silent sentries stood. Expecting them to try to stop her, she prepared to deliver a savage karate kick, but much to her surprise, they simply stood motionless and let her pass.

Maggie fled up a set of moist stone stairs and came to a large wooden door. She expected it to be locked, but again surprising her, it opened into the voodoo parlor. As she fled toward the entrance, she chanced to see her reflection in a mirror. The face that looked back horrified her. The voodoo ghouls had painted her with terrible paints and powders to look like an undead horror.

Maggie dashed out the door and onto the street. It was still daytime. The sunlight stung her eyes. Then, she was regaled by the sound of mocking laughter from people on the street. Too terrified to be embarrassed, she dashed down an alleyway. Curious onlookers followed her, calling her strange names. She kept running.

Though her lungs felt as if they had been stabbed by razors, she did not stop running until she was far from the voodoo parlor. She had stared into the face of the Brotherhood's dark sorcery, and terror now stalked her soul. Even as she drank in fresh air a mile from the horrible voodoo parlor, she heard the icy laughter of the Mondra Lava tinkling in the air.

VOODOO DEATH

In the cool of the evening, Agent 13, still disguised as the gambler Barton, stepped from the riverboat onto the dock. The air was clean and fresh. He pulled a short cigar from his breast pocket and lit up, as he cursed himself for the stupid gambling stunt of two nights earlier. In a misguided attempt to gain an ally of dubious reliability, Agent 13 had caused the deaths of at least two men. Far from gaining De-Peaux's trust, he had ensured that the man would not acknowledge him for the rest of the journey.

A moment later, 13 saw the crime boss emerge from the gangway and step across the dock. DePeaux walked straight to a gleaming black sedan guarded by a footman, and stepped in. 13 still marveled at DePeaux. Traveling in the shady circles that he did, the Agent had come across many crimi-nals, but he had never come across one who carried himself with the easy grace that DePeaux did.

When the sedan pulled away, a bag-gage handler stepped up to 13. "Your bags, Mr. Barton. And also, I was in-structed to give you this." The porter held out a gold key. The Agent held it in the sunlight and felt its weight. Unless he was mistaken, the key was 18-karat gold. The letter "D" was en-graved on the key.

The porter continued. "Our friend says that all you need to do is present this to any cabbie in town and you'll be taken to Mr. DePeaux's right away. He said it was his way of saying, 'Thank you.' "

The Agent slipped the key into his pocket. Perhaps the riverboat trip would prove profitable after all. 13 instructed the porter to transport his bags to the Roosevelt Hotel.

He then turned his eyes to Jack-son Square where a statue of Andrew Jackson stood on horseback. The square was surrounded by a wrought iron fence, and reminded him of a cemetery, but without graves.

As he often did when entering any city that was largely unfamiliar to him, 13 probed the crowd for Brotherhood agents. He saw none. New Orleans sparkled with multitudes of lights that warmly welcomed his arrival.

13 scanned the area once again and saw the clumsy movements of Benny the Eye. Benny was standing against a streetpole looking nondescript, shuffling his feet uneasily, scratching his nose. Benny hadn't picked out Agent 13 as he debarked the boat, so 13 knew that his Barton disguise was working well.

13 gestured to Benny in a secret, coded sign language. It took several attempts before Benny responded. The first message established 13's identity, the second told Benny to keep an eye out for tails. Benny sent back a message saying that he hadn't seen any unusual activity.

Loud jazz music and a mysterious and exotic group of people crowded the streets of the French Quarter. The cool breeze, the joyous festive music, and the colorful people captured Agent 13's mind. He felt comfortable and relaxed as he took a meandering path through the city's crowded streets. He switched disguises in a men's room at the back of a jazz club.

By the time he reached the Roosevelt Hotel, he was sure that he had not been followed, and he was refreshed by the summer night. Checking in as Mr. Winter, he awaited the arrival of Maggie Darr and Benny the Eye. He had sent Maggie to investigate voodoo parlors in hopes that she would stumble onto the parlor where the Mondra Lava was staying. He was especially looking forward to seeing Maggie.

Perhaps they would even have a little fun tonight in the French Quarter, he thought, smiling to himself.

A crisp knock came on the door. Grasping a specially modified gas gun, 13 shouted, "Who is it?" There was another knock, and then the sound of a palm rubbing on the door. It was the correct signal. The Agent opened the door, and there stood Benny the Eye. The Agent let him in and then peered down the long warm corridor of the hotel. There was nobody.

When the door closed, Benny started talking. "Come on, boss," Benny said. "I wouldn't be so stupid as to let myself get tailed."

"Perhaps not, but I was that stupid once, and it nearly cost me my life. What do you know?" 13 asked in a commanding voice.

Benny shrugged. "Wish I had more to report, boss. It would make my pay and the train ticket that sent me here worth something. Seems there's something coming down, but nobody knows what. Some kind of a delivery. Also, the police have been keeping hushed about it, a few hookers have been killed. Word is that all the blood was drained from their bodies."

Though this meant little to Benny, it meant a great deal to 13. The high priest of the Blood Ceremony, he thought to himself. The Bludda Dak is here. Reassured, he gave Benny a quick smile.

"Good work," he said enthusiastically.

"You think it's something, boss?"

"I don't know," 13 responded. There was no need to burden Benny's somewhat limited cranial capacity with too much information.

A light tap came on the door. The Agent drew his gun again and crept toward the door.

"Who is it?" He said.

There was a response, but it was so soft that he could barely hear it. Then there was another knock.

The Agent's nerves flared. It could very easily be a trap. Then there was a harsh knock on the door, and a voice bellowed. "Open up! I got a sick woman on my hands!"

Agent 13 took a calculated risk. He whipped the door open ready to blast anyone standing on the other side. What stood before him was a middle-aged maid of gigantic proportions whose stature could have placed her on any professional football team. In the woman's arms, shaking violently, her face streaked with voodoo paint, was Maggie Darr.

"She demanded that I bring her up here. I'll call a doctor," the maid said as she helped Maggie to the bed.

Color drained from 13's face. Something terrible had happened. He came to the bed and cradled her head against his chest. "Oh, Maggie . . . Maggie," he said wearily.

13 had always lived with death. He knew its face well. No words or blind hopes could mask its presence. He held her in his trembling arms.

"I am ill..." she whispered quite simply. She muttered something else that he could not understand and smiled faintly at him. But he saw that she was really very afraid. Tears shone in her eyes. In words as forceful as she could muster, she said, "Mondra Lava ..." Her mouth dropped open, and she let out a final sighing breath.

"Boss, I think she is dead.. . ." Benny said, looking down on Maggie's face, still covered in voodoo paint. Benny's face was ashen gray.

"Dead," 13 said, as though he were slowly comprehending the real meaning of the word. He felt suddenly so intolerably heartsick and sorry. So very sorry. He had been so utterly wrong to have involved her in the Brotherhood.

His bright eyes burned with tears of rage, and overcome by a single-minded fury, he sat holding her. "Dead," he said again with seething hatred. "They will all be dead when I am through," he said simply. The door flew open and with uncharacteristic hesitation, 13 failed to reach for his gun. A heavyset billowy, pink-faced doctor thundered in, rushing to the bed where 13 still held Maggie in his arms. He listened for a heartbeat. As 13 had suspected, he found none.

"She's dead," the doctor said with emotion. "Please accept my condolences . . . Under normal circumstances, I would call it heart failure. But that paint on her face, and her age. I will have to take this matter to the police," the doctor stated with sympathy.

Agent 13 looked into the doctor's eyes. He saw a man who had picked his occupation for its comfort and security. He was not a man who wanted to step into a situation of intrigue and danger. Nor was he a man who wanted his name connected in any way with a scandal.

"I sense you are a man who believes injustice," 13 began, regaining his pragmatic composure.

"Of course I am," the doctor responded.

"Then let me tell you, in truth, that I cared more for this woman than any other person, and will go to all lengths to see justice served. She died of some terrible voodoo death." The Agent uttered the words with undiluted hatred in his voice.

"Voodoo," the doctor said, the words trembling off his lips.

"Yes, voodoo. A dark and evil voodoo bent on wiping out all good people, all people that even know of its existence."

The doctor swallowed and looked over at the trembling maid. Even Benny looked like he was getting the creeps.

"I see..." the doctor said. "I do not know who you or this woman are . . . uh, in her case, were... but I believe you. Would you like me to recommend an undertaker?"

"Yes," 13 said wearily.

The doctor then handed 13 a card from the Steinberg Funeral Home not far away. Benny made the call and then walked the doctor and the maid to the door. The doctor assured him that he would sign any necessary papers, saying that Maggie had died of bad fish. Bad fish indeed.

13 hustled Benny the Eye out with instructions to take careful note of anybody who might be watching the hotel.

In grim silence, he cleaned the voodoo paint off Maggie's face. At moments, he had to stop and regain his composure, so overwhelmed was he by unrestrained grief and anger. Twenty minutes later, three men arrived at the door. Two carried a black stretcher. The third was a proper Southern gentleman in a black suit and top hat. He removed the hat slowly and ceremoniously.

"Doctor Williams," the gentleman began, "has already informed me of the terrible tragedy you have suffered. Let me assure you that I will do everything in my power to be of comfort to you in your time of grief."

In a tone he had obviously practiced

over the years, the funeral director delivered a speech he had probably made a hundred times. "I realize, fine sir, that this is an indelicate time to discuss financial matters, but as you are a transient to the community..."

The Agent quickly pulled several bills from his pocket and placed them in the undertaker's hands. The undertaker quietly established the amounts of the currency. No more was said about money.

While Agent 13 was not a man without religious and certain mystical beliefs, he had no personal desire for a funeral. Nevertheless, he knew that those who had killed Maggie Darr had followed her to the Roosevelt Hotel. His only hope was to hold himself out as bait and hope that they would want to close the trap on him.

Knowing that Maggie had no friends in the community, the Agent asked Benny to hire some of the local talent to arrive dressed as mourners. He vaguely remembered the exotic women and men of the French Quarter, and he felt certain that Maggie would have wanted a colorful funeral.

Peering out the window, the Agent saw Maggie's body loaded into the back of a covered hearse. His arrangements for Maggie's interment would be simple A short graveside service. A short performance for the waiting Brotherhood.

DARK REALIZATIONS

Itsu's journey had become a series of lies, false appearances and camouflaged intents.

A jagged streak of lightning crackled against the deep purple tropical sky illuminating the overgrown ruins of an ancient temple. On this night, however, the temple was not empty. Rather, it housed those who thousands of years earlier had built it.

Inside the temple stood a phalanx of enormous, stone-faced guards. Their faces were hard, unyielding. They reflected no interest in the storm. Behind a door of iron and slabs of stone, the scent of rotted animal was strong, toxically strong. The two Jinda guards who stood in this room were all but overwhelmed by the noxious air.

Here, next to a gold chest, which for millennia had carried two of the Crystals of Uru, the dried-out, shriveled body of Itsu, the Hand Sinister, was deep in meditation that for him served as sleep.

The guards stood as far from the body as they possibly could, as though his corrosion was contagious. They heard nothing, as two darts, lined with a temporary sleep-inducing drug, whizzed silently through the air and lodged in their necks. No eyes watched as a trick stone lifted inside the chamber and a hand reached for the chest. It lifted the lid. The unseen hand took one crystal, then the other...

At dawn's light, a strange and ancient scene graced the southern jungle. A procession, led by scythe-bearing Jindas, then followed by weapon-bearing Jindas, and finally, a black sedan chair, trekked slowly across an ancient stone pathway that had not been traveled in thousands of years. The procession made its way through lush, giant green plants and heavy underbrush.

A large, nondescript cargo ship

known only as the Jargon waited for the party on an obscure dock. There were hundreds like it plying the coasts of South and Central America, the Gulf of Mexico and the coasts of North America. Owned by a shadow company of the Brotherhood, it was properly registered and bore a clean record.

Its journey called for a straight shot from the small, haunted bay near the southern tip of South America to the shores of Louisiana. The course had been specifically charted to avoid territorial waters, as well as treacherous reefs. The course, though slightly unusual, was designed like the Jargon, to be discreet, anonymous.

The Jinda-Dii and three of his Jinda agents piloted the Jargon as it coursed through the brilliant tropical day.

Up on deck, China White leaned against the bulwark, her raven black hair blown back by the warm winds sparkling in the sunlight.

Without warning, the ship suddenly shuddered. The unearthly sound of metal tearing on stone shrieked across the Caribbean. One of the Jindas was thrown so hard against the front window of the ship that the window cracked. The others, including the Jinda-Dii and China White were sent sprawling across the bridge.

A preliminary report indicated that the damage to the ship was minor, but a tugboat would be needed to move it off the reef. China White went for help, and in an hour, a scruffy, poorly clad South American captain of dubious integrity pulled up next to the ship. As he studied the sea charts, he raised a salt-and-pepper eyebrow.

He took a deep puff of his pipe. "Well, if it ain't the strangest thing I've lately seen. Nobody ever published a chart like this. . . . It's been doctored, if you ask me . . ."

China White and the Jinda-Dii looked at one another with uncertainty. Round, china blue eyes met dark black eyes. They held each other for a long moment and nodded.

Nothing would be said to the Hand Sinister. Each one agreed. Each one for his own motives.

Down in the cargo hold, the Hand Sinister felt that the world was rotting around him. He knew. Of course he knew.

The crystals were gone. Deep in the Shadow Zone, he had felt the disturbance. When he had quickly returned to the physical realm and opened his eyes, he knew. Alone and unattended, he put his trembling parchment fingers on the chest, and slowly, ever so carefully, opened it.

Now, he felt the lock of eyes. The deceit. He knew that the threat was absolute.

He opened his eyes. It was bright. Infinitely too bright. For the last thousand years, Itsu had been contracting inward, finding refuge in the hushed dark silence of his throne room. Now he was agitated, morose, terrified amid the growing brightness of day.

And he was tormented by the knowledge of the betrayal.

Who was the Masquerader, the Betrayer? he questioned once again.

Itsu needed an enemy that he could grasp, that he could destroy. Instead, he had only this unidentifiable menace that destroyed his peace of mind. Over the years, Itsu had been intimately acquainted with betrayal. He had betrayed both Brother Du Lac and Sharu eons before, and he had taught his agents the art of political betrayal.

Now his black lips smiled a malignant smile, a desperate one that touched on madness. How ironic, he thought. Somewhere just beyond the periphery of my vision, the Betrayer, one I taught, is planning my demise.

Once again, he considered ordering his entire inner circle to commit suicide, but that, he knew, would leave him completely, desperately vulnerable. Ah, he thought, I am a prisoner of this traitor. He keeps me here while he is destroying me slowly, painfully.

Everything had suddenly become so absolutely unbearable. He was tormented by a force that lurked about on his ship, was paralyzed by failing health, forced to endure this brilliant tropical light, and he could speak to no one of it.

His face darkened. He knew that the noose was slowly tightening around his neck. And so he sat in the brilliant tropical light waiting for what he knew would happen.

FUNERAL IN THE RAIN

The morning began in dead silence. The day promised to be dull, dark and ugly. A dreary rain fell.

Cold eyes watched through binoculars a singularly bizarre precession pass down Bienvielle Street toward the City of the Dead—a name given to New Orleans cemeteries. So much of New Orleans was water that the dead were placed in tombs above the ground. The tombs, varying in degrees of elaborateness, resembled a small city.

This was the second such ceremony of the day. The first was for a prostitute who had been drained of all her blood.

"Damn the Bludda Dak," the Jinda-Gaa thought as he peered through the binoculars. This was a time for subtlety, not brutality.

In sharp contrast to the drab day were the flamboyant members of the funeral procession. The Jinda-Gaa could barely make out Maggie Darr's coffin sandwiched between brilliant orange, red, pink, and vibrant purple robes. He was slightly chilled as he heard the joyful jazz music escorting the casket. It was all strangely atonal. Somewhere under the joy was a bitter sorrow.

The jazz band was composed of a trumpeter, a trombonist, a saxophonist, and a walking drummer with an elaborate drum concoction on his back. The rest of the procession contained young female dancers who were probably prostitutes by night, a gaudily dressed midget with a baton, and a hooded minister on a donkey. As they reached the gates of the cemetery, the young dancers began to sing.

Such primitive people, the Jinda-Gaa thought to himself. He scanned the haphazard collection of mourners for signs of Agent 13. Instinct told him that although 13 was not a super-stitious man, he was fanatically loyal and devoted to his agents. He would not abandon one of them, especially Maggie Darr, on the day she was to be buried.

The Jinda-Gaa felt no remorse for 13. He had despised and envied 13 ever since they had been boys togeth-er at the Shrine. Though he knew that killing Maggie Darr would strike a brutal blow to 13, he had opposed the move. Especially now.

Even the Jinda-Dii feared what the Agent might do were he to decide to end his career in a bloody, frenzied assault. Others, too, had argued that killing Maggie Darr, the most trusted of his agents and the most loved wom-an in his life, might just be the blow that would take 13 over the edge. The Brotherhood, the Jinda-Gaa thought, could scarcely afford this threat dur-ing the Juvita-ta.

He thought of China White. She had stood by her position that Maggie must die, and the Hand Sinister had backed her up. He remembered how, as a young man at the Shrine, his heart had ached desperately when he dis-covered that China White's heart be-longed to Agent 13 alone. Of course, China would want Maggie dead, he thought bitterly, she still has hope that someday she will regain his love. The Jinda-Gaa felt hatred toward China White. Hatred mingled with despair.

The Jinda-Gaa smelled the sickly sweet scent of the Mondra Lava's per-fume and turned. It was a distinctive scent. A mixture of love and death. The Mondra Lava did not acknowl-edge him, nor did the Jinda-Gaa ac-knowledge her. There was no love lost between them. She sickened him. And that said everything. The Jinda-Gaa was by nature a cold, ruthless man. Very few people or actions re-pulsed him.

The Mondra Lava's nostrils flared as she sniffed the air. The Jinda-Gaa could only speculate on her motives.

"He spared no expense on her cas-ket...." she said, eyeing the ebony box that bore the body of Maggie Darr. She laughed cruelly. "His misery adds to my pleasure in killing her."

Mondra Lava was dressed entirely in black. Her skin was flecked with gold. Her deep eyes sparkled with gleeful anticipation like a spider hap-pily eyeing the final twitching of a fly that has accidentally been trapped in the center of the web. The Jinda-Gaa eyed the Mondra Lava with intense disgust, which he repressed with great difficulty.

"What do your magic senses tell you?" the Jinda-Gaa asked sarcasti-cally of his evil companion, fighting a desire to dig a sharp spike into her black breast.

She was not to be bested, however. With a slow, elegant gesture, the Mon-dra Lava raised her right arm, ran her gloved hand up the back of the Jinda-Gaa's neck, and caressed his hair. "No more than your powers of observation." Her voice was cold yet it held just the slightest hint of promise in its huskiness.

For a moment, he stood paralyzed by the conflicting, violent emotions of rage, adoration, hatred and lust. He leered at her cruelly as the funeral procession made its way through the avenues of the City of the Dead.

"He is not one of the musicians...." the Jinda-Gaa said bluntly. "Although I am sure that he possesses the ability to play an instrument, the sounds we are hearing are the products of a life's work. . . ."

"A life's feeling," the Mondra Lava responded.

"I suspect that he is not one of the pallbearers, as it appears they all know each other."

"Then perhaps he is one of the wastrels that tags along," the Mondra Lava whispered.

"That is very possible. . . ." The Jinda-Gaa turned to a Jinda assassin who had stood behind him the whole time sending off no more spiritual energy than a tree. "Arrange to have them all executed," he commanded.

The Mondra Lava turned to the Jinda assassin. "Have their parts delivered to my parlor. No need to have fresh corpses go to waste."

She then removed a gold cigarette case from her small purse, fixed a cigarette in a long, slim ivory holder, and lit it. She inhaled deeply as she faced the Jinda-Gaa. .

"Shall we watch the bloodbath?" she queried. "How quaint that you share my penchant for watching the suffering of others. You deny it. But we are cut from the same cloth, my dear."

The Jinda-Gaa hoped that one day he might watch the Mondra Lava die a hideous death.

TRAPPED IN A CASKET

The tomb was clammy and dark. When the door shut, it was infinitely silent. There was no natural sound at all in the black, humid, lifeless darkness. Spots were dancing in front of his eyes. 13 thought of Maggie. He had been thinking of Maggie all night. Sometime in the early morning hours, his thoughts had once again become sharp and clear, and he had become obsessed with the notion that she was not dead.

Now, as he thought of his decision, he realized what a gamble it was. He was betting that Maggie Darr was still alive, that she was in a deep, drug-induced sleep that had long been rumored to be the result of poisoning with Zombie Powder. He was betting that if the Brotherhood was after her body, it would not check the coffin for secret compartments.

The air was stale. He took shallow breaths. By his calculations, he had an hour's worth of air left. After that, he would have to chance drilling a hole in the side of the coffin.

Because 13 had needed the funeral to be as authentic as possible, he had not tampered with the lock that held the coffin shut. Instead, he left specific instructions for Benny the Eye. If Benny did not see the Agent in the cemetery in two hours, he was to break into the mausoleum and open Maggie's coffin. He had not told Benny the reason for this order. Benny did not ask.

Finally, the Agent felt a faint vibration and heard a soft thud. Placing his ear to the coffin, he heard the distinct sound of feet climbing a ladder. Somebody had broken into the crypt from beneath it.

Concentrating, 13 picked out the sound of two distinct footsteps. Naked footsteps. Skin striking stone. He heard a couple of soft whispers in a language that sounded distinctly like an ancient Mayan dialect.

An instant later, he felt the casket being lifted and carried to what he felt certain was a trap door in the floor of the darkness. The coffin was tipped on its head. Maggie's body shifted above him. Then the casket was lowered into the hole. From the lurching, hesitant motions of the casket, 13 estimated that six men were standing on different rungs of a long ladder, handling the coffin, slowly guiding it down.

Finally, the coffin was laid flat and 13 felt the gentle pitch and roll of a small craft. Faintly at first, then more clearly, he heard the sound of oars slapping water. 13, in unaccustomed awe, concluded that he was being ferried down an underground river by men speaking a dialect that had vanished from the Earth more than a thousand years earlier.

Listening intently against the side of the coffin, 13 could hear a distinct rumble, then distant sounds. There seemed to be an unnatural urgency in the air. After several minutes, the casket was lifted from the raft and placed on a stone floor. The lid was immediately lifted, and 13's ears were stung by the incessant throbbing of drums and chilling, half-human shrieks. Maggie's body was removed. 13 knew this would be the moment of truth. Did the Brotherhood know of the false bottom he had made in the coffin? He waited for a cold moment.

When he felt that attention had shifted from the coffin, 13 opened a pocket knife and drilled a small hole in the side of the coffin. He took a deep breath of the cool, damp air and looked about him.

The scene was a fantastic spectacle. Torches lit the entire room, which was drenched in the deep red color of fresh blood. 13 was certain that this was the room the two Spanish explorers had discovered. In the center of the room, on a low dais, stood a large altar table of ebony, green, red and gold. The top of the table was covered with a gold cloth into which was embroidered an elaborate design. Atop the altar sat a huge chalice, filled with a thick, bubbling, steaming liquid. To the left of the dais, not far from the casket, was a dark pit.

13 grimaced as he watched the lifeless body of Maggie Darr being carried to the altar by five Mayans wearing only loincloths and plumed headdresses. "Forgive me, Maggie," he whispered to himself. "Forgive me."

In a bizarre ceremony, Mayan women wearing only masks danced around the altar.

Using his knife, 13 gouged a wider hole, knowing that the now frantic drums would mask any sound he might make. 13 saw that the primal rhythms were coming from ten Mayan percussionists, glassy-eyed, as if hypnotized by their own sounds. Their bodies swayed like snakes to the horrible music as they danced around the room.

Moments later, heavily muscled men, their faces painted to resemble skulls, entered the room and lifted Maggie's body from the altar.

What 13 had originally thought was one of the walls of the room, proved, on more careful examination, to be a massive stone statue at least fifty feet high. Stretching to see its towering form, 13 hypothesized that it depicted a mythological demon. Around its granite neck hung a gold pentagram on a chain of gold.

In a ceremony that predated history by thousands of years, Maggie's body was shackled to the unholy pentagram. Her neck was chained to the highest point of the star, and each of her arms was stretched to the two upper points. Her legs were then chained to match the two lower Doint.s. Still, nn lifp stirrer! in

As she hung from the pentagram, a savage chant arose. Four more dancers entered, carrying sacred, deadly plants. Each one presented the poison to the bewitchingly beautiful black woman who Agent 13 recognized as the Mondra Lava.

She stood like a statue with her hands open. When all of the poisons were in her hands, she stepped to the golden chalice and dropped the plants into the cup. Her eyes closed, she began to recite in a low monotone an incantation in a strange tongue. In the chalice, the vile fluid bubbled and hissed.

The dancers stepped over to the altar, and with daggers, they jabbed, stirred, and chopped at the concoction in an ancient ritual. When the ceremony was complete, the high priestess, like a cobra, glided across the room and poured the lethal potion into Maggie's mouth. Small droplets spattered on the floor, disappearing to form a foul-smelling mist that slowly filled the room.

All attention shifted to the corpse. The dancers surrounded the body and pulled whips from their backs. They began striking at her flesh, but the lifeless Maggie did not respond to the brutal lashes.

Shadows of concern fell on the Mondra Lava's face. Turning to her left, she muttered something to a cowled figure who seemed to have appeared from nowhere. The Agent caught a few words uttered between them in the ancient language of the Brotherhood. She told the cowled figure that she wondered if it were still possible to revive Maggie Darr, that she had estimated that there would be more air in the coffin.

13's heart jumped with the terrible thought that he was directly responsible for Maggie's death. The Mondra Lava ordered the whippers to strike harder. The cowled figure next to the Mondra Lava said that he could bring Maggie to life. The Mondra Lava turned to him with a threatening tone and told him to ***mouth. The

Bludda Dak. 13 shuddered. Suddenly, there was a roar of excitement from the Mayans. Agent 13 looked over at Maggie Darr. Her body heaved of its own accord. Whips dug into her flesh and large, ugly, bleeding welts began to swell. She was alive.

Maggie Darr opened her eyes, then quickly closed them again. She rolled her head to one side and moaned. "No, no more," she murmured. Her mind, struggling to regain consciousness, vaguely knew that she was being cruelly whipped.

Her throat and mouth felt dry and cottony. Her stomach churned and her head swam with waves of nausea and pain. She was perspiring profusely, and her limbs were weak from continuing muscle spasms.

A dozen dancers surrounded her. Maggie begged for water. A chalice was lifted to her lips and as she took the water, her eyes darted wildly around her, and she let out a terrified scream.

The Mayans gasped. The excitement of the ceremony was overtaking them. The vampire laughed a terrible laugh, spitting blood as he did so. The Mondra Lava watched. She, too, was frozen by the apparition hanging from the pentagram, screaming with mounting despair.

"Leave us," the Mondra Lava commanded the Mayans, and they quickly departed the room. Only the Mondra Lava and the Bludda Dak remained.

Slowly, the full, red lips of the Mon-dra Lava turned upward at the corners. The Mondra Lava was pleased.

"Look into my eyes," she commanded. Maggie, a feverish glow inflaming her cheeks, looked into the dark eyes of the Mondra Lava. "And now, sleep, sleep, sleep," the Mondra Lava whispered softly. "Deep into sleep where there is nothing, nothing at all. There is only my voice, and there is only pain. Only my voice, and only pain." Then Maggie's eyes shut and her body became limp.

The Mondra Lava stepped to the pentagram from which Maggie still hung and released the shackles. She carried the woman's body to the brilliant altar in the middle of the room. The woman turned to her ghoulish companion. "She must sleep now if she is to recover for Itsu ..." the Mondra Lava said, and broke into her tinkling, cold laugh.

The Mondra Lava removed her own black robe and covered Maggie with it. She stood for a moment, next to the Bludda Dak, then they departed. Agent 13 could hear her laughter until the slamming doors cut it off.

13 waited to make sure that he was alone. He then began to lift the false bottom of the coffin. As he was about to rise, he heard footsteps.

They did not come toward him, but stepped toward Maggie Darr. Peering through the hole again, 13 saw that it was the vampire, the Bludda Dak. The Bludda Dak had allowed his demonic thirst to get the better of him.

He was intent on drinking Maggie's blood for his own gratification. What a contemptible creature, 13 thought with mounting anger.

As the demon lowered his hood, and was about to sink his teeth into Maggie's neck, the enraged 13 jumped from the coffin. The vampire, his fangs bared, looked up, and let out a catlike hiss.

13 leaped across the large pit near the altar and charged the ghoul. Agent 13 and the Bludda Dak landed in a heap.

The Agent was startled to discover that his opponent was unusually light but that his strength was much greater than the weight behind it. Mustering all of his power, 13 kicked upward savagely catching the Bludda Dak squarely in the stomach.

Enraged, the vampire grabbed 13 by the throat and began to squeeze. 13 gasped for air and the room began to sway. His ears buzzed, his vision clouded. He grabbed at the fingers that held his throat in paralyzing pain. All he could see was the lurid creature's face as the Bludda Dak tightened his death grip on 13's neck.

Using his last strength, 13 heaved himself against the vampire and shoved the creature toward the pit.

Suddenly, the Bludda Dak realized the significance of the unfortunate turn of events. He panicked. His yellowish eyes drew wide with distress. In urgency, he loosened his grip. Gulping for air with tortured lungs, 13

rasped in a bloody hiss, "We're going down together. ...."

The vampire's attempts to escape were awkward and desperate. Despite his thrashing, 13 was able to shove them both over the side of the pit into the water below. The vampire, seeing the reflection of torchlight on the water, let out a blood-curdling scream as he plummeted.

Agent 13 sunk deep into the fetid water and muck. When he rose to the surface, he heard the agonizing screams of the Bludda Dak. The spot where the vampire had entered the water bubbled in a vivid red boil. He watched the vampire's hideous torture as his flesh decomposed in the water.

Frantic drums echoed throughout the cavern again. There could be no doubt that the struggle in the tomb had drawn the Mayan's attention. Suddenly, a strong light was pointed into the well, and 13 swam from it.

Peering from a dark corner of the pit, 13 saw the last traces of the Bludda Dak bubble away like a seltzer tablet. His ghastly mouth still screamed as the mutilated remains of his face turned to runny pus and his body became merely a reddish foam.

DISTANT VOICES

The terrible drumbeats echoed in 13's ears. Though the Bludda Dak had horribly dissolved, the Mayans concentrated their efforts on dredging the water in which he had dissolved. In the beating glare of the torchlights, 13 had discreetly escaped from the pit and painstakingly made his way through an underwater labyrinth. Like many of the Brotherhood's structures, this labyrinth was a complex network of tunnels.

Strangely, the Agent felt as though he were guided through it. Each time he came to a fork in the path, he could feel a beckoning. Peering ahead into the murky water, he saw what looked to him like an old man paddling a rowboat.

When 13 reached a passage that emptied onto the bayou, he was tired. His head felt heavy, his mind clouded. Mist drifted to him like the souls of the dead ascending the heavens.

Moss hung from the trees like sinister wraiths spinning spiritual spiderwebs to catch oncoming enemies. Logs floated like corpses upon the watery brine.

Peering into the distance, he was struck by a singular image. It was that of a solitary oarsman guiding an archaic craft through the bayou by the light of a purple lantern. 13 could not help but be reminded of Charon, the guide of the mythical underworld, who performed the grim task of leading the dead into Hell.

Overcome by weariness, 13 dragged himself toward the figure. As he drew closer, the mist swivel-ed around him, and the man's figure mysteriously vanished. Oddly, however, the boat remained behind. Dragging himself up, the Agent climbed into the rowboat and paddled away from the terrible labyrinth.

By dusk he reached a dock. From

there he walked down a short stretch of country. He was close to the city and soon found a cab. In the back of his mind, he knew that he must contact his men and change his clothes, which were stained with blood. He had the driver release him at Bourbon Street.

The street was crowded. 13 walked quickly with his head down. Only then, as he walked along Bourbon Street, did he allow himself to recall the abominable ceremony.

The image of Maggie Darr stuck with him. He could see her with absolute clarity. Her shivering body gashed with bloody wounds, her eyes registering horror and confusion, her voice screaming in despair. Though he felt certain that he could again find the entrance to the secret underground world, he did not know whether he could once again find his way through the labyrinth.

His mind whirled with dark thoughts. Although he had killed the Bludda Dak, the Juvita-ta would no doubt continue. He knew no more about the Hand Sinister's journey than when he had set out aboard the riverboat.

As the dark, confusing thoughts of a weary mind overcame him, he was struck by the piercing wail of a saxophone. 13, who was raised without music, had no particular passion for it. How strange, he thought, to be so struck by this entrancing melody. It beckoned him along Bourbon Street

the same way the mysterious oarsman had in the labyrinth.

He followed the music into a jazz club. Amid the cigarette smoke, fetid smell of human sweat and stale alcohol, 13 scanned the faces in the room. They Paid the disheveled and somewhat delirious 13 no mind. He took a seat in a dark corner. He was so tired, so very tired of it all.

Slowly, the music overtook him, liberating him from his aching body and weary thoughts. Imperceptibly, from within the music, came a voice. It was not the emotive, abstract voice of a musical instrument speaking to him. Nor was it the thin range of a human voice. It was the voice of Logos, speaking in a haunted language that transcended both emotion and meaning.

Its message was one of urgency. Of ancient powers coalescing at a special time. A time when things could change. A time of opportunity. A time of action. 13 knew at once what was communicated in the voice of Logos. The Hand Sinister must die. The sacred crystals must be recovered. And the evil must be expunged.

And only the Agent could do it. Even now, the evil was begetting more evil, for another dark one had the crystals. One who was young and strong and dangerous. One who was even more powerful than evil, because the one had betrayed evil.

The music suddenly stopped. Agent 13 woke from the bar with a start.

"There'll be no sleepin' in here," a voice said hoarsely. 13 looked up into the face of a barkeep peering down at him. He stepped to his feet and dropped some money on the table.

"Sorry, it's been a long night," he said apologetically. Laughter erupted throughout the small club. 13 turned to look at the saxophone player. But he was gone. "Where did the saxophonist go?" he asked. "To bed... about seven hours ago..."

Agent 13 again stepped out onto Bourbon Street. But now the morning sparkled. The air was fresh and clean, impregnated with honeysuckle. 13 smiled. He felt like a person who had just recovered from a horrible fever. The fever had passed, and he was left energetic, strong, and hopeful.

He paused for a moment. 13 had no doubt that his old ally, Ray Furnow, had spoken to him in a mysterious way in the bar. Who really is Ray Furnow? he wondered, vaguely remembering Brother Du Lac's description of Sharu.

FALSE HOPES

Itsu's spirits had also buoyed. There had been no more incidents since the ship had hit the reef. Time, he believed, was on his side. In a moment, however, he awoke from his meditations with an expression of positive pain. He had the importunate sense that something was wrong. Then, in a flash, he knew. The Bludda Dak was dead.

"Damn him!" Itsu hissed. The Juvita-ta would lose its potency. He could duplicate many aspects of the Ceremony of Blood, but the fresh blood of an enemy would miss its passage through the undead corpse. The ceremony would be flawed.

And nothing could be done. His fate was sealed. Like all mortals, someday he would die. It might be thousands of years away, but the day would come. No matter how hard he fought it, no matter what advances were made in Brotherhood science, his seal of immortality had been broken.

"Damn the Bludda Dak!" The contemptible, miserable bloodluster had betrayed him. He should have moved the creature in a coffin, but he had chosen instead to let the Bludda Dak transport himself, filling his zombie veins with the blood of prostitutes along the way. The Hand Sinister felt threatened from every direction. He gnashed his teeth and winced as one cracked, then crumbled to powder.

To calm his inflamed and terrified soul, the Hand Sinister found secret liberation in thoughts of destroying freedoms and achieving a mastery of the world, a control that would embrace all humanity.

Itsu knew there were no such things as historical accidents, that he had created the invisible order that existed beneath the charade of world events, that he controlled the evil forces that lurked in the world.

The results of his labors, he thought with a momentary sense of strength and superiority, were becoming increasingly evident. The great powers of the Earth stood poised on the brink of a violent conflagration greater in scope and effect than any in the history of humanity. Carefully, the Brotherhood's Bishops and Rooks had nursed Hitler to power in Germany, and Mussolini to the dictatorship of Italy. Behind the scenes, Brotherhood agents had manoeuvred the intricacies of Japanese politics, assuring that the militaristic radicals, fire-breathing warmongers, would rule that island empire.

Soon, at the ceremony of the Juvi-ta-ta, he would become strong again. Immortal, no. But strong, yes. Strong enough to find the Betrayer.... Or perhaps... yes . . . he would exterminate all of his agents, and the Brotherhood would begin anew. The image of mutilated bodies pleased him.

Yes, he smiled in a wicked mood, that is what will happen.

THE BETRAYER

Not far away, the Betrayer stared into the depths of the night from the stern of the ship. "Ah... ah..." the cowled figure murmured softly to the cool night air. "The crystals have revealed so many things, and hinted at so many more."

The crystals had shown the Betrayer how to hide in the Shadow Zone and the physical realm. Although the Betrayer did not yet have the power to enter the Shadow Zone, the figure had learned the art of psychic camouflage. Just as light causes objects to cast shadows, so too, knowledge forces certain ignorance.

Indeed, the Betrayer thought, gloating in the success of the veiled crime, I have the upper hand.

It started with envy, or perhaps, ultimately with evil. It was the envy born of an evil soul. The Betrayer had this envy, an envy that insidiously grips the mind, an envy that demands ac-tion. And one day, the envy changed. It took on new meaning and became betrayal. And the idea of betrayal took shape in the Betrayer's mind. The idea nagged the Betrayer, and the Betrayer contemplated it long and hard, allowing it to flourish. And the plot took shape. The veiled crime. The evil deed.

So far, the Betrayer's plan had worked perfectly. The Betrayer had successfully stolen the Crystals of Uru. The doctored sea charts had run the ship aground, and thus given a clue to distant eyes that were sure to be watching. And the Bludda Dak was dead.

For days the Betrayer had watched Itsu's restless fidgeting. The Betrayer relished every small nervous move. He knows, The Betrayer thought. He knows, but he just doesn't know how. Oh how I love this.

Consumed with the euphoric ecstasy of success, the Betrayer did not speculate on failure. There can be no failure. Soon I will have everything, and smiled inwardly, greedily, gleefully.

Everything.

The voice laughed in the darkness.

ROTTING CARGO

After a steaming hot shower at the Roosevelt Hotel and a change into a crisp white shirt, a Palm Beach jacket and neat pleated pants, 13 headed to the train station to retrieve the bags he had asked Benny to stash after Maggie's death. Then, armed with a new name and identity, he set out for a modest hotel in the French Quarter. 13 had felt the presence of Jindas lurking in the lobby as he had sneaked back into the Roosevelt. He knew he could not stay there any longer.

His first order of business was to check in with his agents. Opening his suitcase, he found a hastily scrawled note from Benny. It was short, to the point, and a grammatical atrocity.

Sorry, Boss. I musta ben spodded bye one of em, cuz a guy came after me and tried to dust me. I got him first. Guess what. He blew up. And then there was a horrible blood bath after the funereal. Everybudy waz killed. It was real bad. When I finely got to the mosselium, you was gone. Hope you's O.K. Leave notice for me.

The Agent picked up the phone and called Karlton Gould. As always, the State Department's throaty voice sounded like somebody had taken a sandblast-er to it. He had some information.

"Some of the dock hands down on an island called St. Swithens said a cargo freighter ran aground off their island last week. They said some woman called in for help but didn't want any attention from the local authorities or Coast Guard. A tug went down there, pulled it off, and then mysteriously disappeared. One of the tug's mates washed up on the shore, more dead than alive. He described men and women wearing strange red cowls, then died."

"What was the ship's name?" 13

asked with acute interest.

"*The Jargon*. It will approach the Louisiana shoreline by Tuesday. That's all I've got. Call me if you need me down there," Gould said and then abruptly hung up.

13 stared at the phone for a minute. Though he was no stickler for social protocol, he didn't believe he'd ever met a man quicker to disconnect than himself. Finally, he thought to himself, I am on to something.

By the time he had reached his destination, 13 felt sticky from the melting heat. He squinted in the strong glare of the sunlight. Large magnolia trees swallowed up the house, which was concealed by the heavy foliage and a large white wall. Within the wall, it was lush, deep, green, and cool, and the sweet smell of honeysuckle permeated the air.

DePeaux sat in the shade of the porch. Nothing more than a shadow, a silhouette in the cool darkness. He moved toward the porch to focus on the darkness and DePeaux's face. DePeaux looked at him without surprise, without even moving. There was no smile, no real greeting.

13 stood in front of him and outstretched his hand. He looked straight at DePeaux, who looked every bit the Southern gentleman, in a crisp, cool, lime green linen suit.

DePeaux stood and accepted the outstretched hand.

"I suspected that one day you'd come to me with a proposition," DePeaux said, eyeing the handsome young gambler he'd met aboard the riverboat. "I didn't know what your game was on the boat when you played the cards in my favor, but I knew at some point you would be here."

Their eyes met. 13, disguised as Barton, was distinctly calm and confident.

He shrugged, saying, "I have something, something I think you will find very interesting."

"Do sit down," DePeaux said with superficial amiability.

After 13 finished with his proposition, he turned toward DePeaux, who sat in silence concentrating on a gardener who was pruning the magnolias.

"*The Jargon*... strange name for a ship, let alone one that's involved in smuggling," he said after several thoughtful moments.

"Why is that?" 13 questioned confidently.

"You said she had an Ecuadoran register."

"So?" His eyes searched DePeaux.

"Just strange, that's all," DePeaux responded with a hint of reservation in his voice. His eyes were noncommittal, and his fingers played with his bourbon glass. "It is an amusing idea."

A white-uniformed butler suddenly stepped from the house, carrying a note on a silver tray, which he presented to DePeaux. Taking the document, DePeaux opened it. After a moment of quick reading, he rose from the table.

"Please excuse me."

"Of course." 13 nodded and looked around the room. Though the mansion appeared to be a relaxed haven, he felt the eyes watching him. The servant who had delivered the message stood in the entryway to the house. 13 recognized the bulge beneath his serving jacket. He also suspected that the gardener, who spent entirely too much time pruning a nearby tree, was also ready for action.

"Money can bring so many pleasures," DePeaux spoke from inside the house. His voice was loud and strong, and 13 knew that the comment was directed at him.

DePeaux was once again on the terrace.

"Yes it can," 13 said briskly. "My plan requires a gambler. You are a gambler, aren't you, Mr. DePeaux?" 13 questioned, a challenge in his words.

DePeaux sat next to him. He bit a cigar and inhaled deeply, a plume of smoke drifting around him. DePeaux let the question pass without comment.

"Well," DePeaux said, "you'll be happy to know that your story has been backed up by my source." He gave the disguised Agent his best gambler smile.

"I didn't know there was a doubt,"

he responded with impatience.

"You need not go on with this charade." DePeaux's eyes were smiling but watchful. "When a ridiculous Yankee gambler rigs a gambling game aboard a riverboat, and then days later turns up at my home to propose that we pirate a smuggling ship, I am going to consult my sources. Frankly, Barton, I think there's more to your story than meets the eye. You have a great many secrets, but so, indeed, do I. We all have personal business and personal scores to settle. That's your business. But know this," he inhaled on his cigar, "one inch out of line and you're a dead man."

13 was not amused. "I understand your caution," he said curtly and convincingly.

DePeaux's tone immediately changed. He smiled. His smile was genuine, and the bourbon glass returned to his hand. "Tell me about the cargo we're preparing to loot."

"It should be a rather interesting and profitable expedition," 13 said firmly. "Rumors have circulated that the *Jargon* is transporting everything from drugs to stolen Inca treasures."

"In our new spirit of candor, Mr. Barton, please level with me."

"Someone connected with the ship has been sending out feelers for a melter."

"A melter?"

"To melt metal ingots and convert them into other shapes."

"What kind of metal?"

The confident Agent sat back in his deep chair and played his hand for all it was worth. After a long thoughtful moment, he said, "Gold, Mr. De-Peaux. Nazi gold."

13 began an explanation. "I'm not going to tell you how or why I know this. The gold is being used to finance a type of fifth column operation here in America. They're using the South American ship because Customs has been giving all the German ships a thorough going over."

"Why the melter?"

"For safety reasons, the gold's been melted down into seemingly worthless brass souvenir statues of the Empire State Building. They need the melter to retrieve the gold and remelt it into measured bars."

"Interesting . . . how much is supposed to be aboard?"

"Three hundred pounds... that's roughly two million, six-hundred thousand dollars worth."

DePeaux sat back in his chair. Even he was impressed. He swallowed his drink.

"Where did you get the information?" he questioned.

"I have my sources."

"Why should I believe you?"

"Maybe you shouldn't," 13 said in a determined voice.

"Where do you propose we take her?"

"We get her at sea."

"That's a big operation, and we risk losing everything if the ship goes down."

The Agent pulled out a map and opened it, conscious that several hands drifted toward their guns as he moved. "Not if we hit them in shallow water. You are familiar with the routes that smugglers take. You must know their vulnerabilities. . . ."

DePeaux thought for a moment. "Jackson's Shoals... that place is dangerous at noon. Many a smuggler has lost his boat there. I say that's the place to strike. There is not a place to hide or to run. They can only die." Then he smiled and sat back, pleased both with the man before him and the prospects of the mission. "When is she due in port?" DePeaux asked, trying not to appear too eager.

"Tuesday," the Agent responded.

"That doesn't leave us a lot of time..."

He turned to his servant near the door.

"Sparrow ... a round of Juleps for Mr. Barton and myself."

"Yes, sir."

"And cancel my dinner plans for tonight with Klein. It seems our meeting here is going to run longer than expected. . ."

SHOALS OF DEATH

The day was a chaotic mixture of fog and rain interrupted now and then by sudden shafts of light as if a spotlight from above was searching the earth. The air was windless and heavy as DePeaux's army of seventy-five Cajuns, pirates, and smugglers assembled on the sandy shores near Jackson Shoals. Their arsenal consisted of three World War I cannons, a large collection of small arms, and a small naval mine.

Agent 13 stood next to DePeaux and FBI Agent LaMonica. All three were wearing deep-green rain coats. 13 looked over at LaMonica. Already 13 had lost one of his best agents, Gunnar Holt, and he knew that this mission would be particularity dangerous. He had not wanted his agents involved in the actual hijacking of the Jargon, but LaMonica had insisted on joining in.

13 reviewed their strategy with painstaking care. He hated surprises. His perfect timing, extraordinary precautions, and thorough planning rarely allowed for them. He usually foresaw everything.

It was drizzling lightly on the men as 13 reviewed the plan. "First, the *Jargon* will strike the mine. Its crew will surface to investigate the disturbance and inspect the damage. From shore, DePeaux, your men will rake the starboard side with machine gun fire and heavy artillery. Your crew should be able to eliminate most of them at this point. LaMonica and I will remain with our men on the marsh over there." He pointed his finger to the other shoreline. "What crew is left will not notice as our boarding party arrives in a boat on the port side. Your men will continue with heavy artillery, thus strengthening our position. It's a simple plan, really."

DePeaux eyed Barton carefully as

he spoke. There was something about him that didn't add up. DePeaux didn't buy anything about Barton. He wasn't a gambler. DePeaux somehow got the impression that Barton didn't even want the money. What did he want? DePeaux wondered.

DePeaux looked around at his men. But they weren't his men anymore—they were Barton's men. It had happened in the course of a single day. He had watched their enthusiastic support of Barton's plan as Barton had briefed them. These were men who respected few. Yet, they seemed taken by Barton, and when the time had come to pick stations, nearly all of them had opted for the company of the gambler from Chicago.

DePeaux felt it as well. Although he could not understand Barton's motives, he had an instinctual respect for the man. He sensed that Barton was a man who long ago had conquered fear. He had a radiant sense of self-assurance. As Barton went over the plan, DePeaux showed no indication of concern. His face was noncommittal, austere, assured.

"Now we must simply wait. Good luck," 13 concluded. DePeaux knew that luck was something the man in front of him never relied on.

As DePeaux returned to his men, LaMonica and 13 were left alone for a brief moment in the drizzling rain. LaMonica touched 13's shoulder.

"Heard about Maggie," he said with unusual feeling. "I'm really awfully sorry about it."

"We lost Gunnar as well," 13 said, looking beyond LaMonica to the faceless collection of men DePeaux had brought together. Quickly, 13 pushed thoughts of Maggie and Gunnar out of his mind. He could not concentrate on them. Not now. His eyes, however, were an intense, angry blue.

Their conversation was interrupted by two Cajuns who emerged from the thick marsh of the shoals, pushing a man in front of them.

"Looky here what we found, boss," one of the Cajuns said, as he kicked the prisoner forward. It was a small, dark man with beady eyes. A treacherous grin played on his lips.

Agent 13 instantly recognized the man's glazed stare. He was a Jinda. He is on a mission to secure the shoals, 13 thought.

13 then had a numbing thought—the Cajuns would kill this man, and his body would burst into flame. This could spook even the coolheaded DePeaux. Certainly, the Cajuns would suspect voodoo and flee the ensuing battle.

"Get down, he has a bomb!" 13 commanded, as he whipped out his Luger and fired.

When the bullet pierced the Jinda's heart, he burst into flames. In a moment, all that remained was dust.

As DePeaux pulled himself from the wet sand, he looked at 13. "I didn't see any bomb," he said with a degree of certainty.

13 disregarded the doubt in De-Peaux's statement and peered into the distance toward where the Jargon would come. "Let us hope they didn't, either. This little man," and he pointed to the Jinda's ashes, "was obviously sent by the ship to secure the area. Be careful; perhaps more were sent."

DePeaux, satisfied with 13's response, raised his eyebrows and said, with a provocative grin, "Must be some very precious cargo."

"Indeed," 13 responded.

LaMonica had watched the incident closely. He knew that there had been no bomb in the man's hand. But then LaMonica had worked with Agent 13 long enough for this to be no surprise. "Damn," he whispered to himself. LaMonica had had quite enough of the supernatural in his dealings with Agent 13. He preferred enemies, and friends, for that matter, of solid flesh and blood—people who did not burst into flames, people who could be charmed by a smile.

Four hours later, Agent 13 and his men still waited in the camouflage of the marsh and sandy shore. The men waited impatiently, and the atmosphere was strained. 13 also hated to wait. But he had trained himself to wait forever, if necessary. Strange images floated by in the fog. 13 knew that across the narrow waterway, De-Peaux and his group of men waited stealthily in the semi-darkness with cannons and machine guns.

"A perfect night," LaMonica said to him. 13 could barely make out LaMonica's form as he turned toward the voice.

"It certainly makes things easier," 13 said softly.

Agent 13 was the first to spot the tiny light in the foggy gloom of early evening. He lit a match and held it up as a signal to DePeaux. Slowly the speck of light on the horizon grew in size and intensity.

"Let's go!" 13 said in a commanding voice that broke the night's stillness.

The *Jargon's* lights had all but been extinguished as it plied the coast as closely as safety would allow.

Clouds drifted before him as the Jinda-Dii scanned the approaching shoreline. There, he saw the vague outline of a human who waved to him, then disappeared from view. Good, the Jinda-Dii thought, the shoals are secure. Everything was falling into place. Or at least they seemed to be. Yet he felt a strange sensation, as though someone had placed a blanket over the night.

Deep in the ship's hold, Itsu felt swollen in the moist air, like a water balloon ready to burst. In reality, the living corpse's gaunt features were dried and shriveled. He smiled an unnatural, twisted smile to himself. Word had come moments before that the Juvita-ta was prepared. Maggie Darr's blood would be used in the Ceremony of Blood. Even now, he could feel fresh blood flowing through his brittle veins.

Then, in a heartbeat, he knew that a terrible mistake had been made, and although the consequences of it had not yet been felt, they were as inevitable as the pain from a deep cut.

"No," he gasped desperately. "Get me the Jinda-Dii!"

His cries were drowned out, however, by the thunder of an explosion at the front of the ship.

13, LaMonica, and their men were a mere hundred yards from the port side of the ship when the machine guns and cannons opened with explosive force. As Jindas on the main deck were hit, they burst into flames, grotesque beacons in the fog.

"It's the devil's work," one of the Cajuns in 13's boat hissed as he watched the spectacle. The outcry angered 13 somewhat, and he glared at the man. He knew that the prevailing mood of the boarding party had perceptively shifted from enthusiasm to fear. LaMonica also cursed under his breath.

Silently, they pulled up along the Jargon. Agent 13 threw a grappling hook and mounted the surging vessel. The deck was a war zone. Shouted orders and gunfire echoed in the darkness. Barely perceptible shadows moved hastily along the starboard side. The rain, which had let up for several hours, returned and was now heavy and cold.

13 saw the shadowy images and re-

alized that many more Jindas moved aboard the deck than he had hoped. However, he pulled himself slowly, quietly onto the deck and helped LaMonica aboard. The others were to wait five minutes before boarding. Enough time, 13 thought to himself, to find Itsu and destroy him. 13 knew that if the Cajuns were found on board at this point, the Jindas would heavily guard the Hand Sinister, and his assassination attempt would fail. He suspected that now only a guard or two would be with Itsu. He hoped he was correct.

The ship was long, a limitless expanse of darkness. Most of the action was taking place on the starboard bow of the ship, allowing for discreet movement in the darkness. 13 and LaMonica groped in the direction they suspected the entrance to the cargo hold would be, found the steel ladder that led below deck. 13 felt certain that all the Jindas would be fighting in the battle above deck. He gave LaMonica a reassuring nod.

"Good luck," LaMonica whispered as 13 began his descent. "I'll make sure nobody gets below."

LaMonica leaned against the bulwark. So far everything had gone well, he thought, remarkably easily. He pulled his raincoat around his face and waited, listening to DePeaux's onslaught and the rain's clangor as it struck the deck. He avoided the occasional flash of light from a burning body.

On the dark, noisy deck, LaMonica failed to hear the approaching Jinda, who now waited for a moment, motionless on the deck. Failing to recognize LaMonica, he silently lunged forward, a chilling expression on his face.

LaMonica felt only a hot, fluid sensation and looked down at his chest before realizing he had been stabbed. Then an incredible, suffocating pain gripped him, and he reeled. Everything blurred, and he swam in agony, spasmodically grabbing the bulwark as death smothered him.

13 did not hear LaMonica's struggle. He had already descended through the dark passageway, and stood in front of the door to the cargo hold. He stood silently, clutching his Luger, and listened. He heard nothing. Slowly, deliberately, he opened the door without a sound. A piercing, foul smell violated his nose, and he held his breath in an effort not to be sick. The room glowed in an iridescent mist. 13 immediately spotted a guard to his left. Before the Jinda even felt 13's presence in the room, 13 had fired. The smell of burned flesh mingled with the overpowering smell of decay as the Jinda became an all-consuming fire in the hold that was the Hand Sinister's room.

The Hand Sinister knew that death was imminent. He felt the presence of Agent 13 in the room, yet his powers had diminished so greatly in the last hours that he was unable to depart into the Shadow Zone. His body shivered in fear. In despair, he attempted to summon the power that would save him, to find the words that would bribe 13 into submission. He made a series of incoherent sounds, half screams, half gurgles, as 13 walked across the room. With what strength he had left, Itsu began to claw the air.

13 felt oddly agitated and exalted as his eyes fixed on the little man in red robes. His cheeks burned as though on fire. He felt heated with his anger. 13 had waited so long for this moment of vindication that he had difficulty believing he would be able to destroy his adversary, or that this little, shriveled man had ever been a threat at all.

13 studied the man's face—malignant black eyes burned viciously from within deep eye sockets. All his life, the Agent had wished to glimpse this face. Now it was before him, like a beacon of darkness, a blackness that absorbs good and turns it to evil, that turns hope to fear, life to death, and draws strength from agony. Bringing death to this almost-dead body would be easy for him.

A sneer of disgust crossed the Agent's face. He pulled the cloak savagely from the man's body, and stood directly before him. 13 unsheathed his knife, planted it firmly against the Hand Sinister's stomach and pushed hard. Itsu screamed as the cold steel slid through his body. He was tormented by the voices of Sharu and Brother Du Lac, as they laughed at him viciously, victoriously.

As if he were lifting a pile of rags, 13 quietly carried the still-twitching, barely alive Itsu down the passageway and up the ladder. Only when he reached the deck did 13 see the mutilated remains of LaMonica, a river of blood spreading across his friend's chest.

A remorseless loathing seethed in him once again. He carried Itsu to the port side of the ship and placed him on the deck. Half dead, the obscene body twisted like a jellyfish. Zealously, 13 tore into Itsu. Meticulously, like a man absorbed in a nightmare, he cut Itsu's decayed body into pieces and threw them into the inky darkness of the shoals below. He dissected Itsu in a strange ritual, until all that remained was his head.

He placed the skull on the deck, and struck his ring on the metal. A strange magnesium light briefly engulfed the corner as he burned the number "13" through Itsu's forehead and skull, and into the brain. He threw the skull overboard as well.

13 turned his face upward and allowed the cold, cathartic rain to cleanse him, to purify him. A change had occurred in 13. Suddenly, he felt incredibly free.

Like a madman returning once again to sanity, he turned slowly to face the confusion on deck. He could make out the forms of Jindas and Cajuns engaged in battle. He focused his attention on the battle, vaguely aware that something was missing. Then it struck him—the unnatural stillness of the night. No cannons boomed. No machine guns rattled. There was no sound of DePeaux's forces in the distance. "The cowards," he whispered to himself, guessing that the men on shore had abandoned the fight.

13 detected a slight movement behind him, and turned. The Agent's eyes met those of his one-time master, the Jinda-Dii. So powerful a hold did the Jinda-Dii's gaze have over 13 that the Agent froze, unable to summon the will even to speak.

"I knew this could only have been a plan of yours, Agent 13," the Jinda-Dii began. "If there is any consolation, know that your demise will be as tragic for me as for you. I do not look forward to what I must do, but alas, for Itsu's protection, it is necessary."

All 13 saw and felt was the deeply evil and darkly persuasive stare of the Jinda-Dii, beckoning him into the caverns of darkness. The Agent could feel himself drowning, sinking into the abyss. Organ by organ, he could feel death spreading through his body, and he was powerless to fight it.

"I express my respect for you, Tredekka, by not inflicting too much pain upon you in death. It shall be as painless as possible," the Jinda-Dii said, his gaze not leaving 13's for a moment. And indeed, the world of shadows seemed to descend upon 13 like the gradual fading from dusk to night.

Suddenly, the ship was hit by a

deafening roar and burst of flame. The Jinda-Dii's body was thrown against the bulwark by the explosion, and he lay unconscious on the deck. 13 tumbled to the deck as well, gasping as life returned to his body. At first, his weary mind was unable to perceive what was happening. He felt only the cold rain against his face.

Gradually, though, his head began to clear. He made out the crumbled body of the Jinda-Dii and saw the blaze of flames. By the firelight, amid frantic screams, 13 made his way back to the steel ladder. He had a plan. A brilliant plan.

DARK GREETINGS

The Hand Sinister was wrapped in a number of blankets when the Jinda-Dii first saw him after the assault on the craft. His eyes appeared brighter than ever before, but his voice was bubbly and weak and he shook violently, drawing no warmth from the drenched blankets.

In the distance, he saw the rotted wreck of *The Jargon* claw at the sky like skeletal fingers. Now all that remained of the secret mission to the Juvita-ta was a ruined ship, five Jindas and a single lifeboat that was beached on the shore of the marshland.

The Jinda-Dii had remained unconscious for quite some time after the explosion. Some Jindas had put him in the lifeboat. Now, as he looked in the direction of the ship, he admired his pupil's attack. 13 had read him perfectly. The attack at Jackson's Shoals was masterful.

Yet, 13 was now dead, he was sure of that—buried with the ship. His thoughts briefly turned to China White. She, too, had disappeared in the turmoil of the attack. No doubt she is dead, as well, he concluded. For a brief moment, the Jinda-Dii wished for the sanctity of the Shrine. I must die, too, he thought to himself.

He turned to the Jinda nearest to him. "Notify the Mondra Lava of the disaster. Tell her to send rescuers."

The Jinda-Dii then turned his eyes upon Itsu. The once-vacant eyes, which earlier had been those of a dead man, were now filled with life, and they glared at him with a fierce intensity.

Terrible words hissed through Itsu's teeth. "You have betrayed me, Jinda-Dii! Seppuku!"

Without hesitation, the Jinda-Dii reached for his belt and drew the razor-sharp blade.

"I offer my life."

"Take it," came Itsu's cold response. The Jinda-Dii did not hesitate. He grasped the long dagger with both hands, placing the tip against his abdomen and fell forward. The cold steel slid easily through his belly. His body twitched violently as he pulled the blade from side to side. Darkness overtook his vision, and as he looked up, he saw a strange and inscrutable expression upon the face of the Hand Sinister.

It was a brilliant morning when the Jinda-Dii regained consciousness. He heard the voices of Jindas moving the lifeless body of Itsu across the swamp. Something was wrong. Contrary to ancient tradition, Itsu had not ordered him beheaded. He had deprived the Jinda-Dii of beheading, so the Jinda-Dii vowed to behead himself.

He climbed to his feet. His own cuts had been faulty, or he would already be dead. Perhaps, even he had swerved at the thought of death, he thought to himself. Slowly, he stumbled across the swamp in search of his sword. It was nowhere to be found. Then he reached the waterline and started to fall. Peering into the water, he expected to see his own face racked with the pains of death, but instead he saw something a million times more terrifying—the face of Itsu!

He trembled, thinking that a living ghost haunted him, but bending down, he discovered that the face was not an illusion. It was Itsu's real head, floating in the fetid marsh, a "13" embedded in the skull. The Jinda-Dii gasped. Then he saw a hand, and other parts that had washed up on shore. Horror welled deep within him.

The impossible had happened. He had been murdered by his own pupil! Agent 13, disguised as the Hand Sinister, had ordered him to kill himself. But he would not die now! Closing his eyes, he summoned all of his darkest knowledge from the mists of his life. And in the blinding sunlight, his blood began to slowly clot.

The smokestack of *the Jargon* protruded from the moonlit ocean like a tilted tombstone the following night. On shore, near DePeaux's dead men, a red-robed figure had nearly assembled the entire corpse of the Hand Sinister. The Jinda-Dii smiled weakly to himself.

It was a terrible sight, but the Jinda-Dii knew that Itsu was still very much alive. As he picked up the head, he felt the flow of warm blood.

The Jinda-Dii moved swiftly, purposefully. He knew that he had little time. He was acquainted with an ancient ritual that would allow him to restore the Living Dead. However, the ceremony had to take place within twenty-four hours of death. The Jinda-Dii knew that he must also give up his own body for the ceremony to be successful. He was prepared for this sacrifice.

The moon was bright as the Jinda-Dii prepared the unearthly ceremony.

Itsu's head sat atop a hastily constructed altar. He knelt before the decayed repellent head.

"Forgive me, high master," he muttered to the Hand Sinister, who watched him with seemingly dead eyes. "I have offered you my life, and, even in that, I have failed. Now I offer you my body. Take it, and you shall be strong." He then chanted several words in an ancient tongue.

Itsu's severed head finally hissed, "Empty your mind, I will take your body." Cruel power was etched in every wrinkle of his hideous face.

The Jinda-Dii felt gratitude that he could perform such a momentous task for his master. He gratefully submitted and peacefully swirled into blackness as his thoughts began to flee. He entered the void, a pit of mysterious darkness, where there was ... nothing.

LABYRINTH OF EVIL

Agent 13, still disguised as Itsu, was ferried by Jindas and Mayans into the underground labyrinth. In minutes, the strange procession of boats was deep in darkness. Already, he could hear the faint sounds of drums, could feel the palpable evil, and smell the unmistakable odor of death.

Though he feigned unconsciousness, he feverishly studied every detail of the labyrinth, mapping it out in his mind. He was confident that he could find his way out.

13 realized that it had all come to this. His fanatical quest would soon be over. Only one delicate task remained before him. He must rescue Maggie Darr from the Brotherhood's possession. Then, disguised as the Hand Sinister, he would order all of the Brotherhood's remaining members to take their own lives.

Yes, he thought, this will cleanse civilization and my own soul. The evil organization would soon be destroyed.

It was at this moment that 13 had an unsettling thought. When he had gone below *the Jargon's* deck to disguise himself as Itsu, he had opened the chest that contained the Crystals of Uru. But the sacred crystals were not there, nor anywhere else in the freighter's hold.

He remembered Ray Furnow's message, spoken mysteriously at the jazz bar. Someone had stolen the crystals. 13 knew that the possessor of the crystals had tremendous knowledge of good and evil. He knew that he must discover the identity of the thief — was it the Bishop, perhaps? The Jinda-Gaa? China White?

THE BETRAYER

With critical admiration, the Betrayer gazed at her image in the yacht's full-length mirror. The anticipation of the Juvita-ta added an aura of excitement that radiated from every limb and feature of her body.

China White ran her hands over the smooth, cool, black silk on her body. Perfection, she thought, then turned her attention to her face. There, her beauty was even more evident to her. Her cheekbones were high and delicate, her lips full, her eyes a deep china blue.

China White had schemed and acted with surprising speed and ruthless determination to bring about the events of the day. As she finished admiring herself in the mirror, she indulged, as she had so often in the past, in thoughts of her successful betrayal.

Unknowingly, Agent 13, her former lover, had been her greatest ally in the betrayal. She had sent him to Brother Du Lac with the assurance that once he had spoken to the spirit, he would be able to find the location of the Juvita-ta. After sabotaging the Jargon near St. Swithens, she had contacted the island locals and informed them of the tugboat's demise, as well, and where they might find the crew washed ashore. She knew that the half-dead crew would have a tale to tell. A tale that would reach Agent 13.

Agent 13 had ambushed the ship as planned, and his timing could not have been better. Once all of his men had boarded *the Jargon*, she had escaped in Agent 13's boat. The Crystals of Uru were safely tucked in a bag beside her. She had sat in the rainy darkness and watched gleefully as 13 dissected her former master. She saw the decayed head float past her in the murky water.

She had remained discreetly close by until morning. Peering through binoculars, she could see the entire activity on the marsh. She knew 13 had disguised himself as Itsu. She knew that he had ordered the Jinda-Dii to commit seppuku, and she knew that she had some time before the Mayans would escort the Hand Sinister to the Juvita-ta.

Everything had fallen into place brilliantly. China White used the time she had before the Mayans arrived to join up with a yacht owned by Phillo-polus, a Greek multimillionaire. She knew that there were men like Phillopolus, men of power around the world, who decided the fate of nations daily. They were driven to despair by the thought of her, their longing for her love a greater passion even than their chosen vices of greed or lust for power. Phillopolus had eagerly and without question given her his yacht and several men.

How delicious this had all been! She laughed to herself and turned to the couch, where she had placed her black bag. She sat on the couch and took out the precious crystals. Now she could take her time with them. During the journey, she had pulled them out on many occasions. She had gained intense flashes of knowledge from them. However, she had always been hurried.

The Crystal of Politics and the Crystal of Science were brilliant in the morning light. China White was hypnotized by their dazzling splendor and gazed at them with awe. Her mind reeled. Visions appeared before her. Knowledge filled her mind. But as she looked into the dazzling crystals, something left her. It was the power to love. She felt nothing for Tredekka. She knew that soon she must kill him. She persisted, fascinated with the globes. Ideas formed in her mind as she gained more and more knowledge. Things she had never thought of, or had quickly dismissed, presented themselves in new and startling ways. The world was alive with possibilities. She shivered in excitement. She had had enough.

Quickly, she tucked away the Crystals of Uru and climbed the steps to the bridge. The yacht crept along the walls of the labyrinth, silently following the procession of the Hand Sinister. In the velvety darkness, thoughts of evil deeds brushed against her. She reached out and grabbed them, struck by the immensity of her newfound power.

"I have everything," she said with a contemptuous laugh. "Everything."

CEREMONY OF THE GUILTY

Agent 13's boat passed under a huge stone arch and into a great domed chamber. It was enormous; the top of the dome towered a hundred feet above the water. Before him was a great pool fed by four water channels that radiated out like arms of a Maltese cross and vanished into other dark chambers like the one he had entered.

As 13 was lifted from the boat, he began to worry about his disguise. In the cargo hold of the Jargon, he had only been able to apply ash-gray makeup to his face. Under the blankets that concealed his body were the clothes of Barton, the gambler. He feared that if the blankets were removed, his true identity would be revealed. The firmness of his Luger tucked under his arm gave him small comfort.

13 could feel the ominous powers of darkness that were present in this region of evil. He was led past dozens of chanting Mayans, whose bodies were painted pitch black so that they looked like shadows in the dim torchlight.

As he was carried past, the Mayans dropped to their knees and parted to reveal seven Brotherhood Bishops.

The Bishops, wearing red robes, gazed upon him with eyes of ice. When he was young, 13 had waited for days to catch a glimpse of a Bishop. Bishops were the highest order of political saboteurs. He knew these seven Bishops had influenced many world leaders. He thought he recognized Beria's face among them. 13 knew Beria was a Bishop with a great deal of power in Soviet Russia, and thought back to his failed attempt to kill Beria at Lenin's tomb. 13 made no sign of recognition, no attempt to communicate with the Bishops as they bowed before him.

Agent 13 was once again in the deep red room that connected with the waterway. There was a frenzy of activity. He was placed on the large dais at the center of the room, the altar on which he had last seen the body of Maggie Darr.

The Mondra Lava, high priestess of the Powder Ceremony, stood before the altar at the edge of the deep circular pit. She wore a sheer black robe, and her body was flecked with gold and red, the colors of the voodoo paint she had applied for the ceremony. She stood glistening like the primal goddess of the Underworld.

"Ah, hah, hah, hah!" The Mondra Lava's tinkling laughter floated through the room. "Welcome, Itsu, welcome." The Mondra Lava's eyes scrutinized Agent 13.

13 involuntarily shuddered. Her eyes were an unearthly color. Though he knew nothing of Itsu's relationship with the Mondra Lava, he feared it. It seemed that she knew him too well. Far too well.

"The Bludda Dak is dead," she explained. "However, we still have the blood of your enemy, the beautiful Maggie Darr, to transfuse into your veins. The Ceremony of Blood will not be a complete failure. My Ceremony of Powder and the Ceremony of Water are also well prepared. Soon, Itsu, you will once again be the strong young man I remember you to be. Soon, my darling, soon."

The Mondra Lava turned, and in a high voice she declared in an ancient Brotherhood language, "Mya... comenta... Juvita-ta. So be it. Let the Juvita-ta begin."

Another dais had been prepared on the opposite side of the pit. The Mondra Lava now stood on this altar, a brilliant glow in her eyes. She shivered with excitement. With an elaborate gesture, she grasped a clear chalice in both hands and lifted it high above her head. Her eyes closed, and in a low monotone, she recited an incantation in a Brotherhood tongue.

The Mondra Lava then opened her eyes and gazed at the seven Bishops that now stood before her. They appeared entranced by the beautiful woman before them.

The Mondra Lava spoke to them in a whisper. "Soon, soon, the pain will come. Soon the life will leave your body. Your soul will long leave the elements of its flesh. But it cannot leave without my will. It cannot leave without my will. Remember this: Your soul cannot depart without my will..."

The seven Bishops chanted in response, "We are the souls of evil. We are the destroyers of liberties. We are the souls of evil. High Priestess, receive our sacrifice."

The first Bishop stepped to the altar. He repeated the words. "High Priestess, receive my sacrifice." She concentrated on the man, used her immense and dark powers on him. The Bishop bellowed a deep moan of despair. His face became a frozen statue of unbearable, searing pain, as a blue flame erupted and quickly died in his chest.

The clear chalice began to glow with a deep blue aura. Black-painted Mayans guided the first Bishop off the dais to a spot several feet away. The ceremony was repeated again and again as each of the six remaining Bishops stepped to the altar and offered the sacrifice of his soul.

The Mondra Lava felt a strange excitement growing within her as the aura of evil strengthened. She gleefully accepted the last Bishop's sacrifice, and silence reigned in the red room.

For a moment, the room became dark, illuminated only by the strange, deep blue aura of the chalice. Then, the blue aura disappeared, plunging the room into absolute darkness. As torches were re-lighted, the Mondra Lava stood with the urn over her head. The blue nimbus had turned to a vibrant blue powder in the chalice.

Slowly, the Mayans began the faint murmurings of a chant, and ominous drums began to beat. The Mayans threw the Bishops one by one into the pit, where they violently dissolved into gas.

Suddenly, the entire pit bubbled and roared more than ever. The Mondra Lava stood once again by 13's side. "The Ceremony of Powder is prepared," she whispered in a feverish voice. "The Ceremony of Water is beginning."

Like a volcano, a geyser erupted from the bubbly froth. The water was a molten red. Indeed, 13 thought, he was watching the same ceremony that ancient Spanish explorers had seen. They had called this geyser the Fountain of Youth.

The geyser burst upward. Loud snarls and growls emerged from it as it cascaded downward. An unspeakable, perverted, inhuman form stood before Agent 13. A creature forged of human nightmares. It was fifty feet tall and a cross between human and fish. The Agent knew its name at once. It was the Salamis!

Its bubbled eyes were those of a mammal and a fish. The Salamis's mouth opened and let out a reptilian hiss followed by a mammalian roar. Its jagged teeth still dripped with the blood of others who had summoned him.

13 tried to pull his gun from under the blanket that surrounded him, but before he could fire, a huge claw, webbed and green, grabbed him from the altar. Inside the crushing grip of the foul creature, he lost hold of the pistol. 13 froze as he stared at the creature's fiercely distorted face.

The Salamis let out a roar that was answered by the laughter of the Mondra Lava standing at her dais. 13 was pulled through the air toward the Salamis's mouth. The creature's hot, inflamed breath fell on him, overpowered him. Losing all composure, 13 emitted a final, piercing scream of terror, unadulterated by any other emotion.

As his body entered the dark, tooth-lined cave, a piercing fang dropped into place, tearing into his flesh. Burning-hot venom entered his body and a tide of darkness swept over him. He was conscious of nothing, spiraling downward into darkness. Then there was nothing. A void. From the void came a voice. "Itsu, with life comes hardship. Will you accept hardship?" "My name is not Itsu ..."

"What is your name?" the voice asked. "None you shall know..."

"Very well. Will you accept hardship?"

"Yes."

"Will you accept pain?"

"Yes."

"Will you preserve your life, even though you might grow weary of it?"

"Yes."

"Then I shall bathe you in the powder of rebirth. You will be revitalized by the souls of seven Bishops."

13 realized that he was hearing the voice of the Mondra Lava. Suddenly, from the darkness, came a burning, searing pain. It was as if somebody had poured acid on his chest.

But I have no skin, he thought, I am the void. The burning comes from the void.

13 wanted relief from the agonizing pain. He wanted desperately to rub the burn, but he had no hands to do so. After the burn came the sounds. And they were ear-piercing shrieks turned to cackling laughter. Then came vi-

sion. The fanged demon held him again.

Slowly, the sounds ended and the vision faded. The smell of death stung his nose as the taste of bile scorched his throat. He was alive.

In what could have been minutes, hours or seconds, the emptiness of the void gave way to chanting in the underground shrine, and the Mondra Lava looked down on him with delighted eyes.

"You look as you did five thousand years ago, Itsu," she whispered, almost breathless.

Gradually, 13's vision cleared. She thought he was Itsu! He was supposed to possess the secrets of the Crystals of Uru, but he did not. Surely, he thought, they had seen his face under the hastily improvised disguise, his body under the clothes.

Then it struck him. He had experienced the Juvita-ta! The infernal Salamis had bitten him. Then, when it spit him from its mouth, he was naked and young. Thus, the Mondra Lava and all the others were fooled into believing that he was a young Itsu.

The Mondra Lava fell to her knees before him.

"Truly, you are the Hand Sinister," she murmured.

The Mondra Lava rose and said, "The bloodgiver is prepared." She turned to the Mayans. "Begin the Ceremony of Blood."

The Mondra Lava then presented 13 with red robes, and clad his naked body. He peered into a polished bronze mirror that the Mondra Lava held before him. A mixture of horror and joy filled him, for his face was an evil parody of his own, but his eyes were filled with a mystical power. He felt, for a moment, that he truly was becoming the Hand Sinister.

The Mondra Lava pointed to a stone chair, and 13 went to it and sat. His senses were strangely well-tuned. He was aware of the breathing of those around him. He felt their body temperatures change with each new emotion they felt. He was aware of their hopes and fears.

The floor rumbled with the sound of stone sliding on stone. Beyond the rumble, he could hear the precise workings of gears and levers and pulleys. He could feel movement below him, and could see something descending from the darkness above. First, he caught a glimmer of highly polished gold, then slowly he could see the sinister device itself.

A huge, empty syringe drifted down toward him. It was so large that it could easily hold all the blood in a human body. He shuddered. The Mondra Lava looked at the device with glee, thriving on the savagery of the ceremony.

13 saw the massive polished skull of the gigantic idol rising toward him. He could hear the awed gasps of the Mayans below him. It was the same idol he had seen once before. Slowly, the top of a pentagram appeared on the side of the pillar.

He saw a wave of golden hair, then the twisted, horrible face of a woman driven to the brink of madness—Maggie Darr's. He could see the vicious red welts swollen on her body. Her eyes were inflamed, her teeth gritted. She hissed and shrieked like one driven far beyond sanity.

"Ah, hah, hah, hah..." The Mondra Lava shook her head with delight as she gazed upon the terrorized woman. 13, fearing what would happen if Maggie saw his face, slouched back into the darkness of the cowled robes.

"Her body is full of life," the Mondra Lava uttered in a fiendish voice.

And I intend to keep it that way, Agent 13 thought to himself. But another voice within him disagreed. Ah, this voice said, her blood shall boil well within me. 13 then realized the battle within him. The germ of evil had been planted in him by the ceremonies, and the corruption was beginning.

He summoned all his strength to fight the urge to have Maggie's blood. He thought about the dead—his parents, Gunnar Holt, LaMonica, and countless others. He finally triumphed over the corruption. And he planned their escape.

13 had a finely developed sense of impending doom. As he planned possible courses of action, he felt Maggie's stare. Maggie watched him through inflamed, wild eyes. He knew that an awful outburst was on Mag-

gie's lips but he could do nothing to stop it. She stared at him in absolute bewilderment as she suffered an instant shock of recognition. Somewhere in her feverish dreams, she recognized him.

She groped for words. At first, they were garbled, but gradually they became absolutely clear.

"13! It was you all along! You were Itsu!" she shouted in horror, overwhelmed with confusion.

Silence descended on the room. The drumming of the Mayans below stopped and the Mondra Lava turned to him, her face twisted with accusation.

13 looked at the Mondra Lava with fierce, glaring eyes. "Who is this woman?" he hissed.
The Mondra Lava looked back. "It is Maggie Darr. The fresh one you desired."

"You are either a traitor or a fool! Die!" shouted 13. The Mondra Lava instinctively stepped back, but 13 quickly stood up and shoved her into the pit, the Salamis's lair. The woman screamed a series of curses, not heard in this world for millennia, as she fell through the air. Finally, she hit the foul water. The Mondra Lava surfaced near the side of it. "You are not Itsu!" she shouted.

Suddenly, all eyes shifted to 13. He ignored her outburst, and in a commanding voice screamed in Mayan dialect, "Lower the idol. I wish to inspect the woman."

The remaining Jindas encircled him. One of them spoke. "Show us your palm, worthy master, so that we may know it is you."

"At last, Agent 13, the pleasure of killing you shall be mine!" the Mondra Lava screamed from the pit. Then she broke into tinkling laughter. Her face glowed with maniacal glee.

13 watched as the water under the Mondra Lava began to bubble. He turned to the Jindas and pointed toward the pit. "There is your proof!" he screamed. Suddenly, a slimy, scaled hand rose from the water and grabbed the woman. The Mondra Lava screamed curses in a long-dead tongue, but the Salamis did not listen. Instead, its hand pulled her into the water. There was a ferocious roiling of the water and a brutal thrashing. Then, all was silent until the Mondra Lava's head floated to the surface. Her distorted face looked very much like those she had impaled on poles in Africa weeks before.

13 stood atop the dais. With an elaborate gesture, he swept his hand across the room.

"Unshackle her!" he yelled to the Mayans in their tongue, pointing to Maggie. The Mayans released Maggie from the pentagram. "Put her aboard the boat," he shouted.

He then turned to the Jindas. "You have failed me," he said in a terrible voice. "All of you. I demand Sep-pu-ku!"

The Jindas did not respond to his order for their deaths. They hesitated for a moment, then slowly began to close in on him. In a chant of their own, they repeated, "Show us your palm, worthy master, so that we may know it is you."

13 found his Luger under the dais and moved with the speed of a cheetah toward the waiting boat where Maggie Darr lay in an exhausted heap.

A Jinda guarding the boat launched himself feet first at 13. The Agent squeezed the trigger of his Luger. Even before the Jinda heard the faint "poof of the shot, a .45-caliber hollow-point entered his chest and ripped a red-hot path through the man's body.

In an instant, he burst into flames.

Slugs spattered the ground around him as 13 plunged into the boat and started the motor, while still squeezing the Luger's trigger.

13 roared out of the ceremonial chamber, into the comparative calm of the labyrinth. Once a good distance from the chanber, he stopped the boat to check on Maggie's condition.

"I know not whether to reward you or kill you!" A woman's voice shouted from the water next to Agent 13's boat. 13 dropped his gun in surprise, and turned to face China White. She was standing on the deck of a yacht. A man stood next to her with a submachine gun pointed directly at 13's chest.

"It would not have been possible for me to steal the Crystals of Uru and defeat Itsu without you!" she shouted.

13 thought of China White's saving him in Russia many weeks before. The frantic ride away from Red Square in the Soviet jeep. Her passionate words. Her brilliant acting. She sent him to meet Brother Du Lac, knowing that he would find the Juvita-ta. He guessed that she had even sabotaged the Jargon to draw his attention. The diabolical scheming and elegant treachery overwhelmed him.

"I never believed that you saved me out of love," he responded.

"No, but there was doubt in your mind. It was that doubt that fuelled my plans."

"Nonsense. You could have destroyed the Hand Sinister and the Jinda-Dii yourself."

"Had I done that, I never would have found my way into the Juvita-ta. I needed Itsu for that, but I could never have allowed a living Itsu to do it, therefore I needed an impostor. You were the unwitting actor, and I the choreographer. It was your greatest role, Agent 13, the man of a thousand faces."

China White smiled. "Good-bye, Agent 13. And if it makes a difference to you, take the knowledge to your death that I once did love you."

She then turned to the gunner and muttered something. He started to lift the barrel of his gun, when suddenly, Maggie Darr sat up, raising Agent 13's Luger. She squeezed off three shots, hitting the man in the thigh, shattering the thigh bone. His leg gave way, and with a crunch, he tumbled forward, screaming in pain. His head bounced on the floor of the boat less than six inches from China White.

China White reached for the gunner's submachine gun as 13 roared the engine of his boat, and he and Maggie were gone in a spray of foam.

In minutes, the buzzing confusion was only a distant thunder as 13 and Maggie made their way out of the black, nightmarish labyrinth and into the bayou. They were safe.

Agent 13 put his warm arms around Maggie Darr, and covered her shivering body with his robes. A long moment passed when nothing was said.

"Please," she muttered finally, looking at him through hazy eyes. "You have done all you need to do. You have done more than anyone could ask. Let the rest of the world fight its wars."

He looked in the direction from which they had come. "Don't you understand, Maggie? I have no choice. I must fight them. Before, the end could be measured in decades. Now, it can be measured in millennia because of that damn ceremony. I cannot stop, Maggie."

She trembled a little. "I know," she said. Tears shone in her eyes. "And I am afraid."

He held her tightly to him. "Have no doubts about the love I have for you," he said simply. Never before had he spoken that way, and she knew it.

"I have never doubted it."

"Is that why you spared China White?" he asked.

"No. I was out of bullets," she said with a grin, her face warmed by 13's embrace and the dazzling sunset.

13 smiled to himself. Maggie had passed through death, unchanged.

EPILOGUE

A blood-red sunset illuminated Jackson's Shoals. The Hand Sinister, now in the body of the Jinda-Dii, peered down at the carefully collected remnants of his former body and laughed.

He felt newborn strength. He knew that with the Jinda-Dii's body, he would not need the Juvita-ta for quite some time. The ceremonies could wait. He rubbed his hands together, a malignant smile on his face. There was so much left to do. He would find the Betrayer. He would destroy Agent 13. He would retrieve the Crystals of Uru. And he would conquer the world. Yes, he thought, there is so much left to do.

Then he picked up the head that had formerly been his own for thousands of years, and looked at it. It would be a marvelous souvenir. He dropped it into a bag at his side, and silhouetted against the bloody horizon, he walked to meet his destiny.

AGENT 13: THE DOSSIER

AGENT 13: THE RADIO SERIES

AN INTRODUCTION TO THE RADIO ADVENTURES OF THE MIDNIGHT AVENGER

BY DENIZ CORDELL

In early 2010, Flint Dille and I were working together on another project when I rather brashly broached the idea of bringing Agent 13 to the airwaves as a full-cast radio drama. The idea was enthusiastically received by Messrs Dille & Marconi, and it was agreed that I would write the scripts for the series, which would be based on the three novels you've just finished reading. The Colonial Radio Theatre on the Air, an award-winning company noted for their collaborations with Ray Bradbury and popular original programming - and also a company I've worked with as a writer, actor and composer over the last nine years - would present and produce the shows, with artistic director Jerry Robbins directing the scripts with his usual high style and sharp rhythm.

I thought the character had a number of tremendous ideas attached to him that would work like gangbusters in audio: his constant use of disguise and subterfuge would make the role great fun for an actor who'd have a chance to shroud themselves in various dialects and character types (and would add another element for the audience to actively participate in, too: "that voice wasn't 13, was it?"), and his branding ring (a tip of the fedora to that restlessly questing figure, *The Spider*) would provide a sonic imprint and hook that I felt could be a signature sound for the radio program, much as *The Shadow's* laugh or *Doc Savage's* unearthly trilling provided an immediate and memorable aural stamp for those fine men of mystery. Then, of course, there was the thrill of bringing a modern-day pulp legend to a new audience, and given the Agent's birth as a grand homage to the pulp heroes of yesteryear, it seemed appropriate to me that he make the leap to radio, and join his (literary not

Wold-Newton) grandfather, *The Shadow*, in taking his fight against ill-doers to listeners coast-to-coast. Of course, in the case of Street & Smith's cloaked crusader, his move was from radio to the pulps and back again, but now I'm splitting hairs.

There also existed a more complicated worldview within 13's storytelling than much seen in the magazines of the other pulp heroes. Dille and Marconi took notions from the three major monoliths of pulp, moved them forward a logical step, and in the process, brought a more contemporary storytelling sensibility to the larger-than-life antics. The moral gray-area that 13 sometimes occupies is an integral part of the character's fabric, and is also a part of the kind of storytelling that's in vogue these days - the juxtaposition of his upbringing as an assassin, compounded with his self-enforced moral code provided an internal conflict which you wouldn't necessarily see in a figure like *Doc Savage*, who was always in the right. The tone and breadth of the storytelling in the books also offered up a little bit of everything, which I thought was tremendously appealing, not only as a writer but a listener - here was great heroism, terrible villainy, nailbiting suspense, a melancholy and bittersweet love story, well-placed moments of light humor, and white-hot adventure, all brought to life with well-developed characters (I developed a particular fondness for Maggie in the course of writing the scripts) and a strong sense of internal history.

Writing the scripts for the first nine episodes (which make up the adaptation of *The Invisible Empire*) was consistently exhilarating, sometimes maddening work. Given the extensive number of action sequences in the book, a good amount of time on my part was spent making those inherently visual moments zip and sing in sound - something that would require the meshing of elaborate production design with just the right accompanying dialogue, which would clarify and elaborate on - but not explicitly spell-out - what the audience hears. The stylized dialogue of the books was greatly expanded upon as well - the new medium allowing for a little more time spent with the characters, while also requiring a certain degree of conversation driven storytelling. Throughout it all, I found myself able to indulge in my love for all of the great fiction of the thirties and forties - from Walter Gibson to Raymond Chandler, John Carroll Daly to Damon Runyon - and embraced the style and feel of my favorite films of the era, made by such luminaries as John Huston, Sir Carol Reed, Howard Hawks, Jacques Tourneur, and so on. Throw in a dollop of Chester Gould, the serials put out by Republic, Universal and others, and the sound and feel of the great radio programs of the day, and you get a vague idea of the dramatic stone soup I was happily, heedlessly tossing ingredients into. In this process, the show evolved into a billet-doux to the artistic and pop-cultural landscape of the time - just as the original books were a loving appreciation of the pulp adventure genre, and those dreams of derring-do and nervewracking nightmares the stories evoked in their readers.

In the production, you'll find familiar scenes from the books lying side-by-side with new characters and sequences that fit into the larger scope of 13's universe. Smaller roles from the books are expanded and play greater roles in the progression of the narrative, offering up commentary, new plot-threads, and cementing and emphasizing the connections between the various facets of the story. Also sutured into the fabric of the production are moments and snatches of dialogue from the first graphic novel written by Dille & Marconi, as well as other newly expanded material. Part of the joy in working on the shows were creating something that was faithful to the source, while offering up new treats and delights for listeners familiar with the books - with the advantage of the new medium, we're given more glimpses into the lives of the delightful and distinct characters brought forth in the books, to say nothing of bringing in the wry, acerbic, and knowing voice of Brother Sharu (one of the three original founders of the Brotherhood, for those of you keeping score) into a dramatically necessary role.

Throughout the writing, both Flint and David were extremely supportive of any additions, alterations and emendations that I made to the story - and we were very careful to ensure that anything I did (whether adding an operative to 13's ranks or giving China White a new, terrifying aquatic pet) would play fair within the pulp world, and with the rules and universe established for Agent 13. Flint, in particular, pushed for emphasizing the more mystic-horror and supernatural elements from the text (see the Nephilim in *The Invisible Empire* and the *Bludda-Dak* in *Acolytes of Darkness* for just a few of the pre-existing examples), and this aesthetic figures most prominently in key sojourns to the Shadow Zone, as well as creating a few new grisly grue-somes, such as the Rook seen early in the book. In the radio show, he is not merely a man who rose up through the Brotherhood ranks, but instead a... but I shouldn't give everything away.

The script pages published here come from early in the first episode, and follow the final steps of Colonel Schmidt as he makes his way through the Hagia Sophia to his meeting. Eagle-eyed readers will immediately notice the presence of a second German officer - a necessity for the new medium. By having two characters engaging in conversation, a sense of dramatic motion is created, and some much needed vocal variety for the listener to latch on to and follow is offered up. As opposed to hearing a lengthy internal monologue for several pages (as the book nimbly does), what would be a passive scene on the radio becomes an active one. The reader interested in how such scripts are structured will note that sound and music cues are very specifically noted for the producer and composer.

My friend Nicholas Meyer once told me that "art thrives on restrictions," and while I won't be so presumptuous or naïve as to call these scripts "art," I think his adage holds true. Radio drama - with no corresponding images - not only forces the writer to be creative in getting ideas across, but - more importantly - it makes the listener the director of their own visual component, they are the camera, the stagers of scenes - and the performances and sound design work together to actively involve them in the sweeping, operatic action; allowing them to visualize the characters as they see them - it becomes a highly individual experience, and much like a snowflake, no two listeners will "see" it in the exact same way - I think there's something wonderful about that.

My tremendous thanks are due to Flint Dille and David Marconi for their support and enthusiasm for the series, and to everyone at the Colonial Radio Theatre on the Air, for their belief in the material and for imbuing it with such zest and vitality.

Since he's an unparalleled master of disguise, Agent 13 could just as soon be me or you - and isn't that thrill of vicarious, grandiose heroism one of the reasons we turn to these grand figures anyway? Heroes like 13 provide a gateway into making some sense of a senseless world, of righting the wrongs that seem unrightable, of fighting that which is undefeatable, and yet defeating it anyway, whether through pluck, luck, ingenuity, or sacrifice. It's nice sometimes to have that quick method of escape from reality, and it's nice to think that paragons like that can exist. You've just read the terrific stories that launched our venerable hero's vaunted career, but, to coin a cliché: you haven't heard anything yet.

The rumblings are true. Agent 13 lives, and he's fighting for all of our lives. Join him, won't you?

COLONIAL RADIO THEATRE
ON THE AIR
PRESENTS

AGENT 13
AND
THE INVISIBLE EMPIRE

CREATED BY
FLINT DILLE AND
DAVID MARCONI

COMING 2013

THE
COLONIAL
RADIO
THEATRE
On The Air
© 2013 CRT

THE DOSSIER

AGENT 13:

THE INVISIBLE EMPIRE

Produced and Presented by
The Colonial Radio Theatre on the Air

Based on the novels and characters created by
Flint Dille and David Marconi

Written for Radio by
Deniz Cordell

Directed by
Jerry Robbins

Executive Producer
Mark Vander Berg

Music by
Jeffrey Gage

Editing and Post-Production by
Rich Matheson

Script excerpt presented with the express permission of
The Colonial Radio Theatre on the Air

INT. THE HAGIA SOPHIA

SOUND - A LARGE, REVERBERATING SPACE

SOUND - FOOTSTEPS CONTINUE INTO CHAMBER MUSIC - QUASI-RELIGIOUS, TURNING OMINOUS

> SCHMIDT
> Ah, here we are. Now, you see that statue of Neptune there? Go and...

SOUND - HE STOPS WALKING WITH SUDDEN FORCE

> SCHMIDT (CONT'D)
> (startled noise)
> Back, Schultz!

SOUND - SCHMIDT DRAWS HIS GUN, COCKS IT

SOUND - CONFUSED FOOTSTEPS DARTING BACK

> SCHULTZ
> (darting back)
> What is it, Colonel?

> SCHMIDT
> There! That face... you see it?
> Twisted in pain...

> SCHULTZ
> It's nothing but a statue,
> Colonel... A silly, meaningless
> icon from centuries past.

> SCHMIDT
> Hmm, yes, yes, you're quite right.

SOUND - SCHMIDT PUTS HIS GUN AWAY

> SCHMIDT (CONT'D)
> Go ahead and open up the passageway.
> The less time I am in the same room as this...
> Christ on the cross, the better.

> SCHULTZ
> Jawohl...

SOUND - SCHULTZ FOOTSTEPS HEADING OFF IN THE DISTANCE

                    SCHMIDT
                 (to himself)
                 Strange...

                 SCHMIDT (CONT'D)
            How unsettling it is to behold...
          and yet I cannot help but look at it.

SOUND - FOOTSTEP OR TWO COMING CLOSER

                 SCHMIDT (CONT'D)
            Those nails in its hands... The
            wounds... It is... so real...

SOUND - FROM OFF, A CLICK OF A STONE

SOUND - FROM OFF, THE WHIRRING AND NOISE OF ANCIENT
GEARS AS...

SOUND - A LARGE STONE DOOR OPENS. HEAVY.

                    SCHULTZ
               (calling from off)
            I have opened the entrance to the
            secret staircase, Herr Colonel...
                 (silence)
                 Colonel?

                    SCHMIDT
            There is something about this
          statue, Schultz. I do not like it.
           It is... terrifyingly lifelike.
          Those eyes - see how they appear to
          burn... with anguish, with pain...
            they... they remind me of...

                    SCHULTZ
          Ah, come now, Colonel, a man of
            reason such as yourself...

                    SCHMIDT
                    (a sigh)
                    Yes...

SOUND - SCHMIDT (CLOSE UP) STARTS WALKING OFF, SLOWLY

                SCHMIDT (CONT'D)
                (as he walks)
            I suppose you're...

SOUND - FROM OFF, A SLIGHT SHIFTING NOISE, AND A MILD
CREAK (STOPS ABRUPTLY)

SOUND - FOOTSTEPS STOP, AND WHIRL ABOUT/SCUFFLE QUICKLY

                SCHMIDT (CONT'D)
                (startled)
                Schultz...

                    SCHULTZ
                Jawohl, Colonel?

                    SCHMIDT
            Oh... Nothing, I'm just... letting
            this place get to me -- strange
                that it should...
                (sharp, soft)
            Schultz -- the statue!

                    SCHULTZ
        Colonel, for the last time, it is...

                    SCHMIDT
            No, idiot, listen to me, and look
            for yourself! The left hand...

                    SCHULTZ
                What about it?

                    SCHMIDT
            I would swear by Itsu himself
                that it... it...

                    SCHULTZ
                  (impatiently)
     What?! You desire to live in terror, and keep the
       Brotherhood waiting?! So what is it, Colonel?!

                    SCHMIDT
          The hand... I would swear... a
          moment ago it... it was over...

                    SCHULTZ
               Spit it out, man!

                    SCHMIDT
          His hand... it has moved.

                    SCHULTZ
               (beat, hushed and
                  surprised)
                    What?

SOUND - FROM OFF, A NAIL SHOOTING THROUGH THE AIR
MUSIC - ON A SUSTAINED NOTE AND OUT AS...

SOUND - THE NAIL STRIKES FLESH, HARD, CAUSING A SPURTING
NOISE AS...

CAST AD LIB - SCHULTZ LETS OUT A HORRIBLE SCREAM AND...
SOUND - HIS BODY DROPS TO THE FLOOR, KICKING ABOUT...
CAST AD LIB - FROM OFF, SCHULTZ GURGLES AS...

                    SCHMIDT
               (stunned, terrified)
          A nail! He... threw a nail at...
                 (calling over)
                   Schultz!

CAST AD LIB - FROM OFF, THE END OF SCHULTZ'S DEATH
RATTLE SOUND - WITH THE END OF THE RATTLE, THE BODY
STOPS TWISTING ABOUT ON THE FLOOR

SOUND - CLOSE ON - A SNAPPING OF WOOD AND AFTER A
MOMENT, ANOTHER SNAPPING NOISE...

                    SCHMIDT   (CONT'D)
                    (turning back)
                     Wh...? No.
         (after the SECOND SNAP OF WOOD)
          No... Get back! It can't be...
              You're a statue! You...
                 Stop looking at me!

SOUND - HE DRAWS HIS GUN, AND COCKS IT

SOUND - SCHMIDT STARTS BACKING AWAY

                    SCHMIDT   (CONT'D)
        Those eyes! Gott in himmel, I cannot bear to
            look at those empty, burning eyes!
                   I cannot...

SOUND - FROM CLOSE, ANOTHER NAIL SHOOTS THROUGH THE
AIR... AND...

SOUND - THE NAIL STRIKES FLESH - A HORRIBLE SQUISH/
CRUNCH/CRACK/POPPING NOISE (LIKE AN EGG CRACKING)

CAST AD LIB - SCHMIDT LETS OUT A SCREAM TO WAKE THE
DEAD - SCREAMING AND YELLING, AMONG THE NOISE IS THE
OCCASIONAL CRY OF: "MY EYE!" (AT LEAST ONE "MY
EYE!" SHOULD BE HEARD UNADORNED BY OTHER SOUNDS)

SOUND/CAST AD LIB - SCHMIDT COLLAPSES TO THE GROUND,
STILL SCREAMING, WRITHING IN AGONY...

SOUND - FEET LANDING ON THE TILE

SOUND - HOLLOW, EERIE FOOTSTEPS APPROACHING

                     AGENT 13
                   (sepulchral)
              An eye for an eye, Schmidt.

                     SCHMIDT
                 (screaming, and:)
          No... No... Away from me, ghost!

AGENT 13
I've been tracking you for four
months...Four long months, while
I was powerless to prevent you from
murdering hundreds of people. No
more. At last, your twisted trail
of death ends. With you.

SCHMIDT
(spiteful, spitting)
No! I will not die witnessing Christ
descending from his cross... I will
not be judged... not by you,
not by anyone! I've done what I must,
and you will not have...
(heavy breathing)

SOUND - MORE HOLLOW FOOTSTEPS APPROACHING

SCHMIDT (CONT'D)
(really losing it)
Speak, damn you!

SOUND - METAL RING HITTING STONE FLOOR
SOUND - SOMETHING SPARKING LIKE A FLARE] AND HISSING

SCHMIDT (CONT'D)
(pained noises throughout)
What is... that light... from...
your ring... You!

AGENT 13
(approaching)
Any last confessions, Schmidt?

                    SCHMIDT
                   (gurgling)
    The fallen angel... Nummer Dreizehn...
              (a sickening laugh)
       Go ahead... leave me with your
        mark upon my forehead. I do not
    fear you. No, *au contraire* – I fear
                 for you...
              (quick beat)
    Well?! What do you delay for? Do it!

SOUND - A HISSING AND SIZZLE/BURNING NOISE

CAST AD LIB - SCHMIDT YELLS IN GREAT PAIN, WHICH HITS A
CLIMAX BEFORE HE ABRUPTLY STOPS - DEAD.

MUSIC - OUT

SOUND - A RESIDUAL HISSING FROM THE STEAM, OUT.

                    AGENT 13
         The world's a better place now,
          Schmidt... Even if by a small
                measure. Now...

SOUND - A TOWEL WIPING/SWASH NOISE

                 AGENT 13 (CONT'D)
                  To get this...

SOUND - PLASTIC TEARING NOISE

                 AGENT 13 (CONT'D)
                Make-up off... and...

SOUND - SOMETHING LIQUID-LIKE UNROLLING, SPILLING OUT

                 AGENT 13 (CONT'D)
          Get this insta-derm on Schmidt's
         face... should be active in just a...

SOUND - CLOSE TO MIC, A VACUUM LIKE NOISE, FAST

> AGENT 13 (CONT'D)
> Good. His facial mold should be
> done in just a... ah, his briefcase.

SOUND - BRIEFCASE SLIDING ON FLOOR

> AGENT 13 (CONT'D)
> Hmm.

SOUND - BRIEFCASE SHAKES - A FEW THINGS IN IT JUMBLE UP
AND DOWN (NOT JUST PAPERS, BUT PENS, "HARDER" OBJECTS),
SHIFT, JOSTLE.

> AGENT 13 (CONT'D)
> Booby trapped, no doubt...

SOUND - BRIEFCASE CLOSER - WE HEAR A TICKING NOISE
THROUGH IT

> AGENT 13 (CONT'D)
> Ah, yes... The bomb's designed
> to go off when the wrong man
> opens it, I'd imagine. Well, if I...

SOUND - SWITCHBLADE OPENS

> AGENT 13 (CONT'D)
> slice the case open...

SOUND - SWITCHBLADE CUTS OPEN LEATHER CASE

> AGENT 13 (CONT'D)
> I should be able to pry it
> out, and...

SOUND - SUITCASE BEING PRIED OPEN

SOUND - TICKING NOISE LOUDER FROM INSIDE CASE

AGENT 13 (CONT'D)
Ah. And there it is.
(finding the bomb)
Hel-lo...

SOUND - WIRELESS WAVELENGTH NOISES, FADING IN AND OUT
AS...

ANGLES
(filtered, staticky)
Les Angles calling Thirteen.
Come in Thirteen.

AGENT 13
Just a minute, Les.

SOUND - TICKING CONTINUES UNDER

ANGLES
(filtered, staticky)
Been trying to get you on the
wireless for a bit now, Boss.

AGENT 13
Yeah, I'm a little busy right now...
(softer)
This should dis[arm]...

SOUND - A SMALL CRANK TURNS - TICKING GETS MUCH FASTER

ANGLES
(filtered, staticky)
Our eyes in Istanbul sighted a truck with the
Omega symbol on it quarter of a mile from the
Hagia Sophia. Ten guys got off it, carting some kinda crate...
Whatever's in it - it's big, Boss.

AGENT 13
Les, pick a color - red or blue...

ANGLES
(filtered, staticky)
Uh... Blue?

AGENT 13
All right...

SOUND - A WIRE SNIP

SOUND - BOMB TICKING CEASES

AGENT 13 (CONT'D)
Thanks.

ANGLES
(filtered, staticky)
Sure, uhm, sure thing...

AGENT 13
Now, let's see what's so important
about these papers...

SOUND - PAPERS START SHUFFLING OUT

AGENT 13 (CONT'D)
War plans... Troop locations...
Deployment orders...
Nürnberg Rally speech...

SOUND - PHOTOGRAPH PAPER PULLED OUT OF FOLDER

AGENT 13 (CONT'D)
Hello - an itinerary, and a photo of the
National Security Council in Washington...
so, they would spread their terrible
plague to the New World, eh?
And... What... What's this...?

SOUND - FOLDER SLIDES OUT - OPENS

SOUND - PAPERS SHUFFLING FAST

                    AGENT 13 (CONT'D)
             Doesn't seem to have much to do
             with any... Les - I need you to
             start digging up anything you can
             on a scientist named David Fischer.
             And have Benny check into the
             National Security Council's latest
                      doings...

                        ANGLES
                  (filtered, staticky)
             Right-o. That all, Boss?

                      AGENT 13
                  That's all. Out.

SOUND - RADIO WAVES OSCILLATE VERY BRIEFLY, THEN OUT
AS...

SOUND - THE WIRELESS SET IS CLICKED OFF

                    AGENT 13 (CONT'D)
             All right... The facemask-mold
             should be ready about now...

SOUND - A PEELING PLASTIC NOISE

                    AGENT 13 (CONT'D)
             Perfect. *Danke schön*, Colonel...
                  Now, I'll just...

SOUND - MASK BEING PUT ON

                    AGENT 13 (CONT'D)
                (putting on the mask)
                  Put this on, and...

SOUND - FABRIC UNROLLING AND SNAPPING

                    AGENT 13 (CONT'D)
             Take this ceremonial robe you were
                  kind enough to pack...

SOUND - ROBE ON - QUICK - HOOD OVER HEAD

> AGENT 13 (CONT'D)
> Good. Now to head down to King
> Bizas' secret chamber...
> (German accent)
> *As Herr Colonel Reinhardt Schmidt...*

SOUND - FOOTSTEPS FAST, OFF, FOLLOW TO...

SOUND - A GREAT GONG CRASH!

MUSIC - SINISTER/MYSTICAL

MUSIC - HOLLYWOOD-FAR EAST

> SHARU
> (light reverb)
> What new terror will Agent 13 discover
> in the bowels of the Hagia Sophia?
> Who is David Fischer, and why is the
> Brotherhood interested in him?
> When will Itsu, *The Hand Sinister*,
> make his next, deadly move against
> those who would oppose him?
> The All-Seeing Sharu knows
> the answers to these questions and
> more - and so shall you, when you
> tune in for "Agent 13 and the
> Invisible Empire," coming soon from
> *The Colonial Radio Theatre on the Air.*

MUSIC - CYMBAL SHIMMER, AND OUT

AGENT 13:

CONFESSIONS ON THE ORIGIN OF

THE MIDNIGHT AVENGER

ILLUSTRATIONS BY JAMES CRAIG

"I loaded up on secret societies, lost cities, dangerous women, Chthonic monsters, masked crime fighters and never looked back" - Flint Dille

Pulp was one of those things that I always knew was out there, but never really saw it until I was an adult. My father had a book called *The Pulps: Fifty years of American Pop Culture* by Tony Goodstone who had some connection with his *The Collected Works of Buck Rogers in the 25th Century* project, so I knew the word and liked the lurid covers. I'd read bits and pieces of it when I was younger, but always in things like *Conan* reprints. I didn't know it was a genre or that it came from disreputable magazines, it was always just sort of there.

As an adult, I started looking for it after *Raiders of the Lost Ark* came out. I wanted more like that. I knew that Pulp and old Radio Shows and Cliffhanger serials were all related. Pulps dated better because of the technical and budgetary limitations of the serials and the radio shows. (Though I listen to Classic Radio on XM, and I am constantly amazed by how good some of it is). In any case, when I talk about pulps, I'm referring to this Transmedia blur in my head of magazines, serials, radio shows, comic strips and paperback novels.

Anyway, one year at Comic Con I found some pulp mags sitting in an old bin while I was busy re-buying my childhood. You could buy non-pristine off-brand for $5 at the time. I loaded up on secret societies, lost cities, dangerous women, chthonic monsters, masked crime fighters and never looked back. It was about then that I realized that I was much more familiar with the pulps than I knew I was: *Phillip Marlowe, The Shadow, The Phantom, Tarzan* and all sorts of familiar characters came from the pulps. I liked the off brand ones the most for some reason, *Operator #5, Secret Agent X, The Spider.*

So I came home from ComiCon, probably 1985, with a pile of pulp stuff. Dave was crashed at my couch around that time, and we sat around reading the falling apart magazines and decided we'd take a film story we'd been pitching around do our own pulp. Our story was kind of "Indiana Jones meets James Bond." I conned Gary Gygax into publishing the books at TSR. The movie pitch got us both writing jobs at Amblin', but nobody put it into development...

"The people who populated that world were also larger than life in many ways - much more interesting than the grayness of today's world" - David Marconi

For me, the 20s, 30's and 40s have always been a period of great interest. Good and evil were seen more in terms of black and white and the pulps be-came an extension of that world. The people who populated that world were also larger than life in many ways - much more interesting than the grayness of today's world. The Pulps also reminded me of the Saturday morning action pictures my parents would take me to see at an early age. Many of the scripts I write today are a further extension of that world as well.

I love pulp. Its pure entertainment. In its heyday it was non-literary stuff written by often extremely literate people who were being paid by the word. It was churned out fast, and you can feel it – in a good way. Nothing is labored, its pure inspiration, fully charged and loaded. I guess the best analogy in my mind is that its like a live concert as opposed to a studio album. No months of navel pondering, no rethink, just right there, right out and at its best you can almost feel the energy of some guy writing in a white heat trying to make a deadline.

"Pulps also filled a hole in my understanding of the origins of two important American genres (and pulps are truly and deeply American): The Hard Boiled Detective and the Superhero"
- Flint Dille

It never occurred to me until this moment. Right now as I'm typing this, that at the time I was working in that tradition. I was working in the disreputable medium of animation. We were cranking out *Transformers* and *G.I. Joe* and *Inhumanoids* and *Visionaries* at an amazing rate, it was the kind of sprinting marathon that I get the feeling Robert E. Howard worked in. You can't have written as much as he did and died at such a young age if you spent a lot of time meditating on each word. The thing that's wonderful about Pulp is that you have beautiful, poetic lines side-by-side pure cliché. It's not about crafting the words, its about always cutting to the visceral moment. I was also working on the *Sagard* books with Gary Gygax at the time, and even though they were 'fight a path' game books, they were heavily influenced by the pulps.

And we haven't even mentioned the cover artwork. You look at those covers and you want to read the story. Doesn't matter if it's a western, and in captivity, I don't even read westerns or a spicy mystery or a *G-8 and his Battle Aces,* but you're sucked in.

Pulps also filled a hole in my understanding of the origins of two important American genres (and pulps are truly and deeply American): The Hard Boiled Detective and the Superhero. Something with the 'reality' of our world, but with a hint of the magic of comics – kind of like the way 'Uranus' was found by deduction (*'there must be something there'*). Of course, it was staring me in the face. When I was in 6th Grade, poised on that magical precipice between childhood and adolescence, *The Green Hornet* was my favorite show. It wasn't the show itself, as much as what I felt the show could be: the Black Beauty cruising the rain-slicked streets at night, a fence with a breath mint ad splitting apart, a secret world right inside ours.

What I didn't know at the time, but somehow intuitively understood was that I was seeing a transitional hero – a guy who wore regular clothes and a mask who fought crime by night and ran a newspaper by day. The villains were mobs and gangs and the occasional themed enemy, but they didn't have any powers. Nobody did. Nobody wore costumes that they couldn't ditch in two minutes. Nobody had rays shooting out of their eyes. In short, I could grow up to be this guy. Those heroes wouldn't stay around for long. They would, inside a generation go through a mutational mitosis process into, on one side guys in spandex (though spandex didn't exist then) and on the other side priva te eyes in suits with no mask.

The Green Hornet, some iterations of *The Shadow, The Spider, Operator #5* and *Secret Agent X* all existed somewhere on the edge of reality in that minute when we believed that you could throw on a mask and nobody would know your identity.

I love the artifice of pulp. The suspension. Sometimes you see pulp in real life. The North Hollywood Bank Robbers were simultaneously a modern phenomenon and something out of pulp. Masked men spreading terror,

"Pulp is ground up paper" - David Marconi

Agent 13 was born out of a "pitch" that Flint and I had put together and taken around to the studios to try and set up as a screenplay gig. A pitch is where you walk into a room filled with a bunch of bored studio executives and try to entertain them enough with your verbal story that they will open their wallets and actually pay you to then write the script.

After making the rounds to the various buyers, we had some nibbles, but no bites. But what we did have was a fully flushed out story with characters. So Flint and I looked at each other and said why don't we just write the books as Flint's sister had just acquired TSR and we had access to their Random House deal. And once we started, we couldn't stop.

We discussed and laid out the story together for the pitch. Once we decided to proceed with the books, Flint did his pass on the material. I then took what he had done, and went off to expand it a bit and do my version of it. So the stories became a mashup up of our two minds. Flint is great at coming up with the "outrageous," truly unique idea. My strengths are taking his ideas, grounding them in a reality, and making them somehow believable. Thus we each compliment and bring something unique to "the table" so to speak.

"I remember writing a lot of it up in Carmel" - Flint Dille

Damn. It was a long time ago. Maybe Dave remembers better than I do. I remember that he was in Lake Geneva for a long time doing a lot of heavy lifting (both our families live on the North Shore of Chicago and TSR was up in Lake Geneva about 45 minutes away. I remember writing a lot of it up in Carmel in a place called the Cypress Wordshop, and in a converted stable up at the Dungeons & Dragons mansion in Beverly Hills.

Novel writing is a marathon. There's no set length, and it is truly a writer's medium. Animation and screenwriting are very similar. Comics are a whole thing unto themselves as far as I'm concerned. Movies are about doing a story in time. Comics are about doing them in space – on a page. Very complex medium for somebody with no art skills.

EDITOR'S NOTE: THESE QUOTES FROM CO-CREATORS FLINT DILLE AND DAVID MARCONI ORIGINALLY APPEARED IN AN INTERVIEW MADE FOR THE WEBSITE ALL-PULP WHICH CAN BE FOUND AT WWW.ALLPULP.BLOGSPOT.COM

THE DOSSIER

FLINT DILLE

Flint Dille is a living embodiment of Transmedia: Turning toys into TV Shows with G1 Transformers, G.I. Joe, Inhumanoids and Visionaries; Designing games with Gary Gygax; Writing movies for Steven Spielberg, and selling game design documents as feature films including Venom and Agent In Place. He created the 'Comics Module' for TSR, a comic book with roleplaying and tabletop gaming content. Flint has twice won 'Game Script of the Year'. He has worked on franchises including James Bond, Mission: Impossible, Tiny Toons, Batman: Rise of Sin Tsu (Guiness Book for creating the first Batman villain outside of the comics). He has a degree in Ancient History from U.C. Berkeley and an MFA from USC. Flint teaches a class on Alternate Reality Games at UCLA, and is writing a follow up his The Ultimate Guide to Video Game Writing and Design.

DAVID MARCONI

A native of Highland Park, Ill., David Marconi was passionate about film making from an early age, and was awarded an Alumni Merit Scholarship to attend the USC Film School. His first job was as Francis Ford Coppola's assistant on The Outsiders. In 1993, Marconi wrote and directed The Harvest, premiering as the 'official selection' of the San Sebastian Film Festival and winning numerous awards around the world. Marconi was brought to the attention of Simpson/Bruckheimer who commissioned him to write his original screenplay Enemy of the State starring Will Smith and Gene Hackman. Marconi has built a strong reputation as a top action/adventure writer with Live Free or Die Hard, Perfect Suspect, and the high-tech, sci-fi epic; No Man's Land. Marconi was a featured guest speaker for IADC, International Attorney's Defense Council, and the Department of Defense Cyber-Crime Conference, lecturing on his film Enemy of the State and privacy concerns and cyber-warfare in a post 9-11 world. Holding duel citizenship for the US and EU (Italy,) Marconi divides his time between Los Angeles and Europe.

JAMES CRAIG

Jim Craig was born in Toronto, Ontario, and attended Sheridan College where he studied Media Arts, Illustration, Cartooning, and Graphic Story Arts. In 1974, Craig recreated the Canadian superhero 'The Northern Light'. This definitive version of the hero continued to appear in magazines, and his original artwork resides in The Archives of Canada representing one of Canada's few superheroes of historical importance. During 1975-1995, Craig drew various Atlas, DC and Marvel Comics titles. For the past two decades he has worked extensively as a storyboard artist for Nelvana ('Inspector Gadget', 'Ewoks') and other animation studios, as well as for live-action feature films and TV. Among the many movies are Dead Zone, Sea of Love, Johnny Mnemonic and The Big Hit. His TV credits include Twilight Zone, Robocop and Road to Avonlea. He also served as the director of Nelvana's Mythic Warriors: Guardians of the Legend animated series.

DENIZ CORDELL

Deniz Cordell has worked as a freelance writer, music director, composer, and voice actor for the last several years. An expert on the music of American composer Leonard Rosenman, he has assistant conducted the St. Petersburg Orchestra in Russia, and written liner notes and provided musical analysis for Intrada Records and Film Score Monthly. Deniz has written and appeared in several radio dramas for the Colonial Radio Theatre - including additional dialogue for their two "Zorro" productions, and "Buck Alice and the Actor-Robot," which he wrote with "Star Trek" actor Walter Koenig, based on Mr. Koenig's novel. In addition to writing the Agent 13 radio shows, he can also be heard in them as "Red" Corbett and the Jinda-Dii. He is a one-time "Jeopardy!" loser.

Made in the USA
Lexington, KY
19 January 2018